PATRICK GALE

A Perfectly Good Man

FOURTH ESTATE • London

Fourth Estate
An imprint of HarperCollins*Publishers*
77–85 Fulham Palace Road, Hammersmith
London W6 8JB

This Fourth Estate paperback edition published 2012
1

First published by Fourth Estate in Great Britain in 2012

Copyright © Patrick Gale 2012

Patrick Gale asserts the moral right
to be identified as the author of this work

A catalogue record for this book is available from the British Library

ISBN 978-0-00-746508-8

Quotation from Dorothy Sayers's *The Man Born to Be King* © 1943, reproduced
by kind permission of David Higham Associates

Quotation from U. A. Fanthorpe's 'Atlas', from *From Me to You: Love Poems* by
U. A. Fanthorpe and R. V. Bailey © 2007, reproduced by kind
permission of Dr Rosie Bailey

Typeset in Sabon by G&M Designs Limited,
Raunds, Northamptonshire

Printed and bound in Great Britain by Clays Ltd, St Ives plc

MIX
Paper from
responsible sources

FSC
www.fsc.org
FSC™ C007454

This novel is entirely a work of fiction. The names, characters and incidents
portrayed in it are the work of the author's imagination. Any resemblance to
actual persons, living or dead, events or localities is entirely coincidental.

From the reviews of *A Perfectly Good Man*:

'At his best, Gale is an effortlessly elastic storyteller, a writer with heart, soul, and a dark and naughty wit, one whose company you relish and trust ... A novel which managed to upset and uplift me in equal measure, and which kept me company – and kept me guessing – right through to its slightly bitter and heartfelt end'

JULIE MYERSON, *Observer*

'What Gale does so well is to delineate the unpremeditated spider-web consequences of actions ... The unfolding night-mare for all the family of the consequences of adopting are exquisitely and painfully documented ... The final chapter left me with a lump in my throat'

SALLEY VICKERS, *Guardian*

'He is aided by the warm generosity of his style, which draws the most crabby reader into a position of sympathy, and an irresistible narrative drive. Late at night on the day a new Patrick Gale arrives I am always to be found crouching on the icy bathroom floor, banished from the bedroom for keeping my husband awake, feverishly turning the pages. The pins and needles are terrible, but worth it'

CHARLOTTE HOBSON, *Spectator*

'It's hard to do justice to Gale's lightness of touch in the re-telling: these characters fit together perfectly and something about his ease of manner allows him to flit between one time frame and another ... A heartfelt, cleverly constructed read' VIV GROSKOP, *Independent on Sunday*

'Well-written, cleverly constructed ... This is a thoughtful and moving novel about love, morality and faith. Marvellous' HARRY RITCHIE, *Mail on Sunday*

'Warm and humane, this novel is beautifully written'
HARRY RITCHIE, *The Times*
KATE SAUNDERS, *The Times*

By the same author
The Aerodynamics of Pork
Kansas in August
Ease
Facing the Tank
Little Bits of Baby
The Cat Sanctuary
Caesar's Wife
The Facts of Life
Dangerous Pleasures
Tree Surgery for Beginners
Rough Music
A Sweet Obscurity
Friendly Fire
Notes from an Exhibition
The Whole Day Through
Gentleman's Relish

For Aidan Hicks

All perfection in this life hath some imperfection bound up with it; and no knowledge of ours is without some darkness.

THOMAS À KEMPIS, *De Imitatione Christi*

AUTHOR'S NOTE

The reader is asked to remember that what follows is neither journalism nor history but a work of fiction. The novel's principal settings and church parishes are real ones near my own home but their inhabitants, in particular the priest in their midst, are entirely imaginary. Where such true events as the March for Geevor are included, I have made use of the novelist's prerogative to embroider on the facts for the low purpose of entertainment.

My text quotes from Dorothy Sayers's radio play, *The Man Born to be King*, with the permission of the Sayers Estate, and from U.A. Fanthorpe's poem 'Atlas', with kind permission from Dr Rosie Bailey.

PG

the only resident in the block who wasn't over seventy. He had been there three months now. When a vacancy came up and the council offered it to him, he had seized the chance, spurred on, he was sure, by the grotesque local hero stories in *The Cornishman*.

Away from Pendeen and his mother's stifling concern, given the opportunity to build an independent life for himself in town, where he needed nobody's help to do anything, he was convinced that things would improve. The change of scene, the view, the independence had indeed all brought relief. The problem had moved house with him, of course. If anything it had been heightened. The flat was ingeniously perfect for his needs: a gentle ramp to the front door, all on the level within, and swings to help himself into bed and into the shower. Tables, work surfaces, fridge and cooker, clothes storage were all modified to be usable from a sitting position. There was even a full-length mirror in the hall so that he could check before he went out that, yes, he looked fine, like a perfectly unremarkable twenty-year-old who just happened to be in a wheelchair. The only things out of his reach were the pictures his mother had hung for him – a reproduction of a fiery Rachel Kelly painting he had always liked and a framed enlargement of a photograph he had taken of a sunset at Sennen Cove. This had hung on his bedroom wall ever since he won a prize for it at school and he had agreed without thinking when his mother assumed he would want to take it with him. But now it embarrassed him and was the last thing he needed when trying to muster the motivation to haul himself, literally, out of bed. What had once filled him with teenage pride now reminded him of the motivational posters first on the walls at school and then in the rooms of the rehabilitation centre he had religiously attended. He recalled with particular rancour an image of a soaring seagull with a quotation from Virgil: 'They can because they think they can!'

It didn't matter now. Nothing especially mattered. Unless, of course, he had been ripped off, like the time he had bought Ecstasy tablets that had turned out to be little more than overpriced remodelled Aspirin. He finished the second letter, sealed it and set it beside the first. He had never been comfortable stringing sentences together, still less using a pen, but somehow, as with thank-you letters, a pen had seemed called for. He had been obliged to buy paper and envelopes, which, like the open window on a heated room, seemed wasteful. Some would think it sad that he could think of only two people who mattered enough to him to merit a letter. There were others, of course, but these were the two people who needed to understand. His rugby friends had all pulled together at first, just as one would expect from team players. They had all tried so hard to do and say the right thing but none of them quite arrived at the point of managing to think it, so as to make their words and gestures more than that.

People were gathering on the car park. He saw some children in matching white tee-shirts running with paper fish fluttering on long lengths of bamboo above their heads, and he remembered it was Golowan; local schools and bands were assembling for the annual Mazey Day parade up Market Jew Street.

He checked the time. There was still an hour to go. He wheeled himself over to the kitchen drawer where he had stashed the two deliveries – two small, innocuous, brown, padded envelopes. One from Mexico contained a small polystyrene carton protecting what the label claimed to be veterinary Nembutal. (Knowing no corruptible doctors, vets or nurses, he had found it impossible to source the drug in the UK.) The other, posted within England, bought from an online specialist, was a simple barbiturate-testing kit. He had read the instructions already but read them again now because since the accident he had become that kind of person, a careful reader of warnings and waiter for lights, a measure-twice-cut-once sort of man.

The kit consisted of a tiny translucent plastic case which opened to reveal three small syringes and three tiny, clinical containers of liquid, a mixing vial and instructions. Following the instructions, he carefully used one of the syringes to draw just one millilitre of the putative Nembutal through its sterile seal. He began to shake again – something else that often happened since his accident – and he had to set the syringe down on the table for a second or two to let his hands relax. He breathed deeply twice and watched a lorry edge by, a local steel band mounted on its decorated trailer. Then he took up the syringe again and in a single confident movement added its contents to the vial. Then he did the same, adding to the Nembutal a quantity of one of the containers. Then he drew up the second liquid into a syringe.

'Please,' he thought. 'Please, (just this once)' and he squirted its contents into the mixing vial. At once the testing solution turned a bright, satisfying blue. He felt himself smiling honestly for the first time in weeks. 'Bad news, mate,' he said out loud. 'You're pregnant.'

Finally he took the third syringe, drew up the third liquid and added it to the rest. Nothing happened. No change. No diminishing of the intense, hope-laden blue. He screwed the cap back on the vial and gave it a shake to be sure. Still blue. 'Still pregnant,' he murmured.

Relief stole over him. He had searched and searched online and found only impossible, unconvincing websites offering the drug without prescription, alongside a lurid buffet of antidepressants and sex-enhancers. Blatant scammers were everywhere as were hysterical-sounding victims desperate to expose them.

His salvation had arrived unexpectedly in the course of a purgatorial night out with old friends from the rugby club. It was somebody's stag night. Things had started silly and were sure to get sillier and a rowdy pub was no fun when your head was at the height of everyone else's arse and jokers kept pushing your wheelchair about. Pretending to be staying outside for a smoke as they arrived at the Swordfish, the third pub of the evening, he scored some skunk off a raspy-voiced old hippy to help him cope. The hippy asked outright how he came to be in the chair and Lenny soon found himself matching bluntness with bluntness and confessing the trouble he'd been having finding a trustworthy source of suicide drugs online.

'Nembutal,' the hippy had sighed with welcome candour. 'The paralytic's pal. No problem. I've got a woman friend in Puerto Vallarta. She can get you the kind for dogs. You'll need 100 mil. Yeah. 100 mil and a pause for thought. You go back inside, my friend, and I'll send her a text and let you know.'

He murmured a price in Lenny's ear twenty minutes later as he unexpectedly passed him a drink in the crowd. It seemed worryingly cheap, like the sex he had been offered in Amsterdam, and he had every expectation that the drug would have been diluted to inefficacy or lost its power with age, both of which the chatter on the suicide forums told him could happen.

But no. It was real and full of kindly force.

He needed to get out. Even with the window ajar, the little bottle's potency seemed to be drawing all the oxygen from the flat.

He threw the testing kit into the bin, tucked the Nembutal back in the fridge then hoisted himself onto the loo because excitement was getting to him and he needed to piss.

After the accident he had returned to work at the same Penzance chemist's that had taken him on as a dispensing assistant after school. The grand scheme – derailed by the accident, of course – was to work there, gaining useful experience while he retook his maths and chemistry A-levels with a view to studying pharmacy at university. During the previous day's shift, he had stolen from his employers for the first time, pocketing the dose of prescription-only anti-emetic he now swallowed with a gulp of juice straight from the carton. He wanted to be sure he didn't throw up the precious Nembutal when the time came.

He took the anti-emetic's packaging with him to throw into a bin on the prom; he didn't want anyone at work to get into trouble on his account and had even slipped the money for it into the till in the hope the theft wouldn't be detected. As he pulled the door locked behind him he remembered afresh that he was the only resident, on his floor at least, who had not bothered to prettify the entrance to his flat. All the others, all his elderly neighbours, had planted window boxes or hung wind chimes or even set out garden gnomes or resin meerkats. Everyone but him had done something to mark out their small share of walkway as their own.

Two of the residents whom he saw every day but whose names he had yet to learn had met by the entrance ramp and paused to chat. They watched him with approval.

'Morning, Lenny. Off to watch the parade?'

'That's right,' he told them, although he wasn't. 'Thought I might as well.'

'Good lad,' said the other.

And as he wheeled away from them he knew they would be looking after him and saying pity or waste just as they would over a nice young man who turned out to be gay or a nice young couple whose baby turned out to be autistic. 'Shame,' they'd say, then sigh, then move the conversation on because there was nothing to be done. 'You having that lamb thing you bought, or the chicken?'

He followed the pavement around to the seafront but then, instead of turning left to where the marchers and bands, the fish, mermaids and starfish were preparing to parade up the hill, he turned right and headed away from them, over the Ross Bridge, past the Scillonian dock, around the corner, where the funfair had been set up and the traffic diverted, and onto the promenade.

Provided one could cross the road and find an access point onto the pavement unblocked by thoughtlessly parked cars, it was a good place to exercise, he had discovered. The pavement was broad so that he could pause if he wanted to without feeling he was getting in people's way and there was always plenty of life along there: rollerbladers and skateboarders, dog-walkers, people jogging or pushing babies, or simply sitting on benches or leaning on the railings to watch the sea and one another.

He knew this should change his mind. In the Hollywood version of his story he would see a happy old couple or a beautiful girl, or be asked directions by an elegant woman or catch a ball for an endearingly plain child and be charmed into lingering, seduced by life. As it was, he wheeled himself along the front with no such significant encounter. Sunshine was dazzling on the sea, the brightly coloured banners cracked and flapped in the breeze. Nobody asked him directions or tossed him a hope-restoring ball. The only eyes that met his gaze were those of dogs, and of children in pushchairs, fascinated to find an adult on their level and unashamed of staring.

He crossed the road when he neared the Lugger and wheeled up to Captain's to buy chips, which he took back to the front. They were perfect chips, crisp, hot and salty, and he ate them with slow relish so that his pleasure in the taste of them and his pleasure in the scene around him – water, people, dogs, life – became indistinguishable. He ate carefully. He had learnt the hard way that seagulls registered the wheelchair rather than the adult in it and read him as an overgrown and helpless child, easy to plunder. He had lost the best part of a pasty and suffered a nasty peck to the back of one hand before he learnt to eat with his food tucked beneath a jacket or coat.

As he wheeled himself homewards, the Mazey Day parade started off with a cacophony of steel drums, pipes, school bands and even what sounded like bagpipes and the synchronized chants and whooping of cheerleaders. As he came back over the Ross Bridge he saw the last of a squadron of drum majorettes, in white calf boots and rumpled pink satin, heading round the corner near the station.

It was one of several local festivals that had grown up in his lifetime, cheerful traditions confected to promote tourism and perhaps imbue a pride in all things Cornish. It meant no more to him than the dual-language English-Cornish signs that had begun to appear about the place, but perhaps future Cornish children would feel differently.

He saw Father Barnaby getting out of his impossibly old Rover up ahead and joining the crowd on the prom. He was all in black – a human crow amid the holiday crowd. Lenny had teased him once, about always wearing black, and Father Barnaby had joked that always wearing the same meant one less thing to decide in the mornings. In fact he did wear civilian clothes occasionally – he had a weakness for black, no-label jeans – but he looked strange in them and vulnerable, like an habitual glasses-wearer when he took his glasses off to clean them.

Lenny tailed him for a few minutes, noting how people made way for him, either because of his height or clerical dress, and how many of them stared or even flinched then let out nervous smiles. But then Lenny was held up by a double pushchair with a dog at its side and lost sight of him. It was probably better that way. If Father Barnaby had spotted him he would have offered to push the wheelchair and Lenny would have felt doubly exposed.

Predictably he was in conversation with one of the neighbours as Lenny approached the ramp. On a sunny day like this there was always one or another of them out on the walkway and priests were always good for a chat. Kitty had found him. Kitty who had the foul-mouthed, second-hand mynah bird that so embarrassed her. And now here she was, a schoolboy joke made flesh, all puffed up and aglow from the pleasure of passing the time of day with a handsome vicar. Tense, though, in case he wanted to step inside and heard her bird.

Barnaby was no idler. Lenny was counting on that. His focus on the matter in hand was always total. Sure enough, the moment he spotted Lenny, he broke off chatting.

'Here's the man I came to see. Goodbye – sorry. I don't know your name.'

'Kitty,' she said, preening like a ten-year-old. 'Kitty Arnold.'

'Goodbye Kitty.'

He didn't offer to help, as Lenny had been dreading, but simply strode forward and shook him by the hand. 'Good to see you,' he said.

'Sorry I'm late,' Lenny began, leading the way to his door.

'You're bang on time. I was early. I'd forgotten about Golowan when we spoke and I thought I'd never be able to park but I got lucky.'

'I know. I saw you.'

'You saw me?'

'You don't exactly blend in, dressed like that.' Lenny had his mother's candour. He saw Father Barnaby flinch. 'It's not just the dog collar,' he added. 'You're tall. Sit down. Can I get you anything?'

'A glass of water would be good.'

Perfect. Lenny wheeled into the kitchen, poured him a glass of water and tipped his own drink into a second glass.

'Thank you.' Barnaby took his water and raised it. 'Cheers.' He drank, looked around him. 'It's nice,' he said. 'You've settled in?'

Lenny nodded. This was proving harder than he had imagined.

'It must be a relief to be on your own. Your mum worries and that can be ...'

'Yeah.'

Barnaby stopped talking and let silence fall between them. He looked Lenny directly in the face. Lenny met his gaze for a few seconds then glanced away and fiddled with his glass. He remembered Barnaby as handsomer – Hollywood cowboy handsome – perhaps because of all he represented. In the flesh his jaw was weaker, his nose smaller than in Lenny's memory. But his pale grey eyes had a startling intensity that was unnerving at close range.

'How can I help you, Lenny?' he asked at last.

'I've not been a very ... Does it matter that I never go to church these days?'

'It does if it makes you unhappy. Does it?'

'Not really. But ... Do you pray for us? The people that don't show up?'

'Yes, but that's a pretty impersonal prayer. I pray for you specifically.'

'Do you?'

'Do you mind?'

'No,' Lenny said, 'but why?'

11

'Lenny! Obviously I've been praying for you ever since your accident and during the operations and so on but ... Do you need me to pray for you now for a specific reason?'

Lenny forced himself to meet Barnaby's stare. 'I'm going to die,' he told him.

'We're all going to die. Does dying frighten you?'

'I mean I'm going to kill myself.'

'You can't.'

'Fucking can. Sorry.'

'That's all right. Why?'

'Isn't it obvious? Don't worry. I'm not depressed or mad or anything. I know exactly what I'm doing. It's a decision, that's all. My life, my death.'

'Lenny, your hands are shaking.'

Instinctively Lenny clasped his hands onto his useless knees to hold them still. 'That's because I haven't told anyone this. Not my mum. Not ...'

'Not Amy?'

'Certainly not Amy. Jesus! Sorry.'

'That's quite all right.'

'I just can't do this, OK? Everyone has been brilliant – the boys at the club, the people at work, the council, the physios, the old bats in this place. But I can't do it. I mean look around you. No books. Not even a few. I don't have – what did you call them that time? – inner resources. I know you think I just have to wait and they'll well up in me like a bath but they won't. I've always been a doer, a player. I did OK at school and college but I hate indoors. Working in a dispensary, it's just a job. I lived for the nights out with Amy and practice and matches and ... If I stay here like this I'm going to turn into some bitter old fuck-up

12

downloading porn and taking pictures of girls who pass the window there ...'

Barnaby winced: not as cool as he liked to make out.

'Lenny, I'm so sorry. You should have said you needed help.'

'Yes, well, everyone was being so nice.'

'It'll pass. You'll find new things. New things will enter your life and change it.'

'They already did. They're called incontinence pads.'

'Christ!'

'You swore!'

'Lenny, please. Give life a chance. I've seen lesser men than you work through things like this. When the mines were still open here the accidents could be—'

'I'm never going to run or walk or surf again. I'm never going to score another try again. Or fuck.'

'They kept you a place at the chemist's, didn't they?'

'Oh yeah. They've even installed a ramp so I can get up high enough to see over the counter. But I won't be able to reach the higher shelves so there'll always have to be another dispensing assistant on duty with me. It's charity. It's making allowances. I know they mean well but I don't want that.'

'Please, Len. Think of your mum.'

'I am thinking of her ...'

'And Amy. You've upset her dreadfully already. This'll devastate her.'

'Well she'll get over it. I had to push her away. I couldn't let her martyr herself.'

'But if you'd been married already?'

'I'd have divorced her.'

Barnaby broke off and looked at him with those eyes.

That's shocked him into silence, Lenny thought.

Barnaby glanced at Lenny's untouched glass in a way that made Lenny think he knew. He sighed. 'All I'm saying,' he started.

'Don't,' Lenny said. 'Don't say anything, OK? I didn't ask you here for that. I could have rung Samaritans if I wanted that.'

'So what do you want me to do?'

'Just ... stay here for a bit.'

'I'm here, Len. I'm not leaving until you want me to.'

'It's really fast. It takes two minutes till I pass out and another till my heart stops.'

'Think of the risks. If it goes wrong you could end up—'

'I know the risks. I researched them. Like a fucking chemistry project. I've tested it. It won't go wrong. People do this all the time.'

'And plenty choose not to.'

'Don't. I don't need that.' Lenny pointed to the table where he'd been writing earlier. 'Those are letters to Mum and Amy. And you'll need to call a doctor.'

'Len, I'm a priest. I know what to do when someone dies.'

'Sorry.'

There was a fresh blast of music from outside. Perhaps the front of the parade was already coming around again. Was that possible? Barnaby glanced away towards the sound and Lenny seized the moment to drain his glass. Barnaby didn't see him do it. Lenny knew he had no idea.

It was unbelievably bitter, like drinking a whole glass of Stop'n Grow. Like drinking death itself. He gasped but managed not to retch. He felt utterly calm. A seagull hovered briefly outside the window then rolled off to the side. *They can because they think they can.*

'Not long now,' Lenny said and saw that Barnaby had realized then what was happening.

'No!' he shouted. He took Lenny's hands in his. He kissed one of them. 'Len?'

'You'll send the letters?'

'I'll send them.'

'You can pray now. If you like.'

His mouth was going funny already and he wasn't sure Barnaby had even understood him. Barnaby was gazing at him with those I-will-find-you eyes and he whipped out a little silver bottle and tipped some oil onto his finger, hands shaking, and touched Len's head with it.

'O Almighty God,' he said, 'With whom do live the spirits of just men made perfect, after they are delivered from their earthly prisons, I humbly commend the soul of this thy servant, our dear brother Lenny, into thy hands as into the hands of a faithful Creator, and most merciful Saviour; most humbly beseeching thee, that it may be precious in thy sight.'

Barnaby's voice grew quieter. His face was wet with tears but his words didn't falter. It wasn't like a prayer in church. It was like an important conversation with someone in the room. Someone else. Len's sight clouded and he felt his head grow insupportably heavy. For a short while he was aware of nothing but the continuing voice.

'Wash it, we pray thee, in the blood of that immaculate lamb, that was slain to take away the sins of the world; that whatsoever defilements it may have contracted in the midst of this miserable and naughty world, through the lusts of the flesh, or the wiles of Satan, being purged and done away, it may be presented pure and without spot before thee.'

Without spot, Len thought. That's nice. Like sheets. And he pictured bed sheets on his mother's washing line high above Morvah on a day when the sea down below was deep blue with white horses on it, and the temptation was strong to hold your face in them as they flicked and cracked in the wind and the bleaching sun. Pure. White. Without spot.

DOROTHY AT 24

Dorothy would soon marry Henry Angwin. She had assumed this was her destiny for some time now. She didn't love him. She didn't even know him especially well. But she knew his externals – his height, his voice, his shy-making brand of manliness – and she knew his reputation, which was quiet and trustworthy. Her mother was an old friend of his mother – they usually sat together, or at least nearby, in church. They had been visiting each other's houses all her life. The Angwins farmed on the other side of St Just, between Kelynack's sheltered valley and the coast, whereas her father's farm was between Botallack and Pendeen, in harsher, mine-skirted territory. Neither family was exactly rich, but the Sampsons, like the Angwins, had owned their fields, barns and farmhouses for a generation or two so were secure and steady. Although they had a church nearby in Pendeen, her mother continued to worship in St Just, at the church of her childhood, where she had been married. She was too gentle for snobbery but, when challenged, she implied that there was something a little rough about the Pendeen congregation, that it was a miners' not a farmers' church. This was not strictly true, for most miners were Methodists and were well served by the huge chapel in St Just as well as the smaller ones in between. But her main reason was that St Just was where her girlhood friends worshipped – such as had not married chapel men or not been strong enough to change their habits if they had – and since most were kept busy on farms during the week, church was an opportunity to keep in touch.

Dorothy was an only child, however. There were no male relatives to whom her father would have cared to leave the farm and Henry was her mother's godson. Nothing had been said in so many words, at least not in Dorothy's hearing, but she suspected it was an understanding as reassuring to the older generation as a full barn or a dry August.

Henry was six years her senior – a man, in fact – and now that his father had died, he was her father's equal, so called her mother Dulcie these days rather than Mrs Sampson. He and Dorothy barely spoke beyond cheerful greetings and goodbyes and more-cake-Henrys. But occasionally, once she had finally started to fill out, she would catch his eyes on her the second before he looked away and would feel her cheeks redden so that she had to slip away on an errand, fetching more milk for the table or wool for her knitting.

She would not be handed over like a parcel, though. She set no great store by romance – she had seen the messes and bad marriages into which romance led people – but she had sufficient dignity to want him to know her, to choose her at least partly for herself, not simply for what she represented or what acreage she brought with her. She was dreading him asking her out as she could not imagine going for a Sunday walk with him or even sitting beside him in the suggestive darkness of a cinema; she could not imagine what they would talk about or by what difficult process he would steer the conversation from the generally polite to the personally specific. Yet she knew this was a necessary stage and a part of her was impatient for it to begin so that it might become ordinary and familiar rather than a thing of dread.

But then everything was changed in a swift reversal worthy of a Bible story. Her father died. Barely sixty, and with no warning, he was taken from them, felled by a heart attack while hammering in fence posts. He died on a beautiful day – the sort of day that would routinely tempt him to skip his tea and stay out working beyond sundown, so it was only when he failed to appear at supper that they realized something was wrong. Mother and daughter hunted him through the fields with torches and the dog. It was the dog that found him, and barked with a high, frightened rapidity until they came.

He was buried in Pendeen churchyard and all at once her mother transferred her allegiance from her childhood church to his. She and Dorothy sat near the back, shy among people who were not strangers – these were neighbours, after all – but who possibly thought them stuck-up for never having been before. Which was how they came to hear the announcement that the new curate from upcountry would need somewhere reasonably cheap to stay, ideally with board as well as bed provided.

The women had always done the milking and looked after the hens, but it was Dorothy's father who ploughed, topped the pasture, made silage or tended or harvested the barley. Henry came to the rescue, naturally, renting the pasture off them for some of his Devon Rubies. And as their own beef cattle were sold off in twos and threes, he took over the running of the farm. He paid an honourable rent but inevitably this would mean far less income than if the farm were still in family hands. In time, he would help raise them precious capital by organising a dispersal sale of the cows and dairy equipment and farm deadstock. They were advised to leave this until the following tax year, however, which was a relief as Dorothy sensed her mother needed to keep busy. Dorothy's father had no life insurance. Mother and daughter lived simply, were good at making do, but they needed any extra cash they could secure. The curate would pay rent and use the guest bedroom where they never seemed to entertain guests. He would be no trouble.

It was strange having Henry Angwin coming by almost every day, not calling in, just going about his business. Watching him out of her bedroom window or spotting him as she crossed the yard from letting the chickens out, gave Dorothy a chance to get used to having him about the place, to imagine how it would be to be married to him. There were no such discussions, of course, and wouldn't be for a month or two, but she was fairly sure the same idea was flitting through her mother's mind. Without her father there to talk to, man to man, Henry seemed more reticent than ever – what with that and the speechlessness that afflicted most people faced with the recently bereaved. Whereas before it had been she who looked away, red in the face, Dorothy now found it was Henry who dropped his gaze after a mumbled greeting while she felt able to look him full in the face, almost boldly.

And then the curate arrived. She had pictured someone like the vicar only less interesting. Father Philip was old and frail-looking, with papery skin and a high, bloodless voice to match. Childless and long widowed, he lived like a hermit in one end of the rambling rectory and was generally regarded both as a sort of saint and as a figure of gentle fun. He had reached the great age that made it impossible to imagine him ever having been young or been subject to the usual human impulses and appetites.

But Barnaby Johnson was in his mid-twenties, only a year older than her, if that. He was handsome, healthy-looking, funny and – there seemed no other word for it – normal. Her mother had a deep disapproval of what she called *the goings-on in London*, fired by reports she read in her Saturday newspaper or by what she saw on television. She particularly disliked men with flares or long hair or shoes that drew attention to themselves. Barnaby Johnson arrived with a short back and sides so strict it seemed almost cheeky in the circumstances.

He had two suitcases, one very heavy, which was his books, one very light, containing clothes. 'Careful ...' he warned as she took the heavy one from him. 'Oh!' and he laughed at the ease with which she carried it up the stairs ahead of him.

'Farming muscles,' she explained, then thought how silly that sounded but didn't know what to say instead. She showed him his room, with little apologetic gestures. She had prepared it herself, had made his bed, selected his towel, put a new bar of soap in his sink, Roger & Gallet sandalwood, hoarded from Christmas, and cut fresh lining for his drawers out of an old roll of wallpaper. She had thought it looked quite nice when she had finished but now that he was so young and smart she saw it for what it was, a pretty room for a maiden aunt, hopelessly old-fashioned. At least she had resisted the impulse to put lavender bags in the drawers but she had hung a home-made pomander in his wardrobe because it smelled a little musty with disuse.

'Your bathroom's across the landing,' she told him, adding thoughtlessly, 'I put soap in there too.'

'Any rules about hot water?' he asked.

'No,' she said, confused. 'There's always plenty because of the Aga. The only rule I can think of is the phone. It's in the hall and mother hates the noise of it ringing because it startles her and she always thinks it'll be bad news. If you want to make a call you have to plug it in but you need to unplug it again afterwards.'

'Fine,' he said and she saw he was trying not to smile at what she had never thought eccentric until now. 'It's a wonderful old house,' he added as she was leaving him to settle in.

'Is it?' she said. 'I don't know. I suppose it is.'

'It's, what, seventeenth century? Older even.'

'I'm not sure.'

'Have you always lived here?'

She nodded. 'Though I was born in Penzance.' She heard her mother clear her throat downstairs. 'I should, er … Mum says supper's ready when you are. I'll let you unpack then.'

'Thank you, er?'

'Dorothy.'

'God's gift.'

'Who is?'

'It's what your name means. Mine's Son of Consolation, which I always think's a bit like being called Better Luck Next Time.'

She wasn't sure what to say to that so smiled and fled after pointing out the laundry basket on the landing and handing him a back-door key.

She saw fairly little of him at first; just breakfast and the occasional supper, and Sunday lunch – which took the place of supper on Sundays. But he was busy about the parish and she was busy about the farm. Mealtime conversations were necessarily stilted since her mother was present.

Her mother had never been a chatterbox or a gossip and had always tended to concentrate on the food set before her, and now grief and injustice had left her stony and reluctant to please. Besides, Dorothy did not know how to talk to him or what they should talk about. She was no simple farm girl; she had been well educated at some expense at St Clare's, but his directness of manner was unlike anything she had encountered and when he looked she felt he really saw and understood things, perhaps more things than she felt comfortable acknowledging.

But then he came right out with it, in that curiously direct way he had, and asked if he could be shown around the farm that afternoon as he had some spare time. 'I'd walk around on my own,' he said, 'only I wouldn't want to stray onto a neighbour's land or go anywhere I shouldn't.'

'No one'll take you for a cattle rustler,' her mother said; the nearest she had come to levity since her widowing. 'Dorothy can show you round.'

'Of course I can,' Dorothy said. 'If you can spare me.'

'Ooh, I can spare you an hour or two. Go on, girl. Do you good to get some colour back in your cheeks.'

So she met him after lunch, awkward in his clerical black, with shinily new black wellies to match. 'You see,' he said. 'I'm ready for anything,' and he laughed at the boots on her behalf.

She showed him the obvious things at first, the little milking parlour with its antique stools still hanging from wooden pegs, the hen house, the vegetable patch and the two pigs next door to it. She explained how the following spring the vegetables would grow where the pigs had been and new pigs would take the vegetables' place and he chuckled at the simple practicality of it. So she told him how each year's pigs always had the same names – Mary and Martha – regardless of gender, to stop anyone getting too attached – and he laughed out loud.

'Does it work?'

'Not really,' she said, scratching that year's Martha with the old plastic back brush she kept on a hook for the purpose, so that the animal leaned heavily against the fence for pleasure. 'I don't get any less fond and I have to go to Truro for the day when they go for slaughter. Keeping the names just means I sort of transfer my love, so it's as though all the Marys are standing in for the first one. It would make more sense to give them numbers, I suppose, like the cattle.'

She showed him the barn where the straw bales were stacked to the rafters – the last of her father's straw, she thought of it as – and where the milk-fed but ownerless cats hunted mice and held yowling duels for supremacy. He made to stroke an especially handsome grey tabby and she caught his arm to stop him being scratched or bitten. She let go straight afterwards but the warmth of his arm had been a shock. She showed him the shed where some of the beef cattle – Henry's cattle now, not theirs – had gathered to feast on silage. They stood in silence to listen to the softly comforting sound of their munching and to feel the warmth of their huge sighs and yeasty snorts.

'Most summers we get barn owls in here,' she said, and realized she was whispering, as if at a service. She had always loved the cattle shed. It wasn't old – not like the other buildings, which were low and ancient – but had gone up in her childhood during a rare moment of confidence and relative expansiveness of her father's after a peculiarly good harvest of early potatoes. It was an utterly plain, tanalized wooden structure, with a heavy metal door and aluminium grilles through which cattle reached their mounded food. She loved its height, which felt churchlike after the intimate darkness of the granite sheds and barns but principally she loved what it did to the view. The shed was enclosed on three sides to about six feet, to give the animals shelter from rain and wind. For almost the same distance again there was a void before the wooden cladding began. Of course this was purely there to ventilate the shed for the health of the animals, in case especially harsh winter weather meant they had to be shut up there for days at a time. But by a happy accident it composed the view, of fields, hedges, mine sheds and distant Pendeen Watch, into something like a painting. Viewed from outside, the same view seemed disordered and fragmentary; the shed worked a magic on it.

Lent courage by his interest, she led him across their fields towards the lighthouse, pointing out the bits to avoid in winter, where streams made the ground boggy – and where the easiest places were for crossing the hedges so as to avoid having to risk scrapes and cuts by fiddling with the rusting barbed-wire loops with which most of the gates were held shut.

The beef cattle Henry was running on the fields were far more boisterous than her father's had been, perhaps because they had less human contact or had more reasons to be wary of it. She could tell Mr Johnson had a town man's fear of them and she showed him how to intimidate them in turn by raising both his clenched fists in a sort of Fascist salute and shouting *Gaaah!* He laughed when this worked and they backed off in respect, but she could tell he would be embarrassed to try it on his own and would be one of those walkers who turned back or took long detours rather than pass through a field of cattle.

It was a walk, nothing more. She answered all his questions where she could and it seemed to her their conversation had been friendly but impersonal. She had asked him none of the questions in her mind, like what made a perfectly nice, normal man become a priest and did he have brothers and sisters. As they were re-entering the yard, though, they met Henry, who had driven up to drop off some mineral blocks for his cattle, and she felt her cheeks burn as she introduced them, as though the walk had been more than a walk and the conversation more than general.

The physical contrast between the two men as they shook hands could hardly have been greater. Henry's hand seemed twice the size of the curate's, his shoulders twice the width, his skin ruddily healthy by comparison. She knew most girls in the area would have laughed at the way Henry's comfortable Penwith burr made Barnaby Johnson's upcountry accent sound comically fussy and his build made him seem boyishly puny, and she would have predicted her own reaction to be the same. She was surprised, however, to find a sharp impulse of protectiveness rise within her and she saw Henry as she imagined this cultivated visitor saw him: rough-skinned, blockish, of the flesh fleshly, and felt an answering confusion at her disloyalty.

'Barnaby wanted to see the farm,' she said defensively, 'so I showed him around.'

'Wasn't too muddy for you, then?' Henry asked, glancing down at where the muck had worked its way up the new boots and onto the black trousers.

Then she realized she had wielded his Christian name as a kind of weapon and, confused, she left them to chat, hurrying away on the pretext of getting the hens in.

Walking together on his day off became a regular event. She showed him every inch of the parish, from the farther reaches of Morvah to the edge of Botallack. She showed him the mine at Geevor – or as much as they could safely view – and took him to the ancient stones of Chun, the Lanyon Quoit and the Men-an-Tol.

He began to reveal a bit about himself. She learnt that he had a rather strange childhood, with a widowed scientist father, now dead. His only sibling, a much older sister, had gone to Africa to teach and had died out there when he was still a boy. He had read history at Oxford, then trained for his ordination at somewhere called Cuddesdon, where he was still completing a part-time further degree in theology. He worried this had not equipped him to cope as a working priest since the experience had been so remote and scholastic, which was why he had eagerly accepted the invitation to come to Pendeen.

'So he doesn't like it,' her mother said; for although their conversation was so stilted and correct at mealtimes, she was eager enough to hear reports after each week's walk. 'He's only here because he thinks it'll do him good.'

'I don't think that's quite it. Maybe that's how it was to start with. And Pendeen's not obviously pretty, is it? Not picture-postcard pretty, like St Ives or Mousehole. So it's always a shock when people first come out here. But I think he's starting to see there's more to it.'

'You're revealing its hidden charms?' her mother said with something like a smile.

'I think he's finding them for himself.'

She learnt other things, things she didn't like to tell her mother: that he always carried a tiny, red, Victorian book and seemed to read it when alone or waiting, slipping it into his jacket pocket when he sensed her approach; that his shirts, which she had impulsively sniffed twice now when doing the laundry, had a sweet, burnt smell about them, like caramel; and that, having been so solitary in his childhood, he dreamed of having lots of children, at least six, like an Old Testament patriarch.

She too was having her eyes opened. Encouraged by his interest, she began to see that their house was beautiful – old, beautiful and even strange – when to her it had always been no more than home, the house where she grew up, the farm where she woke and slept and worked. He opened her eyes to its details: that not one of its windows was the same as another; that the ancient chimney at its centre was shaped like a barley-sugar cane; that half the house was seventeenth-century, half nineteenth, which implied the family had suddenly come into money or doubled in size. It was the same when they walked; his close attention showed her small wonders afresh: the way starry young thistles formed constellations across the March grass, the way jackdaw cries of 'Pyow! Pyow!' sounded like boys playing at cowboys.

They hardly touched but he was always courteous, offering his support as she came over stiles, and she would thoughtlessly tap his arm now to catch his attention when she thought he had missed something. But then, one afternoon in April, when there was enough warmth in the sun to tempt one to stop walking and linger, they sat, then lay on the banks of cushiony sea grass and thrift flowers above Boat Cove, and quite suddenly he was kissing her and she was eagerly kissing him back.

The kiss was not discussed afterwards but she found it dissolved any remaining diffidence she felt before him. It seemed to release something in him too. He started telling her how old his father's family was, which was a bit strange. 'I mean, every family's old, of course, when you think about it, but this lot stayed put for centuries in the house they built, which somehow makes the continuity, the age, more apparent.'

They headed back soon after this, walking with minimal conversation now because they had dawdled and lost track of time. They paused only to admire the first swallows, which had arrived that afternoon and were diving low across a silage field, eagerly hunting flies.

In her bed that night she found herself puzzling over his words and the story of the old house that wasn't his and never would be, the *might-have-been*, as he put it. She couldn't work out why he had told her.

He had no sooner raised the subject than he dismissed it. 'Might-have-beens are insidious, aren't they, in the way they don't ever quite lie still or go away.' It had seemed almost like a warning, like gently letting someone know you had madness in your family that was likely to be passed on.

He left. He went with bewildering speed, before they could speak again, much less enjoy another walk. He made a sudden announcement to her mother over breakfast, before Dorothy had even come downstairs, and was driven to the station by Henry by half-past nine.

Henry was chatty, by his standards, when he returned from the errand, trying to pass on gossip about how Father Philip had taken against having a curate and found it an imposition. She gave him no encouragement, however, saying only, 'We liked him,' as she paid him for the sack of chicken corn he had brought, which then caused an awkwardness between them which drove her indoors again soon after.

She spent the rest of the day in a numb frenzy of useful- ness but the trouble with practical tasks was that they had a way of occupying the hands alone, leaving the mind free to wander and wonder. As she stripped his bed and washed his bedding for the last time, as she swept and tidied his room and closed it back into the tomblike state in which it lay ready for visitors who never came, she thought over their last conversations, looking for ways in which she might have been to blame. Was she too bold? Was her family insufficiently old?

She paid a visit to the forlorn little back bathroom he had been using. Having cleaned its worn, hip-pinching bath and rust-mottled sink, and retrieved his towel for the wash, she snatched up in a shamefaced impulse the nice soap which she had left in there for him instead of the Wright's Coal Tar her mother was convinced kept disease from the house. Soap lasted a long time with them because their water was so soft but, still, there was something poignant in his not having even stayed long enough to progress to a second bar of it.

It was only as she called in on her room to return the soap to her own sink that she found the envelope he had slipped under her door. The vigour with which he had flicked it through had sent it almost entirely beneath her bedside rug, where it might have lain hidden for weeks. She snatched it up. It was addressed to Dorothy, Pink Bedroom. Inside was a black and white postcard of the Mermaid Chair in Zennor church on the back of which he had simply written, *Write to me!* And his new, grim-sounding address in Portsmouth.

All she knew of Portsmouth came from *Mansfield Park*. Austen's evocation of the crowded, genteel poverty of Fanny Price's home was fairly off-putting and she suspected time and two world wars had made the port less appealing still.

She dropped his towel where she stood, hurried to the ugly Victorian sewing table that had always served as her desk, and wrote to him at once. She wrote four sides of Basildon Bond, what in effect was her first ever love letter, although its tone was almost as guarded as their earliest conversations had been because merely saying things and committing them to paper, where others might read them, were so different. Then she dumped the towel in the twin tub and hurried up to the village letter box. She liked the thought that the letter would soon be travelling upcountry on the same train line that was already carrying him. By the

31

time her mother drove back from a trip into town with a friend, carrying a box of groceries from the Co-op, Dorothy was almost cheerful.

His answer came within the week. He had made a mistake, he wrote, left on impulse and now was in a kind of hell, missing her, the landscape, their walks. Her letter, he said, was precious and she must write more even if he was sometimes kept too busy to write back.

So of course she replied. She had always suspected her letters were like herself: calm and possibly not very interesting. She wrote accounts of her tasks, of news from the village, of developments at the mine or at the Sunday School, where she had started to help out – inspired by him – and didn't feel she could drop out of now that he had gone. She began to keep notes in an old exercise book in her room of things to remember to tell him, things she had seen or that people had said. But she was careful not to write too often. She wrote every other Friday – the day he had gone – and she continued to limit herself to two pieces of Basildon Bond.

But he wrote back to her only that once. For a while she did not mind. She convinced herself he would write if he could and she enjoyed writing the letters anyway; it was the most creative and thoughtful she had allowed herself to be since leaving school. But after three long months of unanswered letters, she dared entertain the suspicion that his first reply had been no more than sensitive politeness, humouring her, and that proved a poison to her hopes and she let their non-correspondence cease.

Then Henry Angwin startled everyone by getting engaged. His fiancée was from the county's wealthy middle.

Her father was a farmer too and when he had died and her brother inherited the farm, which was near Chacewater, she had taken a job as a cashier at Truro cattle market, which was how Henry had met her. He joked he had bought far more store cattle than he could afford over the last weeks in the effort to muster the courage to ask her out.

Since Dorothy's parents had long been as his own, it was only natural that he should bring the girl to visit. The two of them came for Sunday lunch, of course, and were given the best china and Dorothy made them a summer pudding.

Jane was perfect for him; pretty, healthy, clearly a hard worker and a thoroughly nice girl it was easy to imagine befriending. She was nearer his age than Dorothy was, in her late twenties perhaps, and seemed so entirely fitting a partner for him Dorothy wondered how she could ever have imagined herself in such a position, taking his arm and exchanging banter. But thanks to what Barnaby had awoken in her, Henry suddenly seemed the manliest man she knew, of course, and the sisterly happiness she felt for him was borne up on little upswells of erotic regret. She sensed that Jane read the situation correctly as she said her goodbyes, fancied she could smell the disappointment off her, a passing sourness, as of stale sweat trapped in a dress sleeve. Washing up and putting away the china after they were gone, she felt a kind of desolation steal over her.

Her mother's response was brief but heartfelt. 'I should have pushed you together more,' was all she said after they had done the evening chores and eaten a bowl of soup in silence. 'A chance like that won't come your way again. Not here.'

As ever, her mother's emotion was expressed in her attitude to inanimate objects. All that evening and all the day that followed, things made her cross and she spoke to wobbling tables, sticking doorkeys, even a chicken she was stuffing, as though they were deliberately setting out to make her teasy.

Dorothy knew she ought to reach out to her, if only to say something not quite true, like, 'Mum, honestly, it doesn't matter.' She knew her mother was suffering in her way quite as if it were she and not Dorothy who had been passed over. She loved her and hated to see her in pain, but there was a forbidding reserve to the older woman, especially when she was upset, expressed in a tension across her shoulders and a tightness to the set of her jaw that had always made it hard to express whatever warmth Dorothy felt for her. Funnily enough her father had the same trouble with her, never trying to reason or cajole her out of a black mood.

'Your mother's stiff-shouldered,' he used to tell Dorothy with a certain pride. 'All the Treeves were that way. We just have to wait for her to smile again of her own accord.'

In this instance, her mother's spell of growling at sticking drawers or dripping taps or cats in her path at least had the effect of drawing Dorothy's attention away from any pain of her own. She knew, without it being discussed, that when they went to church together now, or into Penzance, her mother was looking around her, assessing any single men on her behalf and finding them all wanting.

They were invited to the wedding, naturally, which was held, rather magnificently, in the cathedral, and gave the happy pair a Morphy Richards toaster. In the months that followed, especially as her pregnancy began to show, Jane took to coming up to the farm with Henry when he had things to see to there, and she would visit Dorothy while he went about his business. She became a friend, a cherished friend even, the nearest Dorothy had enjoyed to a confidante since primary school. When Piran was born and Jane asked her to be a godmother, though, she couldn't help wondering if it was a gesture of recompense or compassion, and she felt a fleeting resentment of her. Her mother mortified her by twice asking Jane if she had brothers and twice being told that she did and that each was already married.

Father Philip died in the autumn of that year, suddenly, if not quite peacefully. He was found slumped across the wheelbarrow in his garden when he failed to appear for an eight o'clock service. He was buried above his wife, in the tiny Morvah graveyard and, after the prescribed period, the vacancy was advertised in the *Church Times*. During the interregnum priests from neighbouring parishes, some of them retired, took services in the old man's stead but Dorothy heard no rumours of who might apply. All she had heard, as she was clearing up the Sunday School books one week, was that applicants were so few the decision was postponed by a further month.

Her mother took against one after another of the temporary vicars and kept threatening to transfer her allegiance back down to the church in St Just, only there was a new vicar there, a permanent one, and she had taken against him too because he had introduced the Peace, which she thought false and embarrassing.

Around this time she became unusually tense and quick-tempered again, lashing out in particular at footstools, buckets, the fiddly plastic compartments in the new fridge

– and turning her impotent fury on Dorothy if Dorothy dared to reason with her. 'Don't use that reasonable tone with me,' she snapped on more than one occasion. Dorothy began to worry she was ill – not in her mind but her body – and that fear or pain was finding voice in anger. But they did not have the kind of relationship in which she could set her mind at rest by asking.

And then Barnaby Johnson appeared in the yard without warning. It was late afternoon. It had been unseasonably warm – oppressive, milk-turning weather that had brought clouds of thunder flies into the sheds. Dorothy was in the act of bringing in laundry from the line in the mowhay and saw him from behind a sheet without his seeing her. He walked up to the front door, shadowed by the dog, and then hesitated, visibly nervous, and went to check the milking parlour instead before heading back to the front door. She watched from her hiding place. He wore extraordinarily shiny black shoes and seemed taller and more grown up, somehow. He seemed to have invested in a new, darker suit, a very well-cut one. It looked expensive.

She slipped off to one side and in through the scullery. Her mother was in the kitchen, furiously rolling out pastry, and she reached her just before the door knocker sounded through the house. Dorothy had never been so decisive.

'It's him,' she told her. 'He's come back. I'm not here.'

Flustered, her mother was taking off her apron and brushing flour from her hands. 'But what should I—?' she began.

'I don't know. I'm not here, that's all. I'm in Truro for the day.'

She had expected a protest on moral grounds – her mother was rigorously truthful – so was surprised that she hurried out directly as he knocked again, and half-closed the kitchen door behind her. Dorothy positioned herself to one side of it so she could hear but could also escape silently through the scullery if need arose. She heard every word of the conversation that followed. Amplified by the hall, perhaps, which was all hard surfaces, she heard it as clearly as a radio play and, just as when she listened to the radio, she found she could picture the facial expressions from tones of voice.

'Mrs Sampson?'

'Hello. Dorothy's not here.' Her mother's voice was harsh with anxiety. Dorothy knew what the lie cost her, but perhaps she convinced herself *not here* could simply mean not in the hall right now.

'Good,' he said. 'That's good because it's not her I came to see. Not really.'

'Oh? Will you come in. Can I fetch you a drink? Tea or something cold? It's warm out there.'

'Er. No. Thank you. I can't stay.'

'Well, let me just …' And her mother must have stepped out to join him in the sunny yard because her words became maddeningly indistinct, then Dorothy heard the front door shut, and the sounds from outside – birdsong, cattle lowing – were abruptly muffled.

She hurried out into the scullery and watched through the window, amid the sharp scents of cheese rind, quinces and cold lamb from the day before yesterday, as her mother walked with him to the top of the yard and back onto the lane. The two of them were talking with some animation.

Then something she said made him stop, shake her mother's hand and, unhesitatingly, plant a kiss on her mother's cheek before he walked away. Her mother stood there a moment, gazing after him, and one hand rose to touch her face. Then she turned and looked, with unerring instinct, towards the scullery window and her expression was as stricken as Dorothy could remember seeing it, worse than when Dad died, and there were tears on her wrinkled cheeks. She had not cried when Dad died, or not in the open, and not like this.

Dorothy ran out and took her in her arms. They were not people who touched; she had not realized her mother had become so very thin and she worried, once again, she might be ill with stomach ulcers, or worse, and not telling her. Her mother did not embrace her back but said only, 'I'm sorry,' pulling back and controlling herself with a kind of shudder. 'I meant it for the best. I was thinking of you. I didn't want you hurt.'

'I don't understand,' Dorothy told her. Some people were approaching on the footpath. She set a hand in the small of her mother's back and gently steered her towards the open front door and privacy.

'As a priest's wife, you'd always be poor.'

Dorothy smiled. 'I never thought to marry money, Mum. Anyway, who says he's interested?'

'And it's a hard life,' her mother went on quietly, ignoring her.

'Harder than marrying a farmer?'

'Oh on a farm there's always work, the work never ends and there's often uncertainty, but you stand together and … He may be exhausted half the time and out of the house the rest but you have him to yourself, girl. The husband who's a priest will never be yours entirely. You have to share him. Your house, your family too. He'll always have a higher duty than to you.'

She could tell this was a speech her mother had rehearsed in her head, maybe even muttered aloud as she milked the cows. 'I know all this,' she told her. 'Do you think I haven't worked this out for myself weeks ago? But it's all by the by now. What did he want, anyway? You still haven't said. Mother?'

'I don't think I've ever met a vicar's wife who was happy, not outside of a novel …' Her mother broke off and looked into Dorothy's face with something like wonder, as though seeing it somehow transformed. 'I meant it for the best,' she said again. 'I was only thinking of your happiness.'

'For pity's sake stop talking in code!' Dorothy told her. 'What have you gone and done?'

Her mother shrank in on herself again, accepting defeat. 'They're all here,' she said and led the way back along the hall to the tall mahogany bookcase which stood at one end, beside the looking glass where she would always give a quick, corrective glare at herself before leaving the house, and the table where the only telephone was, chairless and far from the nearest heat source so that calls were kept short. She reached for the top shelf and took down a volume of the rarely consulted old encyclopaedia that was ranged there. 'They weren't so hard to find,' she said wryly. 'I put them under P for Priest.' She took out a small bundle of envelopes and handed them over then returned to the kitchen and her pie-making.

There were eight letters in all. Only the first had been opened. Presumably discretion had overruled curiosity once her mother had learnt to recognize his handwriting and the Portsmouth postmark. Dorothy sat on the stairs to read them. Blood sang in her ears and burned in her cheeks. She could hear the familiar rhythmic thump of her mother's rolling pin.

The first letter answered hers, of course, and the second, her second, but he had slowly sensed something was wrong as she failed to respond to his specific enquiries or to acknowledge that he had written at all. By the fourth letter he knew that his letters weren't reaching her because her fourth letter must have said something like, *I understand your not writing back because your new post must keep you so busy.* But, like her, he had kept on writing and, unlike her, he had not lost faith. Whereas her letters had been quietly matter of fact, accounts of her days and snippets of news from the parish, his were lacking in specifics but simply about his feelings and thoughts and his hopes and plans for the future.

It was only in the short last letter that a note of self-doubt entered.

I have applied for the job at Pendeen and Morvah, was all it said. And my written application has seen me called for an interview. If you have been somehow turned aside, if, for instance, you have done the sensible thing and married Henry Angwin or somebody like him, someone who can support you and keep you in the way that would no doubt satisfy your mother, I too will turn aside and won't accept the post if they offer me it. I can't imagine living in that great, draughty vicarage without you or seeing you on Sundays coming up to the altar rail with someone else. But I can think of nothing nearer perfection than to build a life there with you at my side. Phoning you is pointless of course, so all I can do is write and hope. I wonder if this will ever reach you. Perhaps all my letters are tumbling into a hole in the lining of that thick curtain on the back of your front door? Perhaps that formidable postmistress with the Jack Russell is collecting them for reasons of her own?

Dorothy read all the letters a second time, so as to be quite sure she had missed nothing, then she pulled on a cardigan, because a cold wind was getting up as the sun sank low over the sea, and slipped out without a word to her mother. The letter said he would have taken a room at the nearest pub, the North Inn. It was thought to be more respectable than the Radjel for some reason. She had never been in there before, although of course she knew who the landlords were. The bar was already noisy with men, miners mostly, she guessed; she could smell the tang of Lifebuoy soap beneath the cigarette smoke. Presumably these were the unmarried ones. The ones with wives went home first to eat as the day's shift finished. It was said wives listened out for the muffled dynamite blast that marked the end of each day's work and lit their ovens at the sound of it, knowing exactly how long it would take their menfolk to reach the surface and head to the dry to wash off the day's grime before walking home.

They made way for her with curious glances and she recognized some of them and nodded hello. She told the landlady she had come to see Barnaby Johnson, ordered herself a half of shandy then sat in the deserted saloon bar to wait for him and it was as though the first sip made her drunk. The strangeness of being in this building she had passed so often and never entered, of waiting there alone for a man she had convinced herself she loved as much as he loved her, although he still felt like a stranger to her, emphasized the sense that she had entered a sort of waiting room, a space of transition, between her old life and her new.

I am waiting, she thought, *for the rest of my life. But I could still step back. I could leave this drink, this sticky table and tired chair and walk home to mutton and carrot pie and nothing need change.*

But then he came in and she rose in such a hurry that she slopped her drink and she was smiling as broadly as he was so that it almost hurt and her future was suddenly blindingly simple. She drew him to her and they kissed for the second time. Her hand that had rested on his shoulder – and it *was* a new suit, she realized – strayed across to the alien material of his dog collar. It was so hard, not like fabric at all. She tapped it playfully with her fingernails.

'Isn't it uncomfortable?' she asked.

'You can pull it off, you know,' he said. 'It comes off as easily as a traffic warden's tie.'

She tugged and gasped to find the symbol of his priesthood so swiftly in her hand like a sort of trophy. And he kissed her again far longer and more deeply this time so that she began to worry someone from the other bar would look in and see them. And as she kissed him back her fingers continued to fiddle with the collar behind his back.

BARNABY AT 60

Lenny's inquest had been organized speedily out of mercy to his mother and perhaps because the evidence had been relatively easy to gather in. A few days ago a middle-aged woman in a dark blue suit had presented herself on the doorstep.

'Are you the Reverend Barnaby Sadler Johnson?' she asked and, because she couldn't seem to stop smiling, he wondered if she were a premium bond emissary sent to tell him he had won a million pounds. When he smiled back and said yes, however, she abruptly stopped smiling and handed over a coroner's summons.

The inquest was held in Penzance, in one of the larger committee rooms at St John's Hall. The coroner, a fiercely intelligent and much-liked Cornishwoman, sat at a large mahogany table with a clerk beside her taking notes. Word had spread and the public chairs were nearly all taken. Barnaby and Dot sat at the front, in the chairs set aside for witnesses, as did Nick Morris the policeman and the ambulance driver who had come to Lenny's flat and the detective who had conducted Barnaby's interview following his arrest. Then there was a man Barnaby didn't recognize, whom Dot murmured was a GP from St Just. The last witnesses to arrive – and they came, impressively, as a group – were Lenny's ex, Amy, and her father and Nuala Barnes. There was another woman who looked startlingly

43

like Nuala and who he realized must be the sister from Australia he had last seen at Lenny's christening.

The coroner's clerk came forward and walked along the row checking names off on a list, then conferred with the coroner before declaring the inquest open. The coroner looked, Barnaby decided, like one of the more approachable members of the royal family. She opened the proceedings by saying she had summoned the inquest to establish the truth of Lenny Barnes's death on Mazey Day. 'This is not a trial,' she added firmly. 'Although sometimes facts revealed at an inquest result in a criminal investigation. I am here to establish the whos, wheres, whens and hows. I feel I must begin by apologizing to Lenny's mother, Mrs Barnes,' and here the clerk indicated which of the women in the front row was Nuala, 'that it is rarely possible to hold an inquest immediately after a death so as to allow the release of a loved one's body for burial or cremation. Mrs Barnes's understanding of the due processes of law and county bureaucracy is appreciated. Some of the things you may hear will be upsetting. However much any of you, or members of the press or public, wish to speak, I must ask you to keep silent unless asked to give evidence. Please respect the difficulty some of our witnesses may feel in speaking before an audience.'

She called the GP from St Just first. He took the oath for non-believers, gave his name and confirmed that he had been Lenny's doctor for most of his life and, at one stage, his weekend rugby coach. Questioned, he described the nature of Lenny's accident, how a collapsing scrum during a rugby match had given him a spinal injury resulting in a temporary total paralysis which two subsequent operations succeeded in reducing to a paralysis of the lower body. He stated that the specialist in charge of Lenny's case had offered no hope of further recovery. He confirmed that Lenny had pursued an exhaustive course of rehabilitation and physiotherapy but had clearly been depressed at the prospect of life in a wheelchair.

'So are you saying he was clinically depressed?'

'Possibly,' the doctor said. 'Although, unlike much depression, his had a clear cause. In that he seemed unlikely to recover from it without medical intervention, I'd be tempted to call it clinical, yes.'

'Did he apply to you for treatment for his depression?'

'No. We discussed the possibility of antidepressant medication but he was wary of that because his situation wasn't going to change and he didn't want to be on antidepressants for life.'

Next she called Nick, who confirmed that on Mazey Day at 12.30 p.m. a call came through to his squad car calling him to Flat 8, Finisterre Court, Ross Lane, Penzance. There he found Father Barnaby – he meant the Reverend Johnson – he indicated Barnaby with a shy smile – evidently in a very distressed state, with the deceased beside him.

'Lenny Barnes?'

'Yes.'

'Where was the deceased exactly?'

'In his wheelchair at the table. Father Barnaby said he had been with him as he took his own life and this meant I should arrest him on a charge of assisted suicide. At this point the paramedics arrived and they confirmed Lenny – Mr Barnes – was dead.'

'Was the manner of death obvious?'

'Not immediately. But Reverend Johnson said he had put something in his water.'

'Sorry. Who had?'

'Sorry. Lenny. Mr Barnes. I then investigated further and found syringes and phials in the kitchen together with a letter of instructions for testing a drug for narcotic strength and purity. I submitted the glass for forensic analysis ...'

'And I have before me the forensics report, which confirms that the glass, like one of the phials, contained veterinary Nembutal which, consumed in the quantities suggested, would have brought about rapid loss of consciousness on ingestion followed by death by stopping Lenny's respiratory system.'

There was a muffled exclamation from someone in the audience.

'Was there evidence of how this drug and the testing kit had been obtained?'

'There were small parcels in the rubbish bin corresponding to both. The Nembutal had come from Mexico and the testing kit from somewhere in the UK.'

The ambulance driver was called next and simply confirmed that he had attended Mr Barnes's address on the day in question and found him dead at the scene. Shortly afterwards Mrs Barnes had arrived and confirmed the identity of the deceased. Given the circumstances, he had taken the body to await a post-mortem.

When the coroner summoned Barnaby to the table, her clerk slid the Bible towards him for the oath.

As he placed his hand on it and began to repeat the words after her, it struck him what a very odd thing it was still to ask men and women to swear on a book with which most of them were now unfamiliar. Even amongst nominal Christians, it would surely have been more potent, more binding, to be asked to swear on a child's life, and yet those same people would have flinched if asked to take an unbeliever's oath instead. It was a navy blue Bible, small, spotless and, almost certainly, he reflected, doomed never to be opened.

Asked to describe his relation to the deceased, Barnaby swallowed and opted for a sin of omission rather than an outright lie.

'Lenny was one of my parishioners, although not a regular attender at church. He came to me for confirmation in his teens and attended for a little under a year after that. I'd known him all his life as he lived nearby and went to the village school.'

He wished witnesses could simply face the coroner and turn their backs on the others in the room. He was conscious of the effort it took not to glance at Nuala.

'How did you come to be with him on the day in question?'

He glanced instead at Dot. She was regarding him with what he privately thought of as her sermon face: attentive and solemn but slightly too anxious to be flattering.

'He asked me there. He rang me at home the day before. We agreed I would call in at twelve, which was the earliest convenient time for both of us.'

'Did he say why he wanted to see you?'

'No. And I didn't ask. I never ask. Parishioners often say they want to see me for one reason, then discover once I'm there that they actually need to talk about something else entirely.'

'So you just go.'

'Yes.'

'You knew nothing about Lenny's suicide plans?'

'Nothing.'

A man at the back of the hall shouted, 'Liar!' and a small commotion flared up. Barnaby could not prevent himself glancing back and fleetingly caught Nuala staring at him. He looked hurriedly forward again.

The two weeks since the suicide and Barnaby's arrest had been horrible and seen Pendeen in turmoil. As was often the way with a young death, Lenny's was labelled a tragedy, with that glib overstatement that brooked no correction, and public response had been correspondingly fulsome, with a spontaneous shrine set up on the railings of the village school. So many flowers and photographs and cards were left that there was soon no room to attach anything else to the railings and a kind of tide of them enveloped the pavement as well so that pedestrians were obliged to cut out into the road to pass by. Lenny in death stood for all youth, so that children too young ever to have known him were encouraged to add to the offerings. Candles were left, and nightlights and the scene after dark took on more than ever the aspect of a site of holy significance, with solemn-faced boys and girls keeping vigil there, reading the messages, photographing the flowers and flickering lights with their mobile phones. Some wept openly. Some hugged their friends. Occasionally, as Barnaby passed, there would be music there, from a phone or guitar or just unaccompanied voices. His daughter, Carrie, told him there was a similar scene in Penzance. The old ladies in Lenny's block rarely saw such excitement and were tending cut flowers, trimming candles and even occasionally serving refreshments like so many practical nuns in attendance at the tomb of a saint.

Meanwhile Barnaby had been demonized in the local then the national press as the Vicar of Death, who had done nothing to help a young man dying. One tabloid even suggested he had brought along the means of Lenny's suicide. The press's worst was swiftly done and it soon lost interest in what seemed a story without future. But the local effects of what was printed rumbled on. Human excrement had been left on their doorstep and rubbed on the door handles of both churches and, after a nasty moment where a petrol-soaked rag was pushed through the letter box, setting fire to the thick old curtain that had always hung there, Dot had set up a continental-style external mail box and nailed the letter box shut with a length of plank. Luckily they had still been downstairs when the fire was started and had put it out with an extinguisher Barnaby had not known they possessed. The taint of burnt cloth still haunted the house days later.

More shouting followed. The coroner waited for the fuss to abate on its own, then said she would clear the room of everyone but the required witnesses if there were any further interruptions.

'How did he seem to you when you arrived?' she asked.

'Cheerful. He had just been for a walk in the sunshine. I mean—'

'We know what you meant.'

'He had just taken himself out in the sunshine in his chair, along the front. I got there a little before him and he seemed calm and relaxed.'

'What happened then?'

'We went inside together and talked and it was then he told me he couldn't go on, that he couldn't see the point of going on. I argued with him. I think I reminded him how many people loved or admired him. I certainly suggested his despair would pass. He ...' Remembering the scene, the dazzlingly sunny little room, the blare of bands and thump of drummers from the distant parade and Lenny's deep, soft voice and the quiet triumph with which he had suddenly said, 'Not long now,' Barnaby became dizzy and had to grip the back of the chair in front of him.

'There's no need to stand,' the coroner said. 'You're not on trial. Please. Sit. Here,' and she reached, with unwitting irony, to pour him a tumbler of water.

'Go on when you're ready,' she said. 'What happened next?'

'I thought it was simply water in his glass,' he said, 'Until he suddenly drained it and pulled a face – I think it was bitter – and then he said ... he said *not long now*. He told me he'd be dead within five minutes.'

'So you rang for an ambulance.'

'Not immediately.'

There were gasps. He tried not to think about Dot watching him from one end of the front row, or Nuala and her sister from the other.

'Why not?'

'I believed him when he said there was no time and I saw he truly wished to end his life and ... I believe he had a right to.'

'So, let me get this right for the record, Mr Johnson. Knowing Lenny Barnes to be dying, you did nothing to help him?'

'No. I helped him.'

'How?'

'By prayer. He asked me to pray for him. And I realized that was why he wanted me to be there at the end. For prayer. I administered Extreme Unction.'

'Could you explain?'

'I anointed him with chrism – holy oil – from this.' He held up his little oil bottle for her to see.

'You happened to have that with you although you didn't know his intentions?'

'I have it with me at all times, as I do my communion set. I never know when it might be needed. I am a priest, not a paramedic or a doctor. I have few skills. I've been on a first aid at work course – everyone on our parish team has – but I'm not confident I could give CPR correctly. But I do know I can pray for a dying man's eternal soul and I am confident that prayer will offer comfort to the dying and will be heard with kindness by God.'

The room was utterly quiet now except for seagulls briefly squabbling on one of its high-up windowsills and the crystalline patter of computer keys as the clerk took rapid notes on his laptop. It seemed to Barnaby that the space was shrinking about him until it was unbearably full of people breathing and listening and waiting. He made himself take another sip of water because nerves were making his tongue stick to the roof of his mouth. He looked up and found the coroner's face turned full upon him. She no longer looked like a sympathetic royal.

'He lost consciousness before I reached the end of the prayer, I think,' he continued. 'He slipped sideways in his chair.'

'Please go on,' she said.

'Lenny had written letters to his mother and fiancée. I'd promised I'd see they were delivered and I was anxious that should happen and that they shouldn't be taken by the police.'

'Why?'

'Because it was his dying wish and they were private letters, not evidence. So I rang Mrs Barnes. She wasn't answering, unfortunately, so I had to leave a message.'

Without thinking he let his eyes stray to Nuala as he spoke, and found her staring back at him, her eyes stricken. He looked back at the coroner and her face of judgement.

'I didn't go into details,' he told her, 'but I said it was bad, that she should ask a friend to drive her. Then I asked a neighbour I had spoken to earlier – Kitty Arnold – to hang onto the letters until Mrs Barnes arrived. Then I dialled 999 and called for police and an ambulance.'

'And you gave yourself up for arrest?'

'I knew the circumstances were ambiguous. I thought it more honest to be arrested and trust in justice than just to slip away. I knew that as an attender of the suicide I might be thought to have assisted it.'

'And as we have seen,' the coroner said, with a severe glance at the public seats, 'that is precisely what some people have chosen to believe. However your honesty in the case was respected and the Crown Prosecution Service decided on the Monday following that there was no case to be made against you and the charge of assisted suicide was dropped. Thank you, Mr Johnson. That will be all.'

She waited, consulting her notes, while Barnaby returned to his seat. 'Mrs Barnes,' she then said. 'There's no need to come up here as my question to you is very brief. Did you receive this letter from your son?' There was no answer. 'Mrs Barnes?'

'Yes.' Nuala's voice sounded high and strained, not like herself at all.

'I know this is very hard for you, therefore I'll word my sentence so a simple yes or no answer will be all you need give. Did the letter Lenny wrote you make it clear he intended to commit suicide?'

'I never read it.'

'You never read your son's letter?'

There was a clatter as Nuala stood up, dropping a bag her sister hurried to pick up for her. 'I was so angry. I burnt it. I never read it. I'm sorry.' Nuala ran out through the swing doors and her sister jumped up with an apologetic glance at the coroner and followed her out.

The coroner checked that the clerk had noted Mrs Barnes's brief testimony, then called for Amy to come up. Derek Hawker came forward instead and Barnaby was struck by the change in him. As a rule Amy's father was maddeningly secure, arrogantly masculine. One of nature's PE teachers, he was just the sort of man to relish being asked to stand up on his own and read the Intercessions. As he had a quiet word with the coroner, however, and handed over a letter, he seemed both nervous and diminished.

'Ms Hawker is too upset to address me directly but she has asked her father to submit the letter she received from Lenny Barnes and is content that this be read out,' the coroner said. She unfolded the letter and read it through in frowning silence before looking over her glasses at Amy. 'You're happy for me to read this out?' Presumably Amy nodded. The coroner cleared her throat. *Dear Amy*, she read. *By the time you read this. Well. You know what the end of this sentence is going to be. I can't cope any more. Everybody is so kind but it's not enough. I said when I broke up with you that I couldn't have you spend your life with only half the man you thought you were marrying. It wouldn't have been right and I stick by that. But please understand when I say that without you and without my legs, life isn't worth my while. I love you and hope you'll move on. Be happy with someone else, someone you deserve and who deserves you. For the record, I did this all on my own, with nobody's help. I'm getting in Father Barnaby as a witness so there's no misunderstanding afterwards. All my love. Len.* She folded the letter back into its envelope and handed it back to Mr Hawker. 'Thank you,' she said.

She thanked the witnesses and composed her thoughts for a moment before standing to address the room. Her verdict was death by suicide and that Lenny's body should be immediately released to his family.

Two days later was a Sunday, the third since Lenny's death. Barnaby rose early as usual. He took Dot her tea then drafted a short sermon on the three resurrections that prefigured Christ's own – those of Lazarus, Jairus's daughter and the only son of the widow from Nain – and went on to write rather challengingly about mourning and how, along with married love, coping with loss was one of life's fundamentals for which Christ left no helpful pattern. He may have wept with his friends at Lazarus's tomb, but he negated that grief with a miraculous resurrection, as though death were no more than a misunderstanding and their grief a failure of faith. And Barnaby quoted Dorothy Sayers's account of Lazarus describing life after death as being the moment of glimpsing the 'beautiful and terrible' front of the tapestry while the living must content themselves with seeing only the tangle of knotted threads at its rear.

Carrie had elected to experience her first Quaker meeting that morning with her new friends so he and Dot drove up alone. The church car park was full and the lane up to it crammed with cars as well, so Dot ended up dropping him off at the church door and driving back to park on the main road.

The robing servers were in a state of high excitement about the crowd and it was the youngest, most computer-savvy of them who explained. Barnaby's testimony at the inquest had been recorded on somebody's smart phone and uploaded to the Internet where it had already been viewed and copied thousands of times. Someone else who had been there, the lay leader of an evangelical church that met in an old warehouse in Penzance, a man Barnaby would have assumed would despise him as comparatively establishment and traditional, had started a Facebook Group called We Love Father Barnaby's Power of Prayer.

'I checked before I came up here,' the server said, 'And you've already got over four thousand likes. Four thousand!' Barnaby had no idea what she meant.

The congregation was the biggest of his career. When he finished his sermon, to which the size of crowd had inspired him to add an improvised sentence or two, there was applause which completely drowned out his request for

God's blessing on it. The sign of peace lasted a good ten minutes. The collection plate was so full that notes drifted off it onto the altar as he held it aloft. They almost ran out of communion wafers, and had to break them into halves and then quarters to eke them out.

In any other circumstances it would have been an answer to prayers: a country-parish equivalent to the feeding of the five thousand. By the time he had shaken the last worshipper's hand, however, his face ached.

He was resolved to call the archdeacon's office the next morning and apply to leave his post and retire as soon as was conveniently possible.

MODEST CARLSSON AT 39

Modest Carlsson had his life, if not his soul, saved in Portsmouth. He had come there on a bleak sort of whim and stayed there through despair. Modest Carlsson was not his real name, naturally. He was raised as Maurice Carver, but the name change had become necessary. And he used to be an English teacher, not a second-hand-book dealer. His life had been balanced, law abiding and uneventful: youth, university, teacher-training college, marriage, daughter.

But then into his sixth-form class had sauntered a girl, whose name he could no longer even bring his mind to shape. Blue-eyed, tawny-haired, extravagantly flirtatious, she had led him on. Even the judge, a woman, suggested as much in her summing-up. The girl had slowly unbuttoned her shirt as he talked to the class, stroked her cleavage with a pencil as he approached her desk, the same pencil she slowly chewed, staring at him, when lost for what to write during a test. She stood so close to him that he could smell the spearmint on her breath, catch the sugary, fruit bowl wafts of shampoo from her hair. It was often said in the common room that if this girl spent even half the attention on her studies that she lavished on that tumble of hair of hers, she would have made Oxbridge material. She was clever but fatally lazy. Something in her background had sapped her self-confidence too, which was perhaps why she set about ensnaring a teacher when she could have taken her pick from the boy-men of the school who followed her every slouching move and hung on her every mumbled word.

Up to this point her behaviour towards him was nothing out of the ordinary. Adolescence was about discovering and flexing one's power over others, or learning to compensate for the lack of it and, as the only adults in range, teachers were natural targets against which that strength could be pitted. Plenty of boys and girls in every class in her year were clumsily flirting with teachers or, usually with more finesse, seeking out their weaknesses and mocking them. Unbeknownst to the pupils, the teachers held regular meetings at which such attacks were aired, even laughed over, and their dangerous potential disarmed by exposure. But then she went further than her peers by starting to write him notes, which she slipped in with her homework. Notes and occasionally photographs. And instead of showing his unsuspecting wife or battle-weary colleagues so as to maintain the moral high ground, he foolishly kept them to himself then, more foolishly still, responded in kind.

Before long they had an assignation. She slipped into his car outside a supermarket several blocks from the school and he drove her out to a notorious beauty spot car park where, among the lovers' litter, she suddenly changed her mind and her successful seduction of him became his violent rape of her.

Had he murdered her, strangled her with her tights and pushed her into the flooded quarry nearby perhaps or even driven her side of the car into oncoming traffic, he might have escaped with only his soul in peril but he was no more

PATRICK GALE

a murderer than, calmly eating toast with his family that morning, he had been a rapist. So he handed her tissues for her tears and wet wipes for the rest of her, drove her back to the end of her street, apologizing the while, and dropped her off.

He had handed over her photographs to the police, thinking their sluttishness would weigh against her but, of course, everyone assumed he had stolen them from her locker, which meant they had the reverse effect from the one he had expected. The evidence, which included his DNA on her skirt, was plentiful and damning and it soon emerged that her lazy cleverness had ushered her into a class a year older than her, so the charge was not just rape but rape of a minor. And in the eyes of the local rag and his colleagues and family he was suddenly not just an unfaithful idiot who had abused a position of trust, but a paedophile. Although he was actually no more a paedophile than he was a murderer or, habitually, a rapist.

In prison, where he was utterly isolated for his own protection and through others' disgust, he shaved off his neat little beard and then his hair, so that his large head was quite egglike and, he fancied, monastic. His only comfort were books – with which the prison kept him well supplied because it was easier than talking to him – and food, of which he ate all he could until he appeared the demon of everyone's imaginings.

On his release, married no longer and apparently no longer a father either, he used his release travel pass to buy a ticket to Portsmouth. After several years with all privilege of choice suspended, the sudden presentation of seemingly endless possibility was overwhelming. So he let the station destination displays do the deciding for him. Wherever he went would have to be a terminus, he decided. Portsmouth Harbour was the destination of the next train due in. It was either that or London, and London frightened him. He had reread the works of Jane Austen on the inside, soothed as much by her moral rectitude as by the elegant plainness of her cadences, and her references to Portsmouth aroused his curiosity to see a place he had never visited.

At once it seemed to him a terrible city, blighted first by the bombs of the Blitz then by the steady erosion of its *raison d'être* and naval pride and lastly by the steady flight of the middle class, but its grimness, its failure, suited his new sense of himself and the blasts of sea air, the scents of salt and car ferry, were a joy after the stale air of his cell.

To his probation officer to whom he was bound to continue to report regularly at first, he remained Maurice Carver, of course, but to the world at large he became Modest Carlsson, product of a Russian/Swedish union, his parents music lovers murdered for their principles, his wife and child dead from carbon monoxide poisoning in the only accommodation he could afford them.

He had not wasted his time in prison. Obviously he was far more highly educated than most, if not all his fellow inmates, so he did not sign up for GCSE courses, but he encouraged visits from a writer in residence attached to the prison, a novelist, who was a believer in the therapeutic benefits of fiction. The novelist was keen he should write about his childhood and family, which he duly did, albeit making most of it up, and that he seek to give his own pain and isolation a context by imagining and describing the pain and isolation of others. And it was from these exercises that Modest Carlsson and his lugubrious history emerged.

He had enjoyed few opportunities to rehearse this story in prison but he had reviewed and embroidered it in private. Once he got to Portsmouth, he released snippets of it in bus queues, on trains, in waiting rooms and in bars until he quite believed it himself and could grow genuinely moist eyed at the mention of his dead wife. Wife and child retained the names of their faithless real-life counterparts – Sylvia and Lily – because it gave him a cheap pleasure to murder them in conversation and because he fancied their unassuming, lower-middle class Englishness lent an added sheen to his sentimental history. Changing the name he went by could not have been simpler and, even though he was obliged to let the probation office know, he felt it made him less vulnerable to anyone from his past life who might seek him out.

He had always been careful with money and, even after the divorce settlement, retained enough savings to start a new life. Returning to teaching was out of the question. Instead, with the savings that had been harvesting a handsome interest in his absence, he took on a rundown secondhand bookshop whose owner had just died in harness. It had a lavatory, a sink, a kettle and there was just room to squeeze a single bed into the office so – probably illegally – he lived in the shop too.

Most of the stock was inferior, paperback stuff, the greasy fruit of house clearances, and it was hard to see how the previous proprietor had made an honest living. The most popular line, he soon discovered, were the tattered old porn magazines in the basement's 'adult' section. Of these he duly sealed the less damaged in cellophane and began to market them at a premium as vintage erotica.

The other healthy market was signed for and unsigned first editions. He soon found there were collectors of these – usually men – who seemed to have less interest in the contents of a book than in its condition. Other dealers' catalogues and prices taught him what to look out for. Every Monday he kept the shop closed to trawl house clearance sales and down-at-heel auctions where books were sold by weight or by the yard. And while he was minding the shop, he would pick through his latest haul, cleaning the better purchases and wrapping them neatly in cellophane. He became an extremely neat wrapper. When it was worth his time, he would visit book festivals and join the long (or sometimes surprisingly short) queues to have a famous writer sign an old copy of one of their books.

'Just your signature,' he would always tell them to prevent them writing *all good wishes* or some such devaluing nonsense.

By degrees his principal income began to come from online sales – a business for which the shop, which was hardly in a prime bibliophilic district, became little more than an office.

His time in prison and the reasons for it had killed off any impulse to form a relationship, even had the opportunity arisen. When his need became distracting he visited a prostitute, of which Portsmouth had such an abundance that he never needed to see the same one twice and so suffer the shame of her recognition or bad memories. Outside again, however, he was assailed by a bitter loneliness he had never felt as a prisoner. Free to move among people once more, he became sharply aware that he was noticed only for the brief registering of disgust. At least disgust involved notice. More wounding was the not being noticed at all, the skating over of eyes, the automatic, impersonal courtesies of transaction. He became obsessed with eye contact. When he paid for something, he would hold back his money a second or two until a salesgirl met his eye. When someone bought a book or magazine off him – especially when they bought a magazine – he would make them – make them! – return his gaze. And he would smile. In prison he was in all probability clinically depressed but now that he was free he taught himself to smile again, practising whenever he faced his spattered mirror. Smiles, he learned, were a challenge less easily ducked than a mere verbal pleasantry. To smile at someone, especially a stranger, was somehow to assume moral superiority until the smile was returned. When he smiled at someone and said a bright good morning to them and they did neither in return, he felt rewarded by a brief flush of angry satisfaction that he was the better person.

He had no illusions about expecting love. He had experienced love and had thrown it away and that kind of true, trusting affection surely only came to each man once. It was not love for which he was lonely, or even friendship, although a friend, an equal, would have been pleasant. He had no such expectations because he knew he was repellent and he knew that the process was cumulative – the more he disgusted people, the more disgusting he would become. What he hungered for was nothing warmer-blooded than significance, he realized: to play a role in people's lives again and know that his decisions and actions affected others. The significance he had known as a teacher, as a head of department no less, this he missed more than his personal significance to his wife and daughter.

He considered suicide frequently. To jump into the sea, cut his wrists or step in front of a train or lorry was a regular temptation and he was ashamed at his fear of doing so and mildly intrigued that he should persist in clinging to life when life had so little to offer him.

He turned instead to alcohol and Jesus. Alcohol found him easily. His appetite had greatly increased in prison and with it his size, to the point where he now had to buy his clothes in a dismal shop catering exclusively to the obese, which in turn so repelled him that he ate more to lift his spirits. He had always liked wine and, now that he lived and worked alone, found that he could easily drink a bottle a day, starting at lunchtime, two if the weather were especially cold or hot.

Once or twice he became extravagantly, falling-down drunk. Waking on the floor of the shop in his own vomit and urine, entirely unaware of how the previous hours had been passed, except for the drinking. But before long he found he could drink steadily with, as he saw it, a measure of responsible control and show no ill effects beyond a generalized warmth of feeling that usually curdled by nightfall into self-pity that his warmth had gone unrecognized and unreturned.

Jesus's approach was characteristically sly and subtle. Modest had never been a Christian, not even, to his knowledge, been christened and certainly not confirmed. Studying then teaching English literature, he had learned enough to understand the broadest religious reference but he had never actually read or possessed a Bible. He had done his best to avoid poets such as Donne or Hopkins, most of whose work was incomprehensible to a reader with neither religious schooling nor spiritual leanings. But then he was called by one of his seedy new work contacts to clear the extensive bookshelves of an elderly cat lover. The books on the lower shelves were unsalvageable, from having been sprayed by generations of tom cats, and naturally he told his contact that all the books were ruined and worthless but that he would deal with them as a favour. Many of the books, needless to say, were in excellent condition – the ailurophile had been a keen book buyer and a blessedly tidy reader, the sort who never folded down a page or read while she was bathing or eating. She had a complete set of mint-condition William Golding hardbacks and a first edition of *The Waste Land*, which he sold for a tidy sum. And while picking through her collection in the shop, sorting trash from trophies, he found a New Testament. It attracted him precisely because it was so unlike a Bible to look at. Printed on good, quarto paper, with a large attractive font and laid out like a novel, with the paragraphs allowed to cross a whole page instead of being crammed into indigestible columns, and with the chapters numbered but not the verses. There were attractive colour plate illustrations too, from the relevant sections of the Duc de Berry's *Très Riches Heures*.

He meant to wrap it in cellophane like the other, better books but then, having poured himself a large glass of Riesling, he began to read and he read on through the rest of the night and the bottle. He carried on reading it all that week, whether there were customers in the shop or not, neglecting all other tasks, even to go to the public baths for his weekly wash. He read a Gospel a day and the Acts on Friday, was alternately bored and baffled by the Epistles on Saturday, when he should have been attending a bank-ruptcy sale in Gosport, and was so disturbed by the Book of Revelation on Sunday that he drank most of a bottle of gin as he read it and would ever after taste juniper on his tongue and feel breathless and a little dizzy when he heard a reading from it.

He had done nothing so intently and consistently since he was a student and the experience left him profoundly unsettled for days afterwards, despite attempting an exor-cism by reading the least biblical texts the shelves could offer, from de Sade's *Justine* to Angela Carter to 'Readers' Wives' Confessions'. He kept having dreams in which Jesus, who had become conflated in his unconscious with the doe-eyed prison novelist, talked kindly to him in words he could not catch, Aramaic possibly, or, most disturbingly, came to sit at the end of his tiny bed, held his foot firmly through the bedding and said, all too clearly in English, 'He sitteth in the lurking places of the villages.'

It was high summer, the sort of sticky August weather that brought out the crudest in everyone. Men paraded in noth-ing but Union Jack shorts. Every child seemed fractious and smeared with ice cream. Pubs spilled threateningly onto the pavements around them and the streets reeked of grilling, sweat and onions.

Out of wine, overcome by thirst, he had gone to the grimly genteel lounge bar of one of the least noisy of the neighbourhood pubs for a drink or two – nothing excessive

– and was walking home in the sodium-lit non-night alternately seething at the rudeness of people and startled by the blare of music from passing cars.

'Oi! Excuse me.'

It was a bunch of sailors on leave. Even without the crew cuts and tattoos, he would have known this from the pub they were leaning against – one few civilian youths would dare frequent.

'Oi! Fatty!'

Used to abuse, he did what he always did, ignored it, crossed the road and quickened his pace without actually breaking into a run.

'I said Fatty. That's you!'

Suddenly they were on the pavement before him. Behind him too. He remembered prison, combs improvised into blades, toothbrush handles patiently scraped to dagger sharpness, and turned so that his back was to the bricks.

'Sorry,' he said, putting on a stammer to make them find him ridiculous rather than offensive. 'I'm a bit deaf.'

'Excuse me,' the leader said again. They were all drunk, unsteady on their feet but fired up. They reeked of beer and noxious cologne.

'We only wanted to ask you a question.'

'Don't be frightened,' another added.

'I'm not frightened,' he lied, wishing he could scale the wall behind him like a spider. 'What's the question?'

'Well, Fatty. We were just wondering … Would you die for Queen and Country?'

'I'm a bit old.'

'Yes. And a bit fat. But would you? Would you die for Queen and Country?'

It was a trick, of course. If he said yes, they would kick him. If he said no, they would kick him. 'Actually,' he said. 'Probably not, these days.'

The punch was so rapid he did not see which one delivered it. It came full in his face so that he flew back hard against the house wall and struck his head. There was another blow to his stomach that winded him and had him doubled over.

'Yup. Really fat,' one of them said. 'Disgusting.'

They kicked him then. He had watched scenes like this in prison; he had known there would be kicking eventually.

In what space was left for thought between pain and pumping adrenaline, he assumed they were going to continue kicking him as he slumped to the pavement and that quite possibly he was about to die. But they broke off and ran away, laughing. He distinctly heard them begin their prank on someone else.

'Hey. Excuse me? We've just got a question we'd like you to answer. Don't be shy!'

He could feel blood bubbling from his nose and then tasted it too. He put a hand gingerly to the back of his head and felt wetness there that sickened him. He tried to stand but his legs would not obey him, robbed of power by shock, perhaps. Besides, he had no idea what he should do next. He supposed he must need a hospital yet knew neither where Portsmouth's hospital was nor how he would reach it. He must leave the street, at least, he knew that much, in case the gang tired of their second victim and decided to return to their first.

'No. Don't try to get up.'

His eyes had closed up, he realized now, and made him temporarily blind. It was a young voice, low, educated, officer-class if it was a sailor's. He felt a hand on his shoulder holding him in place quite firmly. 'An ambulance is coming,' the voice said. 'You're safe now. Did they rob you?'

'No,' Modest managed.

'You're bleeding quite a lot. I'm going to give you a handkerchief and you need to pinch it hard across the bridge of your nose if you can bear to.'

'Not sure I can …'

'Here. I'll guide your hand.'

A folded handkerchief was pressed into his hand then his hand was guided to the middle of his face by large fingers which then clutched his into position. The pain grew no worse so perhaps there was no fracture. Modest felt a great desire to sleep come upon him.

'No,' said the priest. 'You need to stay with me, I'm afraid, in case you've got concussion. What's your name?'

'Modest.'

'How wonderful. Like Mussorgsky. And Tchaikovsky's brother.'

'Yes. Modest Carlsson.'

'Are you Swedish?'

No one had ever asked this before. It made it so easy.

'Half. And half Russian.'

'Your English is very good.'

'I've lived here all my life. I was born in Bayswater.'

'And where do you live now?'

'Allaway Avenue.'

'So you were nearly home! That was bad luck.'

'Yes.'

'Why did they hit you?'

'I wouldn't die for Queen and Country.'

'Ha. That's a new one. Me neither. I'm a terrible coward and I've got flat feet. And I'm a priest. We're much more use alive in any case. Nature's stretcher-bearers.'

Modest was going to ask him his name but suddenly the ambulance arrived and a policewoman and the priest explained briefly that he had seen nothing, just found him, which surely was not quite the truth, then he gave Modest's shoulder a quick squeeze and murmured, 'God watches you, Modest. All will be well,' and seemed to melt away as other voices and other hands took over.

When he told them he was a childless widower, the nurses insisted on keeping him in overnight for observation. He needed stitches to the back of his head. A nurse laid a deliciously cold dressing across his nose and eyes to reduce the swelling but even so, when he could see again properly come morning, he found that his fat face now looked monstrously swollen.

A consultation of the section on stains in the *Reader's Digest Household Manual* – a book which, like the New Testament, he had impulsively removed from stock for his own uses – told him the trick with blood-stained linen was to soak it in brine. He was not particularly interested in hygiene, beyond the preservation of books, but he was due to take a wash to the launderette and salt happened to be one of the few cooking ingredients he had in his possession.

There was something satisfactorily symbolic, too, in redeeming his shirt from the previous night's outrage and in being able to watch the blood slowly lift away as though any lasting wound went with it down the plughole. The next day he bundled shirt and handkerchief, still wet, into the holdall with his rather smelly laundry. When he retrieved it that evening from the pursy-lipped launderette attendant, who resented him for not paying extra to have things ironed, the handkerchief was revealed as sporting a dark blue embroidered B on one corner. He had an M one just like it, a long-ago Christmas present from his daughter, Lily, which miraculously had been waiting for him in the pocket of his court-case suit when it was handed back to him on his release.

He was tempted to keep it, naturally, but the Jesus dreams began to trouble him again and he sensed the two things were connected. 'I gave you my hanky,' the honey-voiced Jew kept saying. 'I died for Queen and Country and you gave me nothing in return. Thy paths drop fatness.' On and on until Modest began to punch and kick him.

Eventually he began investigating churches around Paulsgrove and then further afield, in Cosham and Portchester, rarely far from the dreary thunder of the M27. He held a picture of the priest in his head, of course, but all he actually had to go on was his distinctive voice and the feel of his hands. And the letter B. He knew this was foolish behaviour, erratic even, but the challenge of it diverted him from his aching face and he was obsessive by design, one of nature's librarians, he had come to realize, systematic and relentless in seeing a task through to its conclusion.

And then he felt inhibited about simply showing up and asking questions, so he attended services as a cover for his research, one church, one Sunday, at a time. In a few weeks he was forgetting even to take the handkerchief with him to hand over should he find the right priest. The Anglican cathedral was too pale and impersonal, the Catholic one, too full of trinkets, like a common Christmas tree. The Methodists felt too low, the happy-clappy brigade friendly in a worrying way, the Christian Scientists felt insufficiently like a church, the United Reformed too like a bank. The Jehovah's Witness' literature was so full of judgement and righteousness that he came no closer than the Kingdom Hall's car park, then he lost nerve and went to the Society of Friends on Northwood Road instead. But the Quakers met in a place that didn't even pretend to be a church and he grew so bored by the hour's silence that he fell asleep, and then was so irritated by the kind smiles they gave him at the hour's end that he left with gratifying rudeness, spurning with a wordless sneer their offer of coffee and biscuits.

Then he found the perfect fit. It wasn't even a Sunday but he was passing and the doors were open. It was a piece of shabby, sidestreet Victoriana, all pitch pine and brass memorials; the sort of place that in a wealthier city might have become a cinema or carpet warehouse by now but in Portsmouth was simply limping on towards dereliction and redundancy.

An old woman was arranging brutish chrysanthemums on a hideous brass pillar. The spicy scent of their discarded foliage piled on a sheet beside her reached him as he passed and she offered her muted greeting. The building's Blitz-broken glass had been crudely replaced with not quite matching panes that were mainly a nasty, watery green.

With its unplastered brickwork and humble, stunted proportions, the place felt like the ecclesiastical equivalent of his shop in Paulsgrove – unloved, undervisited.

'Can I help you?' The woman had followed him and timidly apologized for making him jump. 'The next service isn't until Sunday,' she said. 'I'm afraid our congregation's so small now that there's only one evensong a week and that was yesterday. And it's only spoken now.'

'I'll come back on Sunday, then,' he told her. 'What's the vicar here like, by the way?'

'Oh. Young Mr Johnson,' she said and her unremarkable face briefly lit up. 'He's lovely. We were terribly lucky to get him. We'd been making do with all sorts of people, some of them not suitable at all.' As if feeling she had said quite enough, she returned to her flowers.

When he returned on the following Sunday morning, there were barely twenty people present. The same woman handed him his prayer book and hymnal as he entered. He sat well apart before he noticed that everyone else seemed to have done much the same. This was a church for the private and single, apparently.

The priest was by some way the youngest person in the room, so even had he not been good-looking, his presence would have carried a certain charge. Modest was immune to male beauty. What he found compelling was vulnerability. From the moment he began to give out suitably threadbare parish notices, young Mr Johnson was laying himself wide open to mockery. The other priests Modest had been studying on Sundays past were absurd sometimes, often even, with their robes and posturing and portentousness.

Most drew a defensive haughtiness about them, as though judging before they be judged. This man, by contrast, gave the impression of having no such defensive layer but radiated an innocent certainty. His was the unquestioning belief of a child, like belief in Father Christmas, or fairies, or a mother's beauty or a father's love. This was belief that compelled one to fall in with it and follow because to do otherwise would be a kind of cruelty.

As the service began in earnest with a hymn and the priest processed in, fully robed, with one elderly acolyte carrying a cross before him and another bringing up the rear, Modest glanced around and saw that the people there loved their vicar. Man and woman alike stole shy glances at Mr Johnson as he passed them and stared boldly at him once he was before them. With his robes he had not assumed pomposity, like the prison chaplain, or the priest in the hideous council-estate church Modest had attended the previous week. He merely assumed an utterly sincere solemnity. He was, Modest decided, like a considerate child who had begun performing a magic trick only to discover that the magic was real and possibly dangerous. One could imagine him, resolute yet terrified, conducting an exorcism. His voice – unquestionably the same he had heard from the gutter that terrible night – filled him with an unsettling desire to confess all and be absolved.

His sermon, all the more effective for being barely five minutes long, was on the subject of righteous violence, inspired by a nasty outbreak of vigilantism on one of the city's estates that week. He cited the texts of the woman taken in adultery and the striking off of the high priest's servant's ear and he pointed out the curious fact that the registering of feelings of disgust, however righteous, invariably made the human face temporarily less attractive, as though God had left it.

When they made their general confession and he granted them absolution, he did it after a short hesitation and in a thoughtful tone, as though the process were not glibly automatic but required communal effort. When the time came to receive communion, Modest was slow to leave his pew and found himself at the back of the short queue. Then, by an accident of maths, he found himself kneeling at the beginning of a new row, a second sitting, as it were, so all alone at the altar rail.

Those merely asking for blessings were supposed to carry their service booklets before them as a sign. Modest saw no reason why he shouldn't receive communion since he had read the Bible and come to church so often in recent weeks. It wasn't as though his being unconfirmed showed in any way, and the small thrill of transgression was a compensation for the tedium he had been enduring, and all the troubling dreams.

When the priest came to give him the wine, he paused for a second or two, so that Modest instinctively looked up. He found the priest's bright grey eyes looking directly into his as he said, 'Christ died for you,' with just the hint of a smile.

Did he know, somehow, the deception being practised against him? Modest was so startled he had tucked the wafer into the roof of his mouth before he remembered he should have replied with an Amen first.

*   *   *

As they were all filing out and handing back their prayer books and hymnals, the flower arranger greeted him again.

'That was a very good service,' he told her.

'We're lucky to have him,' she said.

'I'm sorry. What was your vicar's first name again?' he asked, although she hadn't said.

'Barnaby,' she said. 'Barnaby Johnson. I hope we'll see you again.'

As at the altar rail, he managed to be the last in line at the door. Before he shook Johnson's hand, he handed him back the handkerchief. It was immediately evident that Johnson remembered the incident but not the face that went with it.

'How are you?' he asked, concerned, 'I should have recognized you straight away.'

'Perhaps with a bloody nose I'd have looked more familiar,' Modest said and they shared a laugh.

'Let me introduce you,' the priest said. 'This is Patience, who's attended this church all her life so can always tell me who people are or where things belong.'

'How do you do?' said an elegant old woman in a purple summer coat. 'What's your name?'

'Modest,' he told her. 'Modest Carlsson.'

'Of course it is,' Mr Johnson said. 'I remember now. You had a Swedish father and a Russian mother.'

'Full marks,' Modest said and they laughed again.

'Well I do hope you come back,' Mr Johnson added. 'Now that you know where we are. Patience will show you the ropes. She knows everything about everybody.'

The old woman clucked to herself and batted a hand at him so it was plain she was as deeply in love as the rest of them. Mr Johnson had slipped away, clearly adept at parishioner evasion.

The old woman had fixed on Barnaby a gaze of comfortless enquiry. 'Would you care for a sherry?' she asked.

Modest noticed her magnificent amethyst brooch and accepted.

Patience – Miss Boyle – lived in a house that would easily have accommodated a family of six. She lived alone, curator to what was in effect a museum to her parents. Born to expect more out of life than Portsmouth, her mother had married a dashing naval officer and somehow become stranded there on his death. She had left their sole child not only the guardian of a houseful of treasures and memories but the sole repository of a lifetime of prejudice and suspicion. Bitter in outlook and acid of tongue, Patience Boyle had not been granted even the compensation of a husband and children and, now, had no friends.

'We have a friend in Jesus,' she told Modest with startlingly naked cynicism.

She appeared to accept him entirely at face value. It also seemed that, for all his carefulness, she recognized in him a kindred spirit: another lost soul. He grew pleasantly dizzy on her excellent Wine Society sherry while she regaled him with unflattering portraits of every member of the congregation. All were found to be hypocrites in some way or other, neither as sweet nor as pious as they appeared.

'It's a good thing you found me first,' she said. 'Saved you so much time and effort.' Only young Mr Johnson was spared her judgement. 'Anyone can see he's the real thing. Far too good for us to hold on to him for long. Not like Mr Xavier.' She made a face.

'Who was he?' he prompted.

'Oh. Another priest. Ghastly little man. Quite ghastly. You'll meet him before too long. Breath that would bring down a bustard.'

She made him share a tin of the better quality chicken soup, to which she added yet more sherry and a carton of cream, then sent him on his way with the odd sensation that, although she had asked him not one question, he had just made a friend.

It was no Road to Damascus moment; he did not change perceptibly. He continued to run the shop, making his best money from selling pornography snatched from the shame-faced and first editions tricked from the innocent. He continued to drink heavily and to lead a life of barely concealed squalor. All that had altered was that he now attended church and, with the minimum of effort it seemed to him, sustained a friendship.

He attended on Sundays, sitting within glancing distance of Patience but not with her, but he soon began also to attend occasional morning or evening services, the stripped-down ones without time-consuming music, at which he was frequently the only person present besides the young priest. If Mr Johnson was surprised to see him, he didn't show it, which gave Modest a powerful sense of these morning and evening offices being observed for their own sake, inexorable as the motions of sun and moon, regardless of who watched them. It was as though, assisted by the priest, the dour, undistinguished building were pray-ing to itself. He took the opportunities these services afforded to watch Barnaby Johnson openly, to notice his very clean nails and clumsily cut hair. The way there was often a catch in his voice when he said the Grace. There was nearly always a small red book about him, either in his hands or on his prayer stall or, when he was in his civilian clothes, jutting out of his jacket pocket. Modest itched to ask him what it was or even to pick it up and hold it for himself. It was not a Bible or a psalter and he had never seen him read from it, yet it was plainly important to him.

Sometimes Johnson spoke with him briefly afterwards. More often he hurried off about his work.

'I'm glad Patience has found you,' he confided one morning. 'You're doing her good.' This made Modest realize she was a parish burden; prickly, difficult, a source of guilt to the kinder souls who failed to love her. And that in turn led him to see how effortlessly he might become such a burden too, unloved, unlovable, yet ineluctably among them, like a moist, secretive toad. And how all around might continue to be repelled and to turn aside yet God and this young man, his vulnerable avatar, were compelled repeatedly to forgive and welcome him.

It didn't work, of course, this difficult magic, lovely though the idea was. He became no better. He regarded his fellow men with no more forgiveness and accorded the women around him no more respect. The wand of loving-kindness was waved and he was no different for it. Like Patience, who remained nasty Patience, with her brutal system of checks and balances in which all were found wanting and the pleasures of life were sherry and spite. He still had disquieting dreams about the pale, beseeching God who by now had acquired the face and voice of his priest. It wasn't sexual but it was, perhaps, a kind of fixation, and he sensed that turning his back would bring no resolution.

He regretted, too late, his fraudulence in pretending to have been baptized and confirmed, once he saw the opportunity confirmation classes would have given for regular, private access to the man.

Besides, the church had found a use for him. Patience wished to retire as secretary of the PCC and saw to it that he was chosen in her stead. He became a regular reader of lessons and taker of collections. No children or parents came near the church, as it had no Sunday school, so there was no risk of him having his background investigated. In less than a year, he found he had become quite drawn in. Patience had some of her late father's suits let out and turned up to fit him. With these and a selection of the dead man's shirts and ties he was almost respectable again. Outwardly, at least.

Then Barnaby Johnson left them. Modest had often wondered why his name and phone number were not displayed on the painted board beside the church door, as it seemed the one area in which he did not lay himself entirely at the parish's disposal. He had not grasped it was because Johnson had only ever been an interim appointment, a stop-gap, like ghastly Mr Xavier, during the necessary interregnum between full incumbents. He could have applied for the job formally, of course, but had been drawn back to his curacy parish in the far west instead.

While Mr Xavier resumed the reins for a while, and proved just as ghastly as Patience had promised, Modest sat with the other PCC members to interview the few priests from whom they would be obliged to make a selection. They were uniformly of the long married, long-serving variety, diplomatic, hard-skinned and uninspiring but then, one could hardly list 'worryingly trusting' in the Parish Statement of Wishes.

'I believe you were slightly in love with him,' Patience said when they were, yet again, picking over his doughty replacement.

'No,' he said firmly. 'You're wrong. It was nothing like that.'

She turned her cold blue eyes on him, arrested by his tone and took a thoughtful sip. 'So? What was it like?'

'It was like ...' he began. He remembered the monogrammed handkerchief staining brine with blood, remembered that voice murmuring, 'God watches you, Modest. All will be well.' 'I feel we have unfinished business,' he said at last and enjoyed the sensation of holding something back from her. 'What do you make of the wife?' he asked, easily diverting her.

'Can you stay to lunch?' she asked. 'It's only soup, mind you.'

'Soup would be lovely,' he told her. 'And what about those hulking children? That girl's head is disturbingly large.'

BARNABY AT 52

They hardly saw Jim in his first year at university. They all dropped him off initially, including Carrie, with a great heap of books and belongings he claimed he couldn't do without, his clothes all crammed into the much-decorated rucksack he had taken on his travels. And he e-mailed them once or twice in his first weeks. Barnaby attended a church conference and took him out for lunch near the end of term at a grown-up wine bar Jim recommended. He seemed fine, almost chatty. But then he dropped the bombshell that he was unlikely to come home for Christmas. He needed money and he could make easy overtime by agreeing to work on Christmas Day and Boxing Day. And if he did come home, it would be with his restored Vietnamese name, Phuc, not as Jim.

Choosing not to rise to this, Barnaby joked that even priests got Boxing Day off, then wished he hadn't because it caused Jim to pull what Dot called his *battening-down-the-hatches-face* and the subject was closed. Barnaby couldn't help but remember the way he had pulled back from his own father when even younger, and how part of him had felt relief at his father's seeming acceptance of it and part of him had been deeply wounded at it. So, although he accepted that Jim, sorry, Phuc wanted distance, he didn't let him believe that he wasn't missed or wanted. He wrote to him thereafter, every week, not e-mails, which he had learnt could so easily be blocked or deleted, but proper ink and paper letters, which could be reread and saved, and stack up to form a physical proof of love. Thinking of his own father's constipated, codified offerings, he always wrote two sides, never hiding behind clippings or cuttings, though occasionally including photographs. He wrote early every Sunday morning, immediately after he wrote the day's sermon when he hadn't found someone else to preach in his stead. And he made an effort to be entirely himself on paper, entirely honest. He wrote about his religious doubts, if not quite admitting to loss of faith, and his impatience with church politics. He told stories of parishioners and neighbours, like Dot's scary librarian friend or pathetic, fat Modest Carlsson who nobody could quite like or trust. He told stories too of his own boyhood and difficult, eventually broken, relationship with his father. He hesitated before writing, 'I don't want that to happen with you and me, Phuc. In fact I won't let it happen.'

Jim responded only very occasionally, and only ever by e-mail or telephone, and when he rang it was always on Sunday morning when he could be sure of only speaking to the answering machine.

He came home for Christmas after all, for the bare twenty-four hours of the feast. He refused to attend church, saying it was all lies, he got drunk and he was consistently horrible to Dot in a sneering, needling way he'd rarely been as a sixth-former, which made her nervous so she kept calling him Jim instead of Phuc. He talked incessantly. He talked to himself. He never finished what was on his plate, although he was worryingly thin. He dressed as though he was going clubbing, immune, apparently, to the cold. If either Barnaby or Dot referred to any of these oddities, he lashed out.

Only Carrie was spared, and she seemed frozen, afraid to intervene and lose whatever attachment of his she retained. It was as though, having already wounded them by threatening to stay away, he had decided to come home only because he realized he could behave more hatefully that way.

Speaking to his parishioners about the Christ child's message of love and how a baby was the perfect symbol of that obligatory, undeniable love within families, Barnaby tasted the sourness of deceit on his tongue more than ever before.

It was a measure of how tense and watchful the visit left the three of them that not one of them succumbed to the temptation to joke about the similarity between Jim's new name and the expletive his behaviour surely made them all want to say.

Barnaby resumed writing to him immediately – it seemed more important than ever – and sent what was probably regarded as a pitiful cheque to help with the spring term's rent. He grew angry afresh as he wrote, remembering how Phuc had spoken to his mother, so found himself apologizing for whatever they had done wrong in raising him. Silence followed, total silence into which Barnaby continued to send his letters as pebbles into a cold, dark shaft, until the end of term, when Carrie told them both he'd be spending the Easter break working in the wine bar.

No one expressed surprise. It was expensive being a student now, they reminded each other, and he didn't have well-off parents to subsidize him. Then the hall of residence returned one of Barnaby's letters with a note to say that Phuc was still a student of the university but had been obliged to move out. This was far more worrying, especially since Barnaby feared he would have moved out in an effort to save money. He e-mailed the contents of his letter instead, asking for Phuc's new postal address. There was no response. He e-mailed again, and this time the e-mail bounced back with a message that Phuc's e-mail account had been closed. At least, the only one that Barnaby and Dot knew about.

As spring unfolded into a glorious summer, they had no news and, Barnaby noticed, took to avoiding speaking of Phuc because the cycle of recrimination and equally useless worry the mere mention of him stirred up was too upsetting. He began to suspect how it might feel to have a loved one in a coma or on a life support machine for week after week, to the point where one would avoid speaking of them because every possible conversation about them would have been had and a kind of mourning delicacy would become preferable to further discussion.

Then he came back from an afternoon of parish visits to find a note from Dot in the usual place, leaning on the kettle.

3 p.m. Jim's in hospital, she had written. Gone to fetch him home.

He had supper ready and had alerted Carrie by the time Dot brought Phuc home after dark. Phuc was in no state to eat anything. He had slept for the two-hour car journey but still looked like a walking corpse. Freezing all enquiries with a glance, Dot left father and daughter in the hall and put him straight to bed.

It was by the sheerest fluke she had even found out he was ill. The daughter of a woman in her book group was a junior nurse on the psychiatric ward at the Royal Devon and Exeter and recognized Phuc, despite his name, as she had been in the year below him at Cape Cornwall. She took the initiative, when he came round from sedation and finally started making sense. He had claimed to have no next of kin, but she went behind the ward sister's back and rang her mother, who rang Dot.

Dot was late back because she had to wait to talk to a doctor. They had explained that he showed signs of addiction to amphetamines, which had left needle tracks, and sclerotic veins, on both his arms. He had been brought in temporarily psychotic from the effects of crystal meth. It had taken three policemen to control him sufficiently to get him into the back of a van and bring him in and it had taken a large dose of Largactil to sedate him to the point of safety and stop him repeatedly shouting, 'You can't do this to me. I'm the Son of God!'

Phuc had looked merely unkempt at Christmas but now his appearance had deteriorated shockingly. He was emaciated, sweaty, dirty and had the sort of acne he had managed to avoid throughout his teens. Dot's only thought, her instinct, had been to bring him straight home without trying to collect his things. She dressed him in Barnaby's pyjamas and Barnaby found her weeping over the state of his clothes as she put them to wash with agricultural quantities of liquid soap. Neither she nor Barnaby slept much that night because she kept tiptoeing across to his old room to check he was still there and still breathing.

He stayed in bed for two whole days, barely speaking, only waking to drink and to toy with the meals she took in to him. They made sure one of them or Carrie was always in the house so that he was never alone and had their GP look in on him too. On the third day he dressed in the basic clothes Barnaby had bought in one of the big supermarkets in Penzance and supplemented with a bag of more colourful things from charity shops. He sat in the garden, enjoying the sun and the cat, whose wordless love was doubtless welcome respite from the anxious expressions of the humans in the house. They conducted small, careful conversations about unthreatening matters in the present: the garden, the weather, the house, the cat. When Barnaby went to sit with him, Phuc would give a crumpled smile and say, 'Hey, Dad,' which made Barnaby feel things might be bad but were not quite broken.

He was more forthcoming with Carrie, admitting to having flunked his course, to being expelled from his hall of residence for stupid stuff, to living in a squat whose address he claimed not to be able to remember. To having no money left, and owing some to a man who scared him. He was nervous the hospital would know his parents' address and pass it on so that the man might come after him.

'It won't all be true,' Dot said, poring over the booklet the nurses had given her. 'We can expect paranoia and mood swings, it says.'

'It's so good to see you,' they told him, and 'You must stay as long as you like.'

'I don't care about his degree,' Barnaby told Dot in bed that night. 'Or the police or anything. I just want him to stay here and get well, however long it takes.' And he dared imagine a few sunny weeks, months even, of having both their adult children back in the nest, of Phuc rebuilding his health and his family relationships, with them in careful, loving, undemanding attendance; a prolonged and peaceful rehabilitation.

He knew this was naïve and that addiction was something about which he was shamefully ignorant for someone who had prided himself on taking a pastoral interest in the more wretched and less law-abiding households of the parish. At the end of the second day of sun and cat and careful conversation, he told Dot this was unlikely to last, that she must ready herself; they couldn't keep Phuc prisoner, even for his own good. But it was still a shock when he vanished the next day and reappeared, high and barely able to speak, an hour or so after Dot had realized he had emptied her purse. Barnaby was still feeling wounded when Phuc disappeared the morning after that and didn't come back.

He discovered the graffito when he went to say evening prayers in Morvah. Curiously these solitary services – when they were indeed solitary, for Modest Carlsson had an irritating way of showing up with something like glee, as though he had stumbled on some precious secret – were never as troubling to his evaporated faith as the better-attended ones. Speaking the words on his own, whether in the barnlike expanse of Pendeen church or the mossy tranquillity of Morvah, continued to feel like a ritual with significance, perhaps because, Modest apparitions aside, there was no one needing anything of him. Ideally it was just him and these buildings he now knew so intimately and for which he had come to feel such deep affection he no longer truly saw them, any more than one continued to see in detail friends one encountered every week of one's life.

Even in high summer, Morvah church felt damp. Sometimes there were puddles on the floor, as though a stream were rising there, but the church wardens assured him it was simply the granite *geeving*. The whitewash was due for a fresh coat as it had marked green patches here and there but still the four words painted across it in blood-red gloss were plainly legible from yards away. They had been carefully placed to be the first thing he would see on letting himself in from the porch. *Fuck Jesus*, they said, *Love Phuc.*

Thank God Modest Carlsson was otherwise engaged that evening. Barnaby said the service as usual, adding in a prayer for Phuc, wherever he might be and whatever he might be doing. He examined the defacement closer to and touched it. The paint had not quite dried so stained his fingertips. He pictured his son leaving the church and throwing the paintbrush over the nearest hedge. And the paint? This could not have used an entire tin. He locked the church and walked around the graveyard, fearing some obscenity splashed across a headstone or on the rough granite of the building's outer walls where it would be that much harder to clean away, but there was nothing. He found brush and empty paint tin under a bush and bagged them up to dispose of at home. The paint had been leftovers; he recognized the tin from earlier in the year when Dot had repainted a wooden, ride-on train from the women's refuge.

He drove home. Dot came out to meet him as he pulled up in the yard.

'He took my wallet,' she said at once. 'Stupid of me to leave it in my bag.'

'Have you stopped the cards?'

'Yes. And he took the Action Aid box from the hall table.'

'Even if he caught the bus, he can't have got far.'

'He'll have hitched,' Carrie said, coming out from her workshop. 'He could be miles away by now. Little bugger.'

Barnaby told them what Phuc had done besides and showed them the paint can. At once Dot was all practicality, as he knew she would be. She packed a wicker basket, as if for a bizarre picnic, with a bottle of solvent, a scrubbing brush, rubber gloves, paint brushes, a can of undercoat and a can of white emulsion. He was amazed afresh at the beautiful order of the big understairs cupboard where she kept her hardware. It gave one the same heartening sense of method and plenty as her larder, but instead of jewel-bright jams and chutneys, displayed identical jars of screws, nails, washers and Rawlplugs all sorted by size and neatly labelled. She kept paint in there too, despite the fire risk it posed, because tins kept in the sheds turned rusty in weeks and the fluctuating temperatures outside ruined the contents.

'We had better change,' she said, so they changed into clothes that didn't matter, gardening clothes, and he drove her out to Morvah. 'How bad is it?' she asked, waiting beside him in the porch as he took the key from its hiding place in the rafters.

'Pretty bad,' he said. 'But it's only words, not pictures.'

He let her in and went to turn on the lights while she stared, taking in what Phuc had done. 'It could be worse,' she said as he came back to her. 'He hasn't touched the altar – most people would have done something to the altar – and he didn't do anything to the flags.'

'Or start a fire.'

'Or start a fire.' She actually smiled a little at that, then sighed. 'Come on. If it's not dry yet we can scrub a lot off with white spirit and at least blur the words a bit before we paint over them.'

They shut the door behind them and worked there all evening. They scrubbed off the worst of the paint with solvent then dried off the patch of reddened wall with an old towel from the car boot. Then they painted over it with undercoat to stop any traces of red coming through.

Carrie called by as they were cleaning the brushes. She had driven down to St Just to fetch fish and chips for them and had also brought a bottle of red wine, glasses, fruit cake and the radio. 'Thought you might as well make an evening of it,' she said, then left them alone as she was playing in a euchre drive for the lifeboats back in one of the pubs.

They listened to a Prom while eating their supper and waiting for the undercoat to dry a little at least, then they painted on two coats of emulsion. They broke off in between to do something they had not done in years, taking a moonlit walk across the fields behind the church to the view out to sea from Chair Carn. It was an unusually still night, retaining some of the day's warmth. The air bore the sweet scents of hot grass and honeysuckle and, nearer the sea, the foxy musk of bracken. They saw a barn owl hunting and, as they stood to watch it, she took his hand and kissed the back of it, which somehow felt as intimate a gesture as if she had unbuttoned his shirt and kissed the skin above his heart.

They painted the second coat to a series of motets by Tallis, who was Composer of the Week, barely speaking as they worked, then cleaned up in bitterly cold water from the graveyard tap. They drove home in silence but with the car windows open so that the smell of paint about them was rinsed by the warm night air.

For the first time in nearly fifteen years they made love. (He would not realize it had been that long until the morning, when he took in her tea and went to shave.) It was not earth-shatteringly passionate – they were both too surprised for that – but for him, at least, it felt like a deep restoration, at the roots of his being, a true forgiveness from the flesh rather than a light and easy one from the tongue.

DOROTHY AT 34

Nearing the end of her first decade of married life, Dorothy felt she must have aged more rapidly in the last ten years than in the twenty-four preceding them. This was odd in that, compared to those of most new wives, her life had outwardly changed so little. She lived in the farmhouse she had grown up in, she still lived with her mother, who had created a kind of flat for herself, with its own front door, at one end of the house, and she still knelt in the same pew in church and taught Sunday School there. Ten years on it was still a surprise to receive a letter or invitation dignifying her as Mrs Barnaby Johnson for she secretly still felt like Dorothy Sampson or simply *Dulcie Sampson's Girl*.

Her mother, she was coming to realize, was always right. Her stern predictions of what lay in store for the wives of priests had all come true: the lack of privacy, the lack of money. But her mother had soon acquired a deep respect, almost an awe, for her son-in-law and never breathed a word of *I-Told-You-So* when she and Dorothy were alone. Becoming a grandmother and sloughing off all responsibility for farm or buildings, had made her biddable, almost sweet. On Dorothy's worst days, when the door knocker and telephone were barely silent and her kitchen seemed constantly invaded by smiling strangers, days when Carrie contrived to be ill or an ancient radiator sprang a leak or a Mary or Martha escaped and rooted up all her seedlings, she would think back to her mother's former shortness of temper and wonder that she had never actually shouted or been violent.

Challenged by life, Dorothy discovered she was stronger than she knew. Poverty, or the constant threat of it, made her ingenious. She reminded herself how to knit and picked up a second-hand electric sewing machine so as to make her own and the child's clothes. The Angwins helped too, discreetly, encouraging her to 'invest' in one of their beef calves every year or two, to keep the freezer stocked with mince and stews. She had always been able to change fuses and paint a room. Now that she was plainly never going to have a husband who could shift for himself in such matters, she pored over a *Reader's Digest* manual, acquired a power drill and lost her ignorant fear of plumbing and wiring.

As for the privacy question, she learned assertiveness. It was she who decided that the family would live in the farm-house and that the former rectory would serve as the office. It was she who pointed out that there were two rooms in the latter not used by the women's refuge or mother and baby group or any of the other worthy organizations to which Barnaby had offered house room there, which would serve as a far more convenient parish office and confirmation classroom than her kitchen and sitting room. People continued to show up on the doorstep of course – Barnaby insisted their home address and phone number continue to be displayed on the church signs – but at least these tended to be people in need: the poor, the fearful, the guilty rather than the officious and busy.

She had fallen pregnant with Carrie soon after they were married and her adoration of, and concern for, the baby and the exhaustion attendant on new motherhood had mitigated most of her pain at having to share Barnaby with so many others. (And she did feel she was sharing him. He truly loved his parishioners, and gave so unstintingly of his time and counsel and affection that he often returned home with little surplus to offer.) She had assumed Carrie would be the first of three or even four, as did others. They were a young couple, clearly in love, clearly healthy. Love would take the lead and ingenious poverty would find a way to follow in its glowing footsteps.

Sure enough she fell pregnant again just as she was weaning Carrie onto solids. She was delighted. As an only child of older parents she liked the idea of a small tribe of children transforming the place, supporting one another and, one day, taking over the farm again. She worried she was too serious to keep a child amused and assumed children were better at doing this for one another. She redecorated the small back bedroom Barnaby had once occupied as a paying guest, replacing its spinster chintzes with bright images from Beatrix Potter and Kate Greenaway. She planned how they could turn what was currently a box room, full of junk, into a play room children could keep toys in and make their own, unchecked by vicarage decorum.

But she lost the baby, inexplicably, just as it was beginning to show. Her grief at this astonished her. It wasn't as though the baby had yet become a person or acquired a personality; it was more that she felt a kind of fury at herself for failing at something requiring no effort, at something she had already proved she could do perfectly well.

The third pregnancy lasted longer but she was so worried about another miscarriage she made Barnaby join her in telling no one, not even her mother. Which meant that when she miscarried this time it felt like a secret shame – worse than a public grief – and she couldn't tell her mother now for fear of hurting her by having been so secretive.

Inevitably all this, and the demands of a toddler, affected their love life. Barnaby started to treat her like something delicate, a patient almost, whereas she had previously gloried in what felt like an equal possession, a passion that, if not exactly careless, at least wasn't constantly watchful.

When she fell pregnant the fourth time, as a result of the giddy freedom of a camping holiday on Bryher, they left nothing to chance. Barnaby was solicitous. He insisted on taking her to a specialist – calling in favours, in a way he never usually did, so that she saw the archdeacon's obstetrician sister, who had a private practice, free of charge. All went well, all her test results were fine, the baby grew until everyone could see. The scans revealed it was a boy. She became so big that people kept asking if she was expecting twins and she had to assure them that, no, it was simply the one, very well-cushioned baby.

Her fingers swelled so, she was obliged to leave off first her wedding band and then the engagement ring Barnaby had given her – a lovely antique amethyst one which had come down through his family. It was so splendid, in its quiet way, she had taken to wearing it inside out most of the time, with its jewels facing inwards, for fear she might somehow lose or damage them. Perhaps because of the story attached to it, of all the Johnson women who had worn it before – none of them farmer's daughters – she had always felt a little fraudulent wearing it, but putting it off entirely made her jumpy, as though the action were an unsaying of vows or unknitting of love.

The archdeacon's sister had said arrangements could be made to admit her a whole week early so as to have mother and baby under observation, but then agreed that there was no cause for worry since neither of her previous two pregnancies had proceeded this far. When the last week approached, though, Dorothy had her overnight case packed and waiting in the hall and Carrie was sent down the road to stay with the Angwins' cousins, the Polglazes at Kelynack, whose boy Pearce was something of a hero to her.

Her waters broke in the dead of night so the roads were still quite empty as Barnaby drove her to Treliske. But then it was clear something was wrong. She was examined and her bump repeatedly listened to by a midwife, then her doctor was called. There was no pulse. No one could say exactly at which point the baby's heart had stopped but it had been pumping away when her GP had called in on her the previous afternoon. Now she had to endure all the pain of labour knowing she was giving birth to a little corpse.

From the moment they were told until after the birth, Barnaby stayed at her side, holding her hand when she let him, kissing it when the pain was at its peak. He had got up in his dog collar for some reason, security perhaps, or habit. It peeped out above the hospital gown they had tied about him and comforted her. She knew he was praying, even though he didn't want to attract attention so was doing it in his head. She could always tell. His beautiful stare lost its focus and he pursed his lips slightly in his effort not to move them.

The staff could not have been more sensitive or considerate. They cleaned and examined the baby as they would have done a living child and wrapped him in a towel and gave him to her to hold. She cried then, to see the perfection and shockingly blue stillness of him, cried far louder than she had done during labour, but could see she frightened Barnaby so controlled herself as soon as she could. He kissed her, kissed the baby and began to weep too, but silently, the first tears she had seen him shed, so that she knew the other losses had not reached him as this one had.

'You can pray out loud now,' she told him. 'I think it might help,' although this was a kind lie and she felt herself beyond all succour.

They had agreed he would be called Harold, for her father, so he said a prayer for Harold as though he were dying between them and not already dead. It was a beautiful, complicated prayer she had never heard before – never having been present at a deathbed – and she marvelled at his ability not only to carry it in his memory but to be able to recall it without stumbling at such a moment. And he surprised her by producing his tiny silver flask of Chrism and making the sign of the cross on Harold's rumpled forehead. Then she let him take the baby, feeling suddenly drained of all energy, and she joined in with the Lord's Prayer. It left her hungry for more and she asked him to say the Grace for them all before he handed Harold to the midwife.

* * *

She had assumed Harold would be quietly cremated along with all the other sad hospital waste – the other dead, incomplete babies, the severed limbs, the cancerous organs. This did not bother her remotely; she had a farmer's lack of sentimentality about the swift and hygienic disposal of the dead and she had said her goodbye simply by cradling that small parcel that so clearly was never him. Barnaby surprised her, however, by arranging that the baby was collected by undertakers and given a tiny, plain wooden coffin, like something one might store letters in, or family silver, under a bed.

She drew the line at involving anyone else, or at telling Carrie, for fear of traumatizing her. A hole was dug in the Sampson plot, over where her father lay, and where her mother would one day join him, and they held a pared-down funeral and committal service very early the following Sunday morning when no one was about. They returned home, breakfasted with her mother and Carrie and then he went to finish the day's sermon and she to start Sunday lunch and nothing further was said.

Carrie seemed disappointed rather than distraught, having already learnt the farm's lessons in mortality from pigs, calves and chickens, and was easily diverted with a kind gift from Jane Angwin of some ducklings to raise. Carrie kept them in a pen under a warm light in the old dairy and spent hours talking to them and seeking ways – impossibly – to tell them apart.

Dorothy was not a glutton and she could not recall actively eating for comfort but she never lost the weight she had gained with Harold. It spread from her belly to settle on her hips, and her previously neat breasts remained heavy and pendulous and seemed doomed to stay that way. She avoided looking at herself in the full-length bedroom mirror, especially when naked, and took to making a point of hurrying into bed before Barnaby came upstairs to join her so that he need not see her undressing or hear the treacherous complaint of bedsprings as she climbed in and arranged herself.

It was around this time that he took to calling her Dot, which she had never liked or encouraged, and the name stuck and soon spread around the parish. It was born of the jokey way he liked to make Carrie giggle by greeting mother and daughter together as *Dot and Carry One*, but she could not help feeling the ease with which her diminutive was taken up was in part a jibe at her growing girth. It was like calling a tall man Titch or a short one Lofty.

He began to pay her less and less attention physically, or rather, to concentrate his touches of affection to her face, ears, throat and hands – ironically those very areas magazines clucked that larger women should adorn in order to distract attention from their other parts. In truth she was content to receive no more strenuous attentions and not just because size had made her self-conscious but for fear of being made to lose another baby. Possibly he shared her dread. Certainly he shouldered a share of blame, for she had never forgotten how he repeatedly apologized as she laboured to give birth to Harold's corpse. They could have taken the usual precautions, she could have gone on the pill easily enough or suggested he have a vasectomy, but there seemed no point when there was nothing to take precautions against.

In the first years of their marriage they often fell asleep in each other's arms. Now, just ten years on, he always turned his back on her to sleep. He kissed her first usually, and murmured good night, but then he settled with his back to her. She wasn't unhappy – nothing so dramatic or definite – it was simply that she occasionally felt called upon to pretend she was happier than she was. People liked to make out all marriages foundered or were founded on sex but she knew there was more. She knew from the stories she heard in the women's refuge and from the unhappy people who often sat at her kitchen table – people whom she would never have met if she had married Henry Angwin – that sex without love, or sex with love gone wrong, could be horrific and tantamount to violence. She knew she was lucky in love, that she loved him and he her. It was simply that they had arrived at the companionate, two-old-shoes stage of marriage earlier than she would have predicted.

Carrie was her consolation. A needy, clingy baby, she became a self-reliant and independent-minded child, thoroughly her own person, still tomboyish in her idolizing of Henry Angwin and Pearce Polglaze and in her ideas of pleasure, but reassuringly girlish in her devotion to her father and her passionate friendships.

That she despised dolls had been a mercy when Dorothy was going through the pain of repeated baby-loss, and that she seemed so good at forming friendships lessened her mother's worry that she would be lonely as an only child. Aside from Pearce, who would soon be too old to pay her any attention, her best friends were a pair of miners' daughters from the village school. Carrie didn't seem to mind their hours of play with their Barbies because, rather touchingly, they understood that she had a special understanding of Barbie's open-topped sports car, which she would solemnly 'service' while the dolls were being dressed and reclothed. The three of them were keen little cyclists, pedalling up and down the village, from the miners' terraces in Boscaswell, along Church Road and down the lane to the farm. The girls' parents were not churchgoers, which made it all the more amusing that Carrie persuaded her friends to start attending Sunday School with her, often in wildly inappropriate clothes which they had picked out for themselves as their parents lay sleeping.

All this reminded Dorothy of her own childhood in all the same places and made her glad that they were far too poor even to consider wrenching Carrie away from these local friendships to send her to a private school in town when the time came. Grateful though Dorothy was to her education in Penzance, the process of being sent to St Clare's, where girls with accents were encouraged to lose them and where she was certainly the only pupil in her year who had grown up among miners' daughters, had opened a rift between her and her Pendeen friends at the worst possible age, a process it had proved impossible to reverse.

There were women she often met in the lanes or at the shop or at the school gates with whom she used to play, swap secrets and make serious promises, who now greeted her cheerily enough but maintained a formal distance, turning back from greeting her to chat amongst themselves, with the friends who had never wavered. Quite possibly Carrie was befriending their children too by now and Dorothy was determined to allow those friendships to endure; any shortfall in Carrie's education could always be made up for at home.

Dorothy's other consolation, in a very quiet way, was God. Shortly before Carrie's birth she had given up the Sunday School to an old schoolfriend of hers recently married to a policeman. Tabby Morris was eager and less encumbered. Dorothy had always guiltily thought that Sunday School and the excuse it gave to miss the sermon and the larger part of the Eucharist service suited her, that she could be busily useful in another room rather than quietly, even passively, contemplative in church, but something had shifted within her in becoming a mother and she found herself noticing and feeling the meaning of words she had long been reciting with her mind unengaged. Once or twice Barnaby persuaded her to read a lesson now but she hated that, hated standing up in front of everyone else and being the only one speaking. What she loved, she discovered, was prayer and an unaccustomed stillness that came over her as she knelt and covered her eyes and either murmured familiar words or focused her thoughts as a speaker directed.

She also loved Barnaby's sermons. He always worked on them in his study very early on Sunday mornings after waking her with a cup of tea. He never discussed them with her or seemed to fret about them and she enjoyed the element of surprise on the occasions where she could recognize how some incident from the preceding week had prompted a particular subject. She had not great experience – the only other preachers she had heard were the old vicar she had grown up with, Father Philip, and their occasional guests – but she suspected that Barnaby's sermons were relatively simple. They invariably took a text from one of the day's readings or its psalm and, almost invariably, they had the effect of gently opening that text out so that she found herself understanding it better, or feeling a better identification with it. This was especially true when a reading threw up one of the Bible's odder or less comforting moments – like one of Christ's harsher pronouncements about separating child from parent, or one of the Old Testament heroes' less edifying exploits. His sermons were never long and sometimes they were very short indeed but involved significant pauses in which he directed everyone to think about or imagine something before he continued. He was, she came to realize, unlike most priests in his use of silence. The idea that sprang to mind when one thought *priest* was of someone talking, probably too much, of someone imposing his voice on one. Yet to conjure up Barnaby's priesthood, his sermons or his services, was to remember the quality of their silences.

He was strongly against missionaries who sought to convert people away from an existing religion. This had been a cause of some conflict when he first took on his post, because one of the more forceful members of the PCC was of the saving the heathen mind-set and for some years money had been regularly sent to a mission specifically for the conversion of Muslims in Paris. Barnaby put a stop to that and he encouraged donations to missions whose emphasis lay on practicalities, improvement of sanitation, housing, education. He fostered connections with a mission in Sudan, where his sister Alice had died.

One of his projects supported a beleaguered nun who focused on the rescuing of street children in Hong Kong from labour or worse. Sister Bernard was an old-school letter writer and responded to each year's cheque with four sides of closely spaced onion skin. She knew the Penzance area, having passed part of her long-ago girlhood at Porthcurno, where her father worked for Cable and Wireless, and she took an overseas subscription to *The Cornishman* so as to know a little about the lives of the people supporting her work and to follow the fortunes of the Cornish Pirates, of whom she was a surprisingly passionate fan.

One day she wrote out of the blue for once, and not in acknowledgement of a donation. She was desperately worried about the plight of children, many of them only babies, in the refugee camps set up in the colony for the Vietnamese fleeing the regime in their homeland. The first wave of Vietnamese refugees, fleeing war, had tended to be better off, often well-educated and with the skills, including languages, necessary to help an immigrant negotiate their legal and social way into a new culture. Now, however, the refugees were fleeing the oppression following the hostilities and were coming from the other end of the social scale, taking incredible risks and often spending whatever savings they had simply to escape in criminally overcrowded boats. Unlike the earlier waves of refugees, these arrived with almost nothing to pave their way into a new life. Many died in trying to make the journey, leaving orphans behind them. Other orphans were quite possibly not parentless at all but simply burdens their mothers could not bear or children of rape. Sister Bernard was having the greatest difficulty finding new homes for these children in Hong Kong, whether in families or already crowded orphanages. So she was writing to everyone she knew, literally everyone in her address book, in search of people prepared to take them in.

Margaret Thatcher was limiting the numbers of refugee immigrants the UK would accept, but an adopted child would not have refugee status. Through relentless lobbying of airlines and Hong Kong and Kowloon companies, Sister Bernard had the funding to see any adoptees escorted safely to Heathrow, so now she needed willing families at the long flight's end. Characteristically frank, she enclosed a mixed assortment of available children, little photographs accompanied by whatever scant biographical details she had procured.

'We should,' Barnaby said, 'shouldn't we?' at once invoking their ethical responsibility and passing the onus of decision to Dorothy. 'At least, I think we should be thinking about it.'

He left the letter and photographs where she could see them and of course Dorothy looked them over and was instantly drawn in to the terse, terrible dramas they suggested. They were not all adorable – a couple were particularly plain – and several were quite old, old enough at six or seven to be traumatized and to arrive with a catalogue of challenges for their new parents. But she found herself returning to a one-year-old boy with a winning grin and black hair standing in a tuft. *Parents Unknown*, his notes said. *Found in hold of boat*. So either his mother had died during the dreadful voyage and been thrown overboard or had fallen overboard alive and drowned or, saddest of all, had tucked her baby into what she hoped was a safe place so as to brave her new life unencumbered. Dorothy thought of Carrie at that age, her clinginess, the difficulty of setting her down anywhere for long without having to unpick the tight grasp of her little fingers unless she was asleep. She could not begin to imagine simply putting down a baby and walking away.

'I think this one,' she told Barnaby at lunch. 'Him. PL. He's smiling. I like his face, don't you?'

'A boy?'

'Yes. Then we'd have one of each.'

'You're sure, though?'

'Well … Would you rather have another girl?'

'No. I meant are you sure about adopting?'

'I don't really know,' she told him. 'Yes. I think so. And as you said, we should. There are so many children in need of homes. We should probably all be adopting.'

'Yes. And you think a Vietnamese will cope growing up here?'

'He won't be Vietnamese. By the time he's old enough to know what's what, he'll be as Cornish as Carrie!'

He came round the table to hold her and kiss the top of her head, so that she felt a flush of answering warmth within her and thought, *Yes. The right decision. A good decision. We love each other and we will love him.*

After consulting the unfamiliar international section at the front of the phone book to ascertain the time difference with Hong Kong, which turned out to be eight hours, they worked out that Sister Bernard might not yet have gone to bed. They telephoned. Barnaby did the talking, Dorothy at his side. It was a pet hate of his to have someone chipping in or calling out things when he was on the telephone, so she had to clutch the back of his chair and simply hope Sister Bernard was giving him the information he wasn't requesting. When he said, 'Good. Oh good. That's excellent news. So what do we do next?' she realized her blood was humming in her ears.

PL stood for his Vietnamese name, which his mother had written on a card tucked into his bedding. Phuc Lan. Neither of them was given to swearing and when Barnaby said the first name he pointedly pronounced it to rhyme with book. 'He'd probably need an English name anyway,' he said, 'to help him fit in here. Phuc really would be impossible. He'd be teased to death.'

'So can we have him?'

'Well nobody has moved to adopt him yet. And the period has passed during which his relations can claim him. Bernard will set things in motion at her end. We'll be sent a heap of paperwork to sign and so on. She was most insistent that we're committed to nothing until we sign the papers and send them back, and she wanted us to feel free to show them to a solicitor first.'

'But we want him, don't we?'

'Don't we?'

'Well I think so!' And they laughed and kissed and a giddy excitement came over them.

She told Carrie that evening as she was seeing her to bed. Carrie was confused at first then seemed a little doubtful. 'Are you pleased?' she asked Dorothy.

'Well yes. I've always wanted a brother for you.' Dorothy showed her his picture and she examined it closely, frowning. 'He looks happy,' she said doubtfully. 'Why did you choose him?'

Dorothy wondered. 'He was smiling. He chose us really. And he's still only a baby so it should be easier for us all to adjust than if he was older.'

'Does he speak English?'

'He won't speak anything much yet. But he'll learn English the same way you did.'

'What'll we call him?'

'You have a think and let us know. He'll be your brother as well as our son.'

Dorothy had worried about how to tell other people. The village was no problem. Now that Carrie knew, Carrie told her friends who told their mothers and soon diffident, slightly confused congratulations were being offered. Her own mother was harder.

'What do you want to do that for?' was her immediate, so most honest response. Once she heard that Barnaby, who could do no wrong these days, thought it was right, she changed tack and decided the baby was an object of pity. 'Poor little thing,' she said whenever she looked at his picture. (Dorothy had made everyone copies to assist in the bonding process even before the baby arrived.) 'Poor little monkey.' Like any farmer's wife, she couldn't help her dynastic fantasies and, just as a daughter was not the same, neither was an adopted, Vietnamese son. Dorothy thought it best not to tell her he was called Phuc.

Paperwork came from Hong Kong and London and, a few weeks later, a phone call from Sister Bernard, borrowing a tame banker's phone line, told them that all the formalities were complete and they had a date for the baby's arrival. Happily this was the week after Easter, so both Carrie and Barnaby would be on holiday.

They left her mother at home but took Carrie and travelled up on the sleeper to Paddington, which in itself was an adventure and a new experience for all three of them.

Dorothy did not sleep. She had Carrie softly snoring in the bunk above her and found that every time the train braked, she rolled towards the void on her right and was wide awake again. Barnaby had opted to save them money by spending the night in a seat in an ordinary carriage, but then he had the enviable gift of being able to sleep anywhere, seemingly at will.

So she contented herself with simply lying there in the semi-darkness left by the blue glow of the compartment's nightlight, preparing herself. She imagined him flying across the world to find her, imagined the small, hungry warmth of him, the scent of his hair, the feel of his little hands. She had brought along changes of clothes for him, nappies (because she had no idea how advanced his potty training would be), warm layers because, coming from Hong Kong and the fug of an airplane, his own clothes would almost certainly not be warm enough. She had knitted him a little hat – on the large side because she had no idea how large he would be. All these and a bottle and a selection of baby food were packed into Carrie's old push-chair, which Dorothy had retained as evidence of hope. She could reach out and touch it where she lay, for it filled half the scant floor space beside her bunk. She thought of the photograph and imagined him in the pram looking back at her, smiling, yawning, asking for her.

She slept eventually, at some point in the night when the train came to a halt somewhere, and she had convoluted dreams, all anxiety, in which she was not allowed to take the baby from his Chinese escort's arms at the airport because she could not name him. In the dream he knew who she was and was holding out his hands to her and screaming but the officials and his stern escort wouldn't allow her to step forward and take him because no name she came up with matched what they had written down. Part of the reason the dream was so unsettling was that her dreaming self knew they were in the right, that she was unfit and unprepared to claim him.

Jolted awake as they started out of Bristol, or Reading, or whichever station's siding they had been waiting in, she touched the pushchair for reassurance and thought about names. They had agreed that the right name would come to them the moment he was with them. She had seen the sense in this; she knew it was best not to form too many preconceptions but simply to ready her heart for him like a sort of nest. But now she found herself restlessly trying names on for size. Thinking it might be a good idea to retain his initials, she tried thinking of name combinations starting in PL. Philip. Patrick. Paul. Peter. Piers. Petroc. The Ps came easily enough but she found the finding of L names a worry as she could muster only Leo and Lionel and Leslie, none of which she liked. Relief came as she remembered Lawrence, but she rejected that almost at once for the nasty thought of Lawrence's martyrdom, roasted on a grill. It was almost as bad as Blaise, ingeniously torn apart with metal combs. By the time the steward knocked on their door and passed in their breakfast trays, Dorothy was up and dressed and grateful for the brief diversion of a teapot and some biscuits and the need to rouse Carrie before they arrived into Paddington.

There were hours to kill before they had to be at Heathrow as the flight wasn't due in until one thirty, and it seemed important to give Carrie attention too that day, so they took her for a walk around Kensington Gardens to see the Peter Pan statue and the Serpentine and the Albert Memorial, Albert Hall and Kensington Palace (from the outside, which cost nothing) as it was her first visit to London. Then they gave her a ride in the top of a double-decker bus back to South Kensington where there was the added thrill of a trip on the Underground out to Heathrow.

Dorothy was too embarrassed to admit that it was her first visit to London too and was careful not to betray her ignorance in the face of Barnaby's blithe assumptions. She loved the park, marvelling at the towering size of the plane trees compared to the stunted blackthorn and hawthorn that passed for trees at home and the way they seemed able to grow equally huge when growing out of small holes in the pavements. But she found the noise and crowds on the streets oppressive and was glad when they were back in the relative quiet of a train but out of the frightening tunnels.

His escort was a tiny Chinese nurse, reassuringly nannyish in her white uniform and black cardigan and sensible shoes but not remotely stern. As instructed by Bernard, they had written out a large card with their surname on it, which Carrie was holding up as they waited at the barrier. The nurse shook hands all round, with a slight bow each time, introduced herself as Mary Thien and said, 'And this is your little boy. Fast asleep because the journey has worn him out. And of course he's eight hours ahead of you ...'

He was tucked into a carrycot, furled in a blanket donated by Qantas. He looked immensely solemn in sleep – used as Dorothy was to his laughing photograph – and he was beautiful – why had she not expected that? – with a shock of jet black hair and tawny skin and a dimple in his chin. It was doubly astonishing that nobody wanted him and in the hour that followed the three of them were unusually quiet, awed by the shock of his physical perfection. Mary Thien noticed, it seemed, and joked, as they were completing the last pieces of paperwork in the immigration office, 'Don't worry. He won't seem quite such a little Buddha in an hour or two. He'll start crying soon enough.'

She would be flying back to Hong Kong in a few hours, she told them, but several of her cousins had come out from London to have an airport meal with her and help her pass the time. They weren't to worry about her. 'Off you go,' she said, 'with your little bundle of joy,' and she had them pose with the carrycot propped up between them while she took a few photographs for Sister Bernard on the smallest camera Dorothy had ever seen. Then they all shook hands again, Carrie included, and she waved them on their way, a family of four suddenly.

The trip to the airport and back had taken longer than expected so they had to run across Paddington to catch their train home, Carrie shouting with laughter as Barnaby gave her a ride on her brother's pushchair, and they clambered into their carriage only just in time. The journey back to Penzance took hours, of course, so inevitably he needed changing and feeding. Waking up, he clearly wondered where he was and who these strangers were and began to cry. Dorothy carried him to the lavatory where she changed his nappy. He calmed down after that, especially when she fed him, and he began to take them in, staring at each in turn. She held him for a while, then Barnaby walked him up and down the carriage. But it was when she settled him on Carrie's lap that he finally began to smile and gurgle. Perhaps he had spent so much time with other children recently that it was with them he felt most secure.

He was so attractive, so pet-like, that of course people kept stopping to admire him and inevitably some asked what he was called. 'Phuc Lan,' Barnaby told them. But after the third time he turned to Dorothy and said, 'We have to give him another name.'

Dorothy told him about her experiments with PL combinations and he liked the idea of Peter Lawrence but then Carrie suddenly said he should be James, at which the baby laughed.

'That was the name of your great-uncle,' Barnaby said. 'I'd like that.'

'What about my family?' Dot said, smiling.

'How about James Sampson?' he suggested. 'For my lovely uncle and your lovely parents?'

And so it was agreed and the next passer-by who stopped to admire him and asked his name was told James Sampson and didn't look surprised or say oh, which seemed a kind of blessing on it. So James Sampson he was, and Barnaby christened him the following Sunday in a church still full of daffodils.

Father and son bonded swiftly. James was still so tiny, small for his age, far too small for the knitting she had done for him, that Barnaby could comfortably carry him in a sling and took him on walks and even short bicycle rides around the parish, stopping to introduce him at every opportunity. Dorothy worried his evident pride, which somehow seemed more proprietorial, more overtly fatherly, than any she remembered him showing in Carrie at the same age, would hurt Carrie's feelings but Carrie's only gripe was at being deprived of constant access to the pushchair and its contents. Having had no interest in dolls, a flesh-and-blood brother had her transfixed. She wanted to help change, wash and feed him, do it herself if possible, and was soon parading him, in an echo of her father, before troops of girlfriends from school and their curious hangers-on. She had never wanted a pet – satisfied all her petting urges with the farm animals and semi-domestic cats – and was practical and unsentimental on the subject of the ducks' likely mortality rates and probable deliciousness when cooked. But she cooed over James, whom she rapidly took to calling Jim or Jim-me-lad, as over a kitten, and lit up at his gratifyingly warm responses to her.

Even her grandmother, a woman incapable of dissembling, took to him, demanding he regularly visited her end of the house to sit on her lap and be read to from the battered *Patrick* annuals whose pictures had always left Dorothy faintly nauseous but which seemed to combine with the older woman's lilting accent and the cosy fug of her wood burner to bring a heavy-limbed comfort to her son.

Her son. It was a fact. He was hers now and always would be. Happy photographs had been sent to Hong Kong and published in the parish newsletter to prove it. One had even found its way into *The Cornishman*, showing Dorothy dandling James on her knee on the stone hedge in Morvah churchyard, with the odd caption *My Vietnamese Joy*. But her heart had yet to take him in. She had been under no illusion, she knew that love grew slowly and fitfully between an adoptive mother and her child, that there might always be a shortfall in affection where a mother had not benefited from the long preparation of pregnancy. In the weeks before his arrival she had even thought she might be able to breastfeed him for a week or two. She held him to her breasts to still him when he cried. If milk arrived suddenly, as it had in the past when she had held friends' babies, it would have felt quite natural to unbutton her blouse and offer him a nipple. But none did and, in any case, he stared up at her with that face which, however sweet, offered her back no reflection either of herself or of one she loved, so that what should have felt tender seemed briefly unnatural. And to look at him was only to remember the son who had died. Harold. The true son.

Her guilt at this was savage. Her failure to love him, simply to love him without compunction, revealed a stony side to her nature she had not guessed at. A secretive one too; she kept all this to herself. She prayed more hungrily and selfishly than she had ever done before, that love would yet surprise her, stealing into her heart the way James's little hand often now stole into hers.

Meanwhile she understood that she must be fair and balance out the deficit in her love for him with a compensation of kindness and support. She would never raise her voice to him, as she often felt she must with Carrie, whom she loved unquestioningly and for whom she would die without a moment's hesitation. She would never criticize him. If he at least appeared to be a little god to her, perhaps, just perhaps, the sharp instincts of childhood would not sniff out her treachery.

BARNABY AT 40

For some years after his affair, Barnaby descended into a self-made hell. This began straightforwardly and predictably enough with guilt at what he had done and shock that something blundered into with such giddy thoughtlessness should have such an irreversible effect. But then, far from crumbling with prayer and confession and the mercy of time, the first room of his hell turned out to open into a second and that into two more. It was a windowless, many-mirrored mansion.

He told Dot what had happened and she forgave him. Not immediately, of course. She was upset and angry. She tried blaming herself. But then she could see that it was over, could see that it probably made him a better priest, having discovered he was no less an animal than other men. She could see it had left him unhappy. She did not want to know who the woman was. 'If I don't put a face to her,' she said, 'it won't feel so real.'

He assured her it was no one she knew, no one in the congregation, so at least she would not be tempted to suspect each and every woman with whom she prayed or took communion. Even had he not been sworn to silence, he couldn't have told her about the rest. He convinced himself it would only cause her unnecessary pain but he suspected his true motive was selfish. The omission lodged like a deep splinter in his spirit and festered there. But the longer he put off the telling of it, the less natural it would have seemed and the greater the hurt it would have caused.

Dot forgave him and, in their gratitude at having apparently weathered a crisis, they even made love a few times before subsiding back into exhausted, passionless companionship. Which was when another room in his hell opened as he realized he was in love, and not with Dot.

And then James, or Jim, as he had become, embarked on puberty and – while not actively rebelling the way friends' sons had – withdrew into a kind of secretive, judgemental reserve that was almost worse. Another room in his hell.

Yet another, with infinite little cupboards, annexes and corridors off it, was a loss of faith. It began as something even worse, a sense that yes, God was still there but had ceased to listen or even to care, not to others, just to him; an exclusive withholding of attention, interest, mercy, an idea he would once have thought as impossible as water flowing uphill, and almost sacrilegious.

He let nothing show. He still went about his business, still conducting services, preaching, leading prayers, believing the magic would work for others at least. He even convinced himself he was being tested. But then, on one especially drab February Sunday, when everyone in the room from the smallest, fidgety child to the most devout widow, would surely rather have stayed in bed for all the transfiguration the dull occasion seemed to offer, his faith left him entirely, midway through his reading of the Gospel. It happened so abruptly it was almost a physical change, like the flicking off of a light, and he hesitated in his reading.

God wasn't listening because God wasn't there. No one was but man, who had constructed it all, leaving only hell and desolation and the justification of Barnaby's childhood killjoys. It was like a fairground ride Jim had persuaded them all onto once, a kind of revolving circular room where the floor slowly fell away from under one's feet but centrifugal force held one stupefied in place against its whirling walls. Faith fell away and, surprise surprise, the world didn't end. Everything simply lost its meaning and savour and people looked increasingly dull and stupid.

He went to see the archdeacon about it. Patient and diplomatic, profoundly spiritual but sturdily practical too, as befitted a man much of whose job involved the settling of parish disputes, he would not hear of Barnaby resigning, 'although no parish priest is worth their salt who isn't constantly questioning the value of what we do.' This happened all the time, he insisted, the difference in this case being that Barnaby was honest enough to admit it had happened. It had happened to himself once or twice. It was entirely to be expected, especially in a job so ruled by routine. 'Think how monks and nuns manage,' he said.

'I don't know how they do,' Barnaby replied. 'I don't know how they don't go insane.'

'Oh but they frequently do.'

He prescribed three things: the closer study of Thomas à Kempis, of whom he had impressively remembered Barnaby was a devotee, the patient continuation of sacred routine into which faith and meaning would flood back in time, and a visit to his GP to discuss the distinct possibility that Barnaby was suffering from depression brought on by overwork.

So Barnaby clung to routine. For week after week, month after month, he went through the holy motions, celebrating Eucharist, christening, marrying, burying and consigning to fire, visiting the unpalatable sick and hearing unasked-for, soiling confidences. And he began to take anti-depressants, which he could tell frightened Dot, because she did not discuss the matter beyond his initial, half-baked explanation and accorded his pills the same discretion her mother would have done the family of ailments she regarded as private, women's territory.

The routine didn't help but the medication did. And so did a new concentration on the not specifically religious aspects of his work – the social work aspects – especially the pastoral care of non-believers. But still he felt a fraud and a hypocrite, especially when he preached, which he began to do as little as he could, becoming an ingenious inviter-in of visiting priests. And especially when his path crossed that of his former lover, and he understood that, for all her friendliness, she saw a man in fancy dress; just a priest and nothing more.

This, then, was his season in hell, several seasons, during which he watched Carrie grow up into a worryingly unad-venturous young woman and Jim sail through his exams with chilly detachment, apply to study philosophy in Exeter and plan a gap-year trip. It was a bad, bleak period made worse by the Church making itself especially hard to love and respect by its puerile attitudes to sex and women, its mishandling of assets, its dwindling, elderly congregations.

As Jim grew away from them, becoming independent and studious, Dot blossomed as at a burden lifted. Her faith, which had always tended to the conventional and not been something she was happy discussing, began to sustain her in new ways. With no prompting from him, discovering opportunities for herself from the diocesan magazine, *The Coracle*, she signed up for courses and study weekends. His offence had given her leeway for some significant independence, perhaps. Encouraged by Tabby Morris who, as a non-stipendiary priest had rapidly become an invaluable extra pair of hands about the parish, she started a Julian Group and began to play a more active role in church services, as a reader and server. She joined a book group, run by Molly Rowe, the rather tough St Just librarian she befriended, and regularly withdrew now into long evenings with 'the girls', which he gathered were often as much about wine appreciation and group therapy as literature. When she hosted a meeting, he tried to arrange confirmation classes or PCC meetings for the same night so he could be busy up at the old vicarage, rather than find himself hiding in his study feeling oppressed by the bursts of womanly laughter or voices raised in bibulous argument, or tempted to eavesdrop when he heard just one voice, which might have been Dot's, confiding something that had reduced the rest to silence he imagined to be indignant rather than merely attentive.

Their love life had died, apparently, and he felt powerless to do anything to revive it. She had withdrawn from him after the intimate horror of the still birth; to be honest, they had withdrawn from each other, frightened at risking putting her through such an ordeal again. His withdrawal was only temporary, however, and he dared to assume hers was too. The way she gained weight – or simply failed to lose it – after that did not repel him, as she perhaps assumed, but it registered with him as a turning-aside, almost a burying of self. She gained in stature metaphorically as well as literally and he was intimidated. And then, with his infidelity and confession, he felt he had no right to expect or seek further comfort from her. Any overture had surely to come from her now, and it didn't. He was forever advocating frank discussion between couples and yet found it impossible to practise what he preached.

Far from suffering empty-nest syndrome when Jim took himself off for a year to America and Vietnam, Dot seemed to thrive in his absence. Barnaby found he was missing him keenly, for all that he had been an increasingly withdrawn and fault-finding presence, but didn't like to say as much in case Dot took it as a criticism of some shortfall on her part.

Carrie never left home, of course, not even to go travelling, which perhaps made the sudden lack of their son less painful. From a mixture of familial affection and intense practicality, she moved no further than the other end of the house. Though wary of the terrible old tradition of daughters being kept at home to be their ageing parents' helpmeets, he hoped she had chosen to stay where she was through no pressure on their part and suspected Dot was as delighted by the semi-detached arrangement as he was. He loved being able to drop in occasionally, much as each child in turn had done on their grandmother, and made an effort not to do so too often.

She had never outgrown her tomboy stage, never had a boyfriend so far as they knew. Once it was clear she wasn't academic and wasn't going to pursue some high-flying career, he couldn't help dreaming she would start a family of her own instead, but that was becoming increasingly difficult to picture. She was loving, intensely so, and would have had a lot to offer children, boys especially, but she was also steadfast and nun-like, presenting the world with a personality that managed to be at once friendly and serenely uninviting, innocent in fact. Secretly, Barnaby was bewildered by her eccentricity in becoming a carpenter. He knew how cruel people could be in small communities. He worried people would laugh at her and shame made him all the more proud when she won respect for her craftsmanship, and relieved when that in turn made her friends.

If she was lonely, she hid it well. Just occasionally some parishioner would let something slip when Carrie's name came up though, saying *pity* or simply sighing, that would set him worrying that his and Dot's non-policy of loving non-intervention might have done their daughter harm.

CARRIE AT 11

They had set off at five o'clock; so early it had felt like the middle of the night. Carrie had almost wept when Dad woke her with a gentle touch to her shoulder and the murmur of her name. Jim did cry, of course, furious at being woken next but Carrie had the knack of stilling him, jiggling him quickly on her hip while Dad found him clothes from the chest of drawers. Dad and Mum had argued, in that quiet, insistent way they had, about his wanting to bring Jim on the march.

'It's such a long day. If he doesn't get his sleep, he'll grizzle. You'll not be popular.'

'He'll be good as gold. It's an historical occasion.' And so on.

She knew her mother was actually worrying about practicalities – nappy changing, regular meals, drinks, and had found a moment at bedtime to reassure her. 'I'll look after him,' she said. 'I know what he needs.'

'But you shouldn't have to.' Mum started fretting anew.

'It's fine. It's easy. Don't worry,' Carrie said, willing away the furrows on her mother's brow and kissing them quickly to speed the process.

Most mothers granted a long, family-free day at home, would enjoy a lie-in, go shopping, treat themselves in some way, but she knew hers would use it to catch up on some task she had been wanting, actually wanting, to do, like taking all the jam from the larder and cleaning both shelves and jars, or dusting all the books with the brush attachment on the Hoover or putting in the wiring herself to make a light inside the walk-in cupboard in Carrie's bedroom.

Her mum was unusually practical. She wasn't beautiful, although Carrie had thought her so when she was very little. She had big, heavy limbs. She was immensely strong – Pearce Polglaze claimed he had once seen her with a calf under her arm. Certainly she could always open tightly fastened jars and she continued swinging Carrie up onto her shoulders at an age when Dad had said she was now too heavy. Carrie was aware that, in her peculiar way, her mother, who was her own plumber and electrician, sewed and knitted, kept chickens and made the best sponges in Pendeen, was a kind of goddess. Shell's mother was pretty but could do none of these things and was married to a man – actually she only lived with him, Shell had confided – who she said was good for only one thing, and that only occasionally.

'I wish I was married to your mum,' Shell's mum said once. 'At least during the day.'

So Mum would enjoy herself today, but not in ways any normal woman would recognize as pleasurable.

Carrie had assumed they'd be travelling by bus, as that was cheapest. But a train had been chartered especially, with room for five hundred, more if people were content to stand. Once news got out it was rapidly nicknamed Trelawny's Train. This led to a quick patriotic lesson from Miss Pendarves about Bishop Trelawny and the last time Cornishmen had marched upon London in protest back in 1688. Miss Pendarves had even taught them a song about it. It had a catchy little tune which Carrie had been whistling ever since and had tried picking out on her penny whistle, only she didn't know all the fingerings. 'Trelawny' was a very, very well-known tune, she had discovered. You only had to whistle it to yourself or even quietly hum it, and an adult in the room would instinctively start humming or whistling it too. It worked on Mum every time. In fact Mum actually burst into song, words and all. *And shall Trelawny live? And shall Trelawny die? There's twenty thousand Cornish men will know the reason why!*

'Don't tell your mother,' Dad said, 'But the marchers actually only got as far as Bristol before Trelawny was released …'

So. Not buses or sick-making coaches for once but a proper train in which you could walk up and down and even go to the loo as it went along. Although Mr Gilbert and his team were fully behind the march, pulling alongside the union men for once, there had been a fuss made that the mine management would spare so few men to come on the march. Only thirty employees out of three hundred and seventy-five were coming. But the bosses made the point that closing the mine for the day, or drastically reducing production, would have given out the wrong message when they were marching to let the world know tin mining at Geevor was still a viable industry. Carrie knew all this from Jazz, whose father, being a union rep, was one of the thirty. Carrie had heard her mother call Jazz a little firebrand and was fairly sure it wasn't for her red hair.

At eleven she was finally outgrowing her phase of resenting the continual constraints imposed on them by lack of money and beginning instead to understand, anticipate and worry about them instead. Her underwear, socks and shoes were new. Everything else was second-hand. This did not matter so much at school, where they all wore boring uniforms, but she was conscious of it on days like today when they wore weekend clothes. She had a horror of somebody pointing at her coat or jersey and calling out, 'Hey! That used to be mine!' (A woman had accosted them in Greenmarket Car Park once because she recognized their crummy old Ford as one she used to own when it didn't have all the dents and rusty bits. She obliged them to stand around awkwardly waiting while she sighed over the state of it and, perhaps inspired by the dog collar, launched into a worryingly tearful speech about how time didn't stand still for any of them.) For this reason Carrie always chose the least noticeable garments in charity shops, resisting Mum's nudging to be more adventurous and feminine and avoiding anything with a pronounced feature, like a fake fur trim or fancy buttons. She had learnt that, of all colours, navy blue and dark brown provoked the least notice. Mum disliked her in brown, saying it was like wearing mud or worse, of which they had more than enough around the yard and fields, so she favoured navy blue. Dad seemed to like this. Whenever she wore her blue coat, as she did today, of course, because it was January, damp and perishing, he made some affectionate comment about my little nun or Sister Carrie.

Shell and Jazz, her best friends for as long as she could remember, couldn't understand her tastes and regarded her family's shopping for clothes in charity shops as a kind of disability, to be spoken of only elliptically or in hushed voices. Their fathers, being mine workers now threatened with redundancy (in every sense) were no richer than hers, she guessed, but their mothers preferred new bargains, which they tracked down with a hunter's pride, to any charity clothes, which they regarded as both pitiable and unhygienic. Occasionally she had tagged along with them on a shopping trip to Truro or even far-away Plymouth, and had to bite back the bitter knowledge learned from her parents that new clothes could only be sold so cheaply at human cost, usually to a worker, possibly even a working child. Everything had consequences. Everything a cost. But it did not do to point this out.

As the daughter of a vicar, she was expected to be perfect and superior so had to be forever undercutting this cruel expectation with small evidences of normality and safe displays of ordinary error. Shell's grandmother, whom she called Nan although her name was Clarice, and who never seemed to leave her armchair in her stifling front room in Botallack, took this expectation to sinister lengths, regarding Carrie as somehow holy and powerful, simply by distant association with the Church.

'Here's my little mystic,' she would say and would clasp the hand Carrie obediently held out to her and press it to her head or her elbow or whichever bit of her was currently giving her trouble. 'That's better,' she'd say. 'You've healing hands, my precious. No need to visit church if you can visit me, eh?' And Shell would watch through slightly narrowed eyes and say nothing about it afterwards although it gave Carrie the creeps.

They were late for the train. They were often late for things because Dad always had more things to do than he

precious child and that was all that mattered, the catcher of his occasional indiscreet comments, the sharer of his burdens, sharpener of his pencils, deliverer of his letters. But the rude intrusion of a son defined her anew as a daughter. The polarity of the household changed. Loyalties within the family were subtly but noticeably reassigned. Whereas before she had felt herself united with Dad who, being often absentminded, needed protection from her mother's practical efficiency, now the extra attention her mother paid her awoke her to a corresponding reduction on Dad's part as he became more and more taken up with his son, this sweet, diminutive reflection of himself. Redefined as daughter it seemed she was to start tagging along with her mother with a smaller version of her apron and brush, perhaps. The boys could be hopeless and messy and male but women could only be useful and tidy and resourceful. Carrie might have rebelled and started throwing the sort of door-slamming, come-back-here-my-girl tantrums that were commonplace in Shell's and Jazz's interaction with their families and had often left Carrie feeling such a dormouse by comparison. But then, with what she was beginning to realize might have been some sly instinct to survive in a hostile world, Jim reached out to her. Quite suddenly it began to be her name he called when he was upset, her hand he reached for when something frightened him. To be needed, admired even, was novel, as was the enjoyment of a family relationship in which adults played no part. She found she could make room for him after all.

She woke when Dad nudged her so as not to miss the great bridge over the Tamar into Plymouth. They stared out at the cloudy-grey expanse of Plymouth's tight terraces then he left Jim in her care while he went off in search of cups of tea. Shell and Jazz were tucking into hot bacon rolls from the buffet car. They said they were delicious, even though they smelled like armpits. Then they looked on in fascination when Dad returned and unpacked breakfast from a Tupperware box: marmalade sandwiches, banana sandwiches, all on the dense, homemade bread whose crusts Jazz and Shell always left when they came to tea. The tangerines were cheap ones, so tart they made Jim pull a face.

After breakfast she went for a walk along the train, leaving Dad deep in conversation with the vicar of St Just, who was a prime mover in organizing the march. She saw lots of people she knew, so the walk took a while because they asked questions. Carrie was shy. If it hadn't been rude, she would far rather have ignored everybody. As it was, she knew her mother despaired of her because even her answers to adults she knew tended towards the minimal. 'Yes, thank you.' 'No, thank you.' 'They're very well, thank you.' When people, especially men, spoke to her and asked her things, she felt as though they were taking a part of her. She knew they were friendly, she knew this was simply what people did and that it was her fault and she must grow out of it and stop being silly, but when some man said, 'And what's your name, my lovely?' and, not content with her answering that, asked more questions like, 'How old are you?' or 'What's your favourite band at the moment?' or the dreaded, 'And what are you going to be when you grow up?' she felt as though they were rummaging through her, their questions like bristly hands in a clean chest of drawers.

The girls lingered long enough near both Shell's and Jazz's fathers for money to be handed over for sweets, which shocked Carrie deeply, although she smiled politely and said thank you. They stopped to inspect Pendeen Silver Band's uniforms, and to compare them with the band players from Camborne and Redruth who were joining in out of solidarity. They admired the mine's banners, which Carrie confirmed had indeed been brought into the church to be blessed by the bishop on a recent visit. Then they reached the buffet and bought chocolate. Carrie was still full from breakfast but knew better than to refuse and be thought a goody-goody.

Then they all squeezed inside one of the less dirty loos to play with some lipstick and blusher and even mascara, which the girls had stolen (more shock to be concealed) on a recent trip to Woollies. The train was going fast now they had passed Exeter, so it was extremely hard to keep one's hand steady enough for the effect not to be ghoulish or comic. Carrie's hand slipped with the lipstick so that she ended up with a lopsided smile and she thought the blusher made her look as though someone had punched her. When the others had enjoyed a good laugh, she quietly took a wodge of lavatory paper and rubbed hard to scrub it off. Shell and Jazz were too intent to notice.

She had disliked games like this since they had ceased to feel like games. They were no longer dressing up or painting their faces for the fun of it, as when they had once bicycled all around the village wearing high heels and hats borrowed from Mum's Oxfam collection box. Recently there was a purpose behind it all. There was no great mystery; she knew it had to do with Boys, as was squirting on testers in Boots and hanging around the benches on Causewayhead at tedious length with no apparent end in view. She knew, yet it left her feeling they were following a set of rules nobody had thought to explain to her. It was like maths. When she was off sick once she had missed two crucial maths lessons in which somehow everything to do with fractions was explained in patient, never-to-be-repeated detail so that she had been floundering on the subject ever since.

She relished the heady, polarized girliness of it, the sense that they were never further from boys, never so exclusively a gang unto themselves, than when observing these rites – if only a way might have been found for her to participate in parallel, as it were. What she needed was a make-up equivalent to servicing Barbie's beach buggy. Mum was no help and Dad certainly wasn't; no one she knew could help her. She couldn't decide if the prospect of being excluded and left behind once it was finally noticed that she failed to pass would be a relief or a sadness to her. The uncertainty made her tense and queasy.

At last a guard knocking on the door and demanding they make way for others set her free to return to Dad, leaving the girls, who were all fired up now and possibly set on mischief, to explore the train further. She found Dad wandering the carriages too. He wasn't looking for her, not being a worrier like her mother, but simply using the need to give Jim a little walk as an excuse to go among his parishioners, doing his job.

Just as she now knew her mother wasn't beautiful, so she had recently begun to understand that people weren't always glad to see their priest, that the smiles and friendliness with which they greeted him were often a little tight with good behaviour. She loved the rare days, and the precious weeks, of holidays, when he left his dog collar and black shirts at home and dressed like anybody else, like just a man, because it completely changed the way people behaved around him and dispelled a tension. It was interesting because he was nothing like some of the other priests in the area, who disapproved of things like rock music and alcohol, or even the idea of women becoming priests too. He was mild rather than disapproving and, if he changed people's behaviour, her own included, it was always by displaying disappointment rather than anger.

Jim greeted her with a shout of her name. Perhaps at only three he was already learning that going anywhere with his father meant meeting lots of strangers and having to stand around quietly while they talked. He was showing no signs of shyness, he was boisterous if anything, so she offered to walk him back to their table. Anyone likely to want to meet him had met him already on his journey up the train, so on the way back just a few people called out things like, 'Back already?' and 'Dad got bored, has he?' which she could answer with just a smile or a yes.

Back at their seats she gave him some diluted juice to drink then read to him quietly until it was plain he was far more interested in the novelty of watching trees and hills apparently flying past the window. Then she dug in her rucksack for her book. It was an Enid Blyton mystery from the library – her guilty pleasure. She sensed Dad's disappointment when he saw her packing it. And perhaps it was a bit young for her now but at least it was a book. She had yet to reach the point where reading didn't feel like school.

Both her parents were readers rather than television watchers. The television – laughably old and small – lived in the kitchen, but apart from children's hour, *Doctor Who* and the news, it was rarely on. The rule was that she had to say what she wanted to watch before turning it on, which stopped her watching it just to pass the time, the way normal people did. If she wanted to enjoy being by the fire and with her parents, she had to do as they almost always did and reach for a book, or at least have one to hand in case a studious silence descended. Her mother was busy during daylight hours, always doing something useful: cooking, cleaning, shopping, mending things. And now that Granny had died, Granny who always used to do the darning, she was quite often busy even at the fireside, mending holes in socks and jerseys or knitting. So for her a book, invariably a novel from St Just Library, represented true leisure. Even when reading, she was never quite still. Her fingers often flicked and picked at the page corners as though seeking occupation or her feet flexed and rubbed against each other, walking invisible paths rather than lie idle.

By contrast Dad was never without a book, even when he was working. There was a little red one, a holy one, always in his pocket. He let her look at it once but it was all thees and thous and she couldn't make sense of it. He said it was his best friend but a best friend whose appeal nobody else quite understood. But he always had other books. He had several on the go at the same time. Some upstairs, some down, even some in the car. As he said, you never knew and it was as well to be prepared. He read novels too, but he read history more and books about people's lives. And God books. His reading, she could see, was a direct reflection of how he was interested in everything, prepared to give everyone a fair hearing. Whenever some parishioner lent him a book, however unsuited to his tastes, he made an effort to read it. He had even spent a few evenings recently sighing heavily over a footballer's life story because an enthusiast in the congregation had pressed it on him and he felt it was an enthusiasm he ought to try to understand.

Carrie knew she would never be like him. She found most schoolwork hard. She enjoyed RE, because it was easy as she had been to Sunday School all her life and knew her Bible so well. But it was woodwork she loved.

She couldn't say why carpentry appealed so but it wasn't only because she was good at it. She had been inspired to take it up when a cabinetmaker spent a couple of days in the house replacing some worm-eaten timbers in the staircase. Sent to him to offer coffee and biscuits, she had been transfixed by his skill and slightly formal politeness, by the shiny condition of his old, hessian-wrapped tools which he let her handle and introduced to her one by one once he saw how interested she was, and by the delicious smells of wood shavings and varnish. She was the only girl in the carpentry class but she found she rather liked that. Without a band of girls around, the boys were transformed, approachable and no-nonsense. She had what Mr Ferris, their teacher, called a true eye: when she drew a straight line, it was straight; when she marked the centre of a piece of wood then measured it up, her mark was at the centre. Their first project had been interminable and boring – a model dugout canoe, designed to teach them how to use chisels and spokeshaves – but this term they were each making a small bookcase, with proper mortise and tenon joints. When it was finished, she was going to give hers to Jim to start a little library in.

'Book,' he said, nudging in on her thoughts and effortlessly eclipsing Enid Blyton's emphatic sentences. 'Book!'

When Dad returned, he was obviously pleased to find her reading to Jim, drawing his attention to the pictures and pointing to each word as she said it. Sitting across from them, since Shell and Jazz were showing no signs of returning, he took out his little red volume.

She was glad the girls had found someone else to amuse them when they arrived at Paddington. She was the only one of them who had been to London before and was worried they thought she would therefore know everything about everything when all she remembered about the visit was a big park, a building with a dome and going to the airport to collect baby Jim. They waved to her from the platform but by the time Jim's pushchair had been retrieved and Jim strapped into it beneath a cosy blanket and a waterproof layer that snapped on around the edges, they were nowhere to be seen.

Through contacts in the union, Dad suggested, a fleet of proper red buses – double-decker ones – had been laid on and were lined up in a nearby street. With a cheer from the excited passengers, these finally set off for St Paul's Cathedral. Dad made sure she had the seat by the window. With Jim unwrapped again and dozing on his lap, he kept leaning across her to point things out and she suspected he was as excited to be there as she was.

It was a nasty day – cold and drizzly – and Postman's Park, where they assembled, was neither as eccentric nor exotic as the name had made her imagine it. It was a sunless space, near a postal sorting office, Dad said, and nothing like the other London park she had visited, with its giant, unfamiliar trees. But once the stewards and policemen gave the word and the band started playing and the banners were unfurled and they began to file out onto the streets, the buzz of it all warmed her.

Shell and Jazz found her again and they walked three abreast, arm in arm, laughing and pointing and calling out. There were several other parents with pushchairs, and they walked with Dad as if making a point. The Buggy Alliance, he called them, and Shell misheard and thought he had said Bugger Alliance which was very funny because he was a vicar.

She had thought they would be only the five hundred from off the train but there were far more marchers than that.

'It's all the Exiles,' Jazz said knowledgeably.

'What's an exile?' Carrie asked, thinking of Israelites.

'She means students,' Shell explained. 'It's a posh name for students.'

Just then the band struck up 'Trelawny' and everyone sang along, self-consciously at first, because people were watching from the pavements and taking photographs. A double-decker crawled by in the other direction and when people waved from the upper storey, the girls waved back. Then they burst out laughing again because they simultaneously forgot the words to the song and had to dum-ti-dum it. A couple of very serious men in suits in front turned back to glare at them. Soon after Jazz's father came to claim her.

'Come along, Jasmine,' he said. 'I hear you're being undignified. Trafalgar Square's up ahead.'

And so their little group fractured again as each girl re-joined her father and Carrie relieved Dad in pushing the buggy. As they entered Trafalgar Square Dad started to point things out to her again. He was distracted for a minute by a creepy-looking man with a big, bald head who stepped off the pavement to greet him. Dad gestured towards her and Jim, pointing them out to the man, but something made her prefer to stay where she was than go over politely to say hello.

'Who was that?' she asked, when Dad hurried back to her.

'A former parishioner, from Portsmouth, I think,' he said. 'But actually I've no idea. You know how hopeless I am with names and faces.' Then they followed the band down Whitehall towards the Houses of Parliament.

'Look!' Shell yelled back at her. 'TV cameras!' and her father smacked the back of her head. Carrie knew they shouldn't wave as they passed the camera. It was a solemn occasion, a bit like church, but she didn't know what to do instead so pretended Jim's waterproof covering was coming adrift so as to look busy.

And then, all too soon it seemed to her, the march was over. A handful of carefully chosen representatives, Jazz's father among them, was actually going inside Parliament to lobby MPs who, after all, wouldn't have seen the march. The rest of them had a free afternoon in London before the Trelawny Train for home left at seven-thirty. And the police and stewards were keen for the marchers to disperse quickly now to free up the traffic jam that had built up behind them. Shell's father was taking Shell and Jazz to Madame Tussauds, which sounded fun and Shell said it had blood and murderers and Michael Jackson. With his tight, talking-to-a-vicar manner, he asked if Dad and she wanted to come too but Dad surprised her by saying they had other plans, when so far as she knew they had no plans at all.

'Isn't it any good?' she asked him once the others had gone on their way.

He pulled a bit of a face and said, 'Not very,' so she knew it was either a bit like Enid Blyton or too expensive or possibly a bit of both. 'And we didn't come all this way to see waxworks,' he added.

So they agreed to choose one thing each and one for Jim. For Dad they went around Westminster Abbey. It was expensive and there were lots of tourists. Her favourite thing was all the wood carving in the choir stalls and the special carved seats called misericords, which Dad explained meant mercy because they had a little shelf that discreetly supported monks having to stand for long services in the middle of the night. Before they left, Dad suggested they go into one of the less crowded side chapels to pray that the march and the meeting with the MPs was a success.

She was worried people would stare at them or that he'd expect her to pray out loud, or that he would. But all he did was sit them in a quiet row near a pretty altar.

'Let's just think for a bit,' he said, 'about why we came today, and all the people we know whose lives will be turned upside down if Geevor closes and they have to find work somewhere else. Not just the miners, but their wives and girlfriends and children like Jasmine and Michelle.'

(She smiled at that because no one called Shell that any more than they called Carrie Caroline, but she hid her smile by kissing Jim's head.)

'But let's think too about the mine managers and Mr Gilbert and Mrs Thatcher and her ministers who have to make the difficult decisions for the greater good. Let us pray.' And then he knelt down and shut his eyes, so she put Jim back in his buggy and knelt down too beside Dad.

At first she was thinking about how hard and mean the kneelers were compared to the nice, plump, tapestried ones in their churches at home. Then she was thinking about people peering into the chapel and seeing them praying like a waxworks tableau at Madame Tussauds. But then she found she was thinking about Shell and Jazz and their families and how Shell's mother liked new clothes from Plymouth and how Jazz's family didn't even have a car because they couldn't afford to run one and weren't allowed a cat, like she and Jim had, because of the cost of food and vet's bills. And finally she thought of how very hard it would be to have to make new friends if the girls had to move away so their parents could find other work. And then she dared to imagine if Mrs Thatcher decided that no, the mine could not be saved. And she imagined all of Geevor covered with grass again, the ugly concrete buildings and the head frame over Victory Shaft gone and trees and hedges and munching cattle in their place or just a park. An empty seaside park. There would be absolutely no risk of Jim having to risk his life down in that terrible, frightening pit when he grew up. She opened her eyes, startled, because she had not known until just then that this was even a possibility.

Dad was already sitting back in his chair, just sitting and looking at the Jesus on the altar.

'Better?' he asked and she nodded and understood how a deep calm had come about her like the pillowy quilt in the bedroom that used to be Granny's but was now for best. It was funny his asking if she felt better when she hadn't complained of not feeling well or happy before but as he asked it, she realized she had been feeling strangely churned up inside about all sorts of things but especially her friendship with Shell and Jazz and the difference she felt more and more between herself and them. And now she felt better.

'Time for lunch,' he said. 'And Jim's treat.'

Jim's treat was to eat their packed lunch in St James's Park, where he could feed the geese and ducks.

'Now your treat,' Dad said, when they had shaken out the last of their crumbs. But her mind was a shaming blank. He asked her what she had liked best in the Abbey and she said the misericords. He asked if she meant the carving or the woodwork. She said both, after some thought.

So they caught a bus to the Victoria and Albert, which to her relief was completely free. The County Museum in Truro, which she had thought big, would have fitted into the entrance hall alone. The key thing with a museum this size, Dad said, was to have one thing you really wanted to see, or you got cultural indigestion.

'And today ours is wood.'

They looked at wooden carvings, religious ones of Jesus and Mary and lots of crucifixes, but also ones of people and faces, of flowers and trees. And they looked at wooden furniture, everything from huge four-poster beds to elegant little chairs. She had never seen so many beautiful or ingenious things in one place. She didn't like to tell Dad, or hold him back now that Jim had woken up from his afternoon nap and was grizzling to be allowed to walk, but the things she liked best of all were the newest and probably the least valuable. There were some pieces of modern furniture in blonde wood she could actually imagine in her room. She could see the joins on these and picture them as a sequence of meticulously cut and sanded sections waiting to be assembled by Mr Ferris. There was a low Danish table that made her almost breathless in her desire to touch or, ideally, own it. She wanted to pull its little drawer out and slide it back into place, could imagine precisely the satisfactory little thunk it would make and the feeling of sliding one's fingers into its elegant indentation that served as a handle.

Dad gave her pocket money early so she could buy postcards, although there were none of the Danish table, and asked her to choose something to console Mum for not being there. This was hard as all the obviously feminine presents – beautiful scarves and china and glass – were far too expensive. But she found some pretty jam jar labels she knew would appeal to her practical economy. They changed Jim's stinky nappy then Dad treated them to tea and cake in the basement cafeteria, which put Jim on such a sugar high they decided it was time to take him outside before he started climbing things and pulling things over.

Dad had talked about walking back across Kensington Gardens, the park with the gigantic trees she remembered so vividly, but in the artificial light and warmth of the museum they had forgotten it was winter, and it was pitch-dark when they came out onto the pavement. Dad said the park would be locked at dusk but they could still save on a bus fare by walking to Paddington across the park but why not take in some street life first? He said they could walk to Knightsbridge to see Harrods all lit up like a Christmas tree.

She was enough her parents' daughter to see no point in window shopping – something she associated with a class trip to Plymouth earlier that month when she had not only had to endure window shopping but sit through an interminable pantomime, a nasty, lurid thing she had promised herself never to suffer again. She hoped Dad hadn't suggested Harrods simply to humour her. He probably had, since he didn't even buy his own socks and was even less interested in clothes than she was. She was trying to think of a way to let him know this without hurting his feelings when they came upon a small crowd of people standing on the pavement to watch news footage showing on a bank of televisions in a shop window. Dad was staring.

'It's the Challenger Shuttle,' she explained. He hardly ever seemed to know about news from outside Cornwall, apart from famines, because his head was always so heavy with the problems of people nearby. He looked blank. 'Like a plane but it goes into outer space,' she said. She was well informed because they had been told all about it in science as there was a schoolmistress on board, a real schoolmistress who wasn't a proper astronaut or anything like that.

'Can we watch?' Dad asked.

She nodded and pulled the pushchair close in beside her so they wouldn't obstruct pedestrians.

'Where is it?' he asked her quietly.

'Cape Canaveral, I think,' she said. 'In Florida.'

144

It was peculiar watching the images like something from *Star Wars* but with the throbbing noises of the street as soundtrack. There was a close-up of the jet bits of the launcher rocket then what looked like a shower around them – some kind of coolant, she supposed – and then they fired. For a weird second or two it didn't seem to move and, because of the close-up camera angle not showing all the supports and things above, it was easy to believe the rocket was about to drop downwards onto the launchpad. But then it began to rise.

'We have lift-off!' a woman said to her friend just beside them, trying to sound American.

It seemed to go slowly but of course that was because it was so big and so far away. The camera angle was further off by now so they could see the whole thing. The launcher rocket was like a huge, dull brown bullet. The pure white shuttle on its side looked scarily flimsy, like a boy's toy. In fact, she decided, the whole thing, shuttle, launcher, rocket and the smaller white rockets on its side, looked like something a boy had made up. How could anybody think it was safe? But it had taken off safely several times. If it hadn't, the schoolmistress would never have agreed to set foot in it.

There was a different angle again, with a background of blue sky now, not grey, a deep blue, as though the darkness of outer space were near at hand, pressing in on the other side. And then the whole thing was swallowed up, not by flames and explosions, the way it would be in a film, but in a huge cloud. The cloud extended in more than one direction. For a second part of it looked just like a duck's head. Then like a duck sitting on a mysteriously extending white branch. And then the camera moved and it was hard to make out where the shuttle had gone. There were simply long, thin streamers of cloud going down to the sea.

It was beautiful although it was so frightening, like the film of an atomic bomb being tested in the desert that Miss Pendarves had made them watch.

Dad pulled away suddenly. 'Sorry,' he said. 'You shouldn't have seen that. Let's go.'

'It's fine,' she said.

'It's people dying.'

'I'm not a baby.'

'No,' he conceded. 'You're not.'

'I knew all about it. Jazz told us this morning while you were getting coffee. I thought you knew. I thought everybody did,' although it was completely obvious he had known nothing.

She tore herself away from the televisions to catch up with him. He seemed to be walking purposelessly now and she was worried he might forget where he was and step into the traffic. He could be so absentminded sometimes. Mum had recently told her always to keep an eye out around the house when he did things like put water on to boil or light the grill. He had set fire to some toast, really set fire to it, and not noticed that the kitchen was filling with smoke and he had twice let the bath overflow because he set it running then became too immersed in a book he was reading on the landing to remember to turn the tap off again.

'Those poor people,' he was saying. 'Awful. I'd heard people talking but hadn't understood properly. How many of them were there?'

'I don't remember exactly. Seven or eight, I think. Far more than in the Apollo rocket that blew up.'

They reached a corner and suddenly there was a huge shop up ahead of them ablaze with lights, not just in its windows but all over the surface of it so that it looked like a mad fairy palace.

'What's that?' she asked.

'What? Oh, that.' He was still lost in thought. 'That's Harrods, the shop I told you about.'

It was the most amazing place, just as amazing in its way as the Abbey or the Victoria and Albert had been and she longed to go closer, even though they had no money and shopping of itself didn't interest her. It looked so warm and comforting in the drizzly darkness. But she could tell Dad was feeling quite the reverse, that after the desperation of the miners and then the horrible beauty of what they had just watched on television, the shop and all it stood for disgusted him. So she just stood close to him and waited as he stared. She imagined herself as people must be seeing her, a small, careworn version of her mother, shielding priest and grizzling toddler from a buffeting by passers-by, sensible coat buttoned to her neck, chin set in defiance of mockery, a parody of any vicar's wife. She felt extremely grown up suddenly and resented the feeling.

At last she said, 'I think we're getting in people's way, Dad. It's very crowded here.'

Dad folded up the armrest and they made Jim a sort of nest between them. As the train pulled out and Dad produced the third Tupperware of the day, and they discovered Mum had included homemade sausage rolls and her special chocolate buns in this one, as if knowing they'd be in need of a lift at a long day's end, Carrie was happy to feel a child again, safe on the train, responsibility lifted off her weary shoulders. She found she was happy not to have to spend the long journey home with Shell and Jazz again.

'What?' Dad asked, seeing her smile out of the window.

'Nothing,' she said. 'I'm glad we didn't go to Madame Tussauds.'

'So am I. Here. A little something for you.'

He had bought her a wooden puzzle when she was looking through postcards at the museum. It was a perfect cube, made of wood the exact colour of the Danish table. There were twenty irregular pieces, the instructions said, which somehow fitted together to form the pleasingly regular finished shape.

'It's OK,' Dad said. 'You can take it apart if you like.'

But she couldn't bear the thought of small pieces getting down the side of the seats and rather wished she hadn't taken the cellophane off it already as she could feel the pieces starting to shift between her fingers, chaos trying to break out. 'Thank you,' she said again. 'I love it.'

BARNABY AT 29

When Mr Ewart finally took up their oft-repeated invitation to visit, Barnaby had been married and living in Pendeen for six years and Dorothy was pregnant a third time and insisting they keep it a secret.

At least, he hoped it was only the third time but the moment she swore him to secrecy, he found himself tormented by the thought that she might have had other miscarriages and not told even him. Dorothy's combination of physical strength and emotional delicacy was daunting. He had always assumed marriage would be a process of getting to know a person better and better yet was finding her harder and harder to read as time went on. When she chose to withhold anything – whether a judgement or a piece of gossip she thought best left unrepeated – her self-control was complete and made him feel childishly self-evident by contrast.

Unearthing the very few photographs he possessed, he sketched out Paul Ewart's odd relation to the family for her benefit. His father's oldest brother James inherited the family estate and enjoyed it for some years in the company of first one then another young man, presented to the world as his secretary but plainly, at least in Paul's case, the focus for a deep and enduring love. Dorothy seemed a bit shocked.

'Did you know all this as a boy?' she asked.

'Only in part. I sort of pieced it together. In a funny way Alice and I worked it out because our father had a parallel situation, having taken up with Mrs Clutterbuck, who was officially a sort of housekeeper but obviously rather more than that to him.'

He had been set to inherit one day, he explained, James being childless, but James was profligate and idle and ran up such debts that almost everything had to be sold. In recompense, and possibly to balance out what he saw as the pernicious influence of his father and Mrs Clutterbuck, James set up a trust on his death to fund Barnaby's education and escape from narrowness of outlook.

'Paul was principal trustee so, in effect, a sort of guardian, even when my father was still alive.'

'Your dad must have been furious.'

Barnaby thought back. 'No. He wasn't happy about it.' And he looked more closely at the most recent of the pictures, which showed him as a mop-haired, grief-numbed teenager with Paul Ewart, both of them in very smart suits, eating in a Paris brasserie. He remembered little of the occasion beyond asking a waiter to take the picture for them, which in turn had rather irritated Paul.

'And what about your sister? Wasn't she a bit miffed?'

'Oh, Alice never expected to inherit so she understood perfectly. They were close, though.'

He knew the explanation reduced to tidy plot summary a complex cluster of events and emotions whose challenge he had simply put out of mind rather than confront. He had loved his uncle instinctively, as he had loved no other relative but his sister, but he had been so young and tongue-tied that the feeling had never been expressed. So on James's death the pent-up feelings had been transferred, with no encouragement, to Mr Ewart who had, perhaps, not known quite what to do with them. Arguably the two non-relatives, now only tenuously linked by the witnessing of an undiscussed love and the papery residue of a legal arrangement, had been in retreat from each other ever since. They exchanged annual Christmas cards, with telegraphed updates, but these only emphasized the distance time, as much as geography, was placing between them. Although the older man had been signing himself Paul for years, Barnaby continued to think of him as Mr Ewart, holding him, he realized, at a comfortable distance.

He was glad Mr Ewart had not visited earlier. He was Barnaby's stand-in parent, he had paid for Barnaby's education. Barnaby wanted him to be proud of him and not merely bewildered or disappointed at the choices his protégé had made in life. Barnaby was not yet feeling settled in the parish. Far from smoothing the way, marrying so rootedly local a girl had actually caused some problems because she had been so anxious they continue to live in her family's farmhouse and not have to move to Pendeen's vicarage. After a long incumbency, during much of which his predecessor had been elderly and easily bossed around, the PCC was used to having its own way and unprepared for change. His early request that people call him Mr Johnson rather than the Catholic-sounding Father Barnaby was met with blank incomprehension. He accepted it was an entrenched tradition, common to many Cornish parishes, and decided not to make a fuss about something that seemed to bother him alone. Dorothy was successful, however, in negotiating for them to live on the farm, while he insisted the substantial vicarage be used for worthwhile causes rather than merely let out for profit. After consultation with Social Services to ascertain what needs were greatest and areas least well-funded, he saw the generous upstairs rooms turned into a women's refuge and downstairs space used for couples counselling and adult literacy tutorials. The refuge was not popular, especially when there were occasional ugly scenes with vengeful husbands or partners on the doorstep and the police had to be called, but he had the support of his modernizing archdeacon and the change came to be accepted.

More enduring ructions arose from his insistence that the parish rooms, which lay between the village school and the vicarage and church, no longer be used solely for activities at least tenuously related to Christianity. The buildings needed rent to keep themselves in good repair and the church should be reaching out, not closing in. There had always been charity whist and euchre drives and coffee mornings and meetings of Cubs and Brownies in there, but now there were life classes (the windows were high enough for no shocks to passers-by), yoga, Humanist Society meetings (sparsely attended, he was pleased to see) and Mind Body Spirit Fayres (all too well attended, the church wardens claimed, by 'pagans, witches and woowoos'). There was a near-constant rumble of discontent about the parish rooms, despite the useful money they brought in, which he came to suspect was as much to do with his relative youth and inexperience – he was the only member of the church team under forty-five – as with the violation of any strongly held principles.

Possibly the parish in Portsmouth had been too diffuse or too urban for him to feel so needed, but a real shock of taking up the job in Pendeen had been discovering that only about four tenths of his work involved the things he had learnt at Cuddesdon, procedures which only an anointed priest could carry out. The burdensome rest was social work, a complex of pastoral tasks that might as easily have landed on the desk of MP, policeman or social worker. These were tasks Dorothy grimly called *mopping up*, everything from visiting the sick, to helping with neighbourhood or family disputes, to advising on benefit claims and tenancy issues. He had not been trained in any of these and did his best – armed from the stash of appropriate leaflets – to nudge parishioners towards the relevant public or voluntary body. But there was, he came to see, something about the priest and his vested authority that retained a special weight in areas of the community where church attendance had become minimal. Just as non-attenders, non-believers even, regularly elected to hold funerals and weddings in church and to bring their babies for baptism, so the evidence of a vestigial faith showed itself in other ways, such as calls for him to bless a new home or barn, to perform exorcisms or, indeed, to hear unsought confessions from elderly agnostics suddenly afraid of death and judgements, not ostensibly believed in. Exorcisms he flatly refused but invariably found the call came from a household where there were other troubles, often unacknowledged, for which unquiet souls were an approximate metaphor – an unhappy or frustrated adolescent or an elderly parent showing signs of neglect.

And in the background to all this, or foregrounded by it, was the surprise of family life and the adjustments it required of him: the mixed blessing of a live-in mother-in-law, the exhausting delight of a baby and the see-saw blessing/challenge of taking in marriage a girl he soon realized understood as little of him as he did of her. They loved each other, desired each other – that much was plain and easy – but they would stumble onto sudden voids of comprehension or inequalities of experience which seemed to cast everything in doubt. (Within weeks, his advice sessions to prospective couples coming to him for marriage went from cheerfully formulaic to gravely questioning.)

In fact the James Johnson Trust had three trustees: Mr Ewart, a solicitor and the old friend of James whom Barnaby's father had scathingly referred to as 'First Secretary', but it was only ever Mr Ewart with whom Barnaby dealt directly. Beyond his school fees the trust paid for what might broadly be called educational holidays. This travel money had to be applied for by letter, which in turn had proved a neat way of keeping Barnaby and Mr Ewart in touch.

Over consecutive summers, in between increasingly necessary holiday jobs in restaurants, offices and the back rooms of banks, Barnaby had seen Paris, Rome, Florence, Istanbul and the cultural highlights of Greece. The longed-for cheque was always accompanied by a note or letter from Mr Ewart, usually just a note and, through the telegraphese of these and his equally elegant Christmas cards, Barnaby was able to piece together a sketch of his life after James.

The couple had soon tired of Ibiza and settled in a cheap quarter of Paris, which was where James finally died of cirrhosis of the liver. His having been hopeless with money was, in some ways, a myth to mask a sort of high standards alcoholism. James never drank Muscadet if Meursault were on offer, or Chianti when he could have vintage Barolo. Luckily for Paul, he had found it hard to resist auction houses and antique markets and had equally expensive and unerring instinct in *objets d'art* as in wine. So although the house had to be sold, the proceeds of that and the sale of all but the most portable contents kept them, as James put it, splendidly cushioned.

Despite a legal challenge from Barnaby's father, Mr Ewart inherited everything that wasn't in the trust, precisely because James had converted so much money into things over the years, unitemised and hard to quantify. He left the sad memories of Paris behind and travelled for several years with various men, including the 'First Secretary', under whose tutelage he made excellent investments in property, just before the property market went into a period of massive growth. He was neither spendthrift nor an alcoholic. He would survive.

He settled in New York. When Barnaby announced his ordination, there was a pointed silence from him, but when he was given his interim parish in Portsmouth, a magnificent black suit from James's old tailor, Gieves and Hawkes, and brogues from Church's arrived. Generosity aside, the touching thing about this was that Mr Ewart had clearly noted his size when he last took him shopping in Paris as a grieving teenager. Since then there had been silence. He wrote nothing when Barnaby informed him about settling in Pendeen and marrying Dorothy, merely sending a bouquet so preposterously large it took every vase in Mrs

Sampson's armoury to accommodate it around the house and, on the day, a gardenia plant so large it was in effect a bush, whose sweet, suggestive scent coloured the entire house before it succumbed wretchedly to white fly and was adopted by his mother-in-law, who prided herself on never giving up on a pot plant, however sick or ill-favoured.

The New York Christmas cards since Barnaby's marriage had contained nothing beyond a signature. Barnaby had come to assume he either felt he had done his duty by him or that he felt no sympathy with Barnaby's having married (which would have been sad) or felt disgust at the Church of England's persistently offensive attitude to homosexuality (which would have been quite understandable).

Then he had rung up, out of the blue; something he had never done. The telephone was always left plugged in now, of course, though Dulcie Sampson had held out vigorously against having a second line put into her end of the house. (She claimed everyone she cared about lived within walking distance.)

'Barnaby Johnson? This is Paul Ewart.' It was so long since they had spoken, Barnaby would not have recognized his voice, which now had acquired a transatlantic timbre.

Like an American cat, he thought nonsensically, picturing for the first time in years his late uncle's dark blue swimming pool and his velvety roses.

'There's a painting coming up at auction near you next month, which I particularly want to bid for. I was going to be in London on business anyway and I see I can fly down there so I wondered if I might finally come on a visit?' His voice had both a graininess and a confidence Barnaby could not remember. He was older, of course, and less self-doubting, his own man, not another's secretary. Agreeing enthusiastically and making a note in the diary, Barnaby wondered if he had become immensely fat.

He hadn't, it turned out, but was just thicker in the neck and shoulders and sandy where he had been golden. Fifty or so to Barnaby's twenty-nine, he had become overtly handsome, a man used to people saying yes; there was nothing left of his former, apologetic posture. Meeting him in the tiny airport at Newquay, to which he had brought Carrie along for the novelty, Barnaby held out his hand and found himself tugged into a hug that was somehow assessing.

Introduced to Carrie, who could be shy with strangers, Paul immediately crouched down to her level, admired her dungarees and, saying he had heard a lot about her – which wasn't strictly true, although he had been sent a recent family photograph so knew she was not yet one of nature's frock-wearers – he presented her with a Yankees baseball cap and said that, once he had her size off her mother, he'd post her the jacket to match. She was clearly won over at once, all coy smiles and wriggling once she had said her obedient thank you, and both men laughed when she offered to carry Paul's huge suitcase.

Struck with shyness in his turn, Barnaby had been worrying about what they would find to talk about but Paul talked for two, easy chat, about his journey and the people he was staying with in London and then asking questions about whatever they were passing in the car. Barnaby had not been driving long. He had signed up for lessons on moving back to Pendeen but still tended to use his bicycle within the parish. If Paul was startled at the car's age and decrepitude, he hid it well.

He exclaimed with delight as St Michael's Mount finally came into view and commented on how attractive Penzance looked but then fell silent as they headed sharply inland, away from the soft delights of the bay, and crossed up to the northeast and mining country. The seemingly haphazard scattering of terraces, bungalows and mine buildings always looked grimmer when the sun was in and that day an oppressive lid of grey cloud was bearing down over it all.

As he turned down their lane, passing a stream of men coming away from the mine, Barnaby caught the appraising stare Paul gave them through the car's grimy windows and diverted him by pointing out that Dorothy's family had lived and farmed the spot for hundreds of years.

'Ah,' Paul said with something like relief. 'Like the Johnsons.'

'Sort of,' Barnaby said and knew they were both thinking that, unlike the Johnsons, the Sampsons had not been obliged to sell up.

Paul exclaimed over the loveliness of the house and the gnarled old quince tree sheltering itself by leaning into one side of it. He made Dorothy blush by kissing her on both cheeks and once again, *à la française*, said he loved his room, said of course he understood when Barnaby explained there was only one bathroom that was currently usable, and said Dorothy's lemon curd sponge was better than anything New York had to offer. The sun came out and he cheerfully let Carrie lead him off on a walk around the farm in his unsuitable shoes while Barnaby slipped out to say evening prayers at Morvah.

They saw little of him on the Saturday until late afternoon, as he rang for a taxi to the Penzance auction house – a place neither Barnaby nor Dorothy had ever had cause to visit.

This was fortunate as there had been an accident at Geevor the afternoon before, which Barnaby only found out about on his way back from morning prayers at Pendeen. He had to drive to Truro to visit a miner in hospital and then call in on his wife and family in Truthwall. The man, who never came to church but whose mother-in-law did, had somehow caught his hand under the wheel of one of the trucks used to bring rock to the surface. He himself couldn't explain how it had happened, saying only that it was near the end of a shift and he had been working a lot of overtime – up to his legal maximum – so was tired and not concentrating. He wouldn't lose all the hand, just the two smallest fingers, and it was his left and he was right-handed, but it seemed likely the nerve damage would leave him with little grip and mining was not a job for the single-handed. The hand, presumably greatly swollen, seemed fatter still for bandages and wadding, resembling a useless club. The miner seemed brave and astonishingly cheerful, but perhaps that was the painkillers numbing harsh truths as well as tissue damage and crushed bone. Barnaby asked him what work he could find, if he had to leave the mine, and he shrugged but continued to smile.

'Farm labouring, maybe,' he said. 'Cutting broccoli. Pulling pints in the Radjel. I'll get some compensation, though. The union and Mr Gilbert will look after me. I'll be OK.'

Barnaby cursed his naïveté in assuming the man's relatives were in a position to make their own way to the hospital to visit. For sure enough, when he asked about this, he received a long explanation of how the man had lost his licence and they'd had to let the car go. He had not meant to bother the young wife with a long visit, meaning simply to call by to tell her how he had found her husband and to offer a lift to Treliske Hospital the following week. But, as was often the case, she insisted he come in and have a cup of tea and meet her two small children. Again, as was so often the case, she spontaneously explained how she used to attend church and had only stopped because her husband didn't and it would have been a cause of awkwardness had she insisted. And he told her the half-joke he always told in such circumstances of how the Sunday School was an hour's free childcare and how lots of parents came simply for the guaranteed peace and quiet.

'Except for the hymns, of course,' he added, and she laughed, as people always did and said well, maybe she'd have to come along and see, as people always said when they had no intention of doing so. He gave her one of the free children's books from the literacy scheme, which he carried in the car boot, and checked she was certain about not wanting a lift to Truro. She cried a little when they talked about her husband's job prospects and said she was going to start taking in ironing as that was something she could do from home with toddlers underfoot.

The house was clean and tidy but shamingly small, with low ceilings and no outside beyond the tiny yard where she dried her washing, and would seem even more so once her boys grew. He wondered if the compensation would be

PATRICK GALE

large enough to help them move. He didn't like to ask if
the house were rented off the mine or the council, hoping,
for her sake, it was the latter should her husband lose his
job.

The arbitrary cruelty of it still hung heavily on him when
a taxi brought Paul back to the house. He returned laden.
He had bought them a fig tree to complement their old
quince, a half-case of claret far grander than anything they
ever allowed themselves from the Co-op and a retracting
tape measure and a spirit level for Carrie. 'We had a little
chat about tool kits last night,' he explained. And he had
secured the painting he wanted. Despite their protests, he
insisted on removing its thick layers of bubble wrap and
setting it on the sitting-room mantelpiece, 'So we can all
enjoy it for the weekend.'

It was by a local artist called Tuke. Barnaby knew almost
nothing about the Newlyn School and their contemporaries
but he dimly remembered the name so supposed he had
seen other work by him in Penlee House or the Royal
Cornwall Museum. His work left him so busy he and
Dorothy had precious little opportunity for cultural excursions. They were one of the things he planned to make time
for now Carrie was nearly old enough to start appreciating
them. He had begun to think it a little unlikely that Paul
would have come all this way simply to buy some Cornish
painting; worrying that he had actually come in order to
talk, to lay ghosts and finish business, Barnaby had become
guiltily aware that, aside from their brief trip up the lane
for evening prayers, he had allowed Paul not one minute
alone with him. But as soon as the painting was unwrapped,
he dismissed this as self-absorption.

The painting showed a naked youth – a fisherman or farm labourer, to judge from his pale skin and heavily tanned face and hands – sprawled across a rock on a mattress of emerald green weed that made the redhead's skin look all the more startlingly pale. It was a beautiful object, its vibrant colours crammed into a square of board little bigger than an Orthodox icon's, and it was so much finer than anything else in the room, the murkily sentimental prints of cattle and horses left behind by Dulcie because the wallpaper had faded so around them, the shabby sofa and armchairs, the ugly but practical coffee table and the thickly varnished Victorian desk at which he would write the next day's sermon before anyone else was up, that its beauty seemed to be drawing colour and energy from the things around it, becoming ever more intense at their expense. Even the people. Dorothy looked wan as she peered closely at it and he loved her for the sturdy way she admired Tuke's technique in catching the seaweed and making it look wet.

When Barnaby excused himself to go and say evening prayers, Paul asked if he might come too, and he came to church with the others in the morning, where he stood out as the best-dressed man or woman in the congregation, but throughout the weekend he gave no sign of having understood Barnaby's job or why Barnaby did it. He was surprised at the calls on Barnaby's time away from the church, the frequency with which the phone rang or the door knocker sounded even late into the evenings. He didn't comment, as such, but he didn't need to; Barnaby saw his eyes widen or heard his conversation break off.

'Do you have to do that every day?' he asked, as they were strolling back from the church on the Saturday evening.

'Twice a day,' Barnaby said.

'But nobody's there.'

'I'm there,' he said. 'Which is all that matters. And God, of course.'

And he could tell Paul's idea of priesthood was out of Trollope: weddings and funerals, Sundays, Christmas and Easter but nothing intense or too overtly theological.

Sunday happened to be Barnaby's birthday. The congregation surprised him by singing 'Happy Birthday' in place of 'O Praise Ye The Lord' for the final hymn and quite a few handed over presents as they shook his hand afterwards: pots of jam, wine, flowers, CDs and books. He could see Paul watching and being charmed but bemused by it all.

It was traditional for them to have a picnic lunch and a swim down in Boat Cove. Dorothy had made little sausage-meat and tomato tarts and filled old ice-cream boxes with potato salad and carrot salad, and Dulcie and Carrie had spent the half-hour before church hulling strawberries. The other tradition was to drink the first bottles of the mildly alcoholic elderflower champagne Dorothy brewed every year in old cider bottles whose rubberized lids clamped shut against the gas fighting to escape.

Freed from his suit back into holiday clothes, Paul was full of slightly nervous, funny chat about people they would never meet with more money than they could possibly imagine. He took photographs, including one of Carrie in which he persuaded her to pose in just the right position for the huge, black foghorns of Pendeen Watch to appear to be emerging from her head like Minnie Mouse's ears. Then he took pictures of them all, sitting on rugs against the rocks. Of the sea and cliffs, of some weekend fishermen who came to push their fishing boat out. He drew out Dulcie Sampson the surest way, by encouraging her to reminisce about the Pendeen of her childhood, its church-filled Sundays, tea treats and homemade amusements. He built sandcastles with Carrie and showed her how to make dams. He was the perfect guest.

Yet Barnaby found his very presence felt like a criticism, that the way of life his ward had chosen was impossibly provincial and dull, a waste of ability and education, and would have disappointed Uncle James, even that Dorothy represented a kind of misalliance, a falling-off.

This was utterly unfair, naturally, for he said none of these things, had not even hinted at them; Barnaby knew they were all in his own head. The fact remained, however, that these thoughts had only entered his head with the arrival of Paul and his urbanity, perhaps simply because Paul was like a human manifestation of the road not taken. Ashamed of himself, he made an extra effort with him, asking him to tell Dorothy about his father and uncle, and about the house. Hearing him talk so lovingly about James made Barnaby like him again.

After lunch Barnaby was given presents. Carrie gave him a key rack she had made at school – basically a piece of wood stuck with a line of hooks – to hang by the front door. The charm lay in the little decorated labels she had drawn and glued on by each hook – a house, a car, and two wildly contrasting churches. He was always losing keys, under books or inside newspapers, so it would be genuinely useful if he remembered to use it. Dulcie had knitted him a fisherman's jersey – a proper Cornish garnsey with the Sennen Cove stitch on it, 'to identify your body when you get washed ashore in Padstow,' she said with the unsmiling twinkle he had learnt to recognize as her version of mischief. It had taken her months of secret labour, apparently, and Carrie laughed because she had been in on the secret. She had not brought the jersey all the way down with her – the weather was too hot and the garment too heavy – but she had the pattern in her pocket so he could look at a picture of its intricate, hard-wearing design. She had even made it in unconventional black so that he might wear it over his dog collar and under his jacket on cold days in winter. This touched him deeply. He knew the profound adjustment she must have made to her wishes in accepting him as her son-in-law.

Then Paul produced a little rectangular parcel. Barnaby protested – surely the fig tree and wine had been present enough – but no, those were for the house apparently while this was just for him. It was a painting, a tiny one evidently done on the size of sketchpad an artist could easily take on a walk. It unmistakably showed the hunched silhouette of Morvah church, with the dramatic sweep of coastline beyond it, yet it was almost an abstract, reducing the individual elements to blocks of strong colour. There was a lovely vigour to it, as if it had been done at speed, with enthusiasm or in a race against impending rain.

'That is your other church, isn't it?' Paul asked.

'Absolutely. I love it. You're so kind. It can hang over my desk.'

'It's nothing very grand. A local painter, a woman still very much alive and working, I guess. I just saw the church and knew I must bid for it. Oh, erm, is she OK?'

He gestured over Barnaby's shoulder and Barnaby saw Dorothy had got to her feet and was heading back towards the house. 'Darling?' he called. 'Are you all right?'

'I'll be fine,' she said weakly. 'Don't mind me,' and kept walking.

Barnaby jumped up. Carrie was back with her sandcastles and Dulcie had nodded off in the sunshine with her skirt uncharacteristically pulled up a little to warm her legs. 'Paul,' he said. 'Would you think me awfully rude if I took her back? She hasn't been brilliant lately.'

'Go,' Paul said. 'Leave all this. Carrie and I can bring it up later. Go.' And he waved him off.

Still holding the little painting and Carrie's key-rack, Barnaby ran to catch up with her.

'You didn't …' she started.

'Don't be silly. I'll walk you back.' He realized she was choking back tears. 'Dorothy?'

'I've got a pain,' she said, a hand on her stomach. 'A kind of cramping. Barnaby, I think I'm losing it.'

'No.'

'I don't want to lose another baby …'

'You won't. It'll be fine. We'll get you back to the house and I'll call the surgery. There'll be someone on call we can get out to check on you.' He tried to persuade her to take his arm and lean on him but she was hurrying onwards, focused on some deep imperative compared to which he was a small irrelevance. So he held her up mentally, hurrying at her side, praying they would meet nobody on the way for they'd feel obliged to maintain a front and chat. Luckily they passed only tourist walkers they could greet and pass by.

Back at the house, she almost ran up the stairs and shut herself in the bathroom. He waited for her, sitting on the foot of their bed, marvelling at how brilliantly sunny the room was at this time of day when they were never normally in it. He prayed intently and in silence, as he tended to when he guiltily felt that his prayers were centred on self. But of course this prayer was for her as much as him. And Dulcie. And Carrie. He imagined her mother's intense, quiet satisfaction at a grandson who might eventually take back the farm and revive its fortunes, even with an incomer's surname. He even fantasized that, if they had a boy, they could make Sampson his middle name. He tried to clear his mind then, stilling his thoughts by staring down at the bright little painting of Morvah on his lap. Then he apologized in his head, making a mental gesture of contrition towards Paul, who had been so generous, and couldn't help his urban spirit and practical, worldly values.

The grandfather clock downstairs struck three with its customary hesitancy between the second and third chime, and she came in to join him.

'Darling?'

'Hi,' she said softly. She sat on the bed beside him and kicked off her shoes and lay back.

'Dorothy?'

He lay beside her. She lay as she always did when about to fall asleep, with her back to him and his hand held in hers between her breasts. She smelled of sandalwood soap. She never wore make-up or scent. Soap was her one indulgence. He bought her a box of it every Christmas – a French make from Peasgood's in Penzance, that came in pretty wrapping at which Carrie marvelled.

'I'm fine,' she murmured. 'We're fine.' And she chuckled. 'Reckon I'd just eaten too many strawberries.'

'Oh, Dot,' he said into the back of her hair. 'I was so worried.'

'Well, it's fine,' she sighed. 'Everything's going to be fine. Can't you tell?'

MODEST CARLSSON AT 55

Modest liked the fact that he lived in one of the ugliest bungalows in Pendeen. Its style was all wrong: pebbledash where its neighbours were granite, brown plastic windows where all the tasteful incomers opted for white painted hardwood, and with a nasty expanse of slippery crazy concrete where there could have been at least an attempt at a garden. What he relished especially was its name. Gosport was a harking back to his Portsmouth past that had made it feel as if the bungalow were choosing him the moment an agent sent him its drab particulars.

People – people and bad films – assumed that one hid in a village behind a mask of prettiness, roses round the door, gingham at the windows, bees in the lavender, but he hid in plain sight in a bungalow so undistinguished people's eyes skated over it as they passed. Deliverymen often claimed they had trouble finding it, although it fronted almost directly onto what passed in such a place for the main road, and he knew it was because it was a building one's eye instinctively edited from the scene.

He was not as poor as the shabbily eremitical image he maintained. He had cultivated old Patience so assiduously that she left him her house and all her pretty things and her considerable savings. He donated a new brass collection plate to the church in her memory but that had not stopped a rising tide of unpleasantness towards him there. A move was not strictly necessary – he could simply have stopped attending that church and transferred his allegiance to the newly completed cathedral, but house prices even in the streets of Paulsgrove were rising and he decided that, if he moved somewhere cheaper in his mid-fifties, he would not be too late to start a new life yet not so young for living carefully off his invested inheritance to prove impossible.

Running into Barnaby Johnson and his little girl and Vietnamese toddler on a day trip to a London dealer awakened an old hunger, and the discovery that his Cornish parish was even lower on the economic ladder than Paulsgrove meant it felt like fate. He was fairly certain Johnson knew exactly who he was when they met in London, even though eleven or so years had passed and there was a limit to how far Patience's money and her late father's suits could improve his appearance or hide the obesity he liked thinking of as morbid. Johnson certainly remembered once Modest arrived in Pendeen and began busily attending services there. Like all truly good people, Johnson was no dissembler. When Modest joined the queue at the end of his first Pendeen service in order to grasp his hand in both of his and hold on just too long for comfort, Johnson failed to hide the effort with which he mastered his dread and disgust.

The Pendeen church was less patchily attended than the Portsmouth one had been so it took a little time for a regular to make himself useful. Modest was not living entirely on Patience's money – although he now dealt in books and magazines entirely online rather than endure the drudgery of running a shop – but he had plenty of spare time to offer the church, even allowing for the long afternoons in bed with a bag of cheap chocolates that were one of semi-retirement's chief pleasures.

Since Portsmouth, Johnson had acquired a family, of course, which served to shield him from the demands of his flock. The wife could be implacable where required and had undoubtedly learnt to protect him as much from his impulse to give of himself as from his parishioners' desire to have of him. At Sunday services there was always a crowd of people round him, what with churchwardens, servers and visiting preachers, so that Modest's encounters with him felt insufficiently meaningful to gratify his needs. However he soon discovered that, as at Portsmouth, there were brief, entirely spoken services of morning and evening prayer at one or other of the parish's two churches. The wife had a tendency sometimes to attend the ones at Pendeen, presumably because she could walk to them with one or both children. For some reason she rarely came to the services at Morvah, so Modest made a point of attending these. He decided to make Morvah 'his' church. Although a much longer walk from Gosport, it was easier to love, being older, smaller and with a quaint association with St Birgit of Sweden that explained the attraction to anyone who knew of his Russo-Swedish parentage.

Often he was the only worshipper besides Barnaby and relished the quiet intimacy of these occasions, the way their two voices remained distinct when joined in prayer or to recite a psalm. Barnaby clearly expected nobody to be there and Modest enjoyed the suspicion that his attendance obliged the priest to take a little longer over the services than he would if allowed to mutter through them on his own. Johnson always said good morning or good evening to him before starting and sometimes even handed him a Bible and asked him to give a reading.

Modest loved being asked to read. Especially if there were only the two of them present. He liked to fantasize that their roles had suddenly switched and that, holding the Bible, standing to read, he had become the one with access to God and Johnson, sitting, lost in thought, sometimes with his head resting on and masked by one hand as though in prayer, were the supplicant thirsty for blessing and relief.

Outside these moments of communion, and the ones at Eucharist where it was Johnson's hands that held the chalice to his lips or pressed a wafer to his treacherously sweating palm, he remained teasingly elusive. The vicar was busy, forever cycling off to visit some parishioner or attend some meeting. His departures were always brisk, perfectly friendly but brisk, as though socializing were a kind of tar or birdlime that might hold him fast if he lingered over it.

And yet, when he was amongst them, taking a service, leading prayers, he retained that slightly worrying quality that had so startled Modest when first they met, of laying himself utterly open, of hiding no part of himself. Modest itched to find a fault in him, even a small one – some laziness or a passing discourtesy – but could find none. His first Christmas in the village, several months after his arrival, Johnson surprised him with an invitation to join the family for lunch. He was tempted to refuse, correctly supposing that only the sad and relationless of the parish would be so singled out, but he accepted because surely in the bosom of his family a man was most likely to reveal his faults. Johnson had occasion enough – two of the other guests were especially troublesome old people, one of whom stank of urine and unwashed hair, and the children, the sturdy little girl and much younger, seraphic Vietnamese boy, clearly resented the intrusion of unloved strangers on such a family feast. But Johnson's grace never wavered. Even when Modest talked so earnestly and so long to Dot that she contrived to burn the pudding so that every mouthful bore a bitter overtaste of charcoal, Johnson smothered her protests and apologies by asking for a generous second helping, lavished with cream 'to take away the richness'.

And he still had that little, battered leather-bound book, the red one, perhaps four inches by five, no more, which he carried with him everywhere. It was always in his hand or tucked into his sagging jacket pocket or waiting on the bookshelf of his stall in church. Two or three times when he came across him when walking, Johnson was reading it, perched on a rock or leaning on a gate, but swiftly tucked it away at Modest's approach. It was too small for a Bible and wasn't a prayer book. The more often he saw the little book in his hands or being tucked out of sight, the more convinced he became of its profound significance to him. It was surely the key to his maddening strength or, better still, the text that would reveal his hidden faults. Whatever, it was plainly a book he needed by him always, like a beloved friend, and that was reason enough to want to take it from him.

The chance to steal it did not present itself for two or three years. He remembered the occasion well because it was his birthday and nobody knew. His long-ago wife and daughter perhaps, in whatever crisp new life they had made for themselves, would pause in their day unable to prevent the date from summoning his unwelcome face or voice, possibly without even acknowledging the sullen memory to one another, but that did not count. No one in the village knew it was his birthday and he had drunk a half-bottle of gin the night before then spent half the day in bed in a brief, pointless access of self-pity and despondency. He was fifty-five, which somehow felt more like the farewell to vigour than fifty had, and nobody was marking the occasion.

He forced himself up and along the road to the Radjel, which was deserted, for a chicken pie and a pint of Doom. And then he took himself for a short walk. He was both profoundly unfit and intensely self-conscious, so did not like to walk fast or far enough to bring on a sweat. But a great advantage of the area was that one did not need to walk for more than quarter of an hour to be on the cliffs or crossing ancient field patterns or even mounting up into moorland. Drama and sensation lay close at hand.

He was surprised at how this landscape stirred him. He had gone through life thinking himself lacking because of his failure to be interested in the natural world, as though he had been born without whichever gland it was that generated wonder. Dogs and cats, any pet, disgusted him and he saw love of animals as a sentimental weakness, but he suspected it was a flaw in him that he failed to be drawn to trees and flowers, fields and riverbanks. In his married days, his teaching days, he visited beauty spots imitatively, as a woman with no sense of smell still ducked her head to a bunch of flowers, but he continued to feel nothing but a vague unease at his lack of feeling and worry lest he let it show. This bleak West Cornwall fastness seemingly flung onto a narrow shelf between forbidding rocky high ground and no less savage coast, this scattered community with the ravaged landscape of abandoned mine works at its heart, roused him as no bluebell wood or picture postcard village ever had. He would always prefer buildings to grass but here he had at last found a landscape that confirmed something in his heart. It spoke of death and danger, of failed ventures and a reassuring lack of glory. He thrilled to the stories of local disasters men told him in the pubs: the collapse of the man engine, the perilous device of steam-driven, shifting ladders by which men and boys used to descend to the depth of the mine in the days before lifts, the underground drowning of a whole team of men because of one man's shoddy surveying, ships wrecked with all hands lost as those on shore looked down from the cliffs, powerless to do more than pray. Most of the tales had human error at their heart. He liked that.

He had not intended to walk so far, being weighed down by pie and beer, but then he spotted Johnson. The priest was evidently enjoying a half-day away from wife and children. He was sitting on a sunny rock to read. Modest did not recognize him from a distance because he was in mufti – black jeans and a black tee-shirt. But then Johnson looked up from his book – it was that book again, the small, red one – saw him coming and slid off the rock to continue walking and avoid company.

Piqued and darkly amused at the simple mischief of it, Modest pursued him. He did not call out or anything obvious. He merely quickened his pace and concentrated on narrowing the gap between them. He fancied Johnson glanced over his shoulders a couple of times. He imagined the polite torment he must be going through. A vicar could not openly avoid a parishioner without shame or embarrassment. He would be thinking up a lame excuse – ageing eyesight, a forgotten, urgent appointment at a distant farmstead. He would be wondering whether it might not be less painful simply to turn around and 'meet' Modest on the way back, with apologies but a characteristic briskness, so as to avoid actually walking home with him.

But Johnson didn't turn. He walked faster, almost hurried, so that Modest began to indulge in a fantasy that he was hunting him down, that he had a savage hunting knife in his hand or something subtler, like a cutthroat razor in his pocket. It was a sunny day. The flowers, none of whose names he knew, were densely in bloom along the hedges, yet there was no one around. It was a weekday in term time.

Modest found himself entertaining a graphic fantasy of killing the priest with a swift slice to the jugular. He would watch him stumble, gurgling, into the gorse bushes at the path's edge, pay close attention as the life left those blameless eyes, then walk on just as briskly, returning home by a long, circuitous route taking in a distant quoit and some of the coastal path. He pictured himself going to evening prayers in Morvah, so as to wait there, electrified in the fading light and deepening chill, for the priest who would not come. And so be able to turn tearfully to his neighbours and the police with the pathetic story. He imagined his unflattering photograph in *The Cornishman* as part of the crime report. *Regular church attender, antiquarian book-seller Modest Carlsson (55) waited in vain for the service of evening prayers at Morvah, which he had come to regard as part of his friendship with the savagely murdered vicar. 'I waited nearly two hours,' he said. 'I waited until it was dark, and he never came. It was so unlike him. He was always so punctual.' An added piquancy in the story comes from its having been widower Carlsson's birthday. 'If I had a cake to slice,' he says, 'I'd have wished for the killer to be brought swiftly to justice.'*

But then he was pulled short by an agonizing stitch and had to give up both chase and lurid fantasy to slump against a farm gate, heedless in his pain and sweaty self-consciousness, of whether Johnson hurried on out of sight or turned back, shamed at last into solicitude, to assist him.

The stupid game had led him further than he ever walked as a rule or had planned to come. The view was spectacular but he felt exhausted and absurd and his birthday self-pity redoubled. Mopping his brow, deeply regretting his peacock folly in wearing one of Patience's father's thicker suits and stiff leather shoes quite unsuitable for country walks, he regained something like composure and turned back the way he had come.

The red book was so small he very nearly trod on and walked past it, nestled as it was in the long grass. It must have bounced out of the back pocket of Johnson's jeans in his eagerness to be alone.

Just in case the priest were coming back by now and thus watching him, Modest pretended to retie a shoelace and so was able to slip the book into his fat palm and thence, undetected, to a jacket pocket. He walked all the way back to the safety of Gosport, excited afresh, without daring either to examine it or cast a glance over his shoulder. Behind closed doors he set the book on his desk, hung up the jacket, gulped down two mugs of water at the kitchen sink then came back to look at it properly.

If only he had simply shut it away in a box, unexamined, it would at least have retained its dark price as something precious to the priest bravely stolen, but he turned on the reading light, donned his glasses and was intensely disappointed. The binding was not leather after all but cheap cloth tooled to resemble leather but already revealing its inferiority in a quantity of little scuffs and scars where the cardboard peered out behind the red. It was a pseudo-Victorian 1930s reprint edition of Thomas à Kempis's *The Imitation of Christ*. It could hardly have felt cheaper. It was not even on India paper – whose rustling delicacy could be so pleasing. The font put him in mind of the ugly, mass-produced school prize certificates of the same period, often found pasted in the front of improving volumes with names like *Pride Before a Fall* or *Prudence's Reward*.

He shook it upside down, hoping for notes or private letters, but nothing fell out. He flicked from page to page, looking for annotations but the pages were marked only by the stains of time and casual use. There was not even Johnson's name or a telling dedication. Plainly he had come by it second-hand as the scribble in the front, in browning ink the colour of old bloodstains, said, *Even I found much good sense in here and think you may too! A. Khartoum, November '67*.

Finally he tried reading it but found the thees and thous, the wouldests and couldests of the translation clotted and phonily antique. As far as he could make out it was a set of instructions to one embarking on life as a monk. It was quite unreadable and plainly had so little resale value it was the sort of book he would once have tossed into the grimy bargain bin on the pavement outside his shop, careless of who might steal it in passing. Plainly its only worth lay in its evident preciousness to Johnson so he tore it up and burnt it in his grate, working hard to conjure up a more gratifying sense of iniquity than the oddly flat gesture yielded.

Disgusted with himself after eating the whole of a shop-bought cream sponge, Modest lumbered slowly back along the road to Morvah for evening prayers. He had not forgotten his lurid fantasy of killing the priest and attending the service as a sort of alibi. He would meet his eye and smile, he decided, shaming Johnson for fleeing from him. He would smile and be kind and, as he knelt to pray, as he always did, resisting the growing vogue for simply slouching forward on one's pew, he would catch the whiff of burnt book off his cuff and know and be glad.

But Johnson never showed up for the service. In a strange echo of his fantasy, Modest waited and waited until Brid Williams, the churchwarden, came by with her husband to lock up and, concerned to find him alone there, offered him a lift home.

Modest never said anything but the minor dereliction from duty was odd and he tucked it away as a small, sweet evidence of imperfection.

NUALA AT 36

Nuala had not lived in Morvah for long before she began to feel she was the most exotic person the community had known, simply by virtue of being Australian, an artist and a runaway wife. Not that she told many people about the last part, but in a rural parish one didn't have to tell many people a thing for word of it to spread.

She didn't care. People could know and think what they pleased. The only thing that mattered was that just two people in Australia knew where she was, her mother and her sister, Niamh, and both had hearts like strong boxes and would never blab. Nuala was safe. For the first time since she married, she was safe.

She had been surprised as anyone when she fell for Christos. A wild-child potter who had spent most of her time at VCA doing whatever drugs were on offer and, often as a result, sleeping with pretty much any man who asked, she thought of herself as a rebel. Unlike Niamh, who had always been the good girl and studied hard and ended up working for a bank, for Christ's sake, Nuala had consciously fought against every respectable mould their widowed mother tried to put on them. But this guy had started buying her work and then he had asked her out, and because she was tired of immature men who couldn't return phone calls, still less commit to a relationship, she said yes. He was sexy and rich and because he was a venture capitalist she convinced herself there was risk enough in his life to make up for the worrying detail that her mother approved of him even though he was, as she put it, a *Bubble-and-Squeak*.

Nuala was secretly pleased about this, too. That he was a Melburnian Greek rather than from old Irish stock played to what was left of her inverse snobbery.

Behind his back, while she was still in a position to talk to people behind his back, she joked that she had become a Bride of Christ. He was a churchgoer but claimed not to mind that she wasn't. 'I'll pray for you,' he said and, fool that she was, she thought he was joking. Niamh was a churchgoer and she loved Niamh. All would be well. She let him sweep her off her dusty Bohemian feet and they were married quietly, in Bali, within the year. She moved out of her grungy flat-share in Carlton and into his immaculate loft in an art deco building on Beaconsfield Parade.

Had he been violent from the start she would probably have seen sense and made good her escape sooner than she did. But he began simply by exerting control over her, control always underpinned with sex – at which he was so good precisely because a part of him was always rationally attuned to her every little reaction and reflex – and overlaid with love.

Christos really loved her. She had never felt so loved, so needed, so special, so absolutely at the centre of a man's world. Little by little he isolated her from most of her old friends, subtly encouraging her to fall out with them when they criticized her new life or, worse, her husband, or convincing her they were envious of her superior skill as an artist.

Curiously her pottery was the one area of her life in which he made no attempt to interfere. It took a month or two of marriage, and the first little checks to new love, for her to notice that he actually knew nothing whatsoever about art and would probably have bought whatever work she had produced if it gained him her initial attention and respect. He bought a huge glass display cabinet – a sort of room divider – in which hidden lights showed off her bowls and vases as though they were in a museum. He bought no more pots, of course, and after a while she started keeping even the ones she wanted for herself at her workshop where she could handle them and let them gather dust or fill with flowers or fruit, rather than see another piece of hers immured in his glass tomb.

The first time he beat her it was over nothing she could have foreseen – some imagined slight she had made in a conversation with friends of his – and he was so apologetic, so devastated afterwards that she found herself apologizing for having upset him in the first place. The first time she assumed it would be an isolated incident. And the second time, when she let a pan of rice boil dry. And the third, when she forgot to drop off his dry cleaning.

With hindsight it astonished her that an intelligent, experienced woman could have been so blind, but she could see that what he did, whether by design or the simple instincts of a twisted personality, differed very little from the techniques used to bind people into cults. Only theirs was a cult of two. He destabilized her with love and intense attention, a commitment to her and their marriage that was almost a parody of the behaviour women the world over were despairing of ever finding in a man, and continued the process by isolating her from the usual voices of reason in her life until his were the only available arms to fall into when she lost her balance at his hands. It was because he was so loving, so considerate, so minutely attentive and supportive most of the time that she could so easily convince herself he was worth forgiving, over and over again, so easily persuade herself that he would change.

She became pregnant. Christos desperately wanted children, a boy above all, she supposed, even though parenthood would necessitate drastic changes to his immaculate way of life. He bought her a diamond bracelet, a beautiful, ludicrous thing that would surely spend most of its life in her dressing-table drawer, and took her to look at pretty houses with gardens in St Kilda. The child must have a garden. But then she sighed when he said he had invited his mother on a celebration visit. It was no more than that. A sigh because it had been a long day, made worse by morning sickness, not a sigh related to his mother, who was an adoring, permanently bewildered sweetheart, and he let fly.

He only hit her twice this time, far less than before. The first blow was a punch to the side of her neck, which must have briefly cut the blood supply to her brain or something because she momentarily blacked out, swiftly coming to on the floor at the intense pain of the kick he delivered to her belly.

He cried. He had never cried before and it scared her more than his passing angers because she could not pretend she was in any way to blame. He ran her a bath, helped her into it and washed her all over as tenderly as if she had been his child.

Something had changed, she realized, had cracked and fallen away. As he washed and massaged her, and wept, and kissed her hands and feet and murmured the Greek endearments that normally made her melt within – *se latrévo agápi mou, ómorfi ángele mou* – she said nothing to take a share of blame. She said nothing, in fact, until she woke some hours after he had dried her all over and led her to bed and made love to her in a way that, for the first time, appalled her in its precision.

She was woken by a sharp, unfamiliar pain, and said, into the darkness, 'Please drive me to the hospital.'

He was the soul of attentiveness, of course, frightened as much for the child as his reputation, but at least he had the dignity not to plead with her to keep schtum or even to ask what she was going to say.

He had his answer when they reached Casualty and she told the nurses on reception, 'I had a fall and now I think I may be miscarrying.'

One of the nurses took her into a small examination room. There was a lot of blood as Nuala lifted up her nightdress, which seemed answer enough but the nurse fetched a doctor anyway, another woman, who examined her and gravely confirmed that she had indeed miscarried.

'That's a nasty bruise you've got there,' the doctor said.

'I fell,' Nuala told her. 'It was so stupid. The rug slipped under me and I landed against a coffee table.'

And the doctor gently touched the second bruise, the one Nuala hadn't realized had blossomed all up one side of her neck and asked, 'Are you sure about that?' Nuala said nothing but must have glanced towards the waiting room. 'Do you want me to call the police?'

'No.'

'Have you got somewhere safe you can go, then?'

Nuala thought a moment and nodded.

'Good. You go there.' The doctor gave her a shot for the pain and some tablets to take when it wore off. Then she slipped her the card of a women's refuge in Carlton, just a block from Nuala's studio. 'Ring them,' she said. 'They'll help you see sense in a way family and friends probably can't.' She was an athletic-looking fifty-something with a quick-dry haircut, more priestly than feminine.

Christos was devastated about the baby, there was no doubting that, but she hardened her heart. She had to be kind and sweet and say she forgave him or he would never have left her alone long enough to pack her things and slip away. And it was two days – a whole eternity of weekend – before he went to work and she could spring into action.

She went to Niamh at first but that was hopeless as he knew exactly where to find her and what the phone number was and simply laid siege. She rang the women's refuge who put her onto a lawyer who not only started divorce proceedings but had an injunction placed on him to keep his distance. Yet still he sent anonymous cards, flowers, chocolates, champagne. It would have been funny had it not been so frightening. She had always hated all the trappings of Valentine's Day and this was like having it three times a week. At last she could stand it no longer, especially once he started terrorizing Niamh and even flying down to Adelaide to visit their mother, who knew none of the nasty details so welcomed him in and threatened to take his side.

Nuala escaped to San Francisco, but found that too expensive, and tried London, which was little cheaper. Then she came on a trip to Cornwall to visit a nice ex-hippy couple she had got talking to at an opening in Clerkenwell, and took a room in a B&B in Penzance, hired a car and started house-hunting. Her mother's family were Adelaide-Cornish, something that had always seemed utterly meaningless and irrelevant when she was growing up – a heritage apparently consisting of little more than various unsuitably wintry recipes like pasties and heavy cake, and a tendency to name one's houses and children after Cornish beauty spots. (Their father had been Irish, however, and stronger willed, otherwise they'd surely have been called Lamorna and Endellion.) Her great-grandfather had been a miner from Pendeen who had been lured to the South Australian minefields with the promise of better weather and higher pay. That was all she knew. That and that nobody in Adelaide seemed to call their bungalows or children Pendeen.

Although it was actually only seven miles from Penzance, it felt profoundly remote, especially in the dingy weather in which she first saw it. The linked parishes of Pendeen and Morvah lay along a sort of windswept shelf of land on the north coast, between the forbidding high moorland that screened it from what felt like civilization, and the no more inviting rocky shore, which, to the untrained eye, appeared entirely beachless. Tin mining had begun out at the cliffs centuries ago and steadily progressed inland towards the villages to which it had given rise, leaving an apparently devastated landscape in its wake. She parked the car by Pendeen church. One generation of miners, including quite possibly her ancestors, had helped build it and another, in urgent need of work, had been hired to encompass it with high, fancifully crenellated walls.

After a quick glance around it, idly looking on gravestones for surnames she knew from Adelaide and finding a host of them, she walked down a steep lane to the stumpy lighthouse whose foghorn was blaring at intervals. From there she followed the coast path to bring her as close to the mine workings at Geevor as she was allowed and she admired the lurid green staining on the cliffs from copper traces in the waste water and wondered at the creeping wasteland still caused by a former arsenic works. Compared to the minefields she knew in Australia, it covered a tiny area and damage to the landscape was relatively confined. Pendeen felt hunkered down and grim, its appearance not helped by the drizzle and being strung out along the road rather than picturesquely gathered around a village green. When she had told her new friends she was visiting the place, they had pulled faces and someone had made a joke about how she'd need a passport to get back from there and someone else, with the thoughtless English racism so different from the Australian kind, said Pendeen lay in Indian Country. All of which made her feel instinctively sorry for the place and protective of it. Added to which, the negative perceptions of others had a way of keeping property prices usefully low.

She returned the next day, in better weather, with a map and a sheaf of estate agents' details. Nothing she saw was right. There were several places she discounted from the car and a couple of near-misses. She wanted something built in the vernacular style from granite, not brick or rendered blockwork and she needed somewhere with an outbuilding suitable for a kiln, which ruled out even the more charming of the old terraces as none of these had outbuildings bigger than a privy or cramped washhouse. She had given up and was heading home by what seemed the quickest way, along the road to Morvah and then back inland towards Penzance, when a hawk swooping over the road in pursuit of something led her eye up to the left and she saw the place and lost her heart.

It lay high above the road and up its own long track and appeared to be a farmstead, only with no evidence of continued farming. An ex-farmstead, perhaps. It was not large but stood entirely alone. And it had a couple of stone outbuildings, one of which had a chimney. There was a For Sale sign at the drive's end with a ferociously messy BY APPOINTMENT ONLY! painted on a piece of wood nailed below it.

There was some confusion at the estate agent's as to whether, actually, it was for sale or not. The owner was an old lady with a tribe of cats and no great fondness for her fellow men, especially if they had children, dogs or were merely looking for a holiday home.

'Basically she'll interview you before she'll even let you see the place,' the agent warned her. 'That For Sale sign's been up for two years but most people don't get to see beyond the first room. Either that or they can't take the cats.'

Sure enough, the feline reek was almost overpowering and Miss Eddy, who had the look of a once-great actress devastated by years and misfortune, began by saying the agents had wasted Nuala's time since the house was no longer for sale. But then she softened, when Nuala stooped to pet an antique, white tom who had come to circle her legs and – a further test – accepted coffee in cups that gave no sign of having been washed within recent memory. And then, after quizzing Nuala closely about her plans and prospects and pottery, she relented further and showed her around.

Redworks House was newer than it appeared from a distance, being some rich man's folly built just before the Great War. It was little more than a hunting lodge when Miss Eddy bought it and added a bathroom in the early sixties and she had lived there ever since, apparently doing nothing more to it. It retained its original, leaky, metal-framed windows and Bakelite light switches with, presumably, antique wiring to match. Beneath the cat-shredded rugs, yellowing newspapers and overflowing litter trays, Nuala could see a filthy parquet floor. There was no garden as such, just grass, gorse and incredible views. The two outbuildings were a garage and a stable complete with a rudimentary fireplace, where Nuala could position a kiln, assuming she could have three-phase wiring connected to such a remote address.

'I love it,' she wanted to enthuse but she was wise to the old bird so simply said, 'I can't think how you can bear to leave it.'

'I can't,' Miss Eddy said. 'Probably go in a box when I do.'

She left things maddeningly vague, implying that, if she were to sell, if, then a non-churchgoing, non-dog-owning, childless artist like Nuala would be just the sort of person she'd want to sell to. If she wanted to sell.

Nuala pressed her mobile number on her, promising to have nothing further to do with the estate agents, and Miss Eddy – Constance, as she now became – rang her repeatedly in the weeks that followed. As Nuala found other houses of less and less interest now that she had experienced the one that was perfect, she found herself dragooned into running ever more intimate errands for the old woman who had what she wanted. First she asked her to call in at the estate agents and pass on the message that the house was now definitely off the market. ('Again,' sighed the estate agent, picking the display out of her window.) Then she asked her to collect a prescription and to return some criminally overdue library books, which stank of cat. Then she asked her to take one of the cats to the vet in St Ives for a booster. This was a major test as the creature yowled all the way there and all the way back and, when it emerged that Constance's account had long-unpaid invoices against it, Nuala had to pay for two years' worth of injections.

And then it became clear that a greater change was afoot, as the errands related to something very like housemoving. Sacks of empty food tins for taking to the recycling centre in St Just. Boxes of old books for the Oxfam shop. Boxes of clothes, ditto, though these were so stained Nuala shame-facedly stuffed them into the more anonymous Oxfam bin instead, so that she need meet nobody's eye over them. Then all the cats bar the antique tom (the yowler and favourite) were mysteriously rehomed or rescued. And then, just when Nuala had decided to put in an offer on a perfectly nice and far more practical place on the lane down to Cape Cornwall, Constance rang, early and excited. She would like a lift to St Ives that morning, please.

'Much better, now I'm getting on a bit,' she said as Nuala negotiated the unbelievably narrow lane towards Zennor. 'It'll make a change being down in the sunshine and crowds, like being on holiday. I've paid all the bills and put everything in your name. The key's under the dustbin at the back. You've been such a dear. So patient. I've had to leave you Eustace because he's part of the furniture. He'd never have got on in a twilight home and he'll be a reformed character now all the girls have gone. Otherwise the place is all yours.'

'What about lawyers?' Nuala stammered. 'Bank details? Conveyancing?'

Once she had settled Constance into the council-run home in St Ives, Nuala consulted her lawyer, who soon discovered that the old bird's saying, 'I couldn't possibly sell you the place – it would be robbery,' was perfectly true since she had never owned the house but had been a squatter. This explained both her longstanding reluctance to sell and her cheerful lack of interest in maintaining the property. No living owners could be traced. Perhaps because of the widely-held assumption that Constance owned it, the property had fallen through a loophole when the land to either side was adopted by the National Trust. Having squatted there herself for nearly a year, and spent what felt like a cottage's cost on legal fees, Nuala became established as Redworks House's rightful owner.

Constance hated being in the home, predictably, became ever more peculiar and unruly then, mercifully, died. Nuala and the home's matron were the only attendees at her faith-free cremation. Eustace held on a few months longer then took himself off somewhere in the impenetrable gorse thickets that had been his hunting grounds and never returned.

With what was left of the settlement from her divorce, Nuala turned the old stable into a studio. Inspired by her new surroundings, the radically different weather, colours, rocks and plants, her work took a new direction. Escaping at last from the oppressive influence of her teachers at VCA who, ironically, had been shaped in turn by the St Ives potter, Bernard Leach, she no longer felt the need to produce work that was in any way useful or practical. Or, indeed, brown. Although she still made the occasional bowl that might be prettily filled, her bottles, vases and platters were now far too delicate for use. She began to lose herself in the risky, expensive realms of lustreware.

Fascinated by the colours she could produce with ground-down gold and silver jewellery, picked up in antiques markets, she also experimented with the metal-laden clays that bad weather washed out of the adits of some of the abandoned mine workings, from Geevor to Nanquidno. One especially arsenical shaft often produced an intense sunshine yellow that was all the more pleasing for the knowledge that a poison had been transformed to produce something so cheerful. Inevitably she had disasters, false turnings, entire batches – weeks of work – ruined when the insane winds made her kiln burn too hot and took all the precious glazes up the chimney, but she steadily found a new style that worked for her. She specialized in pieces that looked ancient – their intense colours frayed and foxed so that they seemed like once-bright artefacts clouded by centuries under sand or earth.

She was learning about herself too. Raised in cities, always in noisy crowds even when she escaped to the beach or the bush, she discovered that she preferred solitude and that her apparent gregariousness had been no more than an habitual mask. She enjoyed her own company. Entirely alone, she was discovering she was far more thoughtful than her upbringing had led her to believe. She had always read for pleasure, though never voraciously. Settling into the house, prompted by boxes of Constance's old books that had travelled no further than the garage, she fell into a routine of reading in the evenings, reading for reading's sake rather than merely to fill the time or make her sleepy.

She discovered, too, the old-fashioned pleasure of writing letters – carefully edited accounts of herself to her mother in Adelaide and easier, entirely frank versions to Niamh. Niamh had recently seen her own life transformed when she fell in love with a farmer from WA and had thrown over banking and Melbourne for planting olives and making cheese from their own goats' milk near Margaret River.

She thought about Christos, of course, but not often; it tended to be in dreams that he resurfaced. She was certainly no longer frightened or hiding and she found, when a friend of a friend wrote in a Christmas card about having spotted him with a new woman and a brace of children, that she had to manufacture curiosity and did not greatly care.

Driving home from dropping off some work in the St Ives gallery that had started selling it, hearing the appetizing rustling and clinking of her food shopping on the back seat, powering through rain so punishing her windscreen wipers could hardly cope with it, she listened to the radio telling her about terrible events far, far away and realized she was profoundly happy and very lucky indeed.

Then she had to slam on the brakes and skidded to a halt. A figure had taken her by surprise. It was a man, tall and thin, bunched up on the roadside to peer into the bracken on the verge. He jumped up, grimacing an apology into the glare of her headlights. He had no jacket on and his black tee-shirt and jeans would not have been wetter had he dipped himself in a pond. He stood aside and she began to pass but something in his face made her stop. He looked distraught, like someone who had lost a child. She wound down her passenger window.

'Sorry,' he stammered.

'Christ, I'm the one who's sorry,' she said. 'I could have killed you. Are you OK? Have you lost something down there?'

'Nothing really. The stupidest thing. A little book. It must have fallen out of my pocket when I was walking.'

'Well it'll be ruined after a few minutes of this. Get in and I'll …'

'No. No, I'm sure it's here somewhere.'

He turned aside and continued groping in the undergrowth. Disturbed, she pulled over and parked, grabbed the heavy torch she always carried in the car to light her way from car to back door, and ran back to him through the downpour.

'Here,' she began. 'This might help.' But she broke off because he was weeping. He had been using a stick to prod around in the brambles and ferns which must have just broken as he was still clutching its useless stump in one

194

hand as he hid his eyes with the other. 'Hey,' she said gently. 'Come on. Get in the car and I'll get you something dry to wear.'

'I can't,' he seemed to be saying. 'I know it's …'

'Come on.' She touched his shoulder and was surprised at the warmth of him even in the wet.

He let himself be led back to her car and did not even try to find his seatbelt as she drove the short distance along the lane then turned up the track to home. 'So sorry,' he mumbled.

'Ssh,' she told him.

His soaked clothes had brought the smell of rain and wet earth into the car with them. He fumbled a handkerchief out of his jeans that was as drenched as the rest of him and blew his nose on it. 'Sorry,' he said again and his teeth started to chatter.

'Jesus!' she said. 'How long have you been out here?'

'I couldn't say,' he said. 'A couple of hours?'

'Soon get you dry and warm.'

'I'm wetting your car seat.'

'Doesn't matter. I never sit on that side.'

'You're Australian.'

'And you're not. Come on.' She led the way into the house. One of the first improvements she had made was to install a big hot water tank, a good shower and an Aga that actually worked, unlike Constance's antique Rayburn which appeared to do little but burn money.

She set the shower running and thrust a towel at him. He started to protest. 'You're shivering,' she said simply. 'You seem to be in shock. You might have exposure. Get in there and warm up. Clean towel. Go.'

'But …'

'I've got some overalls and socks you can borrow.'

She had several outsize pairs she had bought at Cornwall Farmers to wear while she cleaned out and began the slow process of restoring the house. She bought boot socks there too in several sizes too large to pad around the house in, in lieu of slippers. She found all these and opened the bathroom door a crack to push them in for him along with a carrier bag for his wet things. Then she lit a fire and smiled to think she had a handsome, naked stranger in the house. She had either taken leave of her senses or turned a corner in her recovery from marriage …

When he emerged, faintly comical in overalls and bright red socks, she put a whisky in his hands. 'Medicine,' she said. 'Cheers.'

'Yes,' he said, and drank then smiled. 'This was so incredibly kind of you.'

'Well I reckoned you were a chump, not an axe murderer. Me Nuala. Nuala Barnes.'

'Barnaby Johnson.'

'Not Cornish, then?'

'Not remotely.'

'Sit for a bit.' She gestured to the second of Constance's dog-eared armchairs across the wood burner from her.

'I'd love to, but I should be getting back to Pendeen. My wife will be worrying.'

'Of course.' She hoped she showed no disappointment. 'I'll drive you.'

'I can walk. It's not so far. And the rain seems to have stopped.'

'You've only just warmed up, for Christ's sake.'

He smiled. 'Accepted.' He met her eyes as she stood. He had the sort of direct gaze that seemed to miss nothing. It was at once kind and unsettling; his wife could have no secrets from him, poor bitch. She liked the way he had looked about him but asked no questions, but villages being what they were, he probably knew everything about her already.

They were both silent as her car bounced back down the track to the road so perhaps he was feeling the oddness of their situation. 'You're thinking about that book again, aren't you?' she teased.

'I am, actually. Sorry. I should do what I'm always telling my children – just let it go.'

'So what was it that was so precious?'

'It has a very off-putting title.'

'Try me.'

'*The Imitation of Christ.*'

'Jesus.'

'Exactly so. It sounds better in the original Latin. *De Imitatione Christi.*'

'Like an Italian wine.'

'Yes,' he sighed.

'Let it go,' she said.

'Yes, yes,' he laughed.

'Was it valuable?'

'Not remotely, in money terms. But my sister gave it to me before she died and, well, I suppose it had become like a talisman. I seemed to take it with me everywhere.'

'A comfort.'

'Exactly.'

'So do you?' she asked, turning left at Morvah. 'Imitate Christ?'

'I ought to, being your parish priest.'

'Ah. Married and a priest. No dog collar.'

'It was my afternoon off.'

'I'm afraid I don't come to church much. I don't come at all.'

'That's all right.'

'You don't mean that.'

'No,' he said and his tone was smiling. 'Of course I don't. But so many more people don't come to church than do that I find it's my default response.'

They were driving through Pendeen now and despite the damp and chill and the welcoming fire and supper waiting for her at home, she realized she was wishing they had another half-hour in the car together. 'Do I turn up to the church?' she asked.

'No, no. We're a bit further on and down the lane to the right, but honestly here's fine and I'll make my own way down.'

She was about to protest but saw that perhaps it would involve him in one less explanation if he didn't have a strange Australian woman in tow.

'Thanks for rescuing me, Nuala,' he said. 'How on earth do I spell that?'

She told him, adding, 'Rhymes with ruler.'

He hadn't shaken her hand or touched her at all, she noticed. As she turned the car round and headed home she told herself jeeringly that he was a typical priest and scared of women, but sensed as she did so that neither of these was true. On the contrary, as an attractive man with constant access to women and their lives and secrets, and with none of the helpful paraphernalia of consulting room and receptionist and professional protocols to protect him, he must have had to work constantly to maintain a kind of glass barrier against overly warm responses to the attentiveness that was his stock-in-trade.

When he cycled up to her door two days later to return the borrowed clothes, she saw at once how the dog collar and black clothes could be as effective an anaphrodisiac as any crisp receptionist. 'Ah,' she said, opening the studio door. 'Now you look the part.'

His wife had washed both overalls and socks. She had even ironed the overalls. 'How does she do that?' she asked. 'They look as though they've just come out of the wrapper.'

'The least we could do,' he said and she felt a passing pang for his wife who possibly ironed all his shirts in the rueful knowledge that he did not begin to understand that clothes did not simply fall into these crisp folds when one unpegged them from the line.

Her being at work led naturally to his asking to see inside her studio and to examine her pottery. For once she did not resent having to explain what lustreware was, because he was so clearly interested and understanding. But then, as her exposition degenerated into self-criticism, she found his gaze on her in that penetrating way he had, a not-quite-smile about his lips. She broke off. 'What?' she said.

'Nothing,' he said, flustered suddenly. 'I should get on and leave you.'

'No,' she told him. 'I'm done for the day anyway. What is it?'

'It's just so nice to hear someone who knows exactly what they're doing and is really good at it talk about their work,' he said, taking a step or two away from her kiln.

'Oh. Yes,' she said. 'But that wasn't it, was it?'

'Er. No. Nuala, I should leave now.'

She could so easily have let him go. He was by the door, after all, and the dog collar and all that black made him a good deal easier to resist, but for want of a more accurate phrase, the devil was in her so she reached up and took him by the lapels of his jacket, which he didn't resist, and kissed him.

They kissed, laughed and, kissing some more, sank onto the catty old sofa she had moved out there and made rapid, greedy love with their clothes on or almost on. He pulled off his dog collar as it seemed to be restricting his breathing and he undid the front of his shirt because she wanted to feel his chest. Most probably if they had been obliged to step apart to undress or even to compose themselves sufficiently to cross the yard to the relative privacy and comfort of her bedroom, reason and morality would have prevailed. But once she had the weight of him on her she was powerless to resist what (she knew) she had started; he was so delightfully not Christos, she was so fearless, so, relatively, in control. Her feelings for the next quarter-hour were so bound up in herself and the novelty of half-forgotten sensations, that the strength of his own responses came as a shock, not just his flattering need of her but the heartfelt sigh he let out afterwards. He hid his face from her on the pretext of kissing her hair.

'Nuala,' he sighed. 'Oh Nuala.'

'Was that the wickedest thing you've ever done?' she asked, genuinely curious.

He sighed again.

'Oh God,' she said. 'Was it the only wicked thing you've ever done?'

'Don't,' he said. He propped himself up on one elbow to look down at her. He appeared utterly miserable.

In a priestly way – all cheekbones and fine feeling – he was handsome, she considered, especially now she had put his hair in disarray and brought a boyish flush to his cheeks. 'I don't even know your wife's name,' she said. 'Only that she irons better than I do.'

'Dorothy,' he said quietly and had to clear his throat. 'Dot,' he added.

'And you love her.'

'Very much.'

'Then this must never happen again,' she told him straightforwardly. 'Fun though it was.'

'Have you been married?' he asked.

'How …?' she began then added, 'Oh,' as he touched her ring finger in explanation, running his fingertips over the callus that remained although she had not worn her wedding ring since impulsively taking it off and losing it while redecorating. 'I was,' she admitted. 'He was a good Christian and a very bad husband. I left him.'

'I'm sorry.'

'I wasn't. If I'd stayed he'd have ended up killing me. Don't let's talk about him. Sorry but my hips are going to sleep and this sofa isn't very … Would you mind?'

'No. Of course. Sorry.'

And in a few minutes they were upright and respectable once more.

As she showed him out he started to apologize again but she silenced him. 'You weren't here as my parish priest as far as I'm concerned. I don't have a parish or need a priest. You were here as a friend returning borrowed clothes and what happened just happened ... It was no dereliction of duty of care or whatever. It just happened. Look around you. No damage. Nobody saw. No thunderbolt. The sun's even shining.'

'You're amazing.'

'Drongo, get back to your flock.'

Once he had bounced off down the track on his bicycle and she had taken a shower and, abruptly hungry, made herself a sturdy cheese sandwich, she let herself think about his visit afresh. She felt sad at her lack of self-control because, for all that he was a priest, she believed he might have become a friend with whom she could agree to differ, a friend off whom she could strike sparks, and she suspected they had now ruined the chances of that.

He came back, however. After a day or two. He had found a replacement for the little, unreadable book that had brought them together – Thomas à Kempis – an exact likeness to the old one apparently, though, of course, without the dedication from his sister, and he had found Nuala a book in the same second-hand shop. It was a long, early-twentieth-century novel, an Australian one she had never read, although she had heard of its author, Mrs Henry Handel Richardson. 'Something for the long winter evenings,' he told her. 'It has one of the most impossible husbands in all literature. And one of the best longsuffering wives.'

'And you thought this would appeal to me because …?' she teased.

'Oh, no. I didn't mean … It's purely for the story and the writing. And she's so good on the formation of an Australian middle class. And the hopeless husband. And it's Australian.'

And they ended up in a bed. Possibly because they undressed one another this time, and went to her bedroom, it felt worryingly like making love, less recreational than the first occasion. And they kept breaking off to laugh or to chat about things occurring to them.

He seemed almost to lose his temper with her when she asked if it was marriage or God making him so guilty and he said the two were extensions of the same.

'Go away, then,' she said, angry in her turn. 'Fuck off and take that bloody novel with you.'

'You don't mean that.'

'No. Leave the book, but fuck off.'

And she stayed in bed all afternoon, because she could these days, in this new life of hers, and she read the giant book. It was dry at first then compelling and wonderful, only she inevitably saw him as Richard Mahony, the doomed, feckless settler antihero, hopeless when poor and even less reliable when rich. She became morose and did no good work for days. She read on into volume two, scavenging meals from her fridge to take back to bed, and on into volume three.

He came back a third time, somewhere in the chapters where Mahony was losing his sanity, and twice more after that. And they came very close to establishing the sort of pattern on which such unofficial relationships thrive, one of feigned indifference and underhand tenderness. But then something utterly predictable and stupid happened, which gave her the strength to call a halt to whatever was building up between them: she became pregnant.

This need not have changed anything, but she realized the moment she next glimpsed him in the village – she unobserved in her car, he on the pavement with the nice-looking, big-boned woman she had guessed was his wife – that she wanted to keep the baby. So she split with him the cowardly way, but the only way in which she could trust herself not to weaken and yield once again, by simply hiding when he visited.

It didn't take much. He only visited twice more that she knew about. Despite the convenience of this, she was miffed at his apparent lack of persistence. He did nothing awkward like sending a letter or ringing her up. He dropped out of her life as abruptly as he had fallen into it, and as she entered her second trimester and morning sickness gave way to the kind glow of progesterone and endorphins, and her bump began to show, any twinge of regret was swept aside as she began to fall in love with her unborn child, made lists of names and held imaginary conversations with it.

Pregnancy began to mesh her into the local community in a way that the solitary pursuit of art had not. As she waited at the surgery in St Just or queued in shops, there or in Pendeen, other women gave her kind smiles or started conversations. She picked up where she had so cruelly had to leave off the first time around, amassing clothes, many of them given by new friends, attending ante-natal classes (including a wonderfully woowoo one involving much mutual massage, goddess contemplation and flapjack eating), teaching herself to knit and preparing and furnishing a little bedroom.

She told Niamh, who told their mother of course, and the two women agreed to be there for the birth, which would be in the spring, a perfect time for visiting Cornwall and escaping the winter back home. Perhaps because a part of her was aware how exhausted and short of time she would soon be, her creativity thrived and she established valuable connections with galleries further afield, in Falmouth and even Totnes.

It was inevitable that they would meet sooner or later. Knowing this, she had it all worked out, how she would simply deny it was his, tell some fib about a new man she'd been seeing on and off. But she met him completely outside his expected context, on a visit to the Tate. He was with a Eurasian-looking little boy, six or seven, whom he introduced as his son. The child was clearly impatient to visit the gallery shop, so he let him slip ahead and turned back to Nuala while her defences were down.

'You look so well,' he said.

'I feel like a galleon,' she said. 'I can hardly fit in the driving seat.'

'Is it kicking yet?'

'And how.' And without thinking she grasped his hand and placed it on her belly. The baby wasn't kicking just then but the sudden warmth of the connection gave him permission to ask.

'Is it a boy or a girl or haven't you asked?'

'It's a boy,' she said. 'I just found out. Hung like a horse, they told me.'

And he laughed. 'Is it mine?' he asked quietly, taking back his hand as people passed them on the stairs.

'Yes,' she said, all lies forgotten.

'I'll tell Dot,' he said. 'I'll ask her for a divorce.'

'But you love her,' she reminded him. 'You love her deeply.'

'Yes, but …' At which point his son came back to find him because he needed his money and Nuala escaped upstairs into the gallery. Her mind was now anywhere but on art. As she walked through the rooms, her eyes slid, uninvolved, over paintings and sculpture and a great curving wall of Bernard Leach pottery, as her thoughts churned over. She found she was becoming almost angry so gave up and stalked downstairs.

He was waiting outside, his son playing on the beach with friends.

'I don't want a husband,' she told him straight out. 'Really not. Never again. And I don't want him to have a father if it means hurting other children and your wife.'

'But don't I—'

'Have a say? No.' She was surprised at the strength of her own feelings. 'Really not. I'm not letting you martyr yourself and them for this and if you do anything stupid, like tell your … tell Dorothy, I swear we'll just vanish so you'll have hurt her for nothing.'

He was looking stricken.

'Barnaby, I'm very happy, honestly. We'll be happy. We'll be fine. And of course you'll be able to see him and know him. Only …'

'Not as a father.'

'No.'

'Can I ...? Will you bring him to me to be christened, at least?'

She smiled at that, at such an easy, meaningless thing to grant. 'Of course I will,' she said. 'If you like I'll do it while Niamh and my mum are still staying. They'll like that. Now. Please, Barnaby. Step away from the foxy pregnant lady. We live in a goldfish bowl.'

He obeyed her and walked slowly down the steps onto Porthmeor Beach, where he was absorbed by the Easter holiday crowds yet remained entirely visible and apart from them, in his incongruous black. He stopped to look back at her and she raised a hand and touched it to her lips, now he was far enough away for no one to link her gesture to his watching.

JIM AT 12

Jim lost all belief in God one June afternoon when he was twelve. There was no warning, no mental equivalent of distant thunder. The drama played out entirely inside his head. They had come away for a rare half-term holiday to spend a week in a static caravan on a farm near Bradford-on-Avon. They had enjoyed several excursions, to Bradford, to Bath, to Lacock Abbey, but that day's outing began with him secure in the love of an all-knowing creator and ended, still in sunshine, with him knowing he was entirely alone.

It was Granny and Carrie he first remembered. Carrie was always there, seemingly at once bossy and adoring, scooping him up, carrying him around, feeding him mashed banana, which was still a favourite taste of his. His other favourite taste, though rarely indulged in now he was growing up, was condensed milk eaten direct from the can in heart-speedingly sweet spoonfuls. This was the treat with which his Granny bound him to her. She kept a sticky can always in her little fridge in her rooms on the end of the house and gave him illicit helpings from it whenever he came to her with a sore hand or scratched knee or simply in search of love.

'Granny's secret, my bird,' she said. 'Does us both a bit of good.' She often had a spoonful herself, closing her eyes in exaggerated pleasure at its deliciousness to make him laugh.

His mother was less demonstrative and expressed her love as solicitude for his every bump and scrape and as immense care for his appearance. She knitted him a new jersey every year. Each had its particular character. He remembered most of them and was usually sorry to have outgrown them. And in each, until very recently, she embroidered three small kisses on the inside neck to show him which was the back. She liked kissing the back of his neck, or perhaps she preferred it to kissing his face. Whatever the truth behind it, that was the maternal touch that immediately sprang to mind. It became a small ritual between them, in the jersey-wearing months at least. She would pause in bidding him goodnight and say, 'Oops. Something on the back of your neck. Look!' Then she'd give him a quick little kiss on the back of the neck and one of them would say, 'Jersey left one behind.'

Secretly he thought of the three women like the beds in Goldilocks – too soft, too firm and just right – Carrie being the one who was just right. But each was beautiful to him for quite a while, at least until he started school at the top of their lane.

As for Dad, he was love itself. When people talked about God, most listeners pictured an old man with a beard, for some reason, an old man at least. Perhaps to differentiate God the Father from God the Son. But when someone mentioned God to Jim, he saw only his own father. He was enthralled by visits to church, especially once he was old enough to understand what Carrie meant when she said what their father did. 'He talks to God and does a kind of magic we can't see. We can watch him do it but we can't see it happening.'

Dad was loving at home, solemn and funny, often funny in ways you couldn't quite understand, and always readier than their mother, it seemed, to give that love simple physical expression in a passing touch or hug or simply in the ready way he came down to one's own level, bending his long legs to hunker down with a game or book on the floor. But at home, and especially in what Jim instinctively thought of as his *own* clothes, as opposed to the black ones, he looked incomplete. He was most himself when he stood before them all in the pulpit or at the altar, transformed by vestments into a dazzling figure who, by virtue of skirts and glittery bits, seemed to be mother and father in a single being. Watching him at work before so many of the villagers filled Jim with a warm pride indistinguishable from a trusting belief in God. He could no more disbelieve in God than he could deny the reality of his own father.

He was a scientific child, questioning and enquiring, reassured by an ever-growing compendium of facts. The earth was round (ish). The moon's gravitational pull caused the waves and tides. There was still plenty of tin under their feet but its value was too low now to justify the cost of mining it out. God knew everything and looked after everybody. Just another fact to help one map out an understanding of the way things were. The women of the house tended not to speak of God or religion when not in church and he noticed that if circumstances obliged them to they used a special tone of voice. A reverent voice. This was a pet word of his mother's. *Reverent.* When they arrived in their pew in church, she would often still any chattering conversation he and Carrie had brought in from outside by tapping his knee and saying, 'A quick prayer, now, to settle your thoughts, then sit up and be reverent.'

He found it hard to believe now but, looking back, scanning the scant evidence of his mother's intermittently maintained photograph album, he could see that he had no sense of being in any way different from his family. He certainly didn't think of himself as being in any way foreign or exotic. He simply accepted that, when they stood side by side to look in the bathroom mirror, Carrie's eyes, high above his of course, were one shape and his were another; grapes and almonds. Their parents must have discussed the matter because the weekend before he started primary school they explained that he was adopted. 'We chose you especially,' his mother said. They said how he came from a long long way away, from an ancient, beautiful kingdom called Vietnam. But at five, he had no comprehension of great distance beyond the fact that very occasionally they expected him to sit in the car for what seemed like an entire day.

Pendeen School represented an abrupt awakening from bliss. It was a cheerful enough place but it was rambunctious compared to home and he felt unprotected and miserable there and other boys teased him, pulling their eyes into slits, putting on silly voices he laughed at too because they sounded nothing like him, and saying *Chinky Chinky Chink* at him. Girls liked and protected him, however, and a pattern was established in which he gravitated to female company because he felt safer there. Girls had a tendency to treat him like a kind of doll or pet and awoke him to his cleverness by asking his opinion, which nobody had ever done before. Boys stole his things or broke them.

Individually boys could be perfectly nice but as soon as two or three were gathered together, something in them polarized against him and they became like members of a gang from which he was excluded for reasons obvious to everyone but himself. There were boys who tried to befriend him but he soon realized they were the ones everyone despised, the ones who didn't wash enough or whose clothes smelled of wee, so with them he tried to be like his father with his more difficult parishioners like Mr Carlsson: friendly but somehow preoccupied.

He wasn't the only adopted child in the school. One of the girls who took a proprietorial interest in him, Teagan Thomas, revealed that she too lived with parents who weren't her real parents. Her situation was unimaginably complicated. Her mother was still alive but ill in some way in her head that meant that she wasn't allowed to have Teagan with her. Loony, Teagan called it, because her mother was scared of things that weren't there and thought everyone was spying on her. Yet her mother still had her *rights*, so Teagan spent time with her and a child-welfare officer. Her foster parents disliked this and wanted to adopt her outright. She was a startling girl, sultry even, with long lashes, dark eyes and a pout beyond her years. Yet, as she showed Jim, beneath her clothes her limbs were raw with bloody eczema and this always got worse when she was due to visit her mother. Torn between two mothers, she was happiest with the surrogate parenting of school.

The family had spent the morning in the American Museum at Claverton Manor. There was a constant need to save money because Dad earned so little so their agreed routine was only to visit one place a day that charged an admission fee and to fill the rest with the free pleasures of walks and churches. But then Mum was reading something called *The Yellow Book*, and discovered that the house where Dad's family used to live had its garden open for charity that afternoon. So they bent the rules, since the next day was to be spent entirely on a long walk from Bradford to Freshford and back via Iford Manor, and drove there next.

Dad's family house was unexpectedly grand; not a castle or a country seat, but not an ordinary person's house either. It stood in the centre of one of the handsome villages that Jim had trouble telling apart; and each village had an old church and several big houses apparently vying to be best. This house was *definitely* best. It held itself symbolically back from village life by having a deep, lily-filled strip of water – a moat in effect – between its front garden and the street. Not a moat, Dad explained, but a carp pond, a once-regular source of protein and a leftover from the medieval abbey whose lands had become forfeit at the Dissolution. The house had large stone balls atop two outer gateposts, which Dad said was how a visitor in the old days could tell which house in a village was the manor. Jim passed over a pretty stone bridge and entered the front garden between two fanciful stone gazebos. In one of these an old man stood guard, taking entrance money. In the other, his wife, who, he loudly confessed, *did everything but mow the grass and trim the hedges* was manning a plant stall.

'Wander wherever you like,' the man told them. 'The house is shut apart from the servants' hall, where our daughters are serving a jolly good tea.'

'Why didn't you tell him who you are?' Mum asked as they walked away from the entrance but Dad seemed not to have heard her.

They followed the gravel path that encircled a deep island of laden rosebushes underplanted with a dusty blue flower whose label she then stooped to admire. 'Nepeta,' she said wistfully. 'Catmint. Lovely. We could grow that but maybe it wouldn't look so good without the roses.'

'I didn't see the point,' Dad told her. They were always doing this, having two conversations at once. 'It would mean nothing to them. They're the second or third family to live here since Uncle James left.'

They carried on around the pretty courtyard garden then under a mossy arch into the garden proper which, by Pendeen standards, was enormous. A sequence of high-hedged sort of rooms, each with a different colour, theme or botanical feature led to a terrace presided over by two barely humanoid statues Dad said were meant to be pre-Roman, and a view across uninterrupted countryside marred only by a rumble from the M4.

There was a large bench where the three of them sat to enjoy the hint of a breeze coming off the fields below, where swallows were skimming the surface of a wheat-field. Not for the first time that holiday, Jim wished Carrie were with them. At twenty-one, she felt the need to assert her independence, at least in small ways, like taking her own mysterious trips rather than coming on family holidays.

He was becoming aware there was something not quite right about his sister, not in the head, just in her life. Something in the tone their parents and other adults adopted when they spoke of her implied she was special, meaning not normal. Certainly it wasn't normal still to be living with your parents at twenty-one, or for a girl in Pendeen at that age not to have a boyfriend, husband or, at the very least, a baby by then. He suspected it didn't help that she persisted in dressing like a boy and made coffins for a living. 'Death and art are my bread and butter,' she liked to say, meaning coffins and picture framing. She had recently discovered there was a market for pet coffins too. She had tailormade three cat caskets and even, which had made Jim giggle, a coffin for a much loved Siberian hamster. He could not understand what kept her living at home. He intended to be off at the first opportunity and had already quietly ascertained that, when the time came, he could aim higher, and further away, than Penwith or Truro College. So he understood perfectly why she would elect to avoid a week in a static caravan with them. But he missed her keenly whenever they ventured out into the world together, not just because she had a surer instinct than their parents for worldly values but because, with her marked similarity to their mother, he felt she made them unmistakably a family. Without her, he worried, they looked like three people selected at random for a social experiment or, worse still, like two unrelated adults with a stolen boy.

At least he no longer looked entirely Vietnamese. Dad had always said that it was likely his father had been a serving American soldier. (He never mentioned rape but Jim was studying warfare at school and knew that this was the most obvious reason for a refugee to have abandoned her baby.) And as Jim grew, a second, more Western face was emerging from behind his mother's. In his first twelve years, he was evidently his mother's son, uncomplicatedly, sweetly Vietnamese-looking, however Vietnamese looked. But now that he finally started to grow, his father's genes seemed to emerge from dormancy and his face and limbs were morphing dramatically and with them his character. Ironically it was only as he started to look less oriental that he felt the need to assert his oriental side and began to feel moments of directionless anger at whoever or whatever had cut him off from all it represented.

He was still small for his age, however. Several girls in his class were already growing tits and Jade Clegg had twice now tugged up her tee-shirt sleeve to grant him a flash of her downy armpit hair, which he found at once deeply shocking and something he hungered to look on again. He had thought a lot about his real parents recently and, after comparing notes with Teagan, decided that he preferred not knowing who they were as it set him free from disappointment and let him fantasize they looked like Keanu Reeves and Gong Li.

He had discovered that adoptive parents with sufficient money could go to specialist agencies that would find them a baby resembling one they might have produced themselves. He had idly fantasized there might be a service offering the process in reverse, whereby parentless children could be given computer-generated approximations of how their father and mother might have looked. He had heard too how adopted children could grow to resemble their non-biological parents. Certainly his accent was something like his mother's if, he hoped, a little more streetwise and a little less Archers. And Carrie assured him he had acquired Dad's laugh. Sadly, mere proximity would never give him Dad's height or Mum's easy strength.

'So did you grow up here?' he asked as they watched the swallows.

'No,' Dad said. 'I grew up in Bristol. My father didn't live here either, but my uncle did. My father's older brother. Your Great-Uncle James was the one who sold it.'

'Wasn't he rich enough?'

Dad smiled. 'Not at all. That's why he had to sell. Back then it was a big concern, not just the house and garden but there was a lot of farmland too.'

'You never told me that,' Mum told him.

'You never asked,' he said. 'Our ancestors built the house,' he went on to Jim. 'One of them bought the land when Henry VIII dissolved the monasteries and her son built the house, or most of it. It was added to a bit over the years.'

'And they lived here all that time?' Jim was appalled at such immobility and lack of audacity.

Dad nodded. 'Farmers don't move. Then they started marrying well and they became gentlemen.'

'Like a sex change?'

'No!' Mum laughed.

'They didn't have to work,' Dad explained.

'They *were* rich, then?'

'For a while. Yes. They must have been. You can look them up in old copies of *Burke's Landed Gentry* in the reference library.'

'What's that?'

'Oh. It couldn't be more stupid. It was a sort of directory of old families with land.'

'So girls knew who to marry and who to avoid,' Mum put in. 'We should tell them, Barnaby. I bet they'd let us inside then.'

'Oh no. They're busy. Anyway, it'll all have changed. It's not as though there are still ancestral portraits.'

'But there would have been,' she said.

'Maybe. I hardly remember. Yes, I expect there were once. I don't think I ever saw them. My grandfather sold some probably and James sold the rest. Who wants tea?'

'Me,' Jim said. He was extremely hungry as lunch had been only warm lemonade and sandwiches in the car and not enough of them. Having tea *out* was a rare indulgence and he knew, long since trained by Carrie, to opt for the least expensive item on the menu. This tended to be scone or toasted teacake. It was never gâteau.

A noisy family party walked out onto the terrace beside them and he was surprised to feel a stab of resentment. The peaceful interval on the bench with no one else in sight had fostered the illusion of ownership. This could have been his father's garden and these people trespassing on his father's lands. He saw the boy stare and knew he was seeing tall thin husband, short round wife and undersized foreign boy who had no business with them. He stared back with as much hostility as he could muster, wishing he had continued saving for reflective traffic cop sunglasses and not blown the money on trainers. He sensed that with sunglasses he would look merely cosmopolitan rather than foreign; the distinction was subtle but definite. He had learnt a trick from would-be tormentors at school, and he now pictured the boy in uncontrollable, babyish tears, snot dangling from his nose and a protective forearm across his eyes.

It worked. The boy visibly flinched and hurried to rejoin his parents who were arguing noisily about whether a tree in the field below was an alder or a surviving elm.

Jim averted his eyes from the unmistakable sight of his mother surreptitiously checking how much cash was left in her purse. Neither parent had a credit card as they shared a belief that spending money you didn't have was fool-hardy and possibly immoral. He overtook her swiftly to follow Dad along the ornamental rill.

'So did you never want to live here?' he asked him.

'There's no point wanting what you can't have. I was never going to have the money to buy a house like this, let alone run it, and it wouldn't have felt right for a priest.'

'But ... say if you hadn't been a priest. Say you'd been a ... a ...' Jim had trouble thinking of anybody rich. 'A footballer.'

'Most unlikely.'

'Or a surgeon.'

'Unlikelier still. Anyway, isn't it nicer to visit and not have to do all the weeding and gutter-clearing?'

'I suppose so,' Jim said, picturing Carrie mowing the grass at home and his mother, only last week, up on a ladder at the side of the house to replace a couple of roof slates that had blown down overnight. To be fair Dad often offered to help with practical tasks, but he was so useless at them people tended to do them slyly and swiftly behind his back rather than have him make a mess of lawn or hedge. Which in turn must have given him the delusion that such tasks only rarely needed doing.

They arrived back at the house's rear, where a fulsome red rose had been painstakingly trained across the tawny stonework. The three of them stood before it breathing in the scent and watching bees reel from flower to velvet flower.

'Not a hope of that with us,' Mum said. 'Not with the winds we get. But I might try some of that catmint under the fig or beneath the windows. I was just talking to a nice woman who said it's tough as old boots and very cheap to spread as it splits so readily in the spring. And maybe some of that pretty wormwood. What was it called?'

'*Artemisia ludoviciana.*'

'That's the one.'

Dad knew nothing about gardening but could be relied upon to remember Latin names on Mum's behalf; she treated him like a human notebook, pointing him towards plant labels or references on *Gardeners' Question Time*, then consulting him months later when poring over seed catalogues.

They followed a painted sign announcing teas into the servants' hall, a barn-like room that had once been the house's kitchen and retained a magnificent range with a clockwork spit mechanism above it. Luckily there was no menu – this not being a regular restaurant – simply the one flat rate for a pot of tea and a slice of cake. Cake, not scone! Scones *out* were never as good as Mum's own, which always led to muttering about money wasted, whereas cake of any kind was an unqualified treat so less likely to be criticized in the eating.

Just after they were served, other groups drifted in, including the noisy family with the gawking son, which was a relief as it felt a bit odd being waited on by the severe daughters of the house and his parents were less likely to draw them into conversation if the daughters were kept busy. Mum pointed to a huge coat of arms emblazoned on an old wooden board hung high over the fireplace.

'Is that yours, then?' she asked Dad.

He glanced at it. 'Not strictly. It's the Palmer family crest – my great-grandmother's. See the scallop shell? And that would have been done several generations ago, so ours would be different again.'

Jim noticed something odd going on in his manner – a show of lack of interest ('Oh. That old thing.') rubbing against a stirring of pride ('My family has a coat of arms.').

'Funny, really,' Mum said. 'Here we are eating tea like anyone else and those girls have no idea you're the lord of the manor.'

'Are you a lord?' Jim asked, startled.

'No,' Dad said. 'But the Johnsons were lords of this manor, I suppose, and the Palmers before they became Johnsons.'

'No suppose about it,' Mum said.

'All right. The Palmers were the lords of the manor. Which meant they were paid tithes by the less wealthy families in return for, well, protection, I suppose. It's utterly meaningless now, though. Although it's the sort of thing you can sell to gullible people. Occasionally there are unexpected duties attached. Some family from London buys a place like this only to find they're now expected to pay for church repairs or to maintain the village school. So far as I know there was no male Palmer heir, which was how great granny inherited which makes me lord of the manor since my uncle died without issue. And when I die it'll be you!'

'Just think of that,' Mum said. 'You'll still have to bring your own dirty laundry downstairs and make your own bed, mind.'

Jim went to the loo afterwards and Dad joined him. In the corridor that led back to the servants' hall they stopped to examine a sequence of old photographs. Each showed servants and family posing with either the front or back of the house as backdrop. The family sat on dining chairs on the gravel or lawn and the servants stood behind them, like staff and pupils in the annual school equivalent. Dogs were also present, sometimes obediently posing to the fore, sometimes wandering in a wilful blur further off. In some there were other people – more staff, or possibly just playful houseguests – smiling from upstairs windows. Dad peered closely, then pointed at the centre of one such group, at a formidable old lady swathed in black with a no less formidable baby, swathed in white, on her lap. The men on her either side were as unreadable behind beards and large moustaches as their ancestors would have been behind armour, but the old woman's face – their wife and mother? – was quite visible and looked like Dad's in the extreme seriousness he assumed when reading.

'Your great-great-grandmother,' he said. 'That baby is my granny. I remember now she used to have a copy of this picture over her desk.'

'Aren't they killing?' It was the owner's wife, come to check on her daughters perhaps or simply on a break from manning the plant stall. She had a rounded, well-fed face, plump pearls and extremely neat clothes. She had a well-maintained look, lubricated against the shocks of life. She was, Jim realized, entirely unlike any woman he ever encountered at home.

'Looking for long-lost relatives?' she asked and Jim saw her do the usual little eye flick at the tall thin man and short foreign-looking boy.

'We've found my father's grandmother,' Jim told her.

'Oh what fun,' she said. 'It's amazing how many people we get doing this. The Internet is going to make all that sort of research so much easier, isn't it? And of course maids were listed on the census returns alongside their mistresses. My favourite's that pudding-faced girl holding the pony.'

And as she clicked on along the corridor past them and pointedly unhooked and refastened a red silk rope that blocked entry into the rest of the house to mere visitors, something small but essential withered within him.

'She thought your granny was a servant,' he told Dad.

'I know,' Dad said. 'But it doesn't matter.'

It had been a long day out by their standards and they drove back to the caravan in silence. One of the good things about not having Carrie with them was being alone on the car's back seat and being the better able to relish the dull passivity of being driven and not having to participate. He stared out at the passing scenery, shops he would never enter, people he would never meet, with the same pleasurable blankness he brought to watching bad television at friends' houses, and felt himself get a hard-on in the same uninvolved way, stimulated by vibration and boredom rather than active thought.

He perceived how typical it was that his father should choose to make nothing of something that clearly mattered to him: the house, the family history, the line of inheritance that had wobbled with his grandmother being the only heir and been as good as wiped out now that the male heir was an American-Vietnamese rape-baby and no relation. It all mattered to Dad or they need not have visited. And yet, challenged, he crumpled into diffidence and denial when he could have said, perfectly politely, *my ancestors built this house so my family would quite like to see round it actually, at least the downstairs*. And then, by a connection that felt entirely natural, Jim perceived that it was the same with God. God clearly mattered to his father, he had built his life and his family's lives around the church and its needs, he was prepared to earn less than even the miners used to, certainly not enough to let him buy back his ancestral home, not even enough to let them have a holiday in a nice cottage, or even a hotel in the Canaries for once, like normal people, instead of a week in a caravan so small you could have a table or a double bed but not both at once, so that they all had to go to bed at the same time, even if they weren't all tired. And yet if challenged, faced, say, with a classmate's father, like Mr Thomas, Teagan's would-be dad, who said he never saw the point of church, Dad never made a fuss, never said, *but you must for the sake of your eternal soul. It matters, Mr Thomas. Truly it does. Just let me explain.* Rather, he would shrug – Jim had seen him do it – and say something inoffensive and basically meaningless like, *well, we all find our own way, don't we*, because however important he thought it was, he thought it was more important not to make a fuss and risk making anybody, even for a moment, feel uncomfortable.

And as they were slowly bumping along the farm track to the pretty field where the static caravan was not quite shaded by an old oak tree, it came to Jim that he would never be lord of the manor or have the sort of wife who manned a plant stall and he would never go to heaven either because God was all rubbish, a bit like cream teas or trips to museums, just something people did and said *how lovely* about, regardless of what they really felt.

There! he said to himself. *I don't believe in God. That's that.* It was more than not believing, he realized. That implied that some people did, that believing might be a valid option. In fact there were no options. There was no God. There was simply life followed at some entirely random point by death. There was, in fact, simply stuff and time. Nothing more. And the excitement, the beauty even of it was that stuff and time were still amazing.

There was no distant thunder and no sudden onset of cosmic terror. He did not in truth feel any more alone that evening than he had that morning, and no less related to his unrelated family. He simply knew he was alone, which he hadn't done at breakfast.

He said nothing. To that extent, he began to realize, he *was* like his father; he would cause no bother for the rest of them. He wouldn't make a scene about suddenly not believing, even though it was depressing to understand that from now on everything about his father's life, its whole basis, would seem pointless to him. He wouldn't even tell them unless they asked him directly, and that was highly unlikely. He would continue to go with them to church, at least until he left home, because that would be about supporting family now and avoiding conflict, nothing to do with God, but he knew he would never be confirmed. But that was fine too because he knew even now that Dad was too diffident to suggest it outright or even discuss it directly unless Jim brought it up.

'Ham and salad for supper, I thought,' Mum said as they came to a halt in the field and there was the caravan before them, a hot, little airless box like an off-white tomb. 'And there are still those nice potatoes I can boil up.'

Terror came later that night. A fox cry woke him and he felt a sensation he had felt before when woken from nightmares or enduring a high temperature, of being too much awake, too much aware, as though the volume control on his senses had been suddenly turned too high for comfort.

He lay there, in the child's bed that was too short and too narrow for him and so hemmed round it felt like a Formica-lined coffin, listening to the scary-sexy shrieks of the fox and the deep, regular breathing of his parents. He remembered in the instant that God no longer existed and began to enumerate in a kind of panic all the other things, the rights and musts, the duties and the oughts which presumably would crumble away without the idea of God and his huge approval (and its rarely mentioned opposite) to shore them up. Family. Responsibilities. Love, even. It was as though God were a vast ocean liner holed beyond repair beneath the waterline and all these other things were little tugs whose crews realized too late they were tied fast to the larger ship and about to be sucked from view.

And his mounting sense of fear was indistinguishable from his growing sense of disgust at the way his parents were simply lying there, obliviously sucking all the air from the caravan, and, just as obliviously, replacing it with their night fug. When he could bear it no more, he slipped out of bed and opened the caravan door as quietly as he could.

He walked away from the caravan and around it, enjoying the shock of dewy grass under his bare feet and against his pyjama bottoms. There was a moon. He saw a hunting owl. His fear and disgust were replaced with bewildering speed by a painful joy, fed by excitement at the realization that these intense surges of feeling must be part of what was involved in becoming an adult.

At last, when the cold in his feet began to hurt, he enjoyed a long, luxurious piss against a tree, because he could, then let himself back into the caravan and returned to bed, as silent and calm as a practised assassin.

BARNABY AT 21

Barnaby's stepmother had left a message with one of his housemates that morning. The housemate had forgotten to write it down on the little blackboard they kept for the purpose in the kitchen, so Barnaby had spent the entire day studying in the history faculty and had even come home for a spot of lunch and returned to the library, all unawares. He rang her back as soon as the housemate had thought to pass on the message, then raced to catch the next train to Bristol. He had felt so disoriented on finally arriving into Temple Meads long after dark and in driving rain that he had to walk back up into the station a few minutes after leaving it and search for a street map because he had momentarily forgotten the route to the hospital. He had the name of the ward written down, at least, so was able to navigate his way swiftly through the corridors and staircases once he got there.

He did not recognize her at first. He had not been encouraged to visit since they had converted their house into flats and apparently had far less room for entertaining. He had done no more than speak to her on the telephone (and then fleetingly) for over two years.

'I look a fright,' she said, 'but make-up takes so long and he can't see me anyway. I still wear scent for him. He likes that.' She kissed him on the cheek, which was even stranger than seeing her without make-up and with her roots growing out.

228

'It makes you look rather sweet,' he said honestly. 'Approachable.'

She made a scoffing noise. Neither of these was an epithet she welcomed but it was true; with her toughly enamelled nails, shiny gold hair and painted features, she had always dressed the part of the wicked stepmother and handed him and Alice neat evidence that she was an interloper on their scruffy family. Living far apart from her, more alienated from his father than ever, he found his memory of her appearance had hardened into unchanging parody, so that it was startling to be confronted with a reality that had, of course, been ageing, and now seemed vulnerable, even motherly.

'How is he?' he asked her.

'Not good. But he's no longer agitated and the pain nurse or whatever they call her has been and adjusted the medication so he's not suffering, or not so as you'd notice.'

'Have you been here all day?'

She nodded.

'You must be shattered, Marcia.' It felt weird to say her name out loud after years of chuckling over it in secret, weirder still that she didn't seem to register the piece of familiarity.

'I'm done in. Would you mind sitting with him for a couple of hours? Just so I can slip home for a bit and shower and change and maybe eat something?'

'Of course. No rush to get back. I slept on the train and I've had loads of coffee.'

'You're so young still.' She touched his cheek and smiled sadly, another unnerving gesture. 'Silly. I'd forgotten somehow. Maybe because your letters were always so serious. I won't be long. An hour at the most. And he'll probably just be dozing. Don't look for one of your old arguments or even anything much in the conversation line. I'll take you in to him.'

His father was in a room on his own. He was an unhealthy, deeply sallow colour and was plumbed into a catheter bag and a machine dispensing painkiller, Barnaby presumed.

'Prof?' she murmured and touched the back of his hand so that his eyelids fluttered. 'I'm just slipping home to freshen up but look who's here to see you.'

'Hello,' Barnaby said, finding himself unable to call his father anything. 'It's Barnaby.'

'Touch him so he knows what side of the bed you'll be sitting,' she said and he touched his father's forearm through his pyjamas and was shocked to find it as hard and skinny as a dog's foreleg. 'Back soon,' she mouthed exaggeratedly and slipped out.

'Sorry you've been in the wars,' Barnaby said. 'I'd have got here far earlier only I only got the … Marcia's message when I got back from the library at about five. Why didn't you tell anybody? They could have operated last year if you'd only said. The pain must have been …'

'My body,' his father said with enough of his old clarity to bring an end to the matter.

There was silence for a bit, broken only by the passing squeak of someone's shoes on the corridor outside.

'Has she gone?' he asked then. 'What did you two call her? The Butterfuck?'

'That was Uncle James.'

'You too.'

'Sometimes,' Barnaby confessed. 'Yes. She's gone but only to shower and change. She's been here all day.'

230

'Tell me about it. Thanks for coming.'

'Don't be silly.'

'Never silly.' His father broke off then to cry out sharply.

'Dad?'

'It's OK. Pain. Amazing machine this. Amazing. Wish I'd had it last night.'

He was clutching some kind of control for the dispensing device, Barnaby realized, and had just squeezed it. There was a soft sound from the machine and his father sighed and closed his now sightless eyes.

Barnaby sat back in the chair. In his rush to pack and leave he had brought only one book and it was a scholarly one on the Manichean heresies, quite unreadable for pleasure or distraction. He pulled it out now from the zipper on his case and tried again but had to read the same paragraph over and over. He was extremely hungry. The train's sandwiches had seemed criminally expensive so he had eaten nothing but an apple since lunchtime. His father had been admitted in a hurry, following a severe rectal haemorrhage, so it was no surprise to find no grapes on his nightstand. He sat on, overriding his own impulses, trying to see in the withered old man in winceyette the fierce but impressive bogeyman of boyhood. It lived on, he realized, only in the voice, implacable, slightly mocking. He could only imagine it had been pride that had driven his father to keep his illness a secret until it was too late to save him from it. It surely wasn't fear.

The eyelids fluttered open. 'Where is she?'

'Gone home for a bit. Not for long, though.'

'Not *her*!' *Stupid boy* was implied in the withering tone. 'Always literal and a bit slow.'

'You mean ...'

'Alice!'

'Alice died, Dad. You remember.'

'Of course I do but where is she? I don't mean ashes. They were put in the garden. Under a fucking car park now, of course. Where ... Where's the essence?'

'Her soul, you mean?'

There was a pause and his father pulled a slow-motion face, as though sucking on the forbidden word and finding it inexpressibly unpalatable. 'Do you still believe?'

'Yes. I wasn't sure for a while after Alice. But it sort of grew back and wouldn't be ignored.'

'Know the feeling.' His father tried to laugh at his own gallows humour but moaned instead and squeezed again for more morphine, or whatever they had him on. The moan became a sigh and he slipped off into something resembling sleep.

Barnaby watched him closely, picturing the two of them in their tiny room in the midst of a huge hospital as two people on a dimly lit sort of platform high in a great, black, concrete forest. He tried to work out what he felt for the man under the sheet before him then backed off from the attempt, fearful it was nothing loving, just an odd mix of heartless impatience and shameful fear. When his father spoke again it surprised him so that he jolted in his plastic seat.

'Do you believe in hell, then? Buy into the whole system?'

'I believe we make hell for ourselves, right here.'

'Marlowe.'

'Sorry, Dad? What was that?'

'Hell is empty.' His father fought to enunciate through the slurring of the drug. 'And all the devils are here.'

'That's from *The Tempest*.'

'Same difference.'

'You're quite safe here, Dad.'

'I don't want to die. Thought I did but ...'

'You won't. Once they've stabilized you they're going to run some—' His puny attempt at comfort was cut short by his father crying out and scrabbling in the air as if for a handle or safety rail. 'I'm here, Dad. Hold on.' Barnaby had barely touched his fingers when his father seized his hands in his and squeezed furiously, continuing to cry out.

A nurse hurried in, swore and hurried out. There was noise, more footsteps. The nurse returned with another.

'Professor Johnson?' she called over his father's wailing. 'Professor Johnson!'

Both nurses seemed crazily young and bewildered, barely capable.

'Where the hell is he?' one of them muttered, glaring over her shoulder. 'You might not like to watch this,' she told Barnaby but he couldn't leave, even had his father let go. The old man gripped so hard and painfully it felt as though Barnaby had all his body weight hanging from his hands, as though he were the only thing holding him back from a chasm.

'It's OK, Dad,' he called, ignoring the nurses. 'I'm still here. I'm with you,' and a great surge of love came up within him out of nowhere, love such as he had never felt, it seemed, and he kissed both his hands on their grotesquely clenching knuckles. And then there was blood everywhere, stinking black blood, like blood mixed with coffee grounds and vomit and finally the doctor came and there was shouting and instructions and exclamations but he stayed put through it all, holding his father's hands because there was nothing else he could do.

The doctor had gone. The first nurse was gently prising his hands clear of his father's and kindly wiping them clean with a delicious wet flannel. The other was opening the window.

'Is she coming back, do you know? Your mother?'

'Yes,' he said, not bothering to correct her.

'If you wait outside, we'll get your dad all nice and presentable for her. Do you want a cup of tea, love?'

'Yes.'

'Fetch him a tea,' she told her colleague. 'I can cope here.'

The second nurse, who looked younger than he was, about eighteen, sat him back in the corridor and brought him a mug of sweet tea and a KitKat. The chocolate was the best thing he had ever tasted and he ate it slowly, relishing the satisfying way it broke into neat fingers under its foil and crumbled on his grateful tongue. 'Are you going to be all right?' the young nurse asked gently, sitting beside him for a moment.

'I'll be fine,' he told her. 'Thank you. That was very kind of you.'

By the time Marcia appeared, some twenty minutes later, he found he was not only all right but entirely composed, so that he was able to be strong for her when she collapsed into his arms when he told her she had missed the end. She cried wordlessly for a minute or two and he could feel little spasms shake her warm, soft frame. Then she blew her nose, composed herself and stood aside a little, tidying her clothes.

'Would you …?' she began to ask. 'Would you come in to see him with me?'

'Of course,' he said.

The nurse had washed him, replaced his soiled pyjamas and unfolded a spotless sheet up to his chest. He didn't look comfortable or peaceful but he was still and looked clean. The room smelled of disinfectant rather than death.

He lied to her. 'It was very peaceful,' he said. 'He asked for you but he was quite calm. He said he loved you.'

'Did he?' She seemed startled.

'Yes,' he lied again. 'He held my hands and said, "I love her".'

But she seemed not to be listening. She touched a plump hand to the handle of the open window. 'Funny how they still always do that,' she said and closed it.

She had come into some money soon after retirement and used it to convert his boyhood home from a large family house into four flats, selling off the basement and upper ones and living on with his father on the ground floor. The garden had indeed been largely tarmacked to provide parking for all the residents, although the larger trees and a fringe of gloomy laurel remained. He had felt no affection for the place before and was surprised rather than shocked at the brutal transformation. If anything it was a relief not to be sleeping in his old bedroom with whatever memories of Alice might have haunted it, but in an entirely new room, clumsily carved from one corner of their old dining room, so that it retained just two strips of original cornice and a fireplace now quite out of proportion and in quite the wrong place.

When they arrived there from the hospital Marcia fetched a bottle of red wine, cheese and crackers and they became rapidly, pleasantly drunk together. Even had she not still been without make-up she would have seemed an entirely different woman from the one he remembered. She was relaxed and frank with him in a way the Buttercluck could never have been. She told him they hadn't married until after Alice's death because Prof had wanted to spare Alice's feelings, since Alice remembered her mother.

'He adored her, you know.'

'Our mother?'

'No! Alice. He hardly ever spoke of your mother. I used to think he was unfair with you.'

'How so?'

'Well he wasn't exactly even-handed. Alice could do no wrong but you could do no right and then when she was killed, well, she became a sort of saint.'

'I was so upset because he didn't have a funeral for her.'

'It was selfishness,' she said.

'How do you mean?'

'He didn't want to share her, or his grief. He'd pretty much shut me out from then on.'

'But he married you.'

'Oh yes,' she conceded. 'He was decent and practical that way. Thanks for fibbing back there. You meant well.'

'It … It wasn't a peaceful death. Not at all.'

'Good. Shall I open another bottle of this? It's rather good, isn't it? He must have been saving it.'

'Why not?'

They drank on, he drinking less than she did because he knew he had a light head, and she let a great flood of reminiscence come out about how she had met his father, how she had stood by while he had affairs, how he controlled who she saw, who she befriended. How he belittled her and how much, despite it all, she continued to love him. She had a little cry then, but cheered up when he made them buttered toast because they had run out of crackers. It was dawn. The familiar thunder of traffic was starting up again. One of the new neighbours drove a little sports car into her parking space and let herself into the basement flat.

'Prostitute,' Marcia said. 'Officially she works as a croupier in some club but she gets her money from sex.'

'Really?'

'She paid her down payment in cash. Unbelievable. Nice girl, though. Very clean. It's spotless down there.'

'Marcia, will you be OK?'

'Listen to you. All of twenty-one in your Oxfam clothes.'

'But will you?'

'I'll be fine,' she said. 'I'll be dandy. Don't worry about me. I'll sell up here after the funeral and find somewhere near Weston. One of my sisters is there. The will's very straightforward. We drew them up together after the wedding. Everything comes to me. But don't worry. I'll be changing mine now so that you get your share when my turn comes.'

He had been thinking about emotions not money when he asked her if she'd be all right but now that she had talked about it, he was shocked to find he resented his father's having effectively disinherited him. He was as poor as any student. Uncle James had paid for fees and travel, nothing more, but throughout his schooling Barnaby had become used to being markedly poorer than his friends and grown adept and bold at ferreting out obscure travel awards and scholarship funds he could apply for. He took a certain satisfaction in living off baked potatoes.

He rang his tutors to explain and was given compassionate leave to remain away from his studies. It wasn't an exam term. He stayed on with Marcia, as he found he now thought of her, until after the funeral. For a little over a week.

He had never been aware of her having much of a family beyond a sister in Bridlington, perhaps because of his father's strict control of their social life, but it transpired she had a huge one. As well as the sister in Weston-Super-Mare, there were three other siblings and Marcia was the only one of them not to have produced several children. For a week various configurations of Clutterbucks overran the little flat, all of them cheerful and bossily helpful. Clothes were cleared out, books boxed up, files of animal research papers and correspondence burnt in an old dustbin behind the laurels, sending acrid smoke into the November fog that had conveniently descended. Alternately overlooked or patronized, Barnaby felt uncomfortably redundant and in the way.

After her night of drunken honesty, Marcia swiftly rebuilt her old self, hair, nails and all and distanced herself at once from him and from anything else she might rashly have told him. Yet he had promised to stay until the funeral so believed he must. He also felt peculiarly his father's representative as the lone surviving Johnson-by-birth. He discovered that his student library ticket was accepted at Bristol University's library, so spent several mornings hidden away in the history section, taking notes. None of Marcia's nephews and nieces was a student. The entire family seemed to be in business or banking and it came as a shock to realize that they regarded her, whose conventionality had cast a pall over such a swathe of his childhood, as the family Bohemian and rebel, merely for having lived *in sin* with a scientist who didn't play golf.

An even greater shock was her arranging for his father to have a church funeral. His own preference was for this but he wouldn't have dared suggest it to his father and assumed Marcia's anticlerical stance had not changed.

'Wouldn't he have hated that? He thought it was all mumbo jumbo.'

'Well it is,' she said. 'But it's nicer somehow than just cremating him and walking away. Anyway, funerals are for the living, not the dead.'

He didn't feel he could argue but, come the day, for which one of the more reliable housemates sent down his suit and black shoes in a bag left at one end of a pre-agreed Bristol train carriage for him, he felt profoundly uncomfortable with being associated with such a flagrant hypocrisy. He was relieved when she insisted he go in and take a seat in the front pew so that she alone should walk up the aisle behind his father's coffin.

The priest did his best, given that he had no prior knowledge of Prof's personality. Barnaby read one of the lessons, the account of Simeon's preparation for death. When he came to the words, *For mine eyes hath seen thy salvation*, he found he was wringing every ounce of meaning out of them to compensate for an occasion he felt was using the church as a wedding party might some themed hotel dining suite. The other lesson, the inevitable gobbet of 1 Corinthians 13, worn by familiarity to bland meaningless- ness, was read by one of what Marcia called *the kitten- mincers*, who had offered himself for the task.

When, in his hopelessly safe address, the priest said, 'I know Mark wasn't one of nature's churchgoers,' somebody further back laughed out loud and Marcia joined in.

Whatever common humanity she had recently revealed was forgotten as all Barnaby's old, reassuring dislike of her came bubbling back. It completely distorted the rest of the service for him. Where he wanted to be thinking of, even praying for, his father, he found he was thinking only of her and, with an inappropriate elation, of how, far from bind- ing his stepmother to him, this occasion liberated him from her forever and forestalled any influence she might other- wise have acquired over him. He was free.

Lenny liked to think his life was simple, his needs few. He thought in pictures, in things, not words, and the things that summed up all that mattered to him were simple and primary-coloured. Grass first, clean, green grass, not the muddy turf of a pitch by mid-March but the well-mown, unscarred promise of a season's start. But grass didn't just stand for rugby but for the land above Redworks Cottage and the hours he had spent walking the carns and moorland since early boyhood. Then blue sea, naturally, the picture postcard blue you got in a sandy bay with bright sun and a clear sky overhead. Then his mum. But his feelings about her were harder to give a colour to, especially recently, when he only had to enter the same room for her to start arguing with him and finding fault.

So. To start again. Perhaps it was easier to have inanimate objects stand in for what matters. Much easier. In fact, with some ingenuity, he could probably have carried all three of them at once.

First his rugby ball, which he spent so many hours throwing and catching as he lay on his bed that any rugby ball now felt like an extension of his hand. Then his surfboard, the salty smell of whose nylon bag summed up the pleasures of summer as neatly as the ball did those of the year's end. Then his racing bike, much modified and added to until, to his immense satisfaction, it was no longer any identifiable brand but looked as though he'd built it from a kit from scratch rather than starting with a well-meant but actually hopelessly cheap and uncool present from Halfords. This represented escape and freedom, of course, but also his primal love of speed and risk, of the wind in his hair (babyish helmet safely in his bag as soon as he was out of sight of home) as he pedalled as hard as he could on the way down No-Go-By Hill so that half the thrill was imagining how he would almost certainly die if he met a car coming out of a side turning. Like all boys his age, he fantasized about having a car one day, and which make it would have to be and what colour and how he would customize it, but still he found cars less exciting than being on his bike. Unless he could have all the windows down so it was good and windy inside, but Mum never allowed that as it ate petrol apparently.

And then his mum. She could safely be represented by the one thing on his list that stayed put. It was a small pot which he used to keep his desk tidy. She had made it for him. Unlike almost all her work, it was square, because that was what he (aged seven) had demanded. It was a prototype, an idea she had taken little further because the shape was so prone to expensive failure. She had often offered to replace it with something better but he liked its intensity and lack of finesse. She joked it was a failure because it was square and that there was something inherently male about it after all her circles. Like all her work it managed to be several colours at once, flickering from a deep red to orange and yellow. Now that he understood the intense concentration that went into her art, and the value of the end product, he suspected he should stop keeping

pens and paperclips in the pot and promote it to the rank
of pure art object. He liked putting art to such mundane
use, however, just as he liked the fact that the woman
people at private views thought so special because art made
her somehow better than everyone else was for him just a
mum, someone who fed him and washed his underwear
and shared his bathroom.

At fourteen and three-quarters, however, at the start of
a new school year, his life became far more complicated
and broke out of these tidy lists and categories. The reason's
name was Amy Hawker. Her family must have just moved
to the area as he would have remembered if he had seen her
before. She looked more Swedish than Cornish, with
perfectly straight blonde hair, blue eyes and skin so pale it
made everyone around her look as though they didn't wash
properly. And her hands. He had never noticed girls' hands
before. Hands were just hands. But hers were so long and
perfect, whether she was surreptitiously texting inside her
schoolbag or discreetly using a pencil to relieve an itch on
her scalp. They had the effect of making him see for the
first time how varied girls' hands were. He had often
noticed how encrusted his mother's hands could be when
she came in from her studio but never how old they seemed.
Really old, compared to Amy's.

Anyway, the new term started, with all the usual familiar
faces, people he had been in Pendeen School with before
coming to Cape. And there she was in his maths class, like
a princess sent to a rural comprehensive to learn humility.
Only she wasn't a princess. She wasn't stuck up or anything.
Just nervous because everyone knew everyone else and she
was new and when you started a new school at fourteen

nobody said, *this is Amy she's new so be nice to her*. They just let you get on with it.

Maths was one of the subjects he enjoyed and was confidently good at. He liked subjects where there were right and wrong answers: maths, chemistry, physics, biology. The ones he hated were those where you were expected to come up with your own opinion, to read some old poem or story or a history book then say, *I think this because this and this*. Subjects like that were like boggy ground to him after tarmac, everything possible, nothing definite, everyone's opinion valid and so no position entirely secure and satisfactory. They also seemed to be the subjects where teachers were especially merciless at singling out anyone who didn't speak much, where the dreaded words, *so tell us what you think, Lenny*, were never far away.

If she was in his English or History class, she'd have thought him an idiot, but girls were good at all the subjects he hated so there was small chance of that. He was sitting a few places to the side of her so he could see her when she leaned forward to write something, which she did quite a lot, and when that plonker Jez Smith wasn't lolling all over the place blocking his view. But the only way he could really get her attention was to ask Mr Gower something, or answer a question.

Suddenly there was an opening for him, an answer he could see for solving an equation. So when Gower asked if anyone had any ideas, he dared to be seriously gay and put his hand up first, actually saying *please* without thinking.

'Lenny! Excellent. Glad to know you're awake. Come up and show us, then.'

And Lenny headed up to the front and took the offered pen to write his solution on the whiteboard. But then he found he was looking straight into her lovely face and she was smiling, really smiling at him, this great smile like the sun coming out after a wet morning, and straight away he forgot what the solution was that he'd seen. He started to write then he paused and, amid jeers and hoots from his mates at the back, had to just stop.

'You buzzed too early, Mr Barnes,' Gower told him. 'That's twenty points to the other team. Go back to sleep. Anyone else?'

And as Lenny walked back, he saw she was still smiling at him, as though she knew her smile had made him forget everything. And she put up her hand instead.

'Good,' Gower said, 'er …?'

'Amy, sir,' she said, neatly introducing herself to Lenny and the rest of them while she was at it. 'Amy Hawker.'

She walked up to the front, not smiling now but very serious and took the pen and balanced the equation. She didn't wipe out what Lenny had written, because it turned out he was perfectly right but had just forgotten. She simply completed what he had started, pausing for thought now and then, and when she finished and Gower said, 'Well done. Round of applause for Amy,' she said what sounded like, 'Team work,' and cast a quick glance at Lenny as she returned to her seat.

So it felt fairly easy to catch her eye as everyone was haring out at the end of the lesson and say, 'I'm Lenny.'

'I know,' she said. 'I'm Amy.'

'Yeah. I heard,' he said and they laughed so he guessed she was as nervy as he was. 'So have you just moved here?' he asked.

'Yeah,' she said. 'Just last week. The house is still full of boxes and my mum's insane.'

'Are you in St Just, then?'

'Ke …' She broke off. 'Kellynack?'

'It's Ke*LY*nack,' he corrected her. 'I'll show you around if you like.'

'Thanks,' she said. 'I'd like …' and then Chris and Tobes, who couldn't even spell tact, blundered back in to see what was keeping him and a whole load of Year Six kids rushed in behind them for the next maths class and he had to leave and go one way and she had to go the other, borne on a human tide.

He looked out for her all day without success. She was in the same year as him for sure but in a different form and possibly with no overlap other than maths. Incomers often seemed to be more advanced, as though used to greater pressure. Perhaps maths was her least good subject which, given the ease with which she had solved the equation, was a depressing prospect. He had rugby coaching that evening so couldn't loiter under the funny, silver-leafed trees by the school gates in the hope of catching her. It was one of those rare situations where having a sister would have been an advantage: a spy in the other camp.

The next day he had no maths and didn't even glimpse her in the distance, or the day after that. Cape had never felt so large. He was beginning to think she might be avoiding him when he stumbled on her in a lunch break. Like most of his friends he walked into Market Square in the lunch hour in search of a pasty or bag of chips or both, usually washed down with a sports drink. He was on his way out, held back behind the rest because the deputy head had fallen into conversation with him about whether he thought his mum would come in to talk about her pottery one assembly, which he considered about the most embarrassing thing imaginable, when he found her. She was on her own, eating a very neat packed lunch which seemed to be nothing but bits of fruit and vegetable, sitting on a low wall where she'd have known, if she'd been at Cape longer, that nobody normal ever sat.

They didn't talk very long because what he really wanted was to hold her lovely face in his hands and kiss her and see if her hair felt as soft as it looked and he couldn't tell her things like that, obviously, but they established that his mother was a potter and that her parents were both teachers. That they had moved to Cornwall from Ghana, which was the only other place she had lived and that she had been home-educated until now.

'So school feels a bit …'

'I know,' he said, although he had no idea what she meant. 'How did you stay so pale living in Africa?' he blurted out.

'Basically,' she said, 'I lived like a vampire.'

And she laughed, which gave him the courage to ask if she'd give him her mobile number, at which she blushed and said her parents didn't let her have one. At least not yet.

'Have you got a bike?' he asked.

'My mum has. I can borrow it probably.'

And he explained that he rode to school and if she did maybe they could do stuff in the afternoons sometimes.

He kicked himself for that *do stuff*, as it sounded sexy and he hadn't meant it to. And then he hurried into town because he was incredibly hungry, enough for double chips, and people were starting to look at them for sitting where only freaks and gays sat.

They had maths that afternoon and she somehow engineered to sit beside him, which was so exciting he could hardly absorb anything Gower was telling them, what with the little wafts he had of her shampoo whenever she moved her head and the chance he now had to take in every little detail of the hand holding her pen and her extremely precise handwriting and the purple ink she used.

She was claimed by a gang of girls right after the class. This was inevitable because she was new and pretty and he'd noticed how girls liked to collect girls who raised their own currency. But she smiled at him as they surrounded her, and he saw other girls notice and glance between them because such information mattered to them and would need to be discussed and analysed.

The next class was English, reading *As You Like It* out loud around the class, which was a kind of torture to him, and he didn't actually think about her at all, even though the scene they were reading was all about love, because he was either busy counting ahead to work out which speech he would have to read and hoping it would be a tiny one, or daydreaming about the rugby XV and whether he was happy to continue as one of the backs – speedy and getting to score tries and show passing skills – or whether he should be trying to bulk up his muscles in weight training in the hope of becoming a forward instead. Hooker would suit him, he reckoned. Nimble but in the scrum, with all the kudos that carried. Girls didn't like their boyfriends in the scrum, he had heard, because they didn't want their ears or noses spoiled and didn't like them getting so up close and personal with other blokes, which was reason enough to want to be in the thick of it in case the alternative was soft by association, tainted by feminine approval.

Dr Curnow, their English teacher, separated them into boys' and girls' teams when they did Shakespeare. This was because it was a play, she said, about masculinity and femininity and she wanted to emphasize that and encourage them to think about their gender differences. But Lenny knew it was also to make it easier when they were reading round the class, one speech at a time, to avoid the riot that would have ensued if a boy found himself having to read a girl's speech.

Lenny quite liked this novelty. It made the class feel more like sport, with opposing teams and all the excitement and competitive banter that engendered, and he'd enjoyed the lesson where they did the wrestling scene and she'd taken them all down to the gym and encouraged them, girls as well as boys, to have a go at Cornish Wrestling, for which she said St Just used to be notorious as miners wagered large chunks of their pay on the matches there.

But then, as he was wheeling his bike out of the school gates, there was Amy, unmistakably waiting for him.

'Hi,' she said. 'Come and say hi to my mum.' And she led the way to a parked car before he had a chance to think of excuses for not following her. It was far newer than his mother's old beast of a Volvo, which had mortifying pinky-grey plastic and soiled beige upholstery. Quite possibly this car was brand-new, but it had plainly been chosen with only economy in mind. ''Lo, Mum,' Amy said, getting in. 'This is Lenny Barnes.'

Lenny stooped to say hello through the open window. He remembered to do as his mother had told him and held out a hand. She resembled Amy, only older, and sun-aged, like his mother, so that she looked like a smoker although she almost certainly wasn't. Unlike his mother, who had sly fatties in the studio which she thought Lenny knew nothing about.

'Lenny. Hello. Thanks for making Amy so welcome. It sounds like a happy school.'

'Yeah. Well. It's just school,' he said. 'It's all right. Are you cold after Africa?'

'No,' she said crisply. 'Just comfortable. Lenny, would you like to come for lunch on Sunday?'

He calculated rapidly, cancelling any plans he might have had for a long bike ride with Tobes, glancing in Amy's face for disapproval and finding none. 'Sure. What time?'

'After church.'

'Er. OK.'

Amy had seen him wondering and added, 'Quarter to one.'

'Right. Thanks.'

'We're at Pear Tree Cottage. Down to Kelynack then left along the lane that heads up the valley from the side of the old chapel. We're on the right a little after the campsite. The house with the big blue gates. I hope you wear a helmet and visibility strip on that thing.'

'They're in here.' He jolted his bag. 'I just haven't put them on yet.'

For a moment he thought she was going to sit there in the car and watch him till he put the hateful things on but she gave a brisk wave and drove off. He was raising a discreet hand to Amy, who was grinning over her shoulder, when he saw they had one of those Christian fish stickers fixed to the left of their rear numberplate. He assumed it was theirs as the car was so new.

He asked his mum what home education was over supper and she went into a rant about judgemental middle-class parents, usually extreme Christians she reckoned, managing to screw up bright children and undermine perfectly good local schools at the same time. Why did he want to know? He gave her a studiedly off-hand account of Amy and said he was going to her place for Sunday lunch. Apparently he hadn't fooled her because she came around the table to give him a quick, winey hug and promised not to pry the way her mother would have done.

'If you like her, I'll like her. If you still like her after meeting her folks, bring her here whenever you want so I can get a good look at her.' Later she knocked on his door as he was doing his English homework and said, 'I know I said I wouldn't pry but I don't have to tell you about condoms and shit, do I?'

'Mum!'

'You don't want to end up having to be stuck here because you got some local girl up the duff.'

'She's not like that. And she's not local.'

'Yeah. Well. She's going to Cape Cornwall School so she's local now. You be careful.'

On one of their bad evenings, he'd have said, 'So she doesn't end up like you?' and they'd have shouted at each other and she'd have slammed his door or he'd have slammed it in her face. But they'd had a nice, quiet evening and he knew she meant no harm by it. So he resisted the temptation to rile her by waving the condom packet he'd been carrying in his wallet for months now in case anyone teased him for *not* having one, and simply groaned, 'Mum, please? Shakespeare ...' which made her ruffle his hair and sigh and leave him in peace so he could go back to Googling Amy's lane to work out exactly which house was Pear Tree Cottage.

He had started to picture their place as some nightmarishly tidy bungalow with everything in its place and crucifixes everywhere you looked, even in the garden, but it wasn't like that at all. It was an old cottage, with gnarled fruit trees around it and the car wasn't in the garage because the garage was still full of overflowing packing cases, and there was unmown grass jewelled with fallen apples.

Amy was helping her mum in the kitchen. They greeted him cheerfully, like an old friend, and then in came her dad, who was in trainers too, so that was all right, and said he wanted a closer look at Lenny's bike so led him back outside out of their way.

He didn't look like Amy. He was darkhaired, with a pointy chin. He wasn't scarily big, definitely a fly-half not a prop, but there was something about his very short hair and insistently shiny wedding ring and precise, confident way of speaking that made Lenny wary. This was a man who was never contradicted, even by his crisp wife. Even as he was admiring how Lenny had fixed up his bike and asking ques- tions about the gears and saddle he reminded Lenny of the

PE coach they had for a year, Mr Bailey, who had been in the Commandos and used to say that when they were old enough he would show them seven ways to kill a man with their bare hands. When Mr Bailey entered a room you felt his own personal thundercloud had come in with him and whenever he left, people laughed and joked, even grown-ups, as it felt as though a weight had been lifted. Amy's father, Mr Hawker, felt similar: definitely one of those fathers that made Lenny glad he didn't have one. There were birds singing in the tree over their head but he felt certain if Mr Hawker told them to, they'd have fallen silent.

'Lunch is ready, boys,' Amy's mum called out to them.

'Here we come,' Mr Hawker said but instead of going in, he appeared to carry on admiring the bike. 'So how old are you, Lenny?'

'Fifteen,' Lenny told him, because it would soon be true and fourteen-and-three-quarters sounded a bit pathetic.

'Right,' he said. 'The same as Amy. Well, I'm sure you're a nice lad and your heart's in the right place but you need to know that Amy's not allowed a boyfriend until she turns sixteen. Friends is fine but nothing more than that. Do I make myself clear?'

And Lenny knew he meant condoms and stuff and nodded and said, 'Friends is fine,' and nearly called him sir.

'Good lad. I know you country boys grow up fast and I didn't want any misunderstanding.'

Amy came out then to find them and her father said, 'We're coming, we're coming,' in a silly, cartoony voice even though she hadn't said a word. He ushered Lenny in before them and pointedly planted a kiss on Amy's cheek as Lenny passed them. Lenny wanted her to flinch or pull away or complain but she seemed entirely content, like a kitten being washed.

They said Grace, which was totally weird. Lenny had made to sit down but Amy had caught his eye and jerked her head to tell him to keep standing while her father said bless oh Lord this food et cetera.

Lunch was the sort of food his mum hardly ever made because so many of her friends had weird food needs: roast beef and gravy and Yorkshire pudding and incredible roast potatoes like chips only better. Amy's mum seemed pleased when he praised it. 'It's food we had guilty dreams about in Ghana,' she said.

'Yes, and the last thing a growing girl needs is to turn veggie on us,' Amy's dad said, slipping an extra piece of juicy meat onto Amy's plate which, to Lenny's delight, made her flinch as the kiss had not.

'So, Lenny,' Mrs Hawker said. 'We gather your mum's a distinguished potter. Where could I see her work?'

'In St Just is one place,' he told her. 'There's usually some at the Great Atlantic, in the middle, across from the clock tower.'

'I must take a look. Is it just a hobby?'

'Er, no. She makes quite a good living from it, actually.' Amy's mum pulled a little face at this, as though it were not quite nice.

'And what about your dad,' Amy's dad countered. 'He potty too?'

'Derek,' she chided.

'I don't have a dad,' Lenny told him, quite unfazed. 'I mean, I must have somewhere but I've never met him and my mum's not telling who he is. It's no big deal. She's

Australian. Very independent. I've always assumed he was either just a donor or married to somebody else.'

'Ah,' Derek said. Derek! What a name! Lenny made a mental note that one day, quite soon, he would call him that and not Mr Hawker, just to wind him up really tight.

Roast beef gave way to crumble made from some of the apples that littered the garden.

'God's bounty,' Derek said.

'And clotted cream,' said Amy's mum. 'Another thing I dreamed about in Ghana.'

'So were you teachers out there too?' Lenny asked.

'Well now I'm a music teacher and Derek teaches maths, but out there we taught everything,' she explained. 'We ran a mission school. It was a lovely place and a very good life.'

'So why did you move back to the UK?'

Lenny saw a glance exchanged between the parents and guessed this had been the cause of some disagreement.

'We decided it wasn't fair on Amy or her education,' Derek said.

'They didn't want me having a black boyfriend,' Amy explained.

'Amy!'

'She's quite right,' her mother admitted. 'I've not got a racist bone in my body but there are limits to everything. Does your mother go to church, Lenny?'

Amy giggled as though she knew what was coming.

'Er. Well.' Lenny thought, feeling slightly high and daring on sugar and delicious fat. 'She had me christened when I was a baby, but now she says it's all patriarchal rot for misogynist drongos.' Amy stopped giggling and her eyes widened. And at that instant she looked so like everything he had never known he wanted and suddenly might never have, that he added, 'But I reckon she's completely wrong, which is why I plan to start confirmation classes this autumn.'

There wasn't quite an audible sigh but he had a definite sense of tension relaxed and then he felt Amy's foot brushing his calf. He thought it was a cat, then realized it wasn't and shuffled his chair a little further under the table, to make himself easier to reach.

'So who will you go to for classes?' her mother was asking.

'Oh …' He thought rapidly. 'Father Barnaby. No question. He's our parish priest. He baptized me. It would feel weird going to anyone else.'

'Where does he stand on women priests?'

'He has a curate who's a woman. Tabby Morris. She's my friend Tobes' mum.'

'Oh. Good. I didn't want to send Amy to someone who thought women were unclean or whatever and I'd heard stories about some of the priests out here which is why we've been going into Penzance. Lenny, would you let Amy know when his classes happen?'

Amy's foot was wriggling like a happy puppy. 'Sure I will,' he said, hoping his voice sounded level. All too soon her mother was asking her to help clear the dishes away.

There was no question of going up to her room with her, of course, the way they might have done a few years before, so he sat and drank extremely strong, black unsweetened coffee with her parents because he sensed a test of her father's, that this was how he liked it, and looking at photographs of their life in Ghana.

They were meeting colleagues of theirs to go for a walk to Land's End and back and asked him to join them, but Lenny didn't want to push his luck on a first visit so thanked them for everything but said he had promised to wash his mother's car.

Amy held open the gate while he wheeled his bike out and ostentatiously put on his helmet and horrible, yellow, Sam Browne belt. Even now they weren't exactly alone because her parents were standing in the porch, like an advertisement for mortgages.

'Thanks,' he said. 'That was fun.'

'No it wasn't,' she muttered through her smile. 'Were you serious? About confirmation?'

'Sure,' he said, feeling the coffee start to make his heart race. 'I'll have a word with Father Barnaby and let you know. He's nice. You'll like him.'

'I bet I will,' she said, tucking her hair behind her ear. She said it in a way that went round and round in his head as he made himself cycle all the way up Carn Bosavern without either stopping or changing down to a gear so low that the pedals would whirl round at comedy speed while the bike hardly moved. He rode down into St Just, where he ignored the gang of boys he knew who were just mooching around in a way he'd have found irresistible during the summer holidays just past, just shouting *hey* so they wouldn't think he was being standoffish. As he plunged down Nancherrow Hill, trying to get up enough momentum to see him at least halfway up No-Go-By Hill before he needed to make a serious effort, he thought of himself hanging around St Just or Botallack or Boscaswell with gangs of schoolmates, thought of the hours he had spent that way in his life so far, doing nothing in particular for hours on end with other boys, and wondered at how just having a pretty girl slide her foot beneath her parents' dining table could so abruptly make all that seem like the irretrievable past.

At Pendeen he swung right to the church, knowing the vicarage was next door. But a notice directed him back the way he had come a little and out to an old farmhouse. He had cycled across the yard, scattering chickens, and knocked on the door before he remembered it was a Sunday afternoon so probably everyone's time off, even vicars.

Mrs Johnson opened the door. 'Hello.' She smiled. She smelled of cake and looked like any Cornish grandmother. He was slightly disappointed as he'd heard lurid stories of her servicing the family car herself and knowing how to strip and reassemble a tractor engine. Perhaps he had her muddled with her daughter. 'Are you after the vicar?' she prompted.

Lenny nodded. 'Yes, please.'

'Won't be a second. I left him doing the general knowledge crossword.' She had the immediately comforting lilting accent of his friends' mothers, the accent that made him acutely conscious of his mum's harshly Aussie voice and its influence on his own. She left him holding his bike and disappeared inside the rambling old house and he reflected that she must get callers like him all the time. He hoped his mother didn't suddenly get religion. It happened. His mate Tobes had perfectly normal parents, if you counted a policeman as normal, and then suddenly his mother announced she was becoming a priest and Tobes' home life had been in uproar ever since. If he wanted peace and quiet, he said, he had to go to St Just library because there seemed to be people around the kitchen table or out in the living room at all hours of the day and most evenings too. Tobes' mum held prayer meetings and Bible study groups during which Tobes invariably took refuge with Lenny to watch horror films as a sort of antidote.

An enormous tortoiseshell cat stalked through the open door, stared at him hard, unnervingly bold, held its ground on the doorstep, more dog than cat, tail thrashing and looking as though it might growl or worse if Lenny took a step further without an owner present. It melted as Father Barnaby appeared and wreathed around its master's legs.

'Lenny Barnes! What a delightful surprise.' He greeted Lenny like a friend.

'Hello. That's quite a cat.'

'That's Abishag. She's an arrant hypocrite. I know she's a monster behind my back.' He tapped the cat lightly with the side of his foot and it darted off and was chased into a barn by chickens. 'Well leave your bike and come on in. We can have an early cuppa.'

'Actually I'd better not. I'm meant to be washing Mum's car and it'll be dark fairly soon.'

'OK. What can I do for you?'

'Well ... Do you give confirmation classes?'

'Of course. The next confirmation service in the area is in two months. That's a bit soon. But we could put you down for one in the summer.'

'Oh. Good. Thanks. And, er, can more than one person come?'

'Of course!'

'Because a girl from my maths class wants to. Amy Hawker. Her parents were missionaries in Ghana. Sort of. And now they're just teachers. I said I thought you liked women priests, having Tobes' m—, I mean Mrs Morris, as a curate. What should I tell them?'

'I'd tell them to ring me. But I … Do I get the impression you'd like to come at the same time as Amy?'

'Er. Well. Yes.'

'Then I'll tell them I can just fit her into my existing class, which happens to include you and no one else, but they needn't know that, and we'll take it from there. Would Thursday evenings at six work for you?'

'Sure. I should think so. I'm not sure about Amy, though.'

'Well how about I talk to her parents then let you know?'

'I'll give you my mobile number,' Lenny said, scribbling it down on a scrap of paper from his wallet.

'Lenny?' Father Barnaby asked, taking it.

'What?'

'Does your mum not know you're coming for confirmation classes?'

'Not yet. No. I thought I'd check with you first.'

'I see.'

'But I'll tell her now, or this evening.'

'Good. Because it's a big step to take without her blessing and precisely because she's not a Christian it might be a big deal for her.'

'But she had me christened, didn't she?'

'Yes.' Father Barnaby smiled in a way that felt private rather than just him being nice. 'Yes, she did.'

*　　*　　*

Lenny's mum was startled at his insistence on both Hoovering out and washing her car when he got home but not as startled as he'd thought she'd be when he let slip as they were settling down to watch a film together, that he'd signed up for confirmation classes with Father Barnaby. In fact she laughed and said, '*Cherchez la fille*, huh?'

'What?' he said, not understanding.

'Nothing,' she said, swallowing her smile.

'So you don't mind.'

'Why should I mind, Lenny? I'd mind if you got a motorbike on eBay or started smoking skunk but you're going to be spending one evening a week with a priest – a good priest, not one of the paedo woman-haters – learning how to be a better person. No. It'll do you good. Just don't expect me to stop fucking swearing or anything like that. And veganism is time consuming. If you go vegan on me, you're learning to cook.'

The classes started that week, not in the Johnsons' house but in the old vicarage next door to Pendeen Church. Although it wasn't used as a family house at the moment – there were homeless women upstairs or something and downstairs was used for all sorts of classes and meetings – the vicar used a room that must once have been a sitting room and was still fitted out as one, with comfy, bashed-up armchairs and sofas that didn't go together and shelves full of books and windows opening onto a jungly garden between the vicarage and the parish hall next door.

It didn't feel like a class, because there were just the three of them. It felt more like a conversation. Barnaby – he encouraged them to call him that – began and ended with a short prayer that named them both so made it feel as though God were being put directly in touch with them for a while, and then he took another bit of the Lord's Prayer each week for them to discuss. He said they'd work their way through that, and then the Creed, and by the end of that they'd either be ready to be confirmed or ready to give it all up. That was typical of him, apparently, always entertaining the possibility of failure, the reality that most people chose not to believe. It had the effect of making Lenny want the process not to fail.

Barnaby discreetly asked them questions about themselves and what they wanted from life and somehow made it all right to say out loud things Lenny had only thought to himself before. He also enabled him and Amy to learn all sorts of things about each other they might have taken ages to find out, if ever. So he learnt that although Amy's parents were so Christian, so certain, that they had allowed it to shape their whole lives, Amy had doubts she had never dared share with them. He learnt that, just like him, she had often wished she wasn't an only child, so that there'd be shared responsibility for pleasing her parents.

In the classes she seemed utterly sincere, talking about God and Jesus and the Holy Spirit and even sin and temptation with no trace of irony. But then, when the class finished and they walked back to the road together, it was as though she had left the business of the class entirely behind her, like the physics in a physics lesson or the verbs in a Spanish one, whereas he took a good hour to adjust and found he needed to take his time cycling home so as to process everything they'd been saying. Perhaps it was simply that she had known religion all her life whereas it was still new to him.

At first one or other of her parents always drove her there and collected her punctually afterwards. But then there was a breakthrough, caused by her dad taking on a full-time teaching post in Hayle that meant he had less time, and she was allowed to ride a bike, both to school and to their classes. It was her mum's and the world's most embarrassing bike – a small-wheeled one designed for pootling along flat suburban roads to a shopping parade then home again, not for battling up long climbs. But she persevered, even though she admitted to giving up and pushing halfway up most of the hills, because her dad had promised her a bike of her own if she could prove it wouldn't be a waste of his money. And of course, like Lenny, she was kitted out with a helmet and a Sam Browne belt, the crucial difference being that she obediently kept hers on even when out of sight of home.

Granted this trust and freedom, they took to doing precisely what her father hoped they wouldn't, loitering in the dark, secluded car park opposite the church to hold one another and kiss and have low, murmuring conversations then more kissing. The effect was doubly destabilizing for happening when his head was full of concepts like transubstantiation and redemption and *deliver us from evil*, but, because it only ever happened just after confirmation class and not behind the outbuildings after school or whatever, he found it hard to think of it as anything but good.

It was odd. They never talked about love. That they loved each other was seemingly a given, although he'd have appreciated a little reassurance. The kissing and holding was a straightforward expression of what they both felt but couldn't show in the rest of the week. He wanted to go a bit further than kissing. He knew exactly what to do and how to do it best, the internet being as useful on how to do sex as it was on how to strip and service a derailleur gear system, but she called a smiling halt to anything more adventurous than being allowed to cup just one breast at a time through several layers of winter clothing. She had a very clear idea of what was possible, of permitted risk, and he trusted her in that, for all his impatience and for all that he was having to smuggle home his own supply of paper tissues to cope with how stirred up their encounters left him. When Amy said, 'Not yet,' he trusted her.

An unexpected development was that Barnaby expected them both to attend church on Sundays, even though they could as yet receive no more than a fatherly hand on the head from him at the altar rail. Her parents had already attended a service in Pendeen before approving Barnaby as a confirmation teacher, or whatever you called it, and were happy to come there rather than going all the way to the church in Penzance which they'd decided was *too high* for their tastes. So they drove Amy up every Sunday and he rode over on his bike and they encouraged him to sit with them as though they were a family of four. He usually ended up with Amy's father beside him in the pew, sometimes her mum, but never Amy, but he could respect that. Given how strict they were, he could appreciate them letting him see much of her at all.

At first, for all that he resented giving up his Sunday mornings when he could have been lying in bed thinking of Amy or playing computer games with Tobes, he decided he liked how church made him feel. Lenny liked to be right, he liked that assurance. Going to church could never be

wrong and, like doing well in sport or understanding trigo-
nometry or being able to join in 'Trelawny' or simply
knowing he was more or less Cornish, it gave him a warm
sense of belonging. His mum had never been less than
loving and supportive, even recently when things he did,
and sometimes the mere fact of his being (nearly) a man,
could make her so ratty, but she preferred to exist on the
edge of the community rather than at its heart and that
could have the effect of isolating him by association.
School, first in Pendeen then at Cape in St Just, had gone
some way towards stitching him in more closely, by giving
him friends in the nearby villages, but in church he was
made to feel part of an extended family.

It was a curious family, with relations of all shapes and
sizes, most of them fairly or outright old and some of them
a bit peculiar, but he liked it that he was sometimes asked
to do things, like carry a vase of water up to the sanctuary
or that he was sometimes greeted in the street by name
now by people from in church. Not just Tobes' mother,
who had often got his name wrong before, but others he
hardly knew, like Miss Jago the organist, with the hair in
a bun, whom he'd always thought scary until he met her
in church and realized she was simply very shortsighted.
Another who took to saying hello was the fat, bald man,
Mr Carlsson, who delivered the parish magazine but
looked like someone who stole girls' knickers off washing
lines.

Nobody teased him about churchgoing, probably
because, apart from Tobes, most of them didn't know he
went and, in any case, were probably only getting out of
bed and wondering what to do with their Sundays when he

was queuing to shake Father Barnaby's hand at the end of services. Even his mum bit her tongue beyond expressing appreciation that she no longer had to get dressed to fetch her Sunday paper. The questioning and doubting came entirely from within himself. His rational side, the side that had always until now dominated his thinking, began to nag him in the moments when his attention strayed. *Yes but you don't* really *believe it all?* it asked. *Not all the details? Not the Holy Ghost or the Virgin Birth? You don't honestly think a prayer works better than medicine, or faith better than knowledge?*

The uneasiness this stirred up in turn fuelled his worry that Amy was simply pretending and the whole caboodle was for her a piece of compliant hypocrisy. After all, that's what it had been for him to start with, hadn't it? He took to looking at the other people in church when he was meant to be praying, looking for signs they were faking it. Whenever he saw someone stifle a yawn or glance at their watch, he registered a small, unpleasant flare of triumph.

The problem was that religion was so irrational, so lacking in physical proofs, so easily denied. In a rugby game there were rules, there were physical properties, there were obvious consequences to every action – a misjudged drop kick, a mistimed pass – and where there was doubt it lay solely in who exactly was responsible when things went well or badly, a condition of functioning as a team being that the team fell or rose together.

In the horror films he enjoyed watching with Chris and Tobes, the powers of good and evil were self-evident, at least eventually. Demons were revealed by glowing yellow eyes or an ability to make furniture block an escape route or knives fly across a room. While the force of good (or at least of anti-demonic power, because, for all the trappings of Christianity, the crucifixes and talk of angels and Jesus, there never seemed to be much actual prayer or churchgoing involved for the good guys) was equally impressive, a heroine muttered some words of challenge or held up a crucifix or a Bible like a weapon and evil retreated in hissed curses and pantomime smoke.

Even a small superpower conferred by saying, 'I believe,' along with everyone else would have helped. But instead it all remained nebulous and doubtable. The only certainties were that it sometimes gave him a nice warm glow in which the sense of belonging was joined by a certain sense of backing the right side, and that it gave him regular, approved access to Amy and her breasts.

His confession was not premeditated. He simply turned up for confirmation class one week to find that Amy had been obliged to stay home so it was just him and Father Barnaby. Barnaby was as friendly and easy to talk to as ever and Amy's absence freed up something in Lenny and he found himself admitting the inadmissible: that he had only signed up for confirmation as a way of getting to see her with her parents' approval.

Barnaby wasn't angry. He didn't even seem especially surprised.

'Would you rather stop coming to classes?' he asked. 'I can take your name off the confirmandi list easily enough.'

'Well, no.'

'Because of Amy?'

'Er. No. Only partly. It's taken me a bit by surprise. I like coming to church. I like how it makes me feel and ...'

'There's an old line about God moving in mysterious ways I could trot out here,' Barnaby said. 'It's pretty apposite.'

'You think he made me fall for Amy so as to bring me to confirmation?'

Barnaby shrugged. 'What do *you* think?'

And then it all came out, all Lenny's worry about not believing everything all the time, not always being sure about all the details.

'Nobody believes all of it all the time, however hard they try,' Barnaby assured him. 'Doubt is good. Doubt shows that your powers of reasoning aren't suspended. It gives your choice its value. Lenny, it doesn't matter about Amy. You're clearly good for each other. I'd say you were well matched. Her parents aren't the most relaxed people but then she's their only child so they're bound to be protective. Your mum can be a tigress, too. I'm aware that you're coming to church every Sunday because of Amy and because I told you to. But that'll change. It always does. Always. Not long after I was confirmed, I stopped coming to church for two whole years.

'After you're confirmed and you're a bit older, you'll probably stop coming, regardless of how things develop between you and Amy. You might stop for a bit, you might stop for several years. But what matters is what you've learned and that you'll know the church will remain there for you whenever you need it. Perhaps you'll be in desperate need. Does that make sense?' Barnaby asked him.

'Yes.'

'You said that very quickly, Len. I'm not a teacher you have to please. Tell me honestly. Has that made you feel less anxious?'

Lenny smiled. 'A bit. Yes. Thanks.'

'If I've done my job, you'll have a bit of church inside your head and that'll be enough to get you through. And you will need it, Len. Everyone does at some point. We all suffer fears and losses. It's what makes us human. It's what'll make you a man.'

Lenny pictured the church in his head and saw it was people rather than a building. 'You've called me Len twice now,' he said.

'Have I? Sorry.'

'It's OK. It's what Mum calls me sometimes. I reckon he was an old boyfriend ...'

Then Barnaby did something he'd never done before and never did again. He went off to the kitchen and came back with a can of beer for each of them. 'Emergency supplies,' he said. 'Class over. Cheers.'

And they simply sat and drank and chatted for a while. He asked about school and what Lenny wanted to do later on and Lenny said he was torn between engineering and something involving chemistry but admitted that all he really wanted was to play rugby for the Pirates.

'I know absolutely nothing about sport,' Barnaby confessed. 'Tell me. How feasible is that? Playing for them. How would you go about it?'

So Lenny told him about how he already played with the junior league and would go on and trial for St Just probably. About trials and scouts and sports scholarships to help with university fees. And Barnaby seemed truly interested in a way Mum never was. All she ever said was, 'Just don't let them bugger up your ears or break your pretty nose.'

And then, when conversation faltered a little, and because unaccustomed beer had made him bold, Lenny asked what had made Barnaby become a priest.

'Ooh. That's a hard one. Sometimes I think it just sort of happened.'

'Nothing just happens.'

'OK, OK.' He swigged his beer and thought a little. 'There was a sort of voice in my head that wouldn't shut up. I'd had a very scientific childhood, with no religion in it all, but a part of me kept going back to … I was drawn in by, well, mystery, I suppose. And by people who showed kindness when they didn't have to. I felt the pain of death when I was still very young and then I saw the terror of it in other people. My father's death was … Sorry, Lenny. That's not much of an answer. How about I think about it and tell you next time?'

'No. It's just …' Lenny had never seen Barnaby so lost for words. His struggle to express something words couldn't seem to cover was more convincing than any smooth theology. 'What are you doing all day on a weekday?'

Barnaby smiled into his beer, let off the hook, perhaps. 'Apart from parish admin? I visit the sick. A lot of people ask for that, even people who hardly ever set foot in a church. Sometimes they want communion at their bedside. They always want to talk. Most people are frightened of dying, and illness, even if it's not especially serious, reminds them of that and they need comfort. And then, when people do die, I visit their families, to see how they're coping. Funerals and weddings both take quite a bit of planning. And if a couple asks me to marry them, I expect them to set aside time to come in here to talk about marriage and what it means.'

'They can't just book the church and pay you?'

'They can try but it's a serious business, it should be, and marriage in church is a sacrament which I expect them to take seriously.'

'What's a sacrament?'

'It's any activity that involves a direct interaction of God's grace – the Holy Spirit, if you like – in our lives. Most obviously Eucharist, when you'll come to the altar for communion. And when the bishop confirms you. And when a different bishop ordained me a priest. And marriage and extreme unction – that's when I pray for a person who is actually dying …'

'Do you do that often?'

'Not really. It's gone out of fashion. But most people die in hospital rather than at home now and if they don't send for me, they'll be visited by the hospital chaplain instead.'

'Does it work?'

Barnaby smiled, glanced at his watch and drained his can. 'That's your last question then we must both go home for our suppers. Does it work? I hope so. It's a comfort. It's a beautiful prayer. And people are often very frightened at the moment of death. They often feel guilty suddenly about things they've done in the past. On one level it's like magic – it's a ritual. We've no way of knowing if it saves a soul until it's our turn to find out the truth for ourselves, but yes, from the point of view of those left behind, it often does work in that it brings peace. Now. Class well and truly dismissed.' He stood up, so Lenny did too. 'But between now and next week I'd like you to think about the next line of the Creed.'

'He descended into hell.'

'That's the one. Maybe you can text Amy to remind her?'

'She still doesn't have a mobile. Not till her birthday.'

He shook his head. 'People like Derek Hawker make me feel very … inadequate. Not fit enough. Not good enough. Not strict enough. Is he bad at anything, do you think?'

'He can't sing. I sit by him in church and he really can't sing.'

Barnaby briefly rested a hand on Lenny's shoulder. 'That's a great comfort,' he said, mock solemn.

He saw Lenny out to his bike and surprised him by insisting he put on his helmet and Sam Browne belt before setting off. He held out his hand for Lenny to shake before they parted on the corner. It felt a bit weird and formal – they had never done this before – but it also felt gratifyingly adult.

Lenny wasn't much given to fancy, outside of horror films, but the ride home that evening felt magical. There was a moon, fat and bright enough to be casting shadows, and he didn't pass a single car or pedestrian from Pendeen to Morvah. At the bend in the track up the hill to home, he stopped to admire the way the moon was drawing glitter from the sea and throwing a distant container ship into sharp relief. Most of the time he took where he lived for granted, resenting what felt like extreme isolation and the myriad small marks of what he was coming to recognize as poverty. And yet there were times like this, or when he came down the track on his bike just as one of the German tour buses was creeping by on the way to Zennor and St Ives, when he saw his life as outsiders might see it and realized he was lucky.

He probably wouldn't stay. He couldn't imagine what he could do as an adult that would give him a reason to – short of playing for the Pirates – and he wanted to travel, he wanted to see the world, he wanted to visit his cousins in Australia and experience life lived in a city like London, or New York, the sort of places you saw in crime dramas on television. And yet he was glad he'd be able to tell people he had grown up in Cornwall.

His mum was out. He had forgotten she had an opening to go to in Truro that night. He was glad to have the house to himself for a change, to be spared the grilling which often passed with her for conversation. It amused him when friends asked if it wasn't scary, living somewhere so remote; it never occurred to him to be scared, because this silence and darkness were what he had associated with home and security all his life. From what he could gather from *The Cornishman*, you were more likely to end up dead or hospitalized, the victim of scary people, if you had neighbours.

Amy and he had to make do with e-mails until her parents let her have a mobile, and he secretly liked the relative formality and calm of it and that she wrote him whole sentences with whole words instead of the textspeak standard among his mates. Tonight's e-mail was quite short because her mother was ill and she was having to make supper with her dad but still it gave him a little snapshot of her evening so that he knew how she was feeling, what she was going to eat and that she had nearly finished the book she was reading.

They were both careful what they wrote. Her parents probably weren't nearly as strict as it suited them to pretend, her father was probably far too tired after a long day's teaching to spend time hacking into his daughter's e-mail account. Amy and Lenny had yet to use the word Love with each other. Sometimes it felt like something just around the corner and possibly to be dreaded, sometimes it felt as though it didn't need saying and that they had such a natural sympathy they could take it as read.

But that evening, excited by starlight and having the house to himself, he didn't want to leave it unsaid any more. *Amy*, he typed. *I think I love you. Really.* He kept it cool by not signing off, thinking she would know who it was from, which was all that mattered. Then he had a moment or two of panic after pressing send, in case she assumed he had merely pressed send too early and had more to say when in fact he had no idea what he should say next.

He calmed himself by fetching his usual home-alone supper: a huge ham sandwich made crunchy with a chopped-up dill pickle and a slab of cheddar whose thickness would have had his mother talking about bills and *do you think I'm made of money*. A huge cheese and ham sandwich and a big glass of chocolate milk. Baby food really, but it was what he liked. And some ice cream to follow with a chopped banana.

There was nothing he wanted to watch on TV and anyway he preferred to be in his room. He loved his room, especially at night-time. It was off on its own at the far end of the house. His bed was the same he had used since boyhood – a kind of bunk with the clothes storage built in underneath. He was getting too tall for it – his feet stuck out at the end if he didn't lie with his head really near the top – but he enjoyed climbing a ladder to go to bed and he liked that he had a little porthole window near his pillow so he could look out at the stars and the distant view. When he was small he would turn out the lights and pretend his bed was a lunar module. Now he just liked turning out the lights and lying in bed.

Tonight he tried something weird and new. Praying. He prayed in church, of course, because you had to and everyone else did but he had lied when he said yes when Barnaby asked if he and Amy prayed at other times. Prayed out loud, at least. He couldn't kneel at the foot of the bed or anything, which would have been unbearably strange in any case, but he whispered the words to the Lord's Prayer out loud while shutting his eyes. He tried doing as Barnaby asked, actually thinking about the meaning of the words rather than simply chanting them. And then he opened his eyes and lay there looking out at the stars and listening to the wind which was starting to get up, whistling in the not quite blocked up chimney of his bedroom fireplace.

The prayer was strange, a bit like how he imagined witchcraft was meant to be; you said words out loud and things changed around you. He waited, feeling for changes, thinking about Amy reading his e-mail, about Amy in her bed.

When his mum came home he pretended to be asleep.

CARRIE AT 35

Carrie fell in love for the first time when she was thirty-five, and the sensation that stole over her was so utterly unfamiliar she could not recognize it for what it was.

It took her a year or two past puberty to begin to suspect that she had no sex drive. As Jazz and Shell and her other friends at school erupted with hormones and developed crushes and either took cautious sips of sex or threw themselves into it with reckless thirst, she found herself more and more isolated from the instincts around her. At first she assumed she was simply a late developer or just developing in different stages to most people. But her body duly underwent all the dreaded, longed-for changes, and still there was no spark to make sense of it all.

She went through the motions. She stared at air-brushed photographs of pop stars, listening to their music at the same time in case that helped. She did her best to see what it was about certain boys at school that made girls suddenly start flicking their hair about or striking unnatural poses, but they were simply boys and often neither the most pleasant nor the most intelligent ones. She listened carefully as girls confided erotic dreams they had, because she seemed to be having none and needed to know the salient detail in case she were ever called upon to pretend. She absorbed every detail of a page of masturbation tips in one of Shell's mother's magazines, in case this was the key that would unlock normality. But quite apart from making her feel completely weird, as though her head were swelling, the business unnerved her because the scenes and faces she should be conjuring up only made her want to stop immediately.

She was fairly sure she wasn't the only one, fairly sure that some of the others must be faking too, and was simply glad that she wasn't somebody people noticed, least of all boys. Difference of any kind was usually brutally turned upon and she dreaded being suddenly accused of being a hypocrite or weird or, even worse, a dyke, which seemed to be the standard label for any girl who chose not to conform, even harmlessly straight punks or Goths. But she was far more cautious of letting her differences show than when she was little and, perhaps because she was perfectly normal-looking but no threat and such an attentive listener, her blossoming friends did not challenge her but seemed to relish the way her sexual blankness rendered them all the more ripe and available.

And then, naturally, there was God. Her parents would never have shirked discussing sex or relationships with her and certainly would never have been especially strict, yet the tacit assumption among her friends seemed to be that, of course, she had to be careful and good and save herself because her dad was a vicar.

Once they all left school, though, things changed. Friends moved away, either geographically or, abruptly, into the foreign, adjoining countries of motherhood and/or marriage. And never even thinking about sex, which in any case seemed to cause far more trouble than happiness, no longer seemed such a problem. She studied for her City and

Guilds in carpentry, catching a bus and a train to Camborne every day, then quietly started her little business. Although she still effectively lived at home, her move into independent adulthood was marked by Dad's suggestion she move into her grandmother's old rooms at the oldest end of the house, so that she had her own kitchen, bathroom, living room and front door.

'You can have all the visitors you like in there,' her mother said, helping her move her things, which was the only comment she ever seemed to make, even indirectly, about Carrie's persistently single state. The family cat, Sapphira – or was it Abishag by then? – elected to move in with her, apparently setting the seal on her spinster status, and that was that.

She did try. A boy on her carpentry course asked her out a couple of times and she went because he was sad and overweight and they got quite drunk and actually kissed, but she panicked when he got all steamed up and wanted to go further and he avoided speaking to her after that. She went to the North Inn or the Radjel occasionally after work, chatting to people she knew and largely avoiding people she didn't. She dressed like a man, in a uniform of jeans and tee-shirts with some kind of jacket or hoodie to hide the large breasts inherited from her mother, because otherwise men stared at them in a way she suspected meant they were mentally detaching the breasts from the rest of her and weighing up in their minds if the breasts on their own were enough.

She wasn't a virgin, at least. A migrant worker, Jaňek, had led her back to his caravan in Trewellard a couple of times after they got chatting and found they both had priests for parents and shared a guilty fondness for the songs of Elkie Brooks. He had been sweet and considerate and unforceful but the sex was unpleasant all the same, each time leaving her feeling she was being suffocated, and it had been a relief when he mournfully confessed he was having to return to Poland to marry his fiancée.

Once or twice women had made passes at her too, which was incredibly awkward as they had misread whatever signals her jeans and biker jacket were giving out whereas Carrie just thought they were being friendly. She apologized profusely, bought them drinks and heard their life stories while parrying any further advances. Sexual fulfilment might continue to elude her but she had somehow known for as long as she knew Simon le Bon and Adam Ant did nothing for her, that she wasn't gay either.

Carrie spotted a space and pounced, swinging her little van over to the right-hand lane in the face of oncoming traffic she coolly ignored while parking and then thanked cheerfully once safely in. A space on the seafront was handy for the job in hand but also for catching the eyes of passers-by. With its neatly painted signage, done in exchange for building the signwriter a tissue box surround for a new, drop-in bath, the van was as good as a free billboard and brought in so much work she no longer went to the expense of advertising in *The Cornishman*.

It was mid-June and Golowan week so the front was looking festive with brightly coloured banners. She wasn't fussed about going into town on a Saturday usually but had quite forgotten it was Mazey Day, with all the traffic and parking problems its parade and street fair would

cause. At the far end of the front, near the lido, the usual
funfair rides had been set up and the road was cordoned
off.

She double-checked the address she had tapped into her
phone. The house had a garden but, perhaps in keeping
with the 1930s severity of the building, it was very simple
and appeared to use only three plants. All along one side,
edging the right of the path, was a thriving hedge of
lavender. The left border of the path was defined by another
fragrant hedge of something lavender-like but not lavender,
with spikes of purple-blue flowers and blue-grey leaves. It
flowed down onto the gravel on both sides, a sort of
botanical wave. The third plant was some sort of tough
rose bush, covered in loose-petalled white flowers.

Carrie knew nothing about gardening, for all that her
mother had tried to teach her, contenting herself with
cutting grass and keeping hedges neat, but she could see the
admirable simplicity of the scheme. So many gardens struck
her as busy hotchpotches, one of these one of those, a
bunch of these because the colour was cheerful and of this
because Doreen gave it for our wedding anniversary and of
that because we're not quite sure. Gardens seemed to be
allowed to happen by accident in a way few people would
consider decorating or furnishing a house, and it seemed to
her it was this mishmash approach that made them a source
of constant and fretful maintenance to their owners. This
garden was pretty and stylish yet could be maintained with
nothing more specialized than a once-a-year going-over
from a hedge trimmer, and still achieved that other gardening goal of being different from all its neighbours. She felt
an instinctive warmth towards whoever had created it.

She rang the bell and waited a few minutes, rang it again and was about to try calling the number she had stored when she heard footsteps approaching inside. An oldish man opened the door and smiled at her mildly. His thick white hair was standing in a tuft as though he had been lying on it.

'Sorry,' he said. 'I'd gone upstairs to fetch something and somehow fell sound asleep. Come in, come in.'

'I'm Carrie Johnson,' she felt she had to tell him first. 'The carpenter? About the bookshelves?'

'Yes. Do come in. You're lucky I heard you. We're discovering it's a quirk of the design of this place that when you're upstairs the sound of the sea becomes louder than noises from the road or the doorstep. Something to do with the concrete overhang at the top.'

She closed the front door behind her and followed him across the black and white tiled floor into a kitchen that gave onto a sunny yard at the back that was lush with exotic plants in pots.

'Far too many plants,' he sighed. 'I couldn't bear to leave any behind. They become like friends. Some of them are probably older than you.' He sat at the kitchen table so she sat too, setting her tool box carefully on the floor beside her. Then, as if remembering some long-ago training he said, 'How terrible of me; I haven't offered you anything. Coffee? Tea? Elderflower cordial?'

'Cordial sounds nice,' she said, thinking it also sounded like less trouble.

'It's homemade,' he said. 'I make it every year but the citric acid is getting harder and harder to find. The chemist looks at one most suspiciously and has to consult a colleague then fetch it from behind the counter.'

'It's a bomb ingredient,' she explained. 'My mother used to have the same trouble. But I made friends with a school lab technician I did some work for at Hayle and he slipped us a big jar of it – enough for years.'

'Absurd,' he said, as if he hadn't been listening. 'As if Quakers made bombs!' And he set a glass of cordial before her.

'Thanks,' she said. 'Delicious.' It was. It smelled of summer. 'So have you not lived here long?'

'No,' he said. 'But I lose count. No thingy, you know, memory any more. One day's much like the one before, which is restful or a kind of hell depending on how you look at it. Less than a year though. I didn't move far. I spent all my life till now about two streets away. Nearer. But, well, my sons both live so far away now and since my wife died I didn't need all that space. There's a family living there again now, which is as it should be. Houses like that need children.'

He broke off, apparently having run out of inspiration and Carrie didn't do small talk, so they just sat there for a bit in companionable silence. She sipped her cordial and looked about her. It was a very tidy kitchen. It probably had to be because it was so small. It was much as she imagined the galley on a ship. The only unruly touch was an explosive little painting on the wall above the fridge. It was an abstract painting, all reds and oranges, like having a fire halfway up the wall. She didn't normally like abstract art as she had no idea how she was supposed to look at it. This was different. It felt deeper, somehow, less scratchy. It was done with the same bold conviction as a small child's painting, and had the same air of the painter understanding perfectly what he was about, as if he was seeing what he painted and not just drily *thinking* it.

'She was furious when she did that,' he said. 'And even more so when she found I'd kept it.'

'Sorry. Who was?'

'My wife. She was a painter. Rachel Kelly.'

'I'm sorry. That doesn't mean a thing to me. I don't really know anything about art.'

He smiled with real warmth at that. 'You really haven't heard of her?'

'Nope. Sorry.'

'But how very refreshing!'

'Is she famous, then?'

'In her way. In that way that writers and artists can be which is still actually hardly famous at all compared to newsreaders or pop singers. She got much better known after she died but then that's so often the case.'

'Could I have a closer look?'

'Of course.'

She stood and went to peer closely at it. There was a protective layer of glass across it but still Carrie could see the furious brushstrokes and the places where the brush had actually torn the paper in the effort to intensify the colour beyond what mere paint could do.

'I'm sorry, Ms Carpenter, but I'm not entirely sure why you're here.'

'Johnson,' she told him again. 'Carrie Johnson. I'm here to measure up for bookcases.'

'Ah.' Again that lovely smile.

'The lady who rang me, obviously that wasn't your wife.'

'My daughter rang you. She's home from Canada and quietly licking me into shape.'

'Right. Do you know where she wants these shelves?'

'Oh yes. Through here. It's quite a project and I said I felt bad spending a lot of money on it.'

'Well it might cost less than you think.'

'I told her I could always offload more books. I got rid of a couple of hundred when we moved. I used to teach English, you see, and texts do pile up rather. Once you start to throw out it gets easier and easier. You soon realize you're hanging onto things just because you've always hung onto them, not because they retain any meaning or value to you. Do you read much, Ms …'

'Johnson,' she told him again. 'Carrie. No, not a lot, I'm afraid. I never seem to find the time.'

He had led the way back to the hall and opened the door into the room at the front. Or tried to open it. There were books in tottering piles and books still in boxes on every side.

Though not a great reader herself, Carrie had grown up in a house where there were always more books than book-shelf space and where a slow, mysterious tide seemed always to be carrying books from table to table and stair to stair, so she found books a comforting presence and thought the sight before her perfectly understandable. 'That's quite a yardage,' she said, totting up the number of boxes and allowing a metre a box to leave room for growth.

The front door opened behind her and a young woman breezed in singing to herself. On closer inspection she wasn't so much young – she was the same sort of age as Carrie – as youthful. 'Hi,' she said. 'I'm sorry. I'd

PATRICK GALE

completely forgotten about Golowan when I asked you to come today and then, like a lazy fool, I drove to my doctor's appointment instead of walking and of course I couldn't park again once I got back. I had to walk from Newlyn practically. Oh Lord! Books. Lots and lots of books. Look at them all! You must be Carrie. I like your van, by the way.'

'Thanks.'

She looked more Irish than Cornish, with fine, pale skin and a tumble of springy hair the colour of wood shavings, which she was forever pushing out of the way.

'I'll have your parking space when you leave.'

'Sure.'

'I'm Morwenna.'

'Tea?' said the father.

'That's a nice idea. Tea, Carrie?'

They did a little shuffle as to who should put the kettle on, which the father won.

Carrie had a long-established habit of mentally categorizing clients according to the dog breed they most resembled. It helped fix them and their names in her memory. The father, with his rangy frame and frank, loose-mouthed expression and eloquent economy of gesture was an English pointer. But the daughter fitted no breed stereotype. If anything she was a cat and not a domesticated one. Her eyes were unusual, hard to define – tawny? Khaki? This, combined with the hair, made Carrie think of lions.

'What we thought was that we could turn this room into a sort of library,' she said. 'Shelves on every bit of wall, right up to the ceiling and even over the door and windows, just leaving the bit of wall over the fireplace bare for a

285

picture or mirror so it doesn't get too much. Would that be do-able?'

'Of course.' Carrie wished that smiling came more easily to her. She would feel a smile but it often felt as though what emerged on her lips was closer to a sneer, especially if she were at all nervous, as she seemed to be now. 'I always think it's better to have more shelves than you need than too few, and built-in ones are more efficient than freestanding ...' *I sound like a boiler salesman*, she thought, and wondered why it should matter now when it never bothered her as a rule.

'And then I thought a wooden curtain pole could simply run from one bookcase side to another rather than being fastened to the wall itself. We're discovering the plasterwork here is really soft and crumbly, especially on the wall facing the front.'

Carrie took out her tape measure and one of the notepads she made herself from the quantities of mail that her father's parish business attracted, and began jotting down the room's dimensions. 'Paperbacks or hardbacks?' she asked.

'Oh. A mixture, definitely, so I doubt we should try squeezing in more than six rows. And it's probably an idea to have an extra-big shelf space along the bottom for things like art books and dictionaries.' She had a curious, breathy accent, lilting, again more Irish than Cornish, and hard to place.

The father came back in with tea and tough-looking flapjacks on a tray that said *NO TO WAR* in multiple languages. 'This seems such an indulgence,' he told his daughter. 'I'm sure I could give away more.'

'We've been over this,' she said patiently. 'There's no need. And why should you? You love your books!'

Almost immediately he was distracted by a book he had stooped to tidy back into one of the overflowing boxes. He flipped it over to scan the blurb on the back – for all the world like a man browsing in a bookshop, then drifted out of the room with it, having started to read.

Carrie caught Morwenna's eye. 'Was your dad a priest?' she asked her.

Morwenna smiled. 'No,' she said. 'Just a very good person.'

'Ah! You have my deepest sympathy. Mine's a vicar. It's not always easy.'

'No,' she agreed, sipping her tea and sitting on one of the boxes. 'Very, very high standards. He wasn't strict, just … impossible to live up to. We were all doomed to disappoint him and he was far too nice ever to let the disappointment show, which somehow made it worse.'

'How about your mum?'

'His polar opposite,' she said, looking aside and a crispness entered her tone so Carrie pried no further. 'He's fine physically. It's just his short-term memory that's going. Rachel was … capricious. So he's always been in the habit of thoroughness. It's no trouble getting him to keep a pad and diary by the phone. And he has forgiving friends so no one takes offence when he forgets a new name or doesn't show up for something.'

'It's a lovely house,' Carrie said, to keep the conversation going.

'Do you think so?' Again that touch of frost. 'I'm not sure I like it. My brothers helped him choose it … The old house was so special and this feels a bit … I'd rather he'd made a complete break and moved away entirely but he was never going to do that. He couldn't. Not now.'

'Had you lived in the other place long?'

'All my life until I went away to uni.'

'Of course. Your dad said.' Carrie thought of the yard at Pendeen, of the strange, vertigo-inducing view over their fields to the lighthouse and of how her mother and grand-mother had lived there before her. 'Yes,' she added. 'I can see how that would be a wrench. This must feel like …'

'… a holiday house. It stopped being fun after a couple of weeks.'

'So you grew up in Penzance?'

'Yes.'

'Your accent's …'

'My accent's weird, I know. Like my mother's. I'm an accent sponge, my brothers say. Wherever I live, I start to pick it up. I lived in Belgium for a while and started talking English with a sort of all-purpose EEC accent like a drunk translator and now I've spent a couple of years with my aunt in Toronto I guess my voice has changed again. Someone said I sound like Jacqueline Du Pre now and I don't think it was a compliment. My accent's weird, isn't it?'

'No.'

'It's weird. I know.'

'No. It's just unplaceable.'

As she said this, Carrie realized she was just standing there holding her mug of cooling tea while they smiled and gabbled at each other. She never did this. She didn't have friends like this. It made her think back with an ache to the fierce little friendships with Jazz and Shell in girlhood, of bikes and creepy, boring dolls and the queasily unstable currency of secrets. 'So,' she said, reminding herself why she was there. 'Bookshelves.' Her mobile started ringing but she ignored it. 'I've done measuring. Let's talk wood. Do you want them painted, in which case I can use nice, thick planks of MDF that won't bend, or would you rather have oak, which'll look lovely unpainted, but will cost your dad a bit more?'

'Could you price for both, including the paint on the MDF?'

'Sure. And maybe for Osmo on the oak. And then you need to decide if you want them fixed or with those little brass strips chamfered in so you can move the shelf supports?' Her mobile was ringing again. She guessed it was her mother, who hated leaving messages and refused to learn to text because she said her fingers were too thick. 'Sorry,' she said. 'Better get this.' She answered, 'Hello?'

'Carrie, it's me.' Mum was in a state. Not crying – Mum never seemed to cry – but worked up, high-pitched with tension.

'Mum? What?'

'It's your father.'

'What's wrong with him?' Her immediate thought of course was that he was dead and she pictured him sent flying from his rickety bike or face down somewhere around the house and her mother unable to move him. But the truth was far stranger.

'He's with the police. I … Carrie, I think he's been arrested. He wasn't making any sense and I can't go because he took the car into town with him.'

'The police station?'

'Well yes. In town.'

'Mum, try not to worry. I'm on my way there now to check.' She realized that, far from leaving the room or at least pretending not to listen, as might have been normal, Morwenna Middleton was watching her, paying candid attention. 'I'll call you when there's news,' she added, 'Bye,' and hung up.

'What is it?'

'It's nothing. But I have to go.'

'All the blood just drained from your face, Carrie. What is it?' Carrie told her and she insisted on coming too. 'I know police stations from my misspent youth. You'll need company. There'll be a lot of waiting around.'

Carrie protested but she insisted and suddenly the situation was so peculiar anyway that Carrie decided it might as well get more so and gave way. Morwenna said they should go in her car, so as to save the precious parking space in front. As they walked the length of the promenade to find it she talked nervously of her time with her aunt in Canada and her work as a children's counsellor, throwing in that she was bipolar but scrupulous about taking her medication these days. 'Sorry,' she finished. 'My car's a tip.'

'It is, isn't it?'

Morwenna threw a pile of books and files and an apple core off the passenger seat and into the tiny car's rear and Carrie climbed in, rightly assuming there was nothing to be done about the passenger foot well, which appeared to function as a dustbin.

'It's also very old and sounds just like an electric sewing machine,' Morwenna sighed as she pulled out of her parking space. She performed a rapid U-turn before speeding them back along the front and up Alexandra Road into the centre of town. She swerved left, up beside St John's Hall to the police station, a utilitarian building almost as ugly and out of place as the town's tax office though lower, at least, so not quite so brutal.

'First time I've been in here in my entire life,' Carrie said as Morwenna parked abruptly beside a patrol car.

'Glad to hear it.'

'You don't have to come with me, you know. I can walk back to my van from here.'

'I'm staying until we know everything's all right. You have to get out first so I can lock from the inside. It's that old.'

'How can you drive this?' The car was in shocking condition.

Morwenna laughed at her. 'You're scandalized, aren't you? It's just a car. There's a Quaker mechanic in Goldsithney who never gives up on a car unless it's a write-off. Dad buys the cheapest thing going in *The Cornishman* small ads and together they keep them going a year or two.'

'But how about long journeys?'

'We take trains. It's quite simple really. The trick is not to have shame, to remember it's just transport and not your immortal soul.'

She held open the police station door for her and, as Carrie went in, lightly touched her back. Because of Carrie's peculiar emotional history, or rather lack of one, any physical contact she was not expecting had a stronger resonance for her than it might have done for other people. As she approached the desk officer, or whatever they were called, she continued to feel the palm against her shoulder blade, picturing it as a brightly painted handprint on her tee-shirt.

'Er. Hello. I'm here to see my father,' she said, 'Barnaby Johnson?' hating the way nervousness of authority made her statement emerge as a question.

'Hang on a tick,' the desk officer said and went away from his window to make enquiries.

Carrie glanced at Morwenna, who smiled encouragingly. In this context, with her raggedy clothes and wild hair and homemade-looking shoes, she might have been one of the hippies that ran hopeless but tenacious little shops in Bread Street or St Just.

As the desk officer returned, she saw him glance across and assumed he was trying to place them as friends or siblings. 'It'll be a while yet, I'm afraid. Your dad was brought in nearly an hour ago but the duty solicitor was held up in Golowan traffic so they're only just doing the interview now.'

'But why does he need a solicitor?'

'It's his right. He's been arrested.'

'But what's the charge?'

'I'm afraid I'm not at liberty to tell you.'

'Can we wait? My … my friend and I?'

'Of course. There are some chairs over there and a coffee machine and so on.'

'I don't understand,' she said as they sat. 'He's a vicar. He never breaks the law. He's not physically capable. What do they think he's done?'

'We'll find out soon enough. The solicitor will be told you're here and will come out to talk to you once the interview's over.'

'How come you know so much about this? Just how misspent was your youth?'

'Not very. Just a bit sad and misguided. One of my brothers – the youngest – died when I was a student. It was an accident but I was there, in the car though not driving, and Rachel, that was my mother, said ... I was left feeling it was all my fault or that the wrong one had died or whatever. I was seriously mixed up and I had no therapy or counselling and no medication. And I ran away. Right away. Sort of lost myself around the slummier bits of London, then Germany and Holland and Belgium. Most of the people I ended up living with were self-medicating addicts of one kind or another or living in squats. Apart from the nuns. They were sweet. And a poor honey in Brussels. She was in love with me and wanted to wrap me in cotton wool and make everything all right. So I know waiting rooms, hospitals, prisons, police stations. It's always the same tired, plastic chairs and greasy-looking magazines. And nasty coffee. Do you fancy one?'

'Not much.'

'Me neither.'

Two small girls dressed as fairies, for the parade presumably, slipped in and presented themselves at the front desk then stood there for a while, whispering to one another. Their mother, a uniformed WPC, came out and took their photograph on her mobile phone before leading them back outside to her car.

'So why did you become a carpenter?' Morwenna asked. She had kicked off her funny shoes and drawn her bare feet up onto the chair beside her and was picking pensively at her dusty toes.

'A man came to mend the staircase at home.'

'And you fell for him?'

'No. I don't even remember his face or if he was young or old.' Carrie thought back, remembering a set of beautifully maintained chisels in a neat pouch he let her roll and unroll while he worked. 'I fell for his tools and the way wood shavings curled away from the wood as he used a spokeshave. I don't think I'd really looked at wood before then, maybe because there were no trees to speak of around Pendeen. He had a sort of display kit for customers. It had identical cubes, no, fingers really, of different woods. He'd cut them himself and varnished them at one end and simply waxed or oiled them at the other, so you could see the different grains and colours and make your mind up. Mahogany. Tulip wood. Oak. Pine. Iroko. Lime. Ash. Beech. I begged my parents for a set like it for Christmas but of course it's not a thing you could buy – you had to make it yourself. They gave me the *Observer Book of Trees* instead and signed me up for carpentry lessons. And that was it. I was lost.'

The solicitor emerged and explained. Dad had been arrested at his own suggestion but whether he would be charged or simply called to give evidence at an inquest was a matter the Crown Prosecution Service would decide in the coming days. Carrie would not have to stand bail since he was plainly trustworthy and a well-known and responsible member of the community.

Dad looked shattered when he emerged minutes later, as if he had aged years in hours, and was respectfully handed his things back by the duty officer. He frowned as he was asked to sign a piece of paper listing them all – wallet, car keys, mobile, the little antique portable communion set he always had in one breast pocket, the even smaller silver flask for holy oil he carried in the other, and his battered copy of Thomas à Kempis.

She introduced him to Morwenna. 'Morwenna will drive us back to my van then we can go and find yours.'

'I …'

'What?'

'I don't remember where I parked it.'

'Oh. Well, Mum and I can pick it up later once you remember.' His shocked pallor and this pathetic forgetfulness and the extreme oddness of the situation cast all three of them into silence and Carrie was glad they didn't have far to drive. He was the first to speak again, as Morwenna pulled up in front of Carrie's van, ready to reverse into the precious space once they left it.

'That was so very kind of you,' he said. 'Thank you.'

To which Morwenna just smiled and kissed him unfussily on the cheek.

'I'll start on those shelves tonight,' Carrie told her.

'No rush,' she said.

'No. But I want to.'

Back in her van, he had trouble fastening his seatbelt, like a much older man, and looked away out of the window as she fastened it for him, as though ashamed.

'Are you sure you don't remember where you parked?' she asked. 'Where were you going?'

'Lenny … Lenny Barnes's flat, just across the Ross Bridge.'

'Ah. So you're probably just along here somewhere.'

She thought of driving slowly the length of the prom but he was in such a state she doubted he'd be safe driving. 'Not to worry,' she said briskly, performing a U-turn as soon as she could. She drove them home the Newlyn way in case the middle of town was still busy. He said nothing and she knew better than to try to make a person talk. He would talk when he was ready.

There was a man at the top of their lane. She slowed when he raised a hand in greeting, assuming he wanted the usual reassurance that the footpath to the coast did indeed run along it and through their yard, but as she wound down the passenger side window the man started taking photographs and Dad let out a soft groan. As she sped away, the man ran down the lane behind them, shouting, which alerted the others who jumped out of vans and a parked car, one with an ordinary camera, one with a nifty video one. There was a blonde woman with a television cameraman whom Carrie dimly recognized from the local news.

'Dad, do you want me to turn right around and take us somewhere else?' she asked, wondering wildly where she could possibly take him these people could not follow.

'No, no,' he sighed. 'If I talk to them they might go away. I'm so sorry about all this.'

And he sat a moment, composing his thoughts or quite possibly praying before opening the door. Then, far more himself than he had seemed at the start of their drive home, he faced his questioners.

He stood with his back to Carrie's van, unintentionally ensuring widespread publicity for her business as her name and phone number and website URL were clearly visible beside his shoulder.

She headed directly for the front door, thinking to have it unlocked and ready for his retreat. Mum was already on the look-out, for the door opened a little as she approached. But then she felt compelled to listen to what he said. He didn't speak at first.

'Mr Johnson?' they called out. 'Is it true you helped Lenny Barnes kill himself?'

'Was that right as a priest, Reverend Johnson?'

'How long have you known him?'

'Vicar?'

'Mr Johnson!'

But then the television woman, wilier or simply having done a little more local research than the others while waiting in her car, called out, 'Father Barnaby?'

At that appeal, so like a parishioner's, he at last spoke to them all. 'Lenny Barnes was a son of this parish. I'd known him all his life. The accident which paralysed him and now his taking his own life are terrible things for his mother to bear. As her parish priest, I ask that you respect her privacy and grief.'

'But did he kill himself? Did you help him?' Her tone was harsh, without respect.

'I was present at his request. I'm not at liberty to tell you more than that but the details will surely become clear at his inquest.'

'Were you arrested?'

'Did you kill him?'

He cracked at that point and swept into the house. Carrie locked the door behind him and quickly stooped to disconnect the doorbell battery. They still knocked, of course, and called through the letter box, now they'd all learnt his name.

'Father Barnaby?'

'Father Barnaby, please!'

There was a heavy velvet curtain that hung across the door for the colder part of the year to block draughts. It had hung there so long – all Carrie's life certainly – that it was no longer any particular colour. It had been packed away for the summer but she knew where her mother stored it in the bottom drawer of the hall chest of drawers and she hung it as fast as she could, to block any views through the letter box or fanlight, where camera flashes were intruding with frightening rapidity.

Turning from the task she became aware that some kind of scene was going on between her parents. She heard her mother plead desperately, 'Tell me. Just tell me and I can help you!' They were in the winter sitting room, small and rather sunless; being on the house's north side, it was the easiest to heat, having a small wood burner and only one small window. It was also the room furthest from the scrabbling and tapping and voices at the front, protected from intruders by the garden walls.

Perhaps feeling he could relax at long last, her father was slumped in the armchair that was too small for him, weeping with the abandon of a child, an already sodden handkerchief clumped in one fist as he attempted to hide his face in the other. She had never seen him cry before. It was as upsetting as if he had lost his temper, another thing he never did. 'I can't,' he said in a odd, dry voice not his. 'I can't. I can't.'

'There,' Mum said, as though calming a startled animal. 'There there,' and she ran a big hand across his hair and had never seemed stronger. But he wouldn't be soothed and continued to weep, sobs shaking his shoulders. Seeing Carrie standing in the doorway, Mum mouthed *doctor* to her and Carrie slipped off to call Dr Murray and put the kettle on.

The doctor said it was shock and suggested tea and something to eat and said he'd drop off some sleeping pills. Carrie made up a tray. (There was always cake unless it was Lent or an Ember Day. Her mother made sponges and cherry cakes with no more effort than if she had been brushing her teeth or making toast.) Then, prompted by Mum, she made up a second one to take out to the journalists. She worried they'd try to take her photograph, scowling at them, tea tray in hand like a bad-tempered waitress, but they seemed disarmed by the gesture and readily downed cameras to accept mugs of tea and said how good the lemon drizzle cake was.

'Hasn't laced it with something, has he?' one of the men asked, at which they all laughed then looked slightly ashamed.

They stood around drinking and eating cake and talking about everyday matters, traffic on the A30, Wimbledon, the local MPs.

'So who are you?' the television woman asked, returning her empty mug.

'I'm his daughter,' Carrie told her. 'You're not going to be here much longer are you?'

'Is he going to talk to us again?' She looked older than she appeared on television, less perky.

'Doesn't seem very likely,' Carrie told her and gathered back the other mugs. Everyone thanked her politely.

He did talk to them again but not in a way they'd have expected. He had calmed down when Carrie returned to the winter sitting room to collect their tea things. He and Mum were both reading on either side of the unlit wood burner. Carrie had just sat down at a nearby table to flick through yesterday's newspaper when Dad suddenly closed his book with a thump and said, 'Right. Evening prayers. You both coming?'

Evening prayers, like morning prayers, wasn't normally a service as such, although it was listed in small print on the church boards and in the parish magazine. Dad often called it *putting the church to bed*. This evening was clearly different and he was asking for their support.

'Are you sure?' Mum hesitated in the hall. 'Tabby would do it for you in a flash if you asked her.'

'I can't hide,' he said.

So they braved the journalists and photographers again, and soon were leading a small cavalcade up to Pendeen Church. While Dad went to ring the bell, Carrie led her mum to their usual pew, with the seabird kneelers made by Granny, near the front but discreetly to one side, while the journalists sat near the back, clumping together as if for courage. There seemed to be more of them than had been down at the house. Perhaps some had been scouting for stories in the two pubs and been alerted by text.

The only other parishioner present was Modest Carlsson, who sat horribly near Carrie and her mother, fairly vibrating with excitement at the drama unfolding around him. He was the ogre of her childhood, the monster it was somehow forbidden to name as such, blighter of otherwise happy occasions by his mere presence. At least two Christmases had been spoilt by Dad's charitable insistence on inviting him for lunch because he had no one in the world. He was one of those people, Molly Bosavern was another, who seemed energized by other people's suffering, who seemed to swell with the diminishing of others and to grow more lively with a death. Yet there was nothing one could point to directly and he forestalled any criticism by good behaviour; he was never so kind or considerate as when someone was taken seriously ill or had a major disaster or disgrace in the offing: a son in prison, an all too shamingly public visit from the bailiffs. The things he said or gestures he made towards others in such circumstances could not be faulted, but, for Carrie, were always undermined by his tangible excitement, like a dog's at the shedding of blood or a cat's at the fluttering of an injured bird.

He caught her eye as she glanced round to see what Dad was doing and his smile was hungry for developments. She steeled herself for speaking to him afterwards.

Mum suddenly let out a heavy sigh, possibly unconsciously. Carrie reached across and laid a hand on hers. Mum took back her hand shortly afterwards, using it to cover her mouth while she cleared her throat, abashed at having betrayed her weaker feelings perhaps. 'Did you tell Phuc?' she whispered.

'Only a text,' Carrie told her. 'I'll tell him more tonight.'

As ever, thinking of Phuc made Carrie feel suddenly vulnerable, churned up inside. It wasn't normal to feel like this about a brother – she was fairly sure Morwenna Middleton wouldn't feel like this about her two. Women usually complained about their brothers, implying they were immature, insensitive or bad sons, leaving their sisters to bear the parental burden. She imagined Morwenna's brothers as reliable extensions of her peculiarly placid father, dependable, even a bit conventional compared to her.

Phuc was at once hopeless and spikily defensive, which tended to leave her feeling uselessly protective towards him, weirdly maternal, in fact. Weirdly because Carrie had never for one minute hankered after children of her own, always preferring to enjoy other people's from an unde-manding distance. The mere thought that she must get hold of him to tell him properly what had happened, giving him yet another reason to feel he might be about to fall short as a son and brother, upset her and she was glad of the sudden distraction of her father's voice, as reassuringly familiar as her own front door, reciting an opening prayer.

Dad had not robed up. She guessed it was this lack of ritual distance combined with the absence of any musical equivalent that made people give these services such a wide berth. She had even overheard one congregant tell a new arrival who was quizzing her about other services in the week, 'Oh, those. They're listed on there but really they're *private*.' The lack of ritual, of masking, made the service feel at once direct and intimate in a way she imagined some people would find a little threatening.

Sure enough, Dad was suddenly walking among them with a couple of Bibles and a prayer book.

'Hello,' he said to one of the journalists. 'We haven't met properly but since you're here I wonder if I could ask you to read the Old Testament lesson when we get to it and …

er ... you to read the New Testament one? Don't worry. Both very short and I'll say when. Thanks.'

He spoke so that his enquiry was actually a direction. The tactic, if that's what it was, paid off. Having been obliged to read the Bible to one another and to hear each other mumbling the sixty-ninth psalm – *Save me, O God: for the waters are come in unto my soul. I sink in deep mire, where there is no standing: I am come into deep waters, where the floods overflow me* – the journalists melted away. Just one lingered to take a photograph as Carrie and her parents emerged from locking up the church. Modest Carlsson had already vanished, in a rare display of shyness or sensitivity.

She saw her parents into their kitchen then left them in peace and retreated to her end of the house. Dad was plainly a husk of himself after the service and would be taking an early night. There was no guest preacher the next day so he would be rising early to write a sermon. Mum was rattled but would calm her nerves by listening to the radio after supper, hands busy with a jersey or some mending. To Carrie's lasting shame, she persisted in mending Carrie's work clothes the way she had once mended her father's.

The latest half-tamed farm cat, a bulky brindle called Jehoshaphat – inevitably known as Phatty – had adopted her because Dad suffered cramp in the night and tended to kick him off the bed. She fed him, poured herself a badly needed beer and sat down to e-mail Phuc as promised, warning him there was likely to be something in the morning's papers, if not on the night's local news. 'Now we just have to wait,' she told him. 'To see if the CPS are going to prosecute and, if not, to wait for the inquest. Whatever happens, he'll be a key witness at that. And then the Church might take action against him, or the PCC. Do ring,' she added, knowing he wouldn't, 'if you want to know more. Cxx.'

While she was dithering over pressing send, her mobile chirruped, which made her jump, which startled the cat off her lap. It was a voicemail alert. Living where they did, the signal came and went, going more often than not. Texts and alerts seemed to make it through with more consistency than calls. She walked out into the yard and stood on the mounting block there, which she had learnt of old secured the best available signal short of walking up the lane towards the village.

'Hi,' said a voice she immediately placed as Morwenna Middleton's. 'Just calling to see how you all got on. Carrie please *please* don't worry about those shelves when you've got all this to deal with. They can be something to look forward to. But oak. Definitely oak and hang the expense! MDF scares me; what goes into *making* that stuff? Ah well. I just wanted to say hello, really, and that Dad and I are thinking of you … Oh, that's it, and to remind you of something my mad mother used to say when she was being funny and mad rather than mad and scary. *Normal family life is seriously weird*. OK. I'll stop wittering on since you're obviously hiding. Hi and bye. Morwenna.'

How strange it was that she left her name at the end! Dad did the same thing in his messages, as though signing a letter. Carrie folded away her mobile, dodging the impulse to return the call since she was unsure what she would say. Instead she returned to her kitchen to make herself a quick

Marmite and lettuce sandwich, then took a second beer across the yard to her workshop.

This lay in what had once been the dairy. Long since stripped of equipment that new regulations had probably rendered obsolete, it was a simple, whitewashed space with a rack along the longest wall for storing timber on as the damp air would have made wood banana if stored on its end. Her grandfather's work bench, complete with his antique vice and several of his tools was placed so she could work on either side of it and enjoy a view across the yard to the seaward fields. There was a tiny second-hand Swedish wood burner, which she fuelled with offcuts tossed into an old wheelbarrow kept for the purpose. Utilitarian fluorescent lighting and a paint-spattered CD player were slung from the beams.

Phatty followed her, wanting company, and immediately settled in the old Parker Knoll by the wood burner from which he had a good vantage over any mice that ventured out from amongst the piles of wood shavings. The wood burner was old and a bit leaky so at this time of year, when it had stood cold for a month or two, it added a tang of charcoal and ash to the comforting smell of wood.

She fished out her notebook and used an old four-ounce weight to hold it open at the page of measurements she had taken that afternoon, then checked her oak stocks before taking out a plank and starting to measure and mark it off for sawing. She found some music on the radio – a night-time sequence she often seemed to catch on Atlantic FM called *Hairbrush Divas*. Up-tempo dance music, it was tailored to people, girls presumably, getting ready for a long night of clubbing. Carrie had never been in a nightclub in her life, even in her late teens, and prided herself on never taking longer than ten minutes to get dressed and leave the house, fifteen if she was showering. She liked the idea, however, of these possibly mythical girls, for whom the getting ready to go out, the trying on of clothes, the experimenting with make-up, the Dutch courage, gossip and occasional bursts of sisterly bouncing on adjacent beds singing along into microphones improvised from whatever lay to hand, was as much a part of the evening's pleasure as the night out that was meant to be its climax. She liked the idea that even when their clubbing was a failure, these girls, sisters under the skin to Jazz and Shell, would have their friends to fall back on.

Glancing across to the house, she saw that all the lights apart from her own were now out. Her parents were both in bed. She hoped Dad hadn't cried again; she knew how much that would have frightened her mother. The situation could quite possibly get much worse. There could be a court case, aggressive media attention. People crowing, the way they always seemed to when a priest was thought to have misbehaved.

She loved him dearly. She should be deeply worried. Intellectually she was. And yet, as she started to saw timber for bookshelves, she caught herself singing along to a bouncy song about heartbreak, a song she didn't even like especially, and was taken aback to realize she was happy.

BARNABY AT 16

Thanks so much for my birthday tee-shirt. So cool! I can guarantee that nobody else here has one with a revolutionary slogan on it in Arabic. I'll wear it on Saturday afternoon – the next chance we have to wear anything but uniform. Most of the time we dress like geography teachers – tweed jackets, ties and flannel trousers, for pity's sake. My chukka boots are the most modern thing I have on unless you count y-fronts. Prof seriously disapproves of suede, as you know. He says only poodle-fakers wear suede shoes and the Butterfuck says suede doesn't wear well. She should talk!!

It was one the few classrooms that ever became warm. Most lay in a purpose-built Victorian block nicknamed Sparta because its minimal heating, ill-fitting metal windows and lack of insulation made for a bracing atmosphere that ensured no boy ever nodded off in it. Mr Gunthorne was lazy, pleasure-loving and senior, however, so taught in a handsome room in the adjacent, eighteenth-century building. Not only was it lined with history books, which provided excellent insulation, but it contained a wood-burning stove Gunthorne kept hot enough to boil a kettle on. Gunthorne was marking essays. He had told them all to pick a book off the walls at random, read its first ten pages, then write a summary in one hundred and fifty words because, he said, précis-writing was a technique they would need as adults.

Barnaby had picked an extremely easy book and had already written his précis, so was writing to his sister in The Sudan. Alice's latest letter had arrived that morning and he liked to respond the same day, so it felt more like a conversation.

I'm glad you're well again after that nasty fever, he wrote, then broke off to look around him for inspiration. A log settled in the stove. Mr Gunthorne yawned and slid another essay off the heap beside him. The bench beside Barnaby squeaked as Fleming Major shifted to allow Cairns better access to his trouser pocket. *I bet the children are all half in love with you*, Barnaby wrote on, *especially all the girls. I love the sound of you getting them to play cricket. A thoroughly ladylike pursuit and the Imam can't possibly disapprove if you play it with no boys allowed to watch. Harem cricket! No,* convent *cricket!*

'Johnson B?'

Barnaby broke off and looked up. The Undermaster's horn-rimmed secretary had come in and Gunthorne was holding a little note she must have just passed him.

'Sir?'

'You're to go back to house to see Dr Powell.'

'Yes, sir.'

'Er. Best take all your things with you ...'

As Barnaby slung exercise book, fountain pen and writing paper back in his briefcase, his neighbours cast envious looks his way. Errands meant one could slip completely outside the timetable for a precious hour and dawdle, even take the rest of the morning off undetected. He wasn't a rule-breaker, however, although he hoped he wasn't a pious goody-goody either. He had recently been confirmed, to his father's outspoken disgust, but kept his faith a private matter and held himself diplomatically apart from the judgemental creeps in Christian Forum. He loved the school, especially now he had reached the fifth form and no longer had to study subjects that bored him. With so little to make him homesick, he was perhaps ideal boarding-school material.

And Dr Powell was the ideal housemaster, avuncular, a user of first names and with an outgoing wife, English setters and young children, so that the boys in his care felt themselves a party to domestic happiness even while living in conditions worthy of a prisoner-of-war camp. Like all the housemasters, he ceded discipline entirely to the prefects, who essentially ruled the house from teatime until breakfast, but he was fair and accessible, while his study was a trusted court of appeal against injustice.

He received Barnaby in his study now, where the smells of an impending fish lunch and the kitchen's institutional clatter were at odds with the cosy armchairs and subdued, autumnal view of Dr Powell's alpine garden. He sprang out from behind his desk and patted Barnaby on the shoulder as he steered him to one of the armchairs. Barnaby suspected he made him a little nervous as he took no interest in team sports or botany, which were Dr Powell's twin passions. They tended to treat one another with the baffled affection of brothers with no common ground.

'I've had a letter from your father, Barnaby.'

Barnaby's immediate thought was that his father was removing him from the school.

It was Uncle James's choice, and Prof had always despised it as too liberal, artistic and expensive for his rigorous tastes. James's money had paid all the fees in advance but perhaps Prof had found a way to revoke the arrangement. He had been furious at Barnaby's getting confirmed, for which he blamed the school, and he was quite capable of removing him to some godless day school more in line with his Darwinian convictions. Alice's long-distance reaction to his conversion was kindly satirical. Their father's had been to give up almost entirely on personal letters. Instead he sent pointed clippings from newspapers, articles on religious war and the like, with double underlinings and a meaningless *love Prof* at the end, words which Barnaby's philosophical friend, Potts, had pointed out, read as both command and endearment.

Dr Powell cleared his throat. 'Your father asks me to hand you his letter and let you read it. It concerns your sister.'

Barnaby kept his breaths shallow; if he breathed deeply, he might cry out. He became sharply aware of his heart-beat. 'Is she hurt?' he asked.

Dr Powell glared down at the folded letter in his hands. 'Worse than that,' he said. 'Alice is dead, Barnaby.'

Now Barnaby did cry out. Dr Powell had a box of tissues at the ready. Barnaby took a couple, astonished that his face could be so wet so rapidly. 'How?' he tried to ask but his throat was so constricted the word came out as a stran-gled sob. He made himself breathe more slowly. 'How?' he asked again. 'Did she get ill again?'

Dr Powell had opened out the letter. 'No,' he said. It was short. It was typed. There was a handwritten postcard tucked within it, at which he stared indignantly for a moment adding, under his breath, 'This is unspeakable.' He stuffed the card into his jacket pocket and handed the letter over. 'Barnaby, I think you'd better just read this.'

Dear Barnaby, Prof wrote. I won't hide the facts from you, as I'm sure it's better you know everything now rather than find details out later on and resent those who withheld them. Alice has been killed. She borrowed her employers' Jeep, without authorization, and took herself off on an overnight trip. She was shot and, the Foreign Office tells me, probably raped. Things being as they are, there's little hope of them finding the perpetrators. I've arranged for her to be cremated out there and her ashes flown home. There'll be no funeral. Alice was not religious and, as you well know, I'd find any such ceremony pointless. I've asked the school to go easy on you for a bit and Marcia and I look forward to having you home for the holidays next month. As ever. Prof.

Barnaby folded the letter up, to make it clear he had finished. He couldn't bring himself to look up. His eyes felt gluey. He took another tissue, blew his nose.

'I'm so very sorry,' Dr Powell said quietly. 'I know you were extremely close to her and this has come as a horrible shock. In fact you'll probably feel completely unreal for an hour or two. In normal circumstances the—' He broke off and cleared his throat. 'Normally a boy's parents would come and take him home for a day or so. But it seems that isn't to happen. I've spoken to the chaplain and the head-master and we've agreed that you be given time off at school instead. It's entirely up to you whether you come into classes or not until you feel ready to participate fully again. Everyone will be told what has happened and will know to treat you kindly. I'll make a brief announcement at lunch today and the headmaster will be telling the other staff.'

Barnaby nodded.

'Food's probably the last thing you'll feel like.'

'It is rather.'

'But Virginia has made up some nice sandwiches for you just in case. She put them in a bag so you can take them off for a long walk into the hills, if you like. I know you're fond of walking.'

'Yes. Thank you, sir. Please thank Mrs Powell.'

'Don't be silly. Stay in here as long as you like.'

He slipped out. Barnaby sat on. He read the letter again then tore it up. Then wished he hadn't. He sat on until the corridor outside grew punctually noisy with boys returning for lunch. He heard dining-room benches being pushed this way and that as boys took their seats. He heard the drop in conversations as Dr Powell and whichever masters were visiting for lunch took their places, and the abrupt clatter of boys standing followed by the relative silence as Dr Powell said Grace.

He did indeed go for a long walk with Mrs Powell's sandwiches, and walked repeatedly in the following days; the school was situated on the edge of a town, its grounds adjoining attractive countryside rich in hills and woodland. Nature was a help, particularly at its more dramatic – strong wind in beech trees, heavy rain, cloud shadows appearing to race across a valley – and easier to take than people. People meant to be kind but they also tended to be lost for words.

Barnaby was driven a little mad by the disorienting sense of being suddenly cut loose from the school's moorings. Everyone else continued to stick to the rigid timetables of the place while he was disconcertingly at liberty among them. If he chose to attend a class, and he soon did, because he did not want to fall behind, people were so scrupulous in not addressing him or drawing attention to him, that he felt more than ever like a ghost in their midst.

Precisely because Alice had always been all in all to him, he had never acquired the trick of male friendship. Or rather, he had never learnt how to confide in other boys. So, while he had several friends, they tended to be matey rather than close. His best friend, Potts, helped the most, simply by recognizing that Christmas with his father was likely to be an ordeal. He invited Barnaby to consider spending the holidays with him and his family in London instead.

A funeral – the tactless candour of a coffin – would have helped. Because Alice had been out of the country for nearly a year already, kept alive to him in her vividly funny letters, his brain could not accept the fact of her distant death. And school religion was no help. He took himself into the chapel when it was empty, and when it was full. He heard the anthems and readings, the prayers and sermons, and he felt nothing but anger. He was furious at God for the unfairness of it. Alice might not have believed in Him but she was good, she was devoting her life to others. *I'd love to have that sense of being held and protected,* she had written about his confirmation ceremony, *of an essential benevolence. I think people are pretty wonderful, though. The love I see here every day, between the children, or shown by the women, in the face of their pretty horrible lives, is miraculous. Can I take that as God without having to take all the paraphernalia too?*

He began to walk out of chapel far more often than he walked out of classes.

Concerned, noticing he had abruptly ceased to come up to the altar for communion, the chaplain sought him out. He suggested Barnaby read Job, but that was insulting rather than a comfort, since Job's loved ones, arbitrarily taken from him, were just as arbitrarily replaced with new ones. He suggested Barnaby's rage at God was really rage at his own father. This made Barnaby so impatient that, for several Sundays in succession, he attended the philosophy classes one of the classics masters offered as a freethinker's alternative to worship.

A book token came from Mr Ewart, who had never reliably remembered the date of Barnaby's birthday. Barnaby had begun to write an automatic thank you letter when he realized that nothing in the accompanying birthday card had made any acknowledgement of what had happened. Relations between the Prof and Mr Ewart had been glacial ever since Uncle James had by-passed his younger brother and established instead a trust for Barnaby's education. The resentment deepened when, on leaving school, Alice had spent life-changing weeks with James and Mr Ewart on holiday in Ibiza. She came back with two Mary Quant minidresses, a tan, and a fantasy that the two of them might adopt her.

It was monstrous of his father not to tell him, petty.

Rather than write, he dared to presume on Dr Powell's kindness and asked if he could put through a call to Paris. He was allowed to ring from Mrs Powell's study, a little womb of a room that was in disarmingly feminine contrast to the hard surfaces in the boys' half of the house. It had

thick blue carpet and chintz curtains and, before she left him
in peace, she settled him at her pretty, ladylike desk, looking
at framed photographs of her wedding and children.

Mr Ewart was startled to hear from him – Barnaby had
never rung him before – but then was so shocked and so
moved by the news that Barnaby was upset all over again
and wept unrestrainedly, in a way he had not managed to
do until then.

Mr Ewart had always been rather ironic and careful with
him but now he was warmly impulsive.

'Why aren't you at home?'

'Well ... I think Prof thought I was better off here.'

'That's dreadful. You shouldn't be there. What was he
thinking? Let me look at the flight timetables ...' Paper
rustled in the background. 'Listen, Barnaby, I could be
there tomorrow afternoon. I could bring you back here for
a bit.'

Voice cracking at the awkwardness of having to point
such a thing out, Barnaby explained that this might result
in Mr Ewart's being arrested for abduction, since he wasn't
his legal guardian. Instead he accepted an invitation to visit
him over New Year, after spending Christmas *en famille*
with Potts. Mr Ewart said he would see that the trust paid
for a return ticket on the boat train from Victoria.

After finishing his history essay that evening, Barnaby wrote
several drafts of a letter home. In the first version he wrote
out all his anger, and resentment at his father and Mrs
Clutterbuck, at the lack of funeral, at their coldness. By his
final draft, all that remained was calm politeness – precisely
the sort of rational tone that would meet with his father's

approval. He told him he would not be coming home in the holidays and explained where he would be instead. He asked Potts to read the letter for him the following morning, to confirm it was entirely inoffensive and clear. He sealed and stamped it but did not post it immediately. There was no hurry; the writing of it was what mattered.

At the end of that week, on the Saturday, two parcels were waiting for him on the post table when he came in from the morning's classes. One had Sudanese stamps on it, with a giraffe design he recognized instantly. The larger one was from Paris. Parcels in boarding school were an event so at once there were friends around him eager to see what he'd been sent. He stuffed the Sudan one into his school bag, saying it was just boring stuff, and tore open the French parcel. It contained an elegant box of chocolate and coffee macaroons from Ladurée and a card from Mr Ewart saying simply, *A foretaste of treats to come!*

He shared out the macaroons after pudding. The second parcel he saved until he was safely in his study and Potts and his other study-mate had clattered away along the corridor in their football boots. There were several layers of thick brown paper which smelled exotic somehow. He half expected sand to trickle out from its folds. Then there was a little red book, fancifully held closed with a purple silk ribbon. And there was a typewritten letter on a familiar school letterhead that made him catch his breath.

Dear Barnaby,
    You don't know me but I rather feel I know you
because Alice talked about you so often and used

to read out funny bits from your letters sometimes. (Hope you don't mind.) Anyway, as you'll
have gathered from the return address, I'm a VSO
colleague of hers at the school.

She was so amazing. She was already here when
I came out and helped me settle in and, although
I'm quite a bit older than she was, taught me so
much. Your sister had an old soul! She has left
a terrible gap behind her. We have a noticeboard
dedicated to her where the children have hung
poems and pictures and we've put up our favourite
photographs of her. We have also decided to
inaugurate a girls' cricket trophy in her name.
It's only silver plate but the first girl to be
awarded it, who has a stroke just as good as
Boycott's so is nicknamed Geoff, was so proud,
she burst into loud tears. Which of course set
the rest of us off as well!

We have also planted a lemon tree for her. She
grew it in a pot from a pip and now it's in pride
of place in a corner of the playground and the
children give it (precious!) washing-up water
every day and I suspect confide their secrets to
it, as she was that sort of teacher.

Barnaby, she may have been taken from us young
but she had already made a difference for the
better in the world and so many of us will grow
old without the same being said of us. I'm so
glad to know you were confirmed last year. Your
faith will help you. It may not seem to at the
moment, in fact you probably hate God right now

and think you have no faith or vision left to you, but trust me: faith is a tough and patient plant that endures long periods of drought.

But enough of my prattle. My real reason for writing is the enclosed book and letter. They only came my way recently and by chance. We found them in the Jeep when it was finally returned to us. The letter wasn't finished but it was clearly meant to come to you with the book so here they are for you. A rather sad, early Christmas present.

With every good wish (and apologies for this ancient typewriter ribbon),

Cordelia Penberthy

Barnaby opened out the brown paper again, mystified, then thought to undo the ribbon tied around the little book. The second letter was folded tightly and tucked between the pages. It was written on the school paper, as usual, and her tone was so happily alive, no other word for it, that he had to break off reading after a couple of sentences and walk around the little study to compose himself.

Dear Barny, she had written.

Oh but it's so beautiful here! Such a magical night. I'm writing this by torchlight and there are moths all around me like little fairies. I have been crazily daring and escaped for a whole weekend away on my own, like an intrepid lady adventurer of the 1860s. First I wrapped up like a local and visited the city and now I'm way out in the countryside, camping out in the school Jeep, with a night sky full of stars for company. There's even a tiny creek where I can swim. Skinny dipping. Scandalous!

Thanks for the lovely letter. *Very* glad you don't have some stuck-up girlfriend from the local girls' school. Stick to your studies, my boy, and to flowers. Listen to your nice housemaster and join Bot Soc. Flowers never disappoint. I have dreams of James's garden sometimes and I swear I can smell those dark red roses. I wonder how his Paul is. Do you ever hear from him? Now *there* was a love!

I'm never coming home. You'll simply have to come out here to see me in your months off before university. Sod going to Florence and Rome like everyone else to look at paintings and bum around with spoilt Americans. Come out here and discover new ways of enjoying goat ...

Khartoum was wonderful. Exhilarating to be completely unknown after months of village life and everyone knowing my every move. I wore an impenetrable veil and strolled around the souk pretending to be a respectable young widow. I found a funny old bookshop. Lots of things in Arabic and the usual sad heap of left-behind Agatha Christies and Desmond Bagleys but then I found this and it sort of spoke to me. Yes, it seems to be a set of instructions to a monk on how to survive and thrive in the religious life, but it's also full of good sense and I thought it would do pretty well for a clever yoof at bording skool. Lots of stuff about the importance of keeping your counsel and not investing too much in the good opinion of others or prizing mere *stuff* over the life of the spirit. He's also very keen on warning against becoming seduced by the beauty and charm of your mortal companions. I think it must have belonged to a missionary, don't you? I wonder what became of him. Roasted or boiled or sold as a sultan's plaything?

Anyway, better early than not at all. It can be this year's Christmas present. Imagine Prof's face if he caught you reading a book with this title! Sorry. Bit pissed. My first beer in about a year. Supper awaits me under the trees. I've got a little fire going and I expect I'll sleep out there rather than locked in the Jeep as it's so warm and there's nobody around for miles. I'm cooking something I bought in the souk today. They said it was chicken. Well, 'bird' anyway. Like nothing you'd ever find in Sainsbury's but I have to say it smells delicious and after such adventuring I could eat rook.

Oh Barny, don't you ever wonder what it's all for? All this beauty and mess! These glorious moths! Sometimes when I'm lying awake here, especially just after dawn, I get such a powerful sense of

And there she broke off. There was no bloodstain, no jagged tailing off of script. She had simply stopped because she was drunk and hungry and the letter could wait to be finished in sunlight. Had she eaten before they found her? Had she fallen asleep? Did she put up a fight?

In an effort to still his mind, he set her letter aside and opened the little book. She had inked him a little dedication in the front. *Even I found much good sense in here and think you may too! A. Khartoum, November '67.*

He turned a page and began to read.

Modest hated to admit it but Johnson's suggestion that he take over the parish magazine was a stroke of genius. Ostensibly he was deemed to be suited to the work, being a retired bookseller, just the stupidly pointless connection people liked to make; actually it suited him because it placed him securely and squarely at the village's heart. Certainly he was handling announcements of the next bring and buy sale or Charles Causley evening, not earth-shaking gossip, but it was surprising how much he learned when gathering in his copy. He passed none of this on; they'd stop confiding in him if he became known as a gossip. It was the possession of the knowledge that excited him. His predecessor in the post had always delivered her newsletter by car, long-suffering husband at the wheel. He had not driven since his pre-Portsmouth days, letting his driving licence and all the related expense go the way of the former identity now known only to the Probation Service.

His crime, punishment and release all predated the Sex Offender Register, of which he had read with mixed smug-ness and relief. The register caught up with him, however, after his move to Cornwall and in the most irritating and demeaning way. He posted a miscellaneous bundle of smutty photographs and magazines to a regular customer who had never given him trouble. A week later the police arrived with a warrant to search the house and carry off his sales records and he was taken in for questioning.

The customer, a Plymothian, had been arrested for exposing himself to schoolchildren on buses and his flat had been discovered to house an array of paedophile pornography. Just one photograph in the drab stash Modest had sold him gave cause for concern. Luckily there were no other such pictures in Modest's stock so he escaped with a fine while the customer was jailed. His court appearance in distant Plymouth, under his real name, went miraculously unreported in *The Cornishman*'s terse column of court reports. However, in what seemed a piece of pure malice, the addition to his record for crimes of a sexual nature led to his name, his real name, being added to the register. Once a year he was required to call in and sign against his name at Penzance police station and, which was worse, to keep him on his best behaviour, the police reserved the right to call in on him unexpectedly. They had done so just once, nearly five years ago. It was a horrible, demeaning experience, reminding him that his new life and new identity were made of fragile stuff, and he lived in dread of its repetition.

Modest Carlsson was a harmless old man to whom people chatted in bus shelters. He delivered the magazines by hand and recipients, seeing him coming up to their doors, breathless in summer or fumbling with his gloves in winter, often asked him in and seemed to enjoy plying a fat man with cake.

This was how he had come to know Nuala Barnes. He was well aware of the Australian potter's reputation as a godless rebel but had always wanted a closer look at her fascinating house. When it suited him, he decided he was not simply delivering the parish newsletter but representing the Church's hand reaching out in fellowship.

A former shooting lodge – some said it had always been a love nest – of a once powerful local landowner, Redworks Cottage lay high above the sea, on the edge of moorland. It was nearer Bossullow than Morvah and must surely have been at the outer limit of Johnson's parish if not actually in Zennor. There was an American-style post box on a pole at the beginning of its lane, alongside the wheelie bin and recycling box, but he had chosen not to see it. The long route to her front door wound between fenced-in pastures and was utterly exposed to view so she would have ample opportunity to see his approach and choose not to answer her doorbell.

He rang twice and there was no answer but then she emerged from the outbuilding where she presumably had her studio and asked him abruptly what he wanted. As he'd expected, she said she did not take the parish magazine but he had done his homework and added, 'It's not for you, it's for Lenny. I gather he was confirmed last year.'

'Yeah,' she said with a scowl. 'Christ knows what that was about. Teen rebellion, I guess. Well …' She grinned mischievously. 'Can't have him losing touch with the flock.' And, claiming she was breaking off for tea in any case, she asked Modest in.

He continued delivering the magazine and she continued asking him in long after Lenny had dropped all claims to a faith in favour of rugby and his girlfriend, who continued coming to church without him. Nuala confessed she read the magazine herself. She had even been known to bring old clothes and books to jumble sales and to donate pots to fundraising auctions. She had no idea where in Pendeen Modest lived, and she never invited him further into her house than her kitchen. (He had once faked a weak bladder and been disappointed to find her downstairs lavatory lay unrevealingly nearby.) But she seemed to regard him with a kind of affection as a fellow outsider and he in turn enjoyed her battered glamour and caustic wit. She took it into her head that he was good, however, profoundly good, even wise. Nothing he said, no amount of scandalmongering or back-biting, would convince her.

'You don't fool me, Modest,' she would say. 'I know you're above all that really.' And after a while he came to feel a better, wiser person when he was in her presence, raised by an unbeliever's faith.

He knew nothing about art but he could see that her bowls and plates and oddly elongated bottles were beautiful. Sitting with her at her slab-like oak table which was never without something of beauty on it – a pile of apples, a piece of driftwood, a ring of snow-white pebbles – he felt he was dipping into a headily different life that could never have been his because he had always lacked the courage. He had tried copying her in small ways but when he brought things home from his walks on cliffs or moor and cleared a space for them on a table they simply looked like junk. He kept hoping that one day she would give him one of her pots, not least for the pleasure it would cause him to be able to say, should he ever have a visitor, 'Oh, that? It's by my potter friend, Nuala Barnes. Effective, isn't it?' Only she never did and he was far too mean to buy one. Simply buying one, like anyone else, would have felt like cheating and not been the same at all.

When Lenny had his accident, Modest had known himself tested. A true friend would have hurried to her side to offer comfort or assistance but he had found himself checked for some reason, by doubt or inhibition and an uncharacteristic fastidiousness. When he did finally use the parish magazine as his usual excuse to visit, a bossy friend of hers, a true friend presumably, had taken it off him at the door and said Nuala and Lenny were busy with the occupational health visitor.

When he called by the following month, she was preoccupied with adapting the ground floor to Lenny's wheelchair and had been woundingly dismissive of him. So he had cut her off his delivery rounds for three months in the hope of punishing her. And then curiosity overcame him and he felt compelled to visit to see how she was coping with the shock of Lenny's insisting on moving out to live on his own in Penzance. He found her brittle and brave and once again content to sit with him at her kitchen table.

He did not make the same mistake twice. As soon as news reached him in the pub about Lenny's suicide, he sent her flowers. He had never sent flowers to anyone in his life, not even his wife, and was scandalized at the expense but he understood that the pain – the sense of sacrifice – was part of the pleasure people took in giving. *I'm so very sorry*, he wrote on the little card the florist gave him to include in the package. *Let's talk when you're ready.*

And now the latest edition of the parish newsletter gave him reason to climb her windswept drive again, whether she was ready to talk or not. He had not seen her around the village since the news broke but then one rarely did, as she did most of her shopping elsewhere. The funeral had been a godless cremation from which she had excluded everyone but her sister from Australia. He had all the salient details.

He was disappointed to see her emerge from her studio. She would take the magazine, he thought, and dismiss him.

'You're working,' he said. 'I'll leave you in peace.' He was slightly shocked that she *was* working. He had pictured her slightly crazed with grief, needing his wise words.

'No, no,' she said. 'It's all coming out badly,' and she surprised him by kissing his cheek. 'Thanks for the flowers, Modest. I should have written. It was very sweet of you. Everyone's been so kind it got almost unbearable. Sympathy is hard to bear. Come in.'

Although death, inquest and funeral were all long past, there were flowers on every surface. Flowers, pot plants, even a small lemon tree. The scent of them all tickled his nose. She saw him look.

'They're starting to go over,' she said. 'I should start throwing them out but that would mean, well, you know.'

'Starting over?'

'Yeah,' she laughed shortly. 'Right. Something like that. We should have tea. Do you want tea?'

'Please don't go to any trouble, Nuala.'

'It's no trouble. I need tea,' she said but having filled the kettle she sat down again without setting it on the hotplate and he did not like to say anything.

'I expect it's the last thing you need,' he said. 'But I brought you the latest ...' and he took a copy of the news-letter from his shoulder bag and set it on the table. She reached out a clay-whitened hand and touched it with something like tenderness.

'You're amazing the way you keep churning this horrible thing out,' she said.

'Oh, really,' he said. 'It's nothing but typing. Other people do far more. They do real work.'

'Yeah. Well. Other people. So what's going to happen, Modest? Will they chuck him out, do you reckon?'

Of course he knew exactly who she meant but he was *Good Modest* when he was with her, *kind, unworldly Modest.*

'Do you mean Father Barnaby?' he asked softly.

'Who else?'

'I really couldn't say. He's very popular despite … What he said at the inquest, about prayer and … I think some people are taking him up as a kind of cause. People from outside the parish.'

'People don't know the half of it.' She sighed with surprising violence and muttered, 'And they probably never should.'

Modest had been about to stand to set the kettle to heat for her, as he was really very thirsty from all his walking and had said no to two previous offers in expectation of tea at Nuala's, but he froze as her words sank in. Speaking very carefully, speaking just as he imagined a priest might in such a situation, and keeping his voice as gentle as he could, he asked, 'Nuala, is there something … something *held back* which the inquest should have heard about?'

She didn't answer him straight away. Instead she looked at him in a way that made him realize how rarely she actually looked at him. Her eyes were a deep blue that seemed hardly faded by age. For a moment she seemed to be examining him and he felt weighed in the balance and uncomfortable. Just when he thought she might be about to curse him and throw him out, she said simply, 'Barnaby was Len's father. It was a mistake. A stupid, silly fling. And I was a bitch. I realized I wanted a kid but I didn't want Barnaby and all the hassle and fuss. So I never told Len who his father was.'

'But Barnaby knew?'

'Oh yeah. He knew. I owed him that much. But I told him if he ever told Lenny, I'd take the kid away, right away, where he and his fucking Jesus and that fat cake-baker couldn't get their claws into him.' She was crying now, shedding tears at least, but seemed not to notice. She had torn a dark blue flower from the pot on the table and was pulling its petals off one by one and laying them in a neat little daisy-shaped pattern.

Modest felt the room had suddenly become as quiet and airless as a tomb and that she was no longer aware of him, not as himself, that he might have been anybody and she would still have talked, simply because the moment had come for talking.

'Oh, Nuala, I'm so sorry,' he began, ever so slightly prompting her to continue. 'It must have been so …'

'And he didn't say a word,' she said. 'He never said a word. I thought it was so obvious. I thought everyone would see how alike they were. But of course he was a priest so it's the last thing anyone would … Even at the inquest. He was so fucking *good*, wasn't he? He didn't even perjure himself in order to keep his promise. He just didn't quite say it all.'

'But if Lenny didn't know, why did he ... Why involve him like that?'

'It was just Jesus. Fucking Jesus. Len wanted Jesus with him at the end!' She did not say *instead of me* but she did not need to. Her anger felt corrosive, unanswerable.

Good Modest, he reminded himself. *Kind and wise and slightly shocked, perhaps, at her bad language* and he held his tongue in case she offered anything further.

But she pulled herself together suddenly, swept the petals into her hand and so to the compost bucket. 'Christ. Sorry. I offered you tea, Modest, and I never even put the kettle on,' she said and something in her tone, a small barb, made him wonder if she had ever really intended to.

'That's fine,' he said. 'I should leave you and your troubles in peace.'

'I shouldn't have told you,' she continued, ignoring him. 'I don't know what I was ... Nobody knows except you. If word gets out, I'll know it was you.'

'I won't breathe a word,' he said, backing away from her sudden frankness. 'I can keep a secret.'

'Of course you can. You're full of secrets, aren't you?' She opened the door for him. She handed him back the magazine. 'Nothing personal,' she said, 'but please don't bring me this thing anymore. I hate it and everything it stands for.'

'Sure, Nuala,' he said. 'Understood.'

'Good,' she said and she closed the door.

He began to shudder uncontrollably as he walked away from her house. Alone between the wide expanses of field he felt vulnerable, as though walking with more riches than he could safely carry. On one level his long patience was rewarded. At last he had the plump, nutritious proof of Johnson's fallibility and fundamental ordinariness. But on another he felt mocked by the hollowness of his triumph, for the proof was so tenuous – no more than hearsay, all too easily dismissed as mere spite – and in any case, after such a long interval, who would remember the justifying details? The broken-backed boy had been, what? Eighteen? Twenty? Modest calculated and realized the affair must have happened soon after his own arrival in the village and first involvement in the parish.

His memory was usually pretty keen but he tried in vain to think of a single occasion when he had seen Johnson and Nuala together. He tried to picture the preposterous, pornographic scene, the tugging off of dog collar, bursting of buttons, her clayey handprints on his hot, demanding flesh, but was troubled to find that the only image that would linger was of the two of them sitting companionably on the sofa in the sitting room she had never shown him. For all the glaring differences in their spiritual lives, they were, he realized, extremely well suited. As a couple they would have been compellingly attractive, even impressive. A couple to bring forth striking, successful children, a couple to inspire coupling in others.

Poor Dorothy, Modest thought. *Dowdy, unbohemian Dorothy*. Dorothy had never managed to conceal her distaste for and suspicion of him. She might have retained her husband in the flesh but she would surely have lost him in spirit, lost his true affection and respect. *Poor Dorothy*. Like the surprisingly unpolished country wife of an urbane politician. A maker of cakes not conversation. *The fat cake-baker*. He smiled to himself at Nuala's bitter little label for her. Dorothy had eluded him until now, secure in her quiet sense of position, her deep roots in the place and the evident affection in which she was held by the parish.

As if his thoughts had conjured her from the gathering evening, he saw her ahead of him as he entered the village. She was walking the same way as him, laden with bags that were probably stuffed with flower-arranging materials, raspy blocks of oasis, ugly, long-hoarded plastic vases retained from funeral offerings. He was an old man compared to her, seventy-five where he assumed she was at most in her early sixties, yet to watch her he felt vigorous by comparison. She had always walked as though weighted down. She had become quite fat, to the point where she seemed to belong to a different race from her husband and skinny, boyish daughter, but it ran deeper than that. She walked as though her flesh were denser that other people's and, it struck him now, as though her troubles were more burdensome.

Until he spotted her, his assumption had been that he was heading home to tea and toast and a quiet drink or two floated on a tide of bad television uncritically absorbed. But when he saw her a terrible idea took shape and acquired direction when she ducked up the lane that led to the church and the building everyone still called the vicarage although Johnson and his family had always lived elsewhere.

He had the perfect excuse, in a load of surplus parish magazines, to turn that way too. If she went into the vicarage, well, then he had business there because he produced the newsletter in the parish offices on the ground floor. If she continued to the church, he could be on his way there to leave the magazines on the table at the church's rear.

She continued to the church and he slackened his pace, enjoying the sense of anticipation. He actively disliked this church these days, compared to its older sister in Morvah. He found its crenellated outer walls forbidding as he did the stretch of rocky land immediately above the steeply sloping graveyard. He had never known such a steep grave-yard and couldn't see it in rain without imagining corpse juices trickling downhill towards the church's foundations. And the church itself was too high for its narrow width, to his mind, so that its dark stained beams seemed steep and unsafe. Then there was its air of cheerful community clutter, which to his way of thinking typified the bit of this, bit of that compromise that was at the heart of all that was misguided in twenty-first-century Anglicanism, the lack of rigour that would surely prove its undoing. There were times recently when he had seriously considered converting to Rome.

There was no sign of her as he came in and he thought for a moment she might have slipped out again by the smaller door on the vicarage side. But then he heard a clatter from the vestry and realized that she was indeed unload-ing materials for the flower-arrangers. He busied himself at the bookstall table, removing the pile of the previous month's magazine and setting up a neat stack of the new one. Then he tidied the other piles as he waited for her to emerge.

He did not need to see her expression. He could tell from the cheerful effort she put into greeting him how little she wished to find him there.

'Dorothy,' he said and boldly reached out to take both her plump hands in his. 'I'm so very sorry for all you're going through.'

'There's no need. Honestly,' she said, taking back her hands after giving his a quick squeeze, and adding in an echo of Nuala, 'People have been so kind.'

'Have they? Good. I'm glad, because, well, not everyone around here is … well … You know how people are and how they talk.'

'My mother brought me up not to listen,' she said stiffly. 'Oh. Is that your new issue? I'd better take one for us. You're so amazing, the way you still deliver it.'

'At my age!'

'Well … I didn't mean …'

'I think it's the only thing that keeps me fit.' He let his glance play over her pillowy silhouette. 'I sometimes think I feel younger now than when I first moved here over twenty years ago.'

'Really? That's good. Ah well, Modest, I must hurry on. I try to walk everywhere instead of taking the car, but it does eat up the day.'

She had turned away and, for a moment, he hated her.

'I took a copy up to Nuala Barnes,' he said.

'Oh yes?' A definite strain in her voice at that.

'Well … Lenny always took one and she carried on out of force of habit.'

'I see.'

'I had no idea, Dorothy. I don't think anyone did.'

'What about?'

'Lenny.'

'Poor Len. Such a terrible thing. People didn't realize but Barnaby was devastated.' She was fiddling with the bookstall, untidying his neat piles in small ways.

'Well he would be.'

'What do you mean by that?' She faced him again and for a moment her expression was openly hostile. He disgusted her but disgust was easier to bear than pity.

'Dorothy, you've been so amazing. Standing by all this time, not speaking out even when the likeness between father and son was so clear to everybody. I just want you to know that, if ever sides had to be taken, I can think of several of us who would be on yours ...'

She made abruptly for the door. Put-downs were not in her repertoire. Merely to leave without saying goodbye was rude enough in her lexicon. But then she sank with a little gasp into one of the rear pews and hunched over. He thought she was crying at first but as he drew closer he realized she was having some sort of attack. Her face was pale and sweaty and she was clutching her upper arm and panting.

'Dorothy?' he said softly. 'Shall I ...? Would you like me to fetch help?'

There was a scene in that play, *The Little Foxes*, where the marvellous anti-heroine watched on, gloating, as her disapproving banker husband slumped in a heart attack on the stairs before her. It had been shocking even when played a couple of years ago by an amateur group in Newlyn with dodgy Southern accents and even wobblier sets. But thrilling too. He would love to have found such murderous presence of mind, to have watched, perhaps even taking a seat in a pew alongside Dorothy, talking half-audible horrors as she slipped away.

He was a coward, however. He was also alive with the unexpected buzz of being swept up in such a drama.

'Stay right there,' he told her with a nervous dab at her shaking shoulder. 'I'm going next door to call for help.' And he actually ran to the vicarage so that he could scarcely speak when he got there. One of the Women's Refuge people was in the office talking as Brid Williams did something to the parish website.

'We must phone for an ambulance,' he told them so abruptly they must have thought it was for him. 'No no,' he went on, flapping a handkerchief. 'I'll do it. You go to church to be with her. It's Dorothy!'

'I'll call Barnaby's mobile,' Brid said, fumbling with her phone as she hurried out.

Modest called the ambulance, calmly gave the directions and his name and, when he said he thought it was a heart attack, noted down their instructions for how best they could help Dorothy while waiting.

He poured himself a large glass of water then took the instructions back to the church. Dorothy was dead by the time he got there. Brid Williams stopped trying to be brave the moment he arrived and sank against him, hooting with grief. By the time the ambulance screeched up Church Lane, too late of course, he felt positively heroic. *Wise Modest. Good Modest!*

PHUC AT 27

Fern had four sons by two previous partners. Aged from fourteen to seven, each of them had sport, music, family and social engagements, all of which required their being driven somewhere and collected again. On top of these Saturday obligations, there was always a long list of food shopping and some DIY to be done. Fern was an adept at compartmentalizing her boys' needs as she would those of her social work clients. Every Friday night, once the younger ones had been seen off to bed, she sat at the kitchen table with a large glass of Pinot Grigio and her mobile and a list of Saturday's obligations and doggedly drew up a timetable. Saturday's arrangements would not have been possible without a second driver, since so many of them were not even near a bus route. When he wondered how she would have managed before she met him, he soon remembered the ex-partners who, however unreliable, would have been pressed into service.

Fern's weekends involved no churchgoing, she was an atheist, but it often seemed that children and their needs had taken the place of religious observance. The moral imperatives invoked were just as unanswerable.

Being nearly fifteen years younger than her and coming into her life freighted with what, in the vernacular of her profession, could be called issues, he strove never to act like an extra son on her timetable or an extra client on her caseload. But today he might have to be both.

The text was from Carrie, announced by the chorus from 'Trelawny', the ringtone he had always assigned her.

```
Hi, Phuc,
```

she wrote. (She was perhaps the only person in the world he would have permitted to continue to call him Jim or James, but she was positively pious in remembering never to do so.)

```
Something really bad. Will B with U 11. Be home.
OK? Good friend driving me now. Hope that's OK.
Love as ever. C. x.
```

The Saturday breakfast table scene was just as chaotic and noisy and rushed as its weekday equivalent, just fractionally later in the morning. Fern was brokering a treaty between Tom and Flynn over who had the last of the orange juice but saw Phuc read the text and sensed in that way she had that something was up.

'Carrie's coming over,' he said, careful to add nothing that would prompt too many questions from the boys.

'Who's Carrie?' asked the youngest.

'Phuc's sister,' Fern told him. 'Great,' she added. 'When?'

'Elevenish.'

She tapped open the timetable on her mobile. 'That's fine,' she said almost at once. 'If you can take Thomas to drama club, I can do the pool run, then we both have a window until about one.'

'Fine,' he told her. 'Good.' But he had to leave the table. 'Phuc?'

'It's fine,' he told her. He took his tea, he only drank white tea these days – fresh, delicious and totally unexciting – and wandered out to the hall, sipping absently, then swiftly shut himself in the downstairs loo to think.

He was confronted by the hugely enlarged framed print Fern had made of a photograph of him. It was taken on a demonstration when the Archbishop of Canterbury had visited Exeter. Phuc looked impossibly young in it, although it was only a few years old, and was grinning at something off camera. His tight black tee-shirt displayed a bold version of the anti-litter logo with a crucifix upside down in a rubbish bin and he held a placard that read: *If Jesus comes again, kill him properly!* For whatever reason, the picture had been adopted spectacularly on Facebook for a while and ended up in *The Guardian* where Barnaby and Dot had seen it and been predictably upset, although not upset enough to contact him and tell him so. He had heard the details from Carrie.

There were rapid steps in the hall. 'OK! We're off!' Fern called out.

'OK!' he called back.

'Tom's drama's at ten and Flynn needs to be at the station car park for nine-thirty.'

'OK! See you!'

He was not in love with Fern, nothing so destabilizing, but he liked her immensely and trusted her and she knew he was reliable in all the ways his predecessors hadn't been. And, quite unpredictably, they were a good fit in bed, which helped. She was so busy and capable, so overworked, so bruised by her emotional history that he could not quite believe she had taken him on and, three years since moving in with her, still felt he must be on probation.

His predecessors, the boys' fathers, she presented as hollow reeds when the boys weren't in earshot, and flattered him by comparison but he couldn't help suspecting that, in some way, he conformed to the same type and fulfilled a need in her to rescue and rehabilitate hopeless cases.

He was no longer a total wreck when they met. He had been clean for over a year. He had stuck with Narcotics Anonymous and somehow got himself back into the university to attain a practical qualification, as a social worker this time rather than aiming for anything so dangerously nebulous as completing his philosophy degree. They met when he was assigned to her unit for his work experience. She had been going through a messy divorce from partner number two and Phuc became a shoulder to cry on. She returned the favour by writing him a glowing report and nudging him to harness his demons, and draw on his now considerable experience as an NA sponsor, by becoming one of the city's drugs counsellors. He was assigned to a rehab clinic but also regularly visited schools to scare children witless, which was easy, and to persuade teenagers there was nothing remotely glamorous about drug addiction, which was well-nigh impossible.

So this was his new life, the rest of his life, he hoped. No longer the screwed-up adopted son of a Cornish vicar but a cool Vietnamese-American with sons of his own – *in-a-way sons*, he and Fern called them – whose affection and approval were coming to matter almost more to him than their mother's.

Carrie was the only link he maintained with his old life, and *maintained* implied more effort than he expended. His love for her was as uncomplicated as breath but expressing it, actually meeting her, was made hard by the weirdness of her still living with Dot and Barnaby. When he tried sharing this with his NA group, responding to a speaker whose talk on making amends to families had touched on conflict with his unaddicted siblings, a bunch of them took him aside afterwards and told him his whole understanding of parenthood was damaged by the knowledge that his own mother had rejected him as a baby. 'That's why you had to make your adoptive mother reject you too,' one particularly irritating newcomer had said. But of course neither Dot nor Barnaby had ever rejected him. That was what was so hard to bear. The more Barnaby forgave him, the worse Phuc felt – until he simply had to make contact impossible.

He had not seen either of them for eight years. He had returned from his gap year trip to Vietnam with a Speed habit as well as a Vietnamese name and a directionless rage at the disconnect between where he came from and where he had grown up. But when he behaved like a little shit when he returned to Pendeen that Christmas, still they forgave him, Barnaby writing a considered letter about Phuc's childhood and actually asking Phuc to forgive any mistakes they had made and enclosing a maintenance cheque he knew they could ill afford.

He didn't go home for Easter, having the excuse of two holiday jobs, in a supermarket and a nightclub, badly needed to fund what was by now an ounce-a-week amphetamine habit. His debts spiralled. He was expelled from his hall of residence for repeatedly starting a fire in a wastepaper basket because he enjoyed the excitement of triggering the alarms and getting everyone out of bed and angry. He attended fewer and fewer philosophy lectures and his mood swings, paranoia and relentless cadging alienated all but his drug friends, who of course were anything but friendly when judged in normal terms. Then he failed his first-year exams and celebrated the news by shooting up crystal he had scored behind the nightclub dump bins in exchange for sexual favours he elected to forget.

The rush it gave him was like a rocket take-off after the fairground ride of Speed. It felt as though immortality were spreading through his veins, transforming him. For a few exhilarating minutes he became the sexiest, cleverest, happiest person he knew. Nothing could touch him. He could have anyone he wanted. Nobody mattered. He could kill. He was God.

Luckily for him, it was a Friday night so there were police everywere.

Dot came to the rescue through some characteristically convoluted Cornish Whispers – the daughter of a second cousin's husband's schoolfriend Betty … She appeared at his hospital bedside with bananas, which she remembered were one of his more innocent weaknesses. She asked no questions, passed no audible judgement, simply hugged him, loaded him into the terrible old car and drove him the two-and-a-half-hour journey back to the only cure she knew: home and family.

He stayed a week, barely speaking, regained his strength, stole from her purse to buy insanely strong skunk from an old classmate's hippie mother in St Just, defaced the walls of Morvah church, which he knew was Barnaby's favourite, then hitched back to his Exeter squat, having first broken into the hippie mother's greenhouse to steal the rest of her skunk to dry in the microwave and trade for the white powder he was craving.

He never heard from them again but was fairly sure it was not because they hadn't tried. He made sure they had no address or number for him. Arrested for burglary, he was sentenced to community service and rehab treatment, which stabilized him and in turn led him to Narcotics Anonymous. NA had weaker religious overtones than its alcoholic equivalent, but he was drily amused to hear that both organizations tended to have their best success rate among people with a strong churchgoing background. He was a sponsee and did sponsoring in his turn, passing on the stern blessing, and he made friends, good friends, who understood him as the non-addicted never could. He retained a thin layer of ice, an ironic distance from them all, from their surrogate piety. And he lied to the group about having apologized to everyone he had hurt while using. He wrote it all down in a letter home but never sent it.

Carrie eventually reached him through Facebook and winkled a mobile number and an e-mail address from him in exchange for a solemn promise never to pass them on. When he finally dared to mention the graffiti incident she said that the matter had never been discussed since, or not in her presence. This he found frankly terrifying.

He had apologized to her in one of his e-mails, not least for having effectively turned her back into an only child, with all the burden of responsibility that implied, but he could not apologize to their parents. He was coming to realize that this was partly because he could not have been sincere since he remained angry with them. Only that anger was distanced from him now, muffled, like a wasp in a jam jar, by his reinvention of himself.

Twice now he and Carrie had tried to meet, first at her instigation, then at his, agreeing on Truro as a safely neutral midway point. However on both occasions he had taken fright at the last minute. The first time he had not even gone, convinced as he was she would bring Barnaby and Dot along, whatever her assurances to the contrary, because she loved them all so wanted them to love each other. The second time he had gone but then just watched from a safe vantage point in a surf shop across the way, like a coward on a blind date, as she waited trustingly on the steps of the Royal Cornwall Museum. He watched her send him a text, of course, saying *Where RU?* Then she waited a few more minutes, scowling this way and that behind her sunglasses before she rang him. And he pressed Ignore, bought over-priced shirts for all four boys in a compensatory flurry, then started to cry and was brought a chair and a glass of water by a kind sales assistant.

He couldn't hide this morning, though, because he had foolishly let Fern know about it and Fern would be thrilled finally to meet the mysteriously influential sister hot on the heels of the fuss over the suicide and inquest. Carrie had not tried ringing him since the second time he stood her up. He knew she'd be angry about it but also accepting and that her withdrawal and ignoring his subsequent *sorry* text was her way of showing that anger.

'Phuc? We're going to be late,' one of the boys called.

'Shit. Sorry,' he shouted back. 'Miles away.'

He drove Flynn to the St David's station car park, where one of the ominously named Football Dads was waiting by his already laden people-mover. Phuc was only an in-a-way dad and was never going to be a football one. Flynn was nominally obsessed with the game, dutifully supporting Exeter City, wearing their red and black strip to bed and sticking monotonously posed pictures of its star players on his walls where they grinned over his slumber, so many carefully groomed, unreliable saints. But he only ever seemed apprehensive on these Saturday mornings when he actually played, and grew breathless with fear if any of the household suggested coming to watch from the touchlines.

Then Phuc drove Thomas on to the disused Methodist chapel that was home to his no less competitive drama club. The oldest and brightest of the boys, he had landed a scholarship to the cathedral choir school when he was little and had not adjusted well to the shock of life in a big, co-ed comprehensive afterwards, seemingly painfully shy. Like the other parents involved, Fern had thought the drama club was a handy way of inculcating confidence while fostering regular healthy contact with the opposite sex, including plenty of useful relationship role play. It seemed to Phuc that Thomas made friends with all the girls all too easily, constantly analysing and recalibrating each friendship as they did, while remaining wary or self-protectively scornful of boys whose friendship he really craved. Surprisingly in someone for whom liberalism was effectively a professional qualification, Fern had yet to notice her eldest was probably gay and Phuc was not going to be the one to point it out for her.

As if to maintain the fiction that the club was genuinely about drama rather than sex education, an exhausting three shows a year were put on, which, unlike Flynn's football, nobody was allowed to miss. Poor Thomas bought into the fiction entirely and was a passionate believer in his talent. He despised their coach's taste for rock-based musicals and had been lobbying for several weeks, raising consciousness among the ranks with the acuity of a born politician, for a production of *West Side Story* or *Merrily We Roll Along*.

As he drove the short distance across town, Phuc talked with both boys, parrying their teasing about his choice of music, defending each from the other's habitually barbed comments, grateful for the slightly manic opportunity their company briefly gave him to avoid thinking about his other family. But then he handed Thomas over to his troop of possessive girlfriends outside the drama club and he was left alone with his thoughts.

He could not get over his stupid impulse to look at Carrie's text in front of Fern. Had he kept quiet he could either have made excuses and hidden yet again or at least kept the meeting private. Now Fern knew she would make it happen, if not turn the whole thing into a big production. And she would be sure to analyse it exhaustively afterwards.

She had been hungry for every detail of the Lenny Barnes assisted suicide drama, and could not understand either why Phuc didn't take the excuse to visit his parents or how he and Carrie could bear to do all their communicating about it by texts, not even by e-mail.

'I prefer texts,' he told her. 'Texts keep things nice and cool. If we e-mailed I'd start ranting and if we talked she might cry or I might and we'd both get upset.'

'And we can't have that, can we? What is it with your family?'

'Carrie's like me.'

'Scared of feelings, you mean?'

'Just … Just calm. She's steady. Not dramatic. She's getting enough drama dealing with her dad. She doesn't need any from me too.'

But of course he had been far more concerned and involved than he let on. Carrie's initial text had vibrated into his pocket during a consultation with a particularly paranoid homeless man and his social worker. Phuc broke all his rules and glanced at it while the social worker was looking something up in the client's voluminous file. It read simply,

Dad just helped young parishioner top himself. I think. Just back from police station. Later. Cx

Phuc was then unable to concentrate for the rest of the session. He began to ring her as soon as he was free then opted for text in case she was with Barnaby when she answered and obliged father and son to talk.

The story hit the local headlines and television news that night and was picked up nationally the day after that. Nobody, not even Fern, knew he was in any way linked to the story and he was tempted to leave it that way. He didn't, of course, and then had to work hard to buy her silence on the matter with full and frank disclosure and regular updates.

He remembered the dead boy's rather sexy mother only vaguely. Pottery did not interest him. What he chiefly remembered was her being Australian. Foreigners who chose to live in the parish were unusual and he was naturally attuned to their presence, even the white ones, unconsciously collecting evidence that he wasn't the only one. She looked a bit like Julie Christie with sun damage. He certainly didn't remember the boy's accident, as it had happened long after he left home, but he knew exactly the sort of warm-hearted fuss it would have caused in the local press. *Local rugby hopeful in sporting tragedy.* The sort of coverage that equated paralysis with death, which could not have helped the boy's psychological rehabilitation one bit. Sure enough, just as he could have predicted, that sentimentality had fuelled coverage of the boy's suicide and Barnaby's part in it, and turned rapidly toxic.

It was so entirely like Barnaby not to defend himself independently but to trust in honesty and the law to do it for him. It would have been a comfort to take refuge in cynicism, to assume that he relished the unexpected opportunity for a kind of martyrdom. But Phuc knew that was not how it was, that Barnaby's impulses might have been misguided but that they stemmed entirely from the good.

And now Barnaby was rewarded with a kind of celebrity on Facebook. The spectacle of the unimportant Cornish parish priest quietly but firmly defending the power of prayer and the existence of immortal souls had struck a chord. Christians with small and large Cs and even increasing numbers of interested Muslims, enshrined his short speech at the inquest on their Facebook pages, usually with the photograph of Barnaby emerging blinking into the sunlight outside St John's Hall and hundreds, then thousands of cyber friends had clicked on the Like button or copied the speech in turn and illustrated it with doves, flowers, crude crucifixes or garish sunsets. *I do know I can pray for a dying man's eternal soul and I am confident that prayer will offer comfort to the dying and be heard with kindness by God.* It was probably already being made into laminated bookmarks and extra-large tee-shirts for selling at church bookstalls and Faith Fayres.

Equally characteristic had been Barnaby's refusal to pander to the attention, to accept invitations onto the *Today* programme or *Question Time* or to grant a single interview. Phuc saw a *Times* piece in which a journalist, visiting on the assumption that he could persuade the reluctant celebrity to talk, had wrung so little out of him he had printed the quote in full. *The Reverend Johnson would say only, 'Our community has lost a much loved and valued young man in terrible circumstances. Please respect its need to grieve and leave us in peace.'* Obliged to dig, they had unearthed nothing, not even a rumour of Phuc's estrangement; whatever the local feelings against assisted suicide might be, they were stronger against outsiders attempting to rake muck. The internet conversation continued but the local fuss had abated as swiftly as Barnaby surely knew it would. No doubt the Evangelicals who briefly invaded the parish had found their instant hero's sermons too modest and old-fashioned, his services too High, his churches insufficiently modern.

Phuc wilfully took the busiest route home, playing for time, and stopped off to do recycling, collect the day's newspaper and buy petrol. Saturday morning was the worst time to leave his home parking space abandoned so he then had to drive around the block a couple of times before chancing on a neighbour who was just leaving for the weekend. He could simply stay there, he thought childishly, hunched down in his seat. Carrie and her friend would come, meet Fern, satisfy curiosity on either side and then go. He need play no part.

Then he saw Carrie's reflection in one of his side mirrors as she came along the pavement. She seemed transformed somehow. Her look was no less boyish, her hair no longer, her face still unmade up. Perhaps it was just that she was in summery clothes, rather than the sawdusty work things in which he habitually pictured her. In his mental image of her she was either driving her van or holding her vast tool box or carrying a plank. Doing none of these, being completely unencumbered, would normally have left her shy and exposed-looking but she seemed uncharacteristically relaxed and happy in her skin. She was wearing new sunglasses, he noticed, old-style ones in a yellowish tortoiseshell that might have been their granny's. She laughed. Carrie hardly ever laughed. Then suddenly she was out of view, then she was crossing the street to Fern's house, their house, and he could see the very striking friend who was with her. It was nobody he knew. She was tall, honey-haired and in a simple summer dress the colour of tinned mandarins.

He hadn't forgotten she was bringing a friend along but he had imagined it would be one of her lame ducks, some hypochondriac whose particular need lent her a sense of purpose or some wan divorcee who, with the unconscious meanness of the survivor, had chosen Carrie as someone who was no threat and would make them feel better about themselves.

He watched as Carrie double-checked the house number on her mobile, then rang the bell and was let in by Fern with an audible hello. Fern glanced up and down the street with a little grimace before closing the door again. He sat on, aware his heart was racing, counting his breaths to centre himself as he had been taught. His mobile chirruped. It was a text from Carrie:

So we're here - where TFRU?

Hiding, he typed in then pressed discard and opened the door of the car. As he let himself into the house, he could hear laughter – including the louder, higher laugh Fern produced when she was meeting strangers.

They were in the kitchen. Carrie came straight over and gave him a bear hug.

'I've missed you,' she murmured in his ear. She held on fractionally longer than felt comfortable, then he remembered to hug her back, which seemed to relax her, and she released him.

'You've met Fern, then?' he said.

'Of course,' Fern said. 'At long bloody last!' She had put the kettle on but was in the process of uncorking a bottle of white wine. He spotted several bags from the delicatessen she sometimes visited when there was something to celebrate or they could be sure none of the boys would be around to wolf the food or reject it half-eaten.

'And this is Morwenna,' Carrie said.

'Hi,' Phuc said, shaking the bony hand she offered him. With the sharpened instincts of a recovering addict, he thought he recognized a fellow troubled soul; not a lame duck, perhaps, but a troubled one. 'I'm Phuc.'

'I like your name,' she said. 'It means Lucky, doesn't it?'

'How'd you know?'

'I worked alongside a Vietnamese boy in Toronto. He taught me to pronounce it like foot with a silent p instead of a t. You know? As opposed to rhyming it with luck.'

'Yeah. Right.'

'Morwenna means sea virgin. Wishful thinking, I reckon.' She grinned at Carrie.

'Just like Phuc, then.' They all laughed. 'My whole name means *lucky-sea-unicorn*. But the circumstances were pretty desperate.'

'Your surname means unicorn?'

'Uh-huh. It's not really my surname. My mother gave birth to me on a boat then gave me up so I never had a formal naming ceremony. In fact I think the three names I got were probably just given me and written on a card by whichever old ladies in the boat helped with the birth. They feel sort of thrown together and unplanned.' He became aware of Fern's eyes on him. 'Sorry,' he said. 'I'm doing that thing, aren't I? Fern says I have no small talk.'

'You don't,' Carrie said. 'He doesn't,' she agreed with Fern. 'Neither do I. I think our parents thought it was pointless, like learning to play cards or drinking for pleasure.'

'Talking of which.' Fern handed the women a glass of wine and Phuc a glass of pomegranate juice then shook out a bag of the fancy crisps they never had if the boys were around.

'You're looking really well,' he told Carrie.

'You too,' she said, studying him.

'So how long have you two been together?' Fern asked.

'Oh we're not …' Carrie began.

'Actually. We sort of …' Morwenna said over her.

So Phuc saw at once that they were together but were only just beginning to realize it.

'Me and my big mouth,' Fern said. 'They don't do small talk, but I don't do tact. Rescue me by letting me show you the garden?' she asked Morwenna, tactfully if not subtly. 'I'm only in my second year of growing veggies and I feel I have to show everybody.'

'I'd love to see your garden,' Morwenna told her and took her easily by the arm as they walked out through the back door.

'About time,' he said. 'Carrie, she's fucking beautiful.'

'It isn't …' Carrie fiddled with the catch on the table drawer beside her in just the same way Flynn did when he was asking for a favour they were highly unlikely to grant. 'I'm not sure it's even a thing yet. I'm not sure what it is …'

'Is she Canadian?'

'She's from Penzance but she's lived all over and she picks accents up like a sponge apparently. Jim, Morwenna left us because I've got some really tough news.'

'It's Dad, isn't it?'

Her unexpected using of his boyhood name had tripped him into forgetting to say Barnaby. He thought of the unimaginable stress Barnaby must have been under recently, the shock for such a modest man of suddenly having all that aggressive attention focused on him.

'No,' she said. 'Dad's fine. Well, he's not, of course, but …' She fixed him with her level gaze and laid a hand on

PATRICK GALE

his forearm. Her touch was work-roughened as ever. He looked down at the familiar scar across her hand's back where a chisel had slipped when she was still learning her trade, and at her grandmother's engagement ring, which, like her watch, she always wore turned cautiously inward. 'It's Mum,' she said. 'It was completely unexpected and very quick. She had a heart attack.' Her voice wavered as she spoke and she had to stop to breathe before going on. 'It was just like her dad at just the same age.' A tense little laugh escaped her. 'She somehow managed to die in church, which probably gets her a fast track visa to heaven with no questions asked.'

'What? She died during a service?'

'No. I don't know why she was up there. Flowers, probably. Dad was in Truro, being talked to by the archdeacon and I was out on a … on a job for Morwenna's dad, actually. And the first either of us knew was a call from Brid Williams.'

'But she wasn't ill or anything, was she?'

'Well everyone assumed she was as strong as an ox, didn't they? I don't remember her ever taking to her bed even with flu. The most she did was take an early night. But no she was never ill. I think illness embarrassed her, as if she thought it was attention-seeking. Dr Murray says she might have had an underlying weakness, something from a childhood illness – that can happen sometimes apparently – or just a genetic flaw.'

Phuc pictured Dot, her broad, kind face, her strong arms streaked with grass stains and oil as she serviced the rectory lawn mower on an old dining table in one of the barns. He remembered the efficient brutality with which she drowned

353

a trap full of rats in a water butt and her delicacy of touch in lifting a doily off a sponge cake to leave a pattern of icing sugar behind. 'I can't believe it,' he said. He got up to turn off a tap Fern had left dripping. 'She wasn't so old, was she?'

'Only sixty.' Carrie shook out a checked handkerchief and blew her nose. Tears had sprung to her eyes but she rubbed them briskly away. 'It wouldn't have felt right just ringing you.'

'No. Of course it wouldn't. Thanks for that.'

'Aren't you even slightly upset?'

'I don't know,' he told her honestly. 'I think when you said you were coming, part of me thought *Carrie's coming to tell me she has cancer*. I wasn't thinking about Dot at all. I expect it'll hit me later. Can you stay for a bite of early lunch? Fern seems to have bought goodies.'

'Yes please. It's a long drive home again and …'

'Did I miss the funeral?'

'No. Bad luck. It's on Thursday at three.'

'Which church?'

'Pendeen. So she can be buried with Granny.'

'Oh. That's nice.'

'Phuc, where's the loo?'

He showed her, remembering too late the blow-up of the silly picture of him in there, and wondered if it would annoy her.

'I love that picture,' she called through the closed door, so he guessed it probably had. She had almost certainly gone in there for a quick, medicinal cry. Even as a teenager, his earliest detailed memories of her, she had hated showing emotion in public. People thought she was cool. Some chil-

dren at school had even assumed she was autistic. But she
was just as emotionally engaged as anyone, she simply
preferred to keep her feelings private and as reassuringly
compartmentalized as the meticulously size-sorted screws
in the trays of her tool box.

When she returned to his side just as the others came
back from their kindly slow stroll around the garden, he
felt a great swell of love for her that caught in his throat
and made him want to hug her as she had hugged him
earlier, but it was Fern who took him in her arms, evidently
told the news by Morwenna. He was glad of the comfort.
The thought of Dot slumped in a corner of the church had
brought upon him the kind of desolation and insecurity
that would not so long ago have had him scrabbling for a
syringe.

But then the four of them were suddenly sitting down to
an impromptu picnic. The women didn't drink much
because at least two of them were having to drive again
that afternoon, but a kind of desperate hilarity came over
Phuc and the three of them as they chatted and ate that felt
almost like drunkenness. It was deeply strange, he thought.
He knew Carrie was feeling as fragile as he was – their
mother, the nearest person he had to a mother, was dead
– and yet they seemed unable to resist this happiness that
had stolen in amongst them and would not be denied.
None of it had anything to do with Dot's death, which they
had all set aside as a grim thing to be dealt with later. It was
born partly from the uncomplicated pleasure of a reunion
and from the giddy sense of his two lives being allowed to
flow into each other, partly from the faint hysteria induced
by their realization that all too soon they had to re-enter

the usual Saturday routine of fetching and ferrying the boys. But mainly, he felt, it was coming from the understanding begun with Fern's blundering assumption earlier, that Carrie and Morwenna were falling in love.

And then suddenly Fern was setting coffee cups among them and glancing over their heads at the big kitchen clock.

'I hate to break up something beautiful,' she said, 'when I feel we're only just beginning, but it's a Saturday so our lives and cars are not our own.'

'That's fine,' Carrie said, glancing at her watch. 'We're going to visit the cathedral before we head home.'

'But stay,' Fern said as it occurred to her. 'There's no reason, just because we've got to go, you shouldn't …' And her suggestion died off incomplete, possibly because she realized she sounded as though she were offering them a bed and not for sleeping. 'Oh Christ. I'm doing it again, aren't I?'

'No you're not,' Morwenna said, colouring. 'But we shouldn't really linger.'

'I should get back to Dad,' Carrie added.

'Oh. Of course,' Fern said. 'Sorry.'

'And Morwenna doesn't like to leave her dad for too long.'

'Are you a churchgoer too, then?' Phuc asked Morwenna.

'No,' she said. 'I'm a Quaker. And not a very regular one. But I'm not averse to a spot of soul-tourism.'

'You must be close to your father, though, taking such care of him.'

She shrugged and for the first time looked him full in the face. Her eyes were not green, as he had first supposed, but tawny. Hers was a face one instinctively trusted, wanted to confide in. And kiss. 'My brothers both moved far away while he was still independent and I just happened to move back to Penzance in time for his decline. I suppose we are close but, well … I had a problematic youth. There are a lot of things about me he doesn't know. You mustn't worry if you've drifted apart from yours, you know. It's perfectly possible to drift right back again and these things can't be forced.'

'You think?'

'I know,' she said, 'trust me,' and gave him a quick little kiss on the cheek as she stood. 'Carrie, we should be off, I reckon.'

They all left at once, Fern in an especial rush.

'I told Dad that I'd tell you when the funeral was,' Carrie told him, 'but not to assume you'd be there.'

'Thanks,' he said.

'Do you think …?'

'I'll try,' he told her.

Once again he sat in his car watching the two of them walk along the road then he remembered the time and set off. They waved merrily as they saw him passing them. Whatever the nature of their friendship, however far it had advanced, they made a natural pair, even if, or possibly because, Morwenna made Carrie look more than ever like a bloke. He wondered if the little lunch party had been as transformative for them as he expected, one of those occasions where a new couple sees itself for the first time reflected in the welcome of others.

*　　*　　*

All that evening he sensed Fern was keeping a wary eye on him, ready to take action when his grief finally broke through the surface of his composure. But it didn't break. He was waiting for it too, as he remembered waiting when he had taken an unfamiliar drug and was watching, with a mixture of excitement and terror, for its effects and potency to make themselves known. In this odd state of suspense, he found himself freshly appreciative of the four boys, their profound differences of character already so deeply imprinted and their easy acceptance of the domestic stability their lives presented.

For the first time he realized that, if Fern were to die, he had no claim whatsoever on his in-a-way sons and that he would miss them when they were taken from him, for all the formerly private hours they thoughtlessly annexed. Rather than grieving for his mother's death, he found he was worrying about the death of theirs, worrying about her will and fretting because he didn't know how to raise the subject and was afraid she would take it amiss if he did, as a reflection of the age difference between them, of which she was so conscious.

The next day included his weekly NA meeting. Twice a month they had a guest speaker – a fellow recovering addict – and only a limited time for responses. In between they either had a step meeting, where members shared their progress through the twelve steps and helped one another forward, or a discussion meeting, like this one. He rarely felt the need to contribute much at these now.

Members broadly fell into three categories – the nervous newcomers feeling their way, the members who had been clean for two or three years, now high on confidence and their smug sense of achievement and all too keen to become sponsors and pass on their knowledge, and relative old-timers, such as Phuc, content to let others monopolise the airtime. Though broadly a discussion around a given topic, the meeting gave useful space for safe, anonymous avowal.

In practice, Phuc and several of the long-time sponsors now benefited more from their frank conversation over coffee and cigarettes on the fire escape afterwards and he found he resented it when one of the smug loudmouths tried to hang around too. At these informal, after-meeting meetings, any comfort offered tended to be of the glib, Big Book variety. In the spirit of tough love, the friends often said terrible, shattering things to those they knew best – usually at least partly true – yet still they parted on friendly terms and came back for more.

The week's topic was an old favourite, bottomless one: Family. As he took the steps down to the former crypt where the group held its meetings, he wondered if he would talk about the shock of Dot's death and the tide of memories it was stirring up and how tempted he was to avoid her funeral because it was looming over the week like the worst-ever dental appointment. Instead he held back from speaking, glad for once of the loudmouths. But then, five minutes before the end, one of his tough-love mates drew him in saying, 'Phuc? You've got a sister, haven't you?' and Phuc found himself talking.

He said nothing about Dot but told them instead about seeing Carrie again. He spoke of how he loved her more than either adoptive parent and didn't fully understand why he had been avoiding her and why he was still reluctant to see her again too soon. 'She had nothing to do with my drug-taking,' he said. 'I never lied to her. I never stole from her and she's never said a word in judgement about the things I did.'

'Yes, but how does she make you feel?' a sharp-eyed woman asked, who just ten minutes ago had been telling them how she used to drug her baby sister to keep her quiet while she shot up. 'About yourself, I mean?'

'Dirty,' he replied, without a moment to consider. 'Worthless.'

The woman nodded and several of the others did like-wise and he felt tricked into having given them such satisfaction.

On Thursday he set out late from Exeter because of a sudden, stupid indecision about what to wear. He settled on a coloured, open-necked shirt and chinos, then changed his mind in favour of a dark suit, then realized he needed to buy one and then was left hurrying to ever less promising shops in search of a tie that was black but didn't make him look as if he was in school uniform. The drive from Exeter to Launceston took less than an hour but he then had to cover the complete length of Cornwall and, at each of the sections of the A30 where the dual carriageway gave out, he found himself stuck in a queue behind a tractor with a heavily laden trailer. By the time he was edging towards the last little stretch of the dual carriageway between Varfell and Penzance, he knew he had missed the start of the service.

It was a comfortless, unsummery day, intermittently showery and with a nasty north-easterly blowing. *Pendeen weather*, he thought harshly, *weather for weeding out the proper Cornish from the incomers and tourists.* He was half-minded to turn back, confident that no one would blame him, at least not to his face. It was not Carrie that made him press on in the end, up to the Mount Misery roundabout and then up the narrow road through Newbridge towards St Just, with the ordinarily glorious view of Mount's Bay opening out behind him. As a van pulled over to let him pass on the dramatic lane that forked off towards Pendeen from above St Just, he wished he weren't in the brand-new suit and mourning tie after all. It marked him out, he felt, as a man late for a funeral. Worse, in so under-populated an area it probably marked him out as Dot's son late for his own mother's funeral.

It all looked completely unaltered, the inexcusably hideous bungalows facing the attractive granite terrace, the entrance, ever hopeful, to the museum where there had still been a working mine when he was a baby. The two pubs and then, all too soon, the easily missed turning up to the Sunday School and church.

The service was extremely well attended. It shouldn't have surprised him. Dot was of old Pendeen stock and popular in her unassuming way. He parked near the mouth of the church lane behind the other late arrivals. As he walked up he was uncomfortably aware of two undertakers watching him from near the hearse. One of them nodded respectfully and handed him an order of service.

'It's nearly over, I'm afraid, sir,' he said.

Phuc went no further than the porch. There was a crowd of people standing just inside, most of them in bandsmen's uniforms. One of them glanced over his shoulder, saw Phuc, and made to open the door and make way for him but then his neighbour nudged him and he raised his cornet and joined in playing the introduction to the final hymn, which was 'The Day Thou Gavest, Lord, Is Ended'.

Phuc panicked, and backed away. Ignoring the undertakers this time, letting them think what they like, he hurried back to his car and waited in there. Humidity from his drizzled-on suit and the numerous showers he had driven through now rapidly steamed it up, which suited him fine. He sat low in his seat and watched through a spyhole he wiped on the glass as the band grew louder, still playing the hymn, and the cortège led by Tabby Morris, who carried a small black umbrella to shelter her prayer book, wound up into the corner of the churchyard where the woman he couldn't help but think of as Granny had been buried.

The burial service was over surprisingly quickly, perhaps an abbreviated version had been opted for in view of the weather. As it began to drizzle again in earnest, mourners filed away down the lane beside him. Some on foot, most in cars. He slumped low in his seat until the last had passed, followed by the empty hearse. There would be a gathering back at the house. Carrie would have found relief in putting on kettles and slicing donated cakes. Old friends would be rallying round, kindly trying to elbow her out of the one occupation that would help her maintain her equilibrium. And Morwenna? Being new, Morwenna probably felt an intruder on the scene and would be keeping well back, chatting animatedly to some misfit or another spare spouse to make them feel less awkward, or carrying around trays as Phuc had learnt to do as a boy, to avoid having to make more than desultory conversation.

And Barnaby? Phuc could not or would not imagine him. It was too hard. He had a feeling that Barnaby, who could normally be relied upon to stay buoyant, if only to make life easier for others, would be poleaxed by grief, frighteningly incapable even of greeting people.

Phuc let himself out of the car and walked back up towards the churchyard entrance. The sexton had only just finished his work and was walking away from the grave with his shovel over one shoulder like a musket. He was whistling 'The Day Thou Gavest' but stopped when he saw Phuc.

'Hello,' Phuc said but the sexton had evidently forgotten his name or didn't recognize him at all and simply muttered a greeting under his breath.

The drizzle stopped again. Phuc laid his flowers alongside the others on the stony earth, whose smell, close to, was almost overpowering. Granny's headstone said nothing about Dot yet. That would come, presumably. There was plenty of room, room enough for Barnaby too. He reached out to rest a hand on the stone. He had nothing to say, no prayer, no form of words, but he remembered the two women together in the kitchen, the room broiling because the oven was going full pelt, and there was laundry on the overhead drier. They were chuckling at something and encouraging Phuc and Carrie to have a go at stirring the Christmas cake mixture in the enormous mixing bowl that only came out for major tasks. Jim, rather; Phuc had no place in that scene.

He turned away and was heading into the church, thinking he might simply sit there for a while to think, when someone shouted his name. It was Barnaby. He was clutching his bicycle and breathless.

'Dad,' he said automatically.

'Sorry,' Barnaby panted. 'Bit breathless. I thought you hadn't come.'

'Well … I didn't really. Dad, I'm so sorry.'

'But Carrie's new friend, Morwenna, said she'd seen your car parked on the lane so I dropped everything and …'

'You shouldn't have.'

'Don't be silly. Can … could we go back up and have another look? I was a bit misted up earlier, what with the band.'

'Sure.'

Barnaby leaned his bike against the church wall and they walked back up to the graveside. 'Are you quite … still quite well?' he asked.

'Yes. Yes, I think I am. I've been clean for five years next week.'

'That's brilliant,' Barnaby said and Phuc suspected he had no idea what *clean* meant. 'Carrie said they'd been to see you.'

'Yes.'

'And she said how nice your … Fern is.'

Phuc smiled. 'Good. Fern liked her back. And Morwenna.'

They reached the grave and their pitiful conversation petered out. Barnaby crouched. Phuc had almost forgotten how tall and thin he was. He'd always thought he looked like a giraffe next to Dot; tall and benign and never entirely focused on matters at ground level. Phuc thought he was crouching to read the notes on the flowers people had left but then he thrust one of his hands deep into the soil and

364

pressed down hard with a shoe on the spot where his hand had been.

'Her wedding ring,' he mumbled, staring down at the mess as though it were not of his own making. 'Some ninny at the undertaker's had taken it off. She'd have wanted to be buried in it.'

'Have you put it in deep enough? Someone might find it and steal it.'

'Doesn't matter,' Barnaby said and blew his nose, getting earth on his handkerchief. 'Symbolic.'

'Oh. Yes. I'm afraid there's no card with my flowers as I bought them on the way and they're just sort of plonked down.'

'She'd have liked yours best. She liked orange.'

'No she didn't. Stop being kind.'

'I'm so glad you came, Phuc. She loved you so much, you know.'

'No she didn't. You loved me. Mum never quite managed it. She tried but ...'

'She was very proud of you doing so well at school.'

'And afterwards?'

'Afterwards you were ill. She rather blamed herself. Because of her not ... of you not being close.'

'I should have talked to her. I was a coward. Still am.'

'You came, though.'

'Yeah, well. You should get back. Carrie'll be worrying.'

'You're coming back too.'

'Not this time, Dad. Soon, though.'

'That would be good. Bring Fern.'

They walked over to the bike. Phuc got there first and wheeled it for him as far as his car. Holding the battered handlebars gripped by Barnaby every day felt like a way of touching him.

'She has children, doesn't she?'

'Yes. Four. If I ever married her, you'd have four step-grandsons overnight.'

'Wow!' Barnaby said and his forced enthusiasm struck Phuc as the saddest thing all afternoon.

He groped for something to say. 'The band was a nice touch.'

'It was specified in her will. *Pendeen Silver Band to play all hymns.* She'd even set aside a bit of beer money for them. They were delighted to be asked, I think. She also said you were to have this.'

In his still slightly earthy fingers he handed Phuc a ring.

'But shouldn't Carrie have it?'

'She has her granny's and I think she's pretty embarrassed at having to wear even that, don't you think? Take it. You can keep it or sell it or give it to Fern. It's only stuff, after all. It's symbolic.'

'It's beautiful. What's the blue stone?'

'A sapphire. And the smaller stones are diamonds. It was my mother's and her mother-in-law's before that so it's only right it should come to you.'

'Was it … was it a Palmer ring, then?'

'Probably. It's about 1810, I think. Pretty.'

Phuc turned the icy thing in his hand, marvelling that Dot should have worn it day after day yet it should be so completely unfamiliar. He put it on his own hand for safekeeping. Dot's ring finger was thicker than his and he had to move the ring to his index finger to hold it even slightly in place. He caught Barnaby watching this and was drily amused that he would now be worrying that Phuc planned to wear it himself. 'It's just until I get it safely home,' he said.

'Of course,' Barnaby said. 'I didn't think you'd be ...' He broke off.

Rain was starting up again. Proper rain now. Looking instinctively towards the sea, from where bad weather had always seemed to arrive, Phuc saw a thick grey curtain of it coming towards them, hanging in rags. 'Go,' he said. 'Quickly or you'll get soaked.' By setting the bike back in Barnaby's grasp, he forestalled any embrace and simply patted him on the shoulder as he wobbled off.

He tuned the radio to Atlantic FM on the drive home, filling the car's small space with loud love songs, most of which were unfamiliar but had the desired effect of holding off thought beyond whatever was needed to drive. In fact it was as though he drove unconsciously. He travelled for over an hour with no sense whatever of waiting at turnings, negotiating roundabouts or overtaking, yet he must have done all three repeatedly. He had passed Bodmin and was crossing the moor between there and Launceston when he could no longer maintain control. He turned off the blaring radio and swerved in front of a honking lorry to enter a lay-by he had just spotted.

He cut the engine. In place of the rain there was now fog, thinning and thickening as a slack breeze stirred it. He stepped quickly out of the car, not bothering to lock it. The traffic was loud nearby. It was the afternoon rush hour or what passed for one out here, but there was no sense of the harsh immensity of moorland all about, not even a shadow of Brown Willy and Rough Tor, which he knew were only a mile or two away. There was no sense of being anywhere in particular; the empty, fogbound lay-by was a limbo. He walked away from his car to a wooden picnic table, placed for the view that was usually there, sat on it, his feet on its bench, heedless of the damp marks it was surely leaving on his new suit trousers. Giving in to grief was a little like waiting to be sick; the gulping anticipation was horrible but he knew relief would follow.

Only he wasn't grieving. Was he? Or not for Dot. He twisted her lovely, modest ring back and forth on his finger and, instead of receiving the hot balm of tears was merely racked by a few dry, spasmodic sobs. He swore loudly several times, shouting because there was no one to hear and the cars and lorries drowned out his voice. He stripped off the suit, standing by the car, careless of the wet on his socks, and folded it neatly back onto its hanger and into the carrier bag before getting back into the clothes in which he had indecisively left the house.

He drove in silence back to Exeter. The girl in the suit shop remembered him, responded to his flirting and didn't even check for stains or damage.

'You want to try another one instead?' she asked. 'Or get a refund?' It wasn't her business; she didn't care.

'Refund, please,' he said. 'It was an impulse buy and I shouldn't have.'

'That's fine. The card machine's down, though, so it'll have to be cash.'

'Ideal.' Armed with the cash, which felt like free money, of course, rather than merely credit, he walked decisively to an old haunt.

On the face of it the place was a perfectly attractive bar, somewhere young mothers went for lunch and barristers came after work, which was why his dealer had always favoured it. The clients were nice not desperate, the atmosphere was unsuspicious, there was no CCTV and the bouncer was only there on match days and weekends. She also had the perfect cover for paying little visits to every table in the place and stuffing cash into her apron: she worked there as a waitress.

She greeted him like a long-lost friend, even giving him a hug, which was rich given that she had done nothing more amicable over the years than feed his addiction, repeatedly bleed him dry of cash and occasionally seduce into addiction friends he took in there with him. 'Long time no see,' she said. Her name was Vivien. She was extremely pretty – model pretty. He had forgotten that detail. 'I hear you're a poacher turned gamekeeper these days.'

'Well, we all have our weaknesses. You're looking well, Viv.'

She was. One looked in vain at her pretty hair and smooth, lightly tanned skin for any gratifying sign of depravity. Life could surely have offered her so much more? Was that then what drove her; that this smooth surface, this getting away with it, was sufficient pleasure in itself? It was extraordinary. She really did look and sound like someone to whom one could cheerfully entrust small children for milk and cupcakes.

'Thanks, babe,' she said. 'You too. Sad, though. Something sad happen?'

'My mum died.'

'Oh babe, I'm so sorry!'

'It's fine. We ... Viv, could I just have a glass of house red?'

'Sure. Large?'

'Yeah.'

'And the usual?'

He would like to think he hesitated for minutes but it was no more than seconds. 'Sure,' he told her. 'Thanks.'

She slipped away towards the bar, touching shoulders, taking cash and empties and swiftly returned with a glass of wine and, as on nights without number in the years before Fern, a paper napkin carefully folded, which she tucked beneath the glass like a coaster as she set it down. The napkin would not be empty. 'This one's on the house,' she said, touching his shoulder and nodding at someone else who was gesturing for her. 'For your mum.'

He drank the unfamiliar wine indecently fast, in four or five greedy mouthfuls so that he scarcely tasted it, then snatched up the paper napkin and hurried to the gents. He needed the rush, the warmth, the glittering sense of invincible self-confidence. He had missed this! He had missed feeling so attractive and caring so little.

All the cubicles were occupied, though perhaps he only fancied the sniffing sounds coming from inside them. There was a discarded newspaper by the sinks. He had a pee for something to do, then picked up the paper because he felt uneasy and stupid just waiting. It wasn't the proper newspaper but the tabloid insert, the bit with the fluffy stories and the television listings.

As he flicked through, his eye was snagged by a photograph of a strange creature, a little like a gazelle, only thicker-necked, apparently tethered and wretched in a wooden enclosure. *ASIAN 'UNICORN' PHOTOGRAPHED FOR FIRST TIME IN OVER A DECADE,* he read. *For the first time in more than ten years, there has been a confirmed encounter with one of the rarest, most mysterious animals in the world, the saola of Laos and Vietnam.*

He looked again at the photograph, oblivious to men now leaving the cubicles to wash their hands. Even in colour the creature was a ghostly grey with delicate white markings on its face. The two horns rose straight up in a long V from its forehead. It lay unnaturally, with one leg bent out away from its body, a rope wound several times around its neck.

Unfortunately this male animal, weakened by the ordeal of several days in captivity, died shortly after the arrival of a team from the International Union for the Conservation of Nature, who took this photograph. The saola was found in a village's sacred forest in remote Xaychamphon District but it is not clear why the villagers took it into captivity.

Obviously it wasn't a unicorn – it had two horns – but the story had been explained to him on his visit to Vietnam as a teenager. He knew it was the likely inspiration for the myths of the Quilin or Lan, the unicorn whose rare appearances among men conferred heavenly grace. One was said to have appeared at the birth of Confucius. Inevitably another was rumoured to have appeared at the time of the birth of Christ.

It was pathetic, as wretched as any captive animal, and yet there was something in its eyes, even in such a poor-quality photograph, that implied it had bowed its head for the villagers' rope, chosen to leave its sacred forest to spend its last hours amid the stench and smoke, the shouts and prodding sticks of their alien community.

Phuc flushed napkin and unopened paper packet away and left by the back entrance to avoid returning to the bar and the enquiry of Vivien's sweet-sharp gaze. There was a police number stored on his mobile, for a stitch-up-your-mates line. It was displayed on posters around the dependency clinic and in the crypt where NA held their meetings. He had dutifully drawn clients' attention to it and made sure a card with it on was included in their welcome packs when they first registered for his help, but he had always assumed it was a piece of political window dressing and was hardly ever rung. Ringing it now, he pictured an old plastic phone jangling unregarded in a barely used office.

Sure enough, it was answered by a machine. He knew they recorded calls for a reason. For most callers, recording a message was less threatening by far than actually speaking to a policeman. And it saved departmental costs.

He hesitated, doubting his motives. There was a ten-second pause then the machine cut him off.

He drove home through the rain, with great care, feeling light-headed and distinctly drunk but thrillingly alive and in his skin, to present Fern with his dead mother's ring.

NUALA AT 56

Autumn was Nuala's favourite season, especially in West Cornwall where even early October routinely offered golden weather and warm seas without the holiday crowds. The carn above her house was gaudy with heather and gorse and there were so few trees in the area that only fields of barley stubble left for the wintering birds and stretches of browning bracken reminded one the year was entering old age.

The girls had wanted no hothouse flowers in the church so for a month she had been gathering seed pods from her own garden – dramatic ones such as opium poppy, sea holly, acanthus and allium – and had thrown a pair of vases especially, iridescent sea green with quirky handles in the shape of C and M. Her arrangements stood on plain wooden pillars (made by Carrie) on either side of the chairs where the girls were to sit. Now that she knew where the key was hidden, she had been able to slip down the previous night to set them up and thought they looked pretty fine. She reckoned she looked pretty fine too, having had her hair done and chosen her outfit with great care.

When she had realized the sad symmetry by which neither bride had a mother still living, she had jokingly offered herself for the role – mother of the brides – and had been first bewildered then touched that they had taken her in earnest and welcomed the suggestion. Despite their laughing insistence, she had refused to wear a hat. She had bought a new dress, however: a sheath in iridescent blue silk which showed her legs to advantage but not too much cleavage. In case it made her look too sexy or, more worryingly, like some divorcée on the prowl, she found a demure, raw silk jacket with sleeves ending just below the elbow. These were an extravagance – she had actually crossed the Tamar to find them – but a happy one.

She had always known Carrie, of course, though not well and had hired her to build new kitchen cupboards for her once, and another time picture frames, without telling Barnaby, who didn't need to know everything. She had done her best to draw her out and befriend her during the few visits to the house the work entailed. Superficially she was more Dot's child than his – it had been Lenny who looked so like him, if only one knew to look for the resemblance – yet Carrie's equable nature and the careful way she measured her words had clearly been shaped by him. And if she spoke with her mother's accent, it was with her father's voice.

The speed with which Nuala had come to know them as a couple, however, had been Morwenna's doing. Morwenna's nature was quicksilver and enthusiastic and, beneath the surface flutter and fragile charm, there was a steely surety of purpose that reminded one she was her late mother's daughter. Nuala had met Rachel Kelly several times professionally, at gallery openings and the like, and been both envious and afraid of her. She had seen enough to know it would take a certain toughness in a daughter to withstand and survive such a parent. As a pair, the girls – she made a mental note to stop calling them that, it sounded so patronizing – the two *young women* were better matched than they yet realized themselves. They would prove quietly awe-inspiring, she suspected, as they aged together.

A car pulled up outside the church and other guests soon walked in, smiling shyly at her because they were not sure who she was but guessed from her clothes that she had not just dropped in to say a quick prayer. It was Morwenna's married brother, with his severe-looking wife and the three slightly spookily home-educated daughters. The eldest of these took her place at the battered old harmonium, selected music from a tidy leather case and began to play what sounded like Bach, frowning from the unwonted effort involved in having to pump with her feet as she played. The mother talked quietly to the other daughters while the father looked about him, at the damp patches on the walls, the oddity of the Swedish flag beside the altar, the home-grown seedpods. And he glanced at his watch. He jumped up to introduce himself to the next arrival, who she guessed must be the Vietnamese adopted brother with the name she must remember to rhyme with look not luck. He had a pretty, harassed-looking blonde with him, closer to Nuala's age than his own, and four blond boys in dazzlingly clean white shirts, like a soap powder ad, who had clearly just submitted to a going-over with her comb and some hair gel. Nuala met the woman's eye and smiled. The Quaker wife would make mincemeat of her.

Then the lady vicar arrived, Tabby Morris, greeting everyone in turn and thanking Nuala for the flower arrangements and supportively touching the young harmonium player's shoulder before slipping back out to wait in the porch. As she left, she gave an unconvincingly sunny greeting to Modest Carlsson, who slid in and sat near the back, surely uninvited. Nuala imagined he was the sort of person who haunted weddings and funerals to sup second-hand on the emotion and enjoy a transitory taste of being a member rather than an outcast. He was the only one of them, she noticed, who had knelt to pray, pointedly masking his face in his fat little hands, because this was his church, his hour for devotion, and he wasn't about to let a mere wedding get in the way.

Not that it was a wedding. Not officially. Officially the girls had seen their Civil Partnership registered (again, not officially a wedding) in Penzance the previous afternoon and this cosily guerrilla occasion, offered by Tabby Morris, was what Tabby called a 'backdoor blessing'. But they all knew it was a church wedding, which was why nobody, not even the fathers, had been invited to the register office the day before; this was the ceremony that counted.

Outside there was a burst of male laughter at which Modest Carlsson gave a slow glare, then two smartly-suited men came in. From the glee with which the solemn little girls greeted them, including the one trapped at the harmonium, she guessed this was the gay brother from California and his art-dealer spouse – source, no doubt, of many a spoiling, disapproved-of present. This second brother threw her such a dazzling smile when he caught her eye that Nuala had to look down at her hands soon afterwards to ride out one of the surges of grief for Lenny that she had come to accept would now be as much a part of her life as her hay fever or stiff knees. She concentrated on her breathing and the spasm passed. Her spirits were still slightly muffled by antidepressants – she had no intention of crying today, at least not until she was safely home again.

Tabby Morris came back in and had a quiet word with the girl on the harmonium, who stopped abruptly, mid-phrase, which was probably not what Tabby had intended. Nuala thought how much less ridiculous priestly robes looked on a woman than on a man.

'Good morning, everyone. Thank you to Bryony for the lovely playing. Will you all please stand?' They stood. 'Thank you dear,' she said quietly and Bryony played the march from *La Clemenza di Tito*, rather slowly and stumbling slightly over the flourishes. Everyone looked round, of course, to where the two fathers were waiting, each with a daughter on his arm.

Morwenna had on a dramatic, plum-coloured velvet dress, with her hair piled up on her head with a chaplet of brightly variegated ivy around it. Carrie was in a well-cut black suit, offset by a waistcoat in the same velvet as the dress, with a buttonhole made of the same ivy. Barnaby was in his usual clerical black. Morwenna's father – a tall, interesting-looking man – unwittingly echoed his daughter-in-law in a suit with no tie. The aisle was too narrow for them to come up four abreast, of course, so Barnaby and Carrie came first and waited beside the right-hand flower arrangement. As soon as the others were beside them the girls, the *young women*, dropped their father's arms as if spontaneously and held each other's hands. Job done, the fathers stepped back and prepared to to sit down.

'Dearly beloved,' Tabby began. 'We are here today to bless and celebrate the union of our friends, sisters and daughters, Carrie and Morwenna, if not with the full approval of the Church, then in the eye of God …'

*   *   *

Niamh had supported Nuala from two days after Len's suicide until three after his cremation. Her intense sense of right and wrong, combined with her unsparing honesty had made Nuala realize how very English she herself had become. Nuala was hedging herself around with ifs and buts, maybes and perhaps, making allowances on every side. But Niamh shook everything down to a stark simplicity as if to say *these are the facts, my love, and these are your options.*

It was lancing, rather than directly healing, wounding deeper so as to allow poison to emerge so that healing might begin. At first Nuala was furious with Len but Niamh helped her see that, far from cowardly, what he had done took courage and conviction and lacked the element of retribution present in so much self-murder. Reading the copy poor little Amy Hawker sent her of the letter he had written, and bitterly regretting now that she had never read the one he wrote for her, the desolate understanding stole over Nuala that, deep down, she had gone into a kind of suppressed mourning for him from the very day of his accident. Her initial rage against him at his death, she understood now, had been codified expression of a kind of shame at her self-deceit.

She wished the collapsing scrum had simply killed him outright.

Niamh had emptied his little flat for her, since Nuala couldn't face the hideous, insolent shrine outside or running the gauntlet of Kitty Arnold and the other fired-up old biddies tending it like so many wrinkled vestals. His boyhood room at home remained a shrine of her own, and one she found she still could not touch. She had been keeping the door shut but, with Niamh no longer around to preach at her about the unhealthiness of what she was doing, she had taken to sleeping on his bunk bed, marvelling at the view of stars through the porthole window by his pillow, haunted by sweet dreams of his insouciant, bicycling return (sans helmet, naturally) and bad ones of Kitty Arnold, shaking his letter at her. The one she had never read.

Another wayside shrine had sprung up outside the little village school in Pendeen he had left aged eleven. Driving home from the Truro crematorium, giddy from a continuing sense of unreality and an overdose of antidepressants and therapeutic alcohol, she made Niamh stop her hire car.

'I hate that,' she said. 'I fucking hate it. Most of them didn't even know him.'

'So let's trash it,' Niamh said, with the same giggle with which she'd once pointed out that a crack in their Melbourne uncle's bathing box on Brighton Beach let them watch the cute boys in the one next door getting out of their swimmies. 'It's sort of yours to trash, after all. It's your grief, Noolie, not theirs.'

So Niamh swerved alongside it like a bank robber and they swiftly piled her car boot high with rotting bundles of flowers, children's paintings, candles in jam jars and soggy Hallmark cards. A couple of children were standing nearby and just stared back when Niamh told them, in that blunt way she had, 'You can lend a hand if you care to, girls.'

It was extremely satisfying and, fired up, Nuala slipped into the post office, ostensibly to buy milk and bread and the paper but actually to tell the people in there that she'd taken down the shrine and didn't want a fresh one going up, please.

'Len's gone now,' she told them. 'The fuss is over and I need to take him home with me.'

The ashes were delivered by courier the next day. The sisters buried them illegally, high on Watch Croft, near a rock where he liked to sit to look out to sea. At least they buried as much as would fit in the funny red-gold desk tidy she had made him once. She packed it in and formed a rudimentary lid with a section cut from a cork tile. The rest they put into a firework – a huge rocket Niamh had bought especially in Chinatown on her way through London. Niamh expertly slit it open, extended and rebuilt it to include the ashes in a fragile chamber of lining paper near its tip. On the eve of Niamh's departure, they took olives, cold pasties and beer out to the tip of Bosigran Castle so they had sea on three sides of them and, as the sun began to set, launched what remained of Len on a glorious, blue-flamed trajectory over the waves.

Nuala began to go a little mad. Not a half-day passed without another delivery of flowers, or cake, or casserole or art or just another flurry of kind letters and cards and she began to feel immured by it all and panicky.

The low point was a visit from Modest Carlsson, who meant well and could not help being so repellent, and whom she shocked by suddenly burdening with a secret he had surely not come to hear. She was rude to him and felt guilty but not for long; she was glad if what she said kept him and his unwanted pity and genteel curiosity away. And she was confident that a basic insecurity about him would stop his ever risking passing on what she had told him; he was an outsider like her but with the crucial difference, one could see, that he ached to belong.

The one person she wanted to hear from was the only one who kept silent, sent no flowers or letter and never rang. All she had was his stricken message on her answering machine, which Niamh, in her ignorance, had wiped off. Nuala had been humbled by his discretion at the inquest. She knew what it would have cost him to hide the truth, to lie even only by omission. To lie with his hand on a Bible. It was that as much as grief that had caused her to run so melodramatically from the council chamber.

When she came to the flat and saw Lenny dead, the kind paramedics left her alone with him for a few minutes, then were almost in tears at having to take him away from her. Beside herself, she was weeping, talking out loud, pacing around and it was just then that silly Kitty came knocking and oh so respectful in her hour of grief, with a cup of nastily milky tea and the letter. Which was when Nuala cracked and burnt the letter like a witch, burnt it in the kitchen sink, setting off the bloody smoke alarm, and told the frightened old biddy the things she shouldn't have, which started the awful, stupid rumours.

She could see clearly now. She had been envious, grotesquely so, of Barnaby's being with him at the end, and ashamed that she had not proved brave enough to listen to Lenny's mounting despair. She didn't for one moment believe Barnaby had helped kill him but she felt now that she, as the only parent the boy had known, should have offered to, or at least made it easier for him. Mothers were so glib about saying, *oh I'd give him my kidney* or *oh I'd die for him, no question,* but how many would be ready to reach for a smothering pillow or merciful syringe?

She very nearly didn't hear about Dot's death at all. Immediately after Modest's visit she had impulsively booked a flight to Perth. Having emptied and turned off the fridge, and locked all the shutters, she called in at the post office to cancel her newspaper order and make arrangements for her mail to be held for her. She overheard the crucial words in a tillside conversation.

She had not once walked down his lane in twenty years, even to reach the footpath to the coast, but she did so then, did it easily. She gave herself no time to think, to fret or compose suitable words but simply walked down to the lovely old house, knocked and presented herself. It was Carrie who opened the door and Nuala found herself instinctively saying just to give him her love and that they were to ring her if she could help in any way. But Carrie was resolute, for all her croaky voice and red-rimmed eyes.

'No,' she said. 'I think you should see him. I know he'll want to see you,' and she had shown her to a little, dark, book-lined room at the house's rear where Barnaby rose from his chair and took her in his arms.

Helping them in all the small, practical necessities that beset an unexpected death had given a purpose to the weeks that followed. Nothing needed to be explained. Everyone accepted that Barnaby had private dealings with virtually everyone within a five-mile radius. In the strangest, sweetest way, Carrie drew her in and relied on her like an old family friend. Morwenna, meanwhile, formed a swift alliance with her as a fellow alien in Barnaby's close-knit congregation of largely female supporters.

From myriad small evidences and signs, from her daughter's drily Cornish sense of humour to the astonishing order of her kitchen and understairs cupboards, Nuala came to see what a remarkable woman Dot had been. And to regret that she had never felt able to befriend her.

Barnaby was lost without her. 'She was my north and south,' he told her candidly. 'In an odd way, I find she was my reason too.'

On the afternoon of Dot's death, he had been at the Diocesan offices, formally confirming his decision to retire. In a curious way, he confided to her on another occasion, losing Len had restored his faith with one hand and entirely taken away, with the other, any ability to stand before a congregation ever again. 'Your boy humbled me,' he told her. 'Utterly.' At which, naturally, they both had a good cry.

Tabby Morris was to take up his role for the prescribed interregnum and several of them, himself included, were urging her to apply for his post when the opportunity arose. Meanwhile, as with any retiring priest, he would be obliged to quit the parish to make room in every sense for his successor.

He horrified Nuala by saying he was seriously considering entering a monastic order. 'After over half a lifetime's study of Thomas à Kempis, I reckon I'm ready.' Unsure what to suggest instead, she merely changed the subject as soon as she could but she talked the matter over with Morwenna and Carrie when they called in on her during a walk.

The problem was money and property. His stepmother's retirement home bills had used up whatever expectations he had from his father. He had little money of his own, and his pension would be enough to live off – in his habitually frugal style – but not enough to pay much rent. The farmhouse and land had belonged to Dot and naturally came to him as her husband but the long-term plan, set out in both their wills, was that Carrie, as the eldest, inherit both in turn and that Phuc have rent-free use of the end of the house currently lived in by Carrie. All very tidy if Barnaby were to die soon after Dot or indeed to take himself off to Whelm, Alton Abbey, Ewell or wherever but impossible if he needed to sell the farm in order to buy himself somewhere else.

A sly solution presented itself, which Nuala dared not voice just yet. For all Modest Carlsson's assiduity in delivering the parish magazine there, she had recently discovered that her house lay in another parish entirely.

As Morwenna and Carrie's love gradually blossomed and they announced they were going to be civilly partnered and move in together at Carrie's end of the house, so Barnaby slowly emerged from his helpless state and seemed to look around him like the dazed survivor of an aerial attack. A little shy and old-fashioned in the face of the young women's love, he called increasingly on Nuala for company. They took long walks, attended concerts, even, on her sufferance, church. She no longer itched for him as she had when they both were younger, but found his company comforting and congenial. They hugged on meeting and parting, which was enough to remind her they were a good fit, and occasionally held hands when no one was around to see – out on a footpath or sitting on the bench against Redworks House's southerly flank to stare, lost in thought, at the maplike view of fields, and cottages and sea.

'The thing is, Barny,' she finally dared to say. 'We didn't, either of us, waste the time we were apart, of course we didn't, but it would be a fucking awful waste if you did become a monk after all these years.'

'Hmm,' he said unhelpfully. 'You do swear an awful lot.'

'Get used to it. Come on a trip with me.'

'I'm as poor as the proverbial church mouse.'

'I'm not,' she said.

'Well that's nice.'

'Isn't it? Come to WA with me. Just for a month or two. We could stay on Niamh's olive farm. There's a cottage there we can use. And walk and talk and, you know, grieve and make friends with goats and recover.'

'Nuala, I couldn't take—'

'It's not charity, drongo. It would be as much my treat as yours. And there are two bedrooms, so no pressure there either.'

He didn't say yes or no but simply lifted the hand he was holding and kissed its freckled back.

'Your nose is burning,' she said and put her straw gardening hat on him. She saw him smile in its shadow.

'I don't deserve you,' he said quietly.

'Oh … Regard me as a fitting punishment instead,' she told him.

'Carrie has no idea,' he said. 'About, you know … Lenny and me.'

'Jesus, Barny. You did the decent thing for so long, the least I can do is return the favour. He stays our son, even as a secret.'

In the event he would be paying his own way. After announcing the trip, whose duration became ever less definite, he insisted on swapping house-ends with Carrie to give the girls more space. This involved a long September weekend of throwing out, boxing up and tidying away, in the course of which Morwenna let out a cowgirl whoop of surprise that brought Nuala from the adjoining room.

While giggling over a funny photograph she had found of little Carrie posed in front of Pendeen Watch so that the black fog horns turned her into Minnie Mouse, she had come across a dusty little painting tucked within a book-shelf: a rough, colourful representation in oils of Morvah church and the land around it.

'I was given it by my uncle's boyfriend years ago,' he said, as he came to look too. 'It's sat there so long that I've sort of stopped seeing it.'

Having eagerly asked his permission, Morwenna deftly used a fingernail to slit open the brown paper masking its back. This revealed a little red-painted design of a childlike tug. She pointed it out to Carrie who instantly understood and gasped, 'Dad!'

'It's an ark,' Morwenna explained. 'A visual/sonic pun for RK. My mother's little pictogram she used on paintings before she got established and started signing the fronts instead. Do you … do you have any idea what this is worth, Barnaby?'

'Well, as I said,' he began, 'It was a present. Ages ago …'

'It's one of a series she did on a crazy, week-long autumn walk she took with a tent from Penzance to St Ives along the coast once, not long after Antony met her when she was first pregnant. Some sharp-eyed collector bought all the others in one of the early St Just cancer charity shows and at least half of those are now in the Guggenheim. People always thought Patrick Heron's family had the others or that she'd just burnt them in one of her clear-outs.'

'Well,' he said, blatantly humouring her enthusiasm and still not really convinced. 'Isn't that nice?'

Once Morwenna's enquiries followed up by some e-mailed photographs had produced a convincingly staggering estimate from Christie's, he proved honest to a fault, not surprisingly, and called up the picture's donor. His late uncle's boyfriend was now a wealthy old crocodile in Palm Springs, apparently, who retained no recollection of the gift, although he remembered little Carrie's dungarees and hooted with pleasure at the news of her civil partnership plans. He declared himself delighted and said of course Barnaby must sell and enjoy the proceeds.

'Oh God,' Barnaby said, once he'd hung up. 'Wasn't that awful? I never told Paul about Dot. Somehow I just couldn't bear to. They never quite understood each other and I didn't want to hear him say something pat and automatic. Poor Dot. I must write to him at once.'

Nuala had always assumed women priests would be all sugary smiles in their effort not to seem to replicate their male counterparts but, while not stern or pompous, Tabby was unafraid to be solemn. With great tact and a certain wit, she had involved both the sisters-in-law in the joining families so that, after handing over the brides, the menfolk were purely decorative.

The pretty, older woman, Phuc's fiancée with the plant name Nuala had temporarily forgotten, read U. A. Fanthorpe's 'Atlas'. 'There is a kind of love called maintenance, Which stores the WD40 and knows when to use it …' As the woman read she fiddled nervously with an exquisite sapphire ring she could not have been wearing for long, and Phuc put an arm around the smallest of the boys to pull him closer.

Then the Quaker wife, who Nuala suddenly saw was only unsmiling because she was desperately tense and nervous, read a heart-breaking little Charles Causley poem about his dead parents waving to him from a riverbank in Paradise with a homespun picnic beside them. This made Barnaby scrabble secretly beside him for Nuala's hand, so was surely meant as a tribute to Dorothy.

There could be no prayer-book marriage service as such but Morwenna and Carrie repeated the vow from the Book of Ruth.

'Whither thou goest, I will go; and where thou lodgest, I will lodge; thy people shall be my people, and thy God, my God. Where thou diest, will I die and there will I be buried.'

At this it was Nuala's turn to blow her nose and look firmly at the Swedish flag, in an effort not to think of Lenny and Amy and what might have been. Then the girls, dammit, knelt before the altar. Tabby placed her hands on their heads and, referring back to the love of David and Jonathan, called down God's blessing on their lasting union. 'May this marriage in the eyes of their friends and family eventually come to be one in the eyes of the Church,' she said, to which everyone added a resounding Amen.

The two families were lingering to take photographs of each other outside the church porch. Tabby stayed inside to take off her robes, possibly anxious lest this unorthodox occasion see her and her career martyred on YouTube. Modest Carlsson came up to her fairly shining with an odd sort of triumph in his face.

'Lovely to see them so happy,' he said. 'But I can't help wondering what the bishop would say if he—'

Tabby cut him short, not exactly clicking her fingers but giving that impression, and something in her sudden air of authority reminded Nuala that her husband had long served on the local police force. 'Could I have a quiet word?' she said. She led him to the very back of the little church, where a curtain masked the brooms and dustpans and the ringing chamber. Nuala didn't like to watch too closely, as it was faintly embarrassing, like watching a child being dressed down by its parent, but whatever Tabby said had a peculiar effect. He seemed to shrink in on himself, if that were possible, and age visibly. He pushed brusquely out through the laughing little crowd outside and hurried away along the road. Nuala heard Barnaby call out a merry, *Bye, Modest – thanks for coming!* There were curlews calling too. Another sign of winter looming.

She caught Tabby's eye as she followed her to the door. 'He looked as if someone had walked on his grave,' she told her. 'Whatever did you say to him?'

'Oh. Nothing much,' Tabby said, gesturing for her to go out ahead of her. 'Just words to the effect that God knows us for who we really are. And calls us by our true names.'

BARNABY AT 8

Barnaby watched from the shade of a wonderfully red tree he had recently learnt was a Japanese maple, as Mr Ewart, Uncle James's secretary, emerged in his bright blue swimming trunks from the summerhouse, dived into the pool and swam an entire length underwater. The transformation was startling. Dressed, he seemed somehow always to be apologizing for himself, slouching in corners, not meeting one's eye, mumbling when asked a question – all the things Prof and the Buttercluck said Barnaby must never do – yet undressed, he was revealed as utterly confident and a kind of god. He had muscles, which was unexpected because he did no heavy work – he did no work at all, the Buttercluck said – and his body was like the statues around Uncle James's garden, only with all its limbs.

Barnaby liked Mr Ewart, if only because he sensed he despised the Buttercluck, but was shy of him and never sure what to say beyond *how do you do*. Mr Ewart occupied a ambiguous position in Uncle James's household similar to the role of the Buttercluck in their own; officially a sort of employee and yet somehow not, or more than: a servant who often overruled the master. This, a reverence for music, and their big, long noses, were about the only ways in which Barnaby's father and uncle were alike.

Mr Ewart swam a couple more lengths, doing proper crawl, putting his face in the water as Barnaby never could and snatching breaths under his left armpit. He seemed hardly to splash at all. He moved, Barnaby thought enviously, like a sort of beautiful pike.

They were there for the day – Barnaby, his father, the Buttercluck and Barnaby's big sister, Alice – because it was Uncle James's birthday. But they were there for other reasons also and the air in the lovely old house was so tense with the things that might be thought but must never be spoken that he had jumped at the suggestion he run and play in the garden before lunch.

'Swim too!' Mr Ewart called.

'I can't, really,' Barnaby called back. 'Not yet. I'll be learning when I start boarding school.'

'So learn now. It's not deep. You'll be quite safe.'

'I put out my swimming things but Mrs Clutterbuck said not to bring them as it's September.'

'But it's boiling still! Silly cow …'

Barnaby couldn't help grinning at such forbidden language.

Mr Ewart grinned back. 'Swim in your pants. They'll soon dry in the sun.' And he carried on doing lengths.

Barnaby watched a little longer. He was never bad. His role was to be as unobtrusive and as little bother to anyone as possible. This seemed to be getting harder, not easier, as he got older, which was one of the reasons he was secretly excited about starting boarding school next week. He hurried to the summerhouse before anyone might come and stop him, took off all his clothes but his pants, folded them neatly onto a chair the way Mr Ewart had done, then hurried to the pool.

The cool of it was delicious after the sticky heat of the drive from Bristol. He couldn't do anything like the crawl yet and hated putting his face underwater but he did the doggy paddle Alice had taught him last time they went to the Buttercluck's caravan at Combe Martin, and managed one, snorting length to about six of Mr Ewart's.

They paused side by side at the other end, Barnaby to recover his breath, Mr Ewart simply to be kind. He had rather pronounced, caramel-coloured nipples, which fascinated Barnaby as his own were barely there and baby pink, but he knew better than to stare so concentrated on the fun of letting his legs float to the surface in front of him while he kept his arms hooked on the silver rail. It wasn't like other pools. It was dark blue, with a silver moon and stars on the bottom. Uncle James had promised that one day he should see it after dark when it was all lit up, but they never seemed to visit at night, only for these lunches.

'Mr Ewart?'

'Yes?'

'Is it true Uncle James is going to die soon?' It had seemed safe enough to ask this, since Mr Ewart was a secretary and so not *people*. But Barnaby saw a quick frown crumple his face for a moment.

'What gave you that idea?'

'Alice said. She said I wasn't to tell people.'

'Your sister's very clever but she's still a schoolgirl,' Mr Ewart said rather sharply. 'She doesn't know everything.'

'No. Of course. Sorry.'

'But he's not well, no. He may not have very long.'

'Is it his liver?' Barnaby asked, chancing his luck with something he had heard the Prof say to the Buttercluck.

Mr Ewart looked away. 'Yes,' he said. 'Among other things ... If you leave your pants off when you dress again,

I'll get them dry for you,' he added briskly and dived elegantly back into another length underwater.

Barnaby felt himself dismissed. His teeth chattered as he hurried back to the summerhouse, enjoying the spongy grass and daisies under bare feet. There was a pile of towels, which were delightfully plump and soft, not like their hard old ones at home, which were good when you had an itchy back but never a comfort to wrap about you like these were. Dressing without pants on, which felt all the more wildly naughty for being undetectable, he wrung out his pants inside a towel, the way Alice had shown him, and laid them on the mosaic-topped table in the warm sunlight where Mr Ewart could not miss them.

Looking at Mr Ewart's neatly folded things – his *disguise*, as Barnaby thought of them now – he wished he hadn't said anything about Uncle James not being well. It had some-how turned Mr Ewart into a servant when he had perhaps been about to become a friend. The desire to unsay things, he was learning, was as bad as the awful panic that could descend when something important was lost.

Early that summer he had managed to drop the Buttercluck's car keys somewhere on a busy street in Wells. Her anger and fuss, the waiting for the AA man, the *very expensive* process of getting more keys made at the garage, were as nothing compared to the agony of the few minutes before he had to tell her, when his only, hopeless wish had been that he could unpick time and find himself back at the moment when she so uncharacteristically entrusted them to him so he could wait in the car while she slipped into the chemist's for whatever it was she didn't want him to see her buy.

He touched Mr Ewart's sky-blue shirt. You could touch things, or people, very, very slightly and find a kind of tingling there in between, like electricity. This was something he hadn't shared, not even with Alice, whom he loved and trusted, because the rest of his household had such deep scorn for anything that wasn't scientific. His father, Prof, was far too polite ever to call anyone a silly moo, even behind their backs, but you could tell when he wanted to, when he really despised someone, because he would call them *irrational* or *sentimental*, the two rudest words in his armoury.

Leaving the summerhouse, glancing in vain for a parting peace gesture from Mr Ewart, who continued to swim, oblivious, he passed through the high copper beech hedges of the pool garden, with its clusters of ornamental trees just entering on their autumn splendour and crossed over the herbaceous walk to take the other, parallel route back to the house. This was bare by contrast, containing no flowers at all, only shades of green that were more refreshing on a hot day than the blazing variety of flowerbeds, and a severe, ornamental rill, slowly running from one end of the green corridor to the other, creating an optical illusion that the house lay at the top of a gentle slope when the approach was, in fact, perfectly level.

Enjoying the novel sensation of no pants under his trousers, he did what he always did on visits here, jumping back and forth across the rill a few times, then walking with one foot on either side of it, then staring at the water closely as he walked in an effort to convince his brain it flowed by gravity and that he was indeed walking uphill.

Uncle James's house was special. It was nearly four hundred years old and dated from when an enterprising ancestor, Olive Palmer, acquired land and barns off Malmesbury Abbey when it was dissolved by Henry VIII. Palmers and then Johnsons had always lived there and always would and, although Alice had brought home to him that this was something never to be spoken of, as his childless uncle's only nephew, he would live there himself one day. Prof would probably live there first. He wasn't younger by anything like the nine years that divided Barnaby from Alice, but there was nothing wrong with his liver and the Buttercluck maintained him with a care like that he lavished on his Alvis.

Their own house, in Bristol, was attractive enough but it was Victorian and, even in the gloomy heart of its shrubbery, you could always hear the grumble of traffic. The Buttercluck had a sort of flat on the top floor, where she practised her French horn, but took all her meals with them, which only made sense as she cooked them too. She had been with them all his life. Alice said she had moved in to help when their mother was dying.

She had met Prof in the amateur orchestra in which they both played on Wednesday nights. She played the French horn and Prof the cello, so they would have had ample scope for eye contact before they actually got around to speaking. She worked as a dental technician on Whiteladies Road as well as keeping house. Prof was a research chemist in a big laboratory near Swindon where he experimented on lots of animals. He had taken Barnaby there once and explained that the tanks of mice and puppies and kittens were not pets and wouldn't live long but were giving their lives to help mankind.

God was sentimental nonsense, a primitive myth we had long outgrown, but man was glorious. Prof and Buttercluck were agreed on this and spoke of *Mankind* in a voice similar to the one the lone religious teacher in his primary school used when talking of *Our Lord*. On Sundays, when other boys and girls were made to go to church, Prof or the Buttercluck or both expected Barnaby, and Alice if she were home, to join them on visits to monuments of Mankind's achievements. Art galleries, museums (especially of science, engineering or industry – Barnaby's least favourite subjects), canals, viaducts, huge Victorian stations, castles and even, once, a mine had all been visited and wondered at. Even today, when lunch had broken the usual routine, Prof had pulled over en route to make them admire some old ditch patterns in some low-lying country. Churches and cathedrals, however imposing, were somehow mentally edited out of the picture since, for all the brilliance of their construction, they were built in the name of irrationality and thus represented a *Blind Alley* in mankind's glorious ascent. There were several big churches near their road in Bristol. Were it not for the energy the Buttercluck put into complaining about the noise their bell ringers made, Barnaby might have believed she was unaware of their existence.

Alice didn't believe in God either but she was characteristically calm about it, so more persuasive. She simply said there was a scientific explanation for absolutely everything that happened in our lives and that explanations were reassuring and made sense in ways that religion wasn't and didn't. She cited Darwin so frequently that Barnaby suspected she had a crush on him. Science, she said, had never been used to persecute people. Unless you counted the Nazis, which was pseudoscience. And while science had its heretics, it didn't burn them but simply trounced them with fact and *meticulous research*. At the moment she wanted to be an economist when she grew up. There was nothing wrong in the world, she said, that might not be righted by redistribution of wealth and resources, and the steady erosion of religion and the strife it caused. As she was the nearest thing he had to a mother, he worshipped her and sought to emulate her in this and all things.

Barnaby bravely echoed her reasoning in the playground at school and even in the classroom occasionally – his primary school having been chosen for its free-thinking philosophy and lack of church affiliation – but he knew he could never convince as she could and suspected it was down to his weakness at maths. When he was stuck on his nine times table for weeks even after Prof pointed out the way every number in it added up to nine and how one numeral went up a stage while the other went down one, he saw how the difference in him was confirmed for them. Prof said he was a changeling because he had no aptitude for science and was given to dreams and pondering. When he protested to Alice, 'But I'm only eight! I might change!' she pointed out that she could do mental arithmetic for fun before she could read and was doing basic algebra by his age.

'But that's all right,' she said kindly. 'You can be a theorist when you grow up. We can't all be practical. The world will always need men of vision too.'

The gong sounded, which meant he was already late. He sprinted along the length of the rill, across a courtyard at the house's rear where the fig tree's late fruit had fallen on the flagstones and gathered drunken wasps around it, and into the little lavatory at one end of the dining room corridor where he quickly pissed, washed his hands and tidied his hair with a wet nailbrush that was a bit soapy.

'Welcome, wanderer,' Uncle James called out. They were already seated at the round dining table, even Mr Ewart, who must have slipped in by the other route while Barnaby was daydreaming. 'Sit by me and tell me everything.'

This was by way of a joke, since Barnaby was always peculiarly tongue-tied with Uncle James. He liked him, though, his immaculate clothes and florid, ruined face and the way he asked questions whereas Prof made statements.

He sat in the tapestried dining chair left vacant between James and the Buttercluck and did as the Buttercluck indicated, smothering his lap in a big, white napkin.

'Have you been swimming?' she asked, turning her horrified stare on him.

'I wet my hair just now to tidy it,' he said, which wasn't a lie, and remembered to fill her water glass before he filled his own. Mr Ewart caught his eye and winked quickly. 'Why are your roses still flowering, Uncle James?' Barnaby asked. 'When ours have all stopped?'

'I deadhead every day from June till October,' James told him. 'And have no useful occupation.'

Uncle James was a very good cook and grew all his own vegetables. Every time something was praised, from the little cheese mousses to the cold tarragon chicken to the pudding he called mulberry tumble, the Buttercluck said, 'You must give me the recipe,' in a way that sounded less and less pleasant and James answered her, 'Of course I will,' and somehow you knew he wouldn't. The grown-ups drank, of course, even Alice, since she was seventeen, which made them noisier and funnier than usual and even Barnaby was given a tiny antique glass of champagne so they could all toast James's birthday.

By the time they had left the table and crossed the hall to the drawing room for coffee, whatever tensions Barnaby had sensed when they arrived had evaporated. Mr Ewart was telling Alice stories that were making her smile and blush and Mrs Clutterbuck actually sat very close to Prof on a sofa, which was something she never did, at least not when Barnaby and Alice were present, and was actually giggling.

But then Uncle James tapped his spoon on his coffee cup for silence. 'Sorry to break in on the jollity,' he said, 'but there's news I have to share with you and this is as good a time as any.'

'James, are you sure …?' Prof began, with a pointed glance at Barnaby but James went on.

'Oh absolutely. This is something the young things should hear too and directly from me.' It was strange. He never normally seemed the older brother because he was jollier than Prof and what the Buttercluck called *frivolous*, but now he seemed much the oldest and most serious person in the room. 'This is, I'm afraid, the last time I can gather you all here for lunch,' he said. 'As you probably all know, I've not been well. What you probably didn't know is that I've had increasing problems with money and the debts have got out of control. In the end I had no option but to sell up.'

The Buttercluck drew in her breath so sharply Barnaby could hear it from the other end of the Persian rug between them.

'Contracts on the house sale have been exchanged and Christie's have sent down a team to do a valuation and draw up a catalogue for a contents sale next month. Obviously I'll hang on to a few things, and there are a few good family bits that should eventually come to Alice and Barnaby. The plan is to move somewhere warm and cheap – Ibiza appeals – less stuffy than Madeira. And Mr Ewart has kindly agreed to come with me to, er, take care of things.' He raised his coffee cup to Mr Ewart in a kind of tribute gesture but Mr Ewart was folding and refolding a truffle wrapper and not looking.

'You should have told me,' Prof said. 'I could have …'

'You couldn't have afforded the price I needed, and anyway, I couldn't have stood being bailed out by my baby brother.'

'Well I think it's terribly sad,' the Buttercluck said. 'I'd always imagined Alice getting married from here. Four hundred years.'

'Yes, thank you, Mrs Clutterbuck. I'm well aware how long the family has lived here and how I'm letting the side down yet again.'

'I didn't mean,' she started to protest and then everyone seemed to be speaking at once.

All the horrible atmosphere that had been there when they first arrived came rushing back tenfold and all the air seemed sucked from the room. Barnaby jumped up, upsetting a coffee cup across a copy of *The Burlington Magazine*. His hands shook trying to right it and the little spotted thing whirled to the carpet where it broke neatly in two. Everyone stopped shouting.

'That was an antique, Barny,' Alice said softly.

'Clumsy oaf,' said Prof.

Mr Ewart swiftly stooped to scoop up the pieces and mop any coffee spill with his spotless handkerchief. It was like the ones with B for Barnaby Alice had given him for Christmas which he kept feeling he must save as they were for best, which meant never blowing your nose on them or mopping up coffee.

Barnaby knew he should apologize. Like everything in the house, the coffee cup had been chosen for its beauty. But all he could think to say, looking at Uncle James's kind, ravaged face was, 'I don't want you to die. It's not fair,' which he knew was a stupid, childish thing to say, an irrational, sentimental thing. As he ran from the room, dodging footstools and startling Uncle James's elderly whippet, he heard the Buttercluck say, 'Too much sunshine and rich food. We should probably be going ...'

Barnaby knew only that he needed to get outside, to breathe freely again and hide his shame. He went out the way he had come in and sat on the stone bench near the fig tree and the wasps. He hated making scenes or losing his temper. It was like running up a flight of stairs to find only a blank wall in the way; the only option was an ignominious return. Luckily Prof and the Buttercluck's way of punishing such behaviour was to ignore one completely for an hour or so, which ironically was all Barnaby wanted just now. He was thinking he might creep out to the car and wait obediently on its back seat in the punishing heat when Uncle James came out to join him.

'Come,' he said, and held out a huge hand. He led Barnaby out of the courtyard and around the side of the house.

'I'm so very sorry about the coffee cup,' Barnaby managed at last. 'Was it a special one?'

'It was rather. It was a Caughley one that came with the house. But you know what? It couldn't matter less. It's only stuff. And I'll give you a tip in life. Never collect china or glass in sets, just collect individual pieces you like. That way there are no obvious gaps to make you sad or cross when things break. Come. I want to show you something.' He dropped Barnaby's hand but steered him with an arm across his shoulders instead. His arm felt dense and immensely comforting.

They stopped beneath an oriel window. 'There,' he said. 'My favourite rose in the entire garden.' He gestured to a rose whose colour was somewhere between purple, red and black, if that were possible. The curling petals looked like something very expensive and soft – velvet, perhaps. 'Souvenir du Docteur Jamain. Isn't it lovely? Go on. Sniff it.'

The scent was as good as the colour. Barnaby felt he was seeing a rose properly for the first time. Its glossy leaves with their purply new growth, the elegantly lime-green bark with barely a thorn on it, the luxurious flowers that grew in ready-made bunches as if offering themselves to one's hand. What possible purpose could such spendthrift beauty serve? 'Why is it your favourite?' he asked.

'Oh. Apart from the colour, which is even better than Nuits de Young, it's that it performs this well even on a north wall where it gets only indirect sun. In fact it actually seems to prefer it. It should have stopped flowering weeks ago but just look at it! Marvellous. I liked it so much I was greedy and planted two more out in the sunshine and they didn't do nearly so well and looked all scorched and sad.

Here.' He took a small pair of secateurs from his jacket pocket and cut a perfect, half-open bud which he handed to Barnaby. 'You can either put it in a glass on your bedside table and enjoy it as it opens and dies or you can squeeze it in a big book between two sheets of blotting paper, the way mad Victorian spinsters did. Choice is yours. Barnaby, dear, I'm sorry about the house.'

'I don't care about the house.'

'Oh. Good.'

'It's only stuff. I care about *you*.'

'Yes, well, I'm sorry about me too. I might go on for ages.'

'But you might not.'

'No. But I don't mind so I don't think you should. Don't tell Mrs Butterfuck but we're not alone.'

'God, you mean?'

'Of course. Call it what you will. I look at a flower like that, or those birds swooping over the grass. And I know everything is going to be all right. All will be well. Walk with me. We've hardly talked. Are you surviving?'

'I start boarding school next week.'

'Hurrah. Is it hurrah?'

Barnaby nodded.

'You'll be a bit homesick at first, even for Mrs Clutterbuck, but that soon passes. I'd say write to me but I'm a hopeless correspondent.'

'I'll write to Alice.'

'A much better idea. And Barnaby?'

'Yes?'

'Please don't feel you always have to be *good*. Sometimes you're so good it hurts to watch you. Now, come along.

The others will be waiting and your father will worry I'm corrupting you with my dying breath.'

Sure enough, Alice and Mr Ewart met them as they returned to the side of the house. Uncle James kissed Alice seriously on the forehead, said, 'Dear girl,' and hugged her so warmly Barnaby knew they would have had a private conversation earlier.

Mr Ewart discreetly handed him his pants when no one was looking. 'Still warm from the Aga rail,' he said kindly as Barnaby thanked him and tucked them quickly into his pocket.

Sure enough, he was ignored on the drive home, even by Alice, but that suited him. He tucked the rose stem carefully into the map pocket on the back of Prof's seat, then pretended to be asleep while his head swam with thoughts of what stayed and what slipped away, of death and renewal. And of the distinct possibility of God, who, having been nowhere and nothing when they set out that morning, suddenly seemed to be glowing out from every surface and every idea, from the quiet magic of the nine times table to the glitter of Mr Ewart's secret muscles in the water.

AUTHOR'S ACKNOWLEDGMENTS

Heartfelt thanks are due to the editorial skills of my first readers: Clare Reihill, Penelope Hoare, Patrick Ness, Mark Adley, Richard Betts and Caradoc King.

I am indebted to the Manussis siblings for tweaking my Greek endearment,

to the Venerable Roger Bush, the Reverend Prebendary Dr John May and the Reverend Stephen Coles for their patient assistance with matters ecclesiastical and theological,

to Sutton Taylor for guiding me through the process of making lustreware,

to Demelza Hauser, for the lesson on the plight of the later wave of Vietnamese refugees,

to Simon Ewart for the inspiring muddy walk and the old photograph of Pendeen Manor,

to Jo Martin for the hours of legal help regarding assisted suicide and standard procedure, to Josephine Warburton and Cyril Honey of Geevor Tin Mine Museum's archive for letting me plunder their fascinating hours of recordings and personal testimonies,

to Jane Finemore and Simon Clews for putting me right on the geographical niceties of Melbourne addresses,

to the wry wisdom of Sarah Meyrick's *Married to the Ministry* and Noel Streatfeild's *A Vicarage Family*,

and, most especially, to the Reverend Alan Rowell, the *real*, and surely spotless, vicar of Pendeen and Morvah: two lovely churches I hope the reader will now wish to visit.

Patrick Gale
Penzance, October 2011